# play buddies

erotic fiction by

## BOB VICKERY

QuarterMoon
Press

San Francisco, California
www.quartermoonpress.com

Play Buddies. Erotic Fiction by Bob Vickery. Copyright © 2004 by Bob Vickery. Published in the United States of America. All rights reserved. No part of this book may be reproduced in any form or by any electronic or mechanical means including information storage and retrieval systems without permission in writing from the publisher, except by a reviewer, who may quote brief passages in a review. Published by Quarter Moon Press, 915 Cole Street, # 377, San Francisco, California 94117-4315 (www.quartermoonpress.com).

First edition: February 2004

Library of Congress Catalog Number: 2003098062

ISBN 0-9745767-0-0

Cover design by Marie LeTourneau
Cover photography courtesy of COLT Studio (www.coltstudios.com)
Interior text design by Jeff Brandenburg (www.image-comp.com)

Printed in The United States of America

To my buddy, Kirk

Anthologies by Bob Vickery

*Skin Deep*

*Cock Tales*

*Cocksure*

# Acknowledgments

Many thanks to all the people who have encouraged me in my writing and helped it to see the light of day: to the succession of editors at Specialty (formerly Liberation) Publications who have published my stories over the years: Pat Califia, John Erich, Austin Foxxe, Alan Carter, and most especially to Fred Goss, the best editor I've ever worked with; to Susie Bright, for her support and warmth and humor; to Jim Eigo, managing editor of Inches magazine, for giving me the best (and most insightful) review I ever got; to the people at COLT Studio for their help, and to the talented smut writers out there who don't get nearly enough appreciation for the awesome stories they write: R. J., Chris, Dale, Horehound, Simon and all the others.

# Table of Contents

# Introduction

January 11, 20**
From: Quarter Moon Press
To: Bob Vickery

Good news, Bob! "Play Buddies" is just about ready to be sent to the printer, and we can't tell you how delighted everyone here at Quarter Moon Press is about this project! We're so happy that you've decided to become a member of our little "family", and we hope this is just the beginning of a long working relationship between you and our small (but prestigious!) company.

Just one final thing: we still need you to write an introduction to the anthology. Do you think you could dash one off and send it to us by the end of the week? That's the last bit of business we need to take care of before we can wrap "Play Buddies" up.

Have a nice day,
*Quarter Moon Press*

---

January 21, 20**
From: Quarter Moon Press
To: Bob Vickery

Hi, Bob. Sorry to be such a nuisance, but we really do need that introduction. Do you think we can have it within the next couple of days?

Best,
*Quarter Moon Press*

January 23, 20**
From: Quarter Moon Press
To: Bob Vickery

Hi, Bob. It's the folks from Quarter Moon Press again. How's that introduction coming along?

*Quarter Moon Press*

---

January 24, 20**
From: Bob Vickery
To: Quarter Moon Press

Look, I'm kind of busy right now. Besides, I can't think of anything to write for an introduction. Nobody ever reads them anyway, so why don't we just bag it and start the book with the first story, okay?

*Bob V.*

---

January 24, 20**
From: Quarter Moon Press
To: Bob Vickery

Hi, Bob, we just got your email. We're afraid we can't just "bag" the introduction like you suggested. Anthologies *always* start with an introduction. That's just common practice. Or haven't you noticed? Look, this doesn't have to be a big deal. All you have to do is just sit down and bang something out. That shouldn't be so hard, should it? After all, you *are* a writer, right? So what's the problem?

We're looking forward to getting your introduction. By tomorrow. Before noon.

*Quarter Moon Press*

January 25, 20**
From: Bob Vickery
To: Quarter Moon Press

Introductions are a pain in the ass to write, and no one ever reads them. I'm not going to do it, so quit bugging me.

*Bob V.*

———————————

January 25, 20**
From: Quarter Moon Press
To: Bob Vickery

Let's just spell out the situation for you, *Bob*. You're under contract with us. You don't have any say in the matter. Write the goddamn introduction.

*Quarter Moon Press*

———————————

January 25, 20**
From: Bob Vickery
To: Quarter Moon Press

Hey, bozos, don't start copping an attitude with me. You don't know who you're tangling assholes with. Keep pushing me, and you'll be in a world of hurt.

*B.V.*

P.S. You can shove your "introduction" up your ass.

January 26, 20**
From: Quarter Moon Press
To: Bob Vickery

You know, Bob, it was just this kind of shit that we were afraid of when we decided to publish your smut. Instead of dealing with a professional, we have to take abuse from some porno hack who is incapable of writing a full sentence that doesn't have the words "throbbing", "spurting" or "cum-drenched" in it.

You should be pathetically grateful that a prestigious publishing company such as Quarter Moon Press would even consider taking on your twisted, sleazy stories.

If we don't get that introduction by noon tomorrow, the next letter you get will be from our attorneys.

*Quarter Moon Press*

---

January 26, 20**
From: Bob Vickery
To: The assholes at Quarter Moon Press

Hey, fuck you! There's nothing in my contract saying I have to write an introduction. All I had to do was deliver the manuscript, which I've done. So you and your attorneys can kiss my "cum-drenched" ass!

By the way, the only thing "pathetic" is your piss-ass little company and the dippy books you were putting out before you were lucky enough to get me to sign on with you. I've seen the shit you've published, all those pitiful "self-help" books, like "Be a Winner, Not a Whiner". Or those cookbooks. Jesus! Who the fuck eats Lithuanian cuisine!? You call that shit "prestigious"? How many copies of *that* did you sell? Two dozen?

*B.V.*

January 27, 20**
From: Quarter Moon Press
To: Bob Vickery

Look, Vickery. Either write that fucking introduction or you're going to be very, very sorry. This is not an idle threat.

*Quarter Moon Press*

---

January 27, 20**
From: Bob Vickery
To: Losers, Inc.

Ooooh, I'm shaking, I'm shaking. What are you going to do? Make me eat a Lithuanian burrito, or whatever the fuck it is they eat over there?

*B.V.*

---

January 27, 20**
From: Quarter Moon Press
To: Bob Vickery

Dear Bob,

Okay, let's all just calm down a bit. Things seem to have taken an unfortunate turn between you and the folks here at Quarter Moon Press, which we deeply regret. What we've got here is just a little communication problem, easily cleared up.

We'd like to explain, Bob, how Quarter Moon Press operates whenever we take on a new writer. You know, give you a little *background*. When we sign somebody on, we first try to learn a little something about that writer, flesh out his past history, talk to some people. Just in case we ever need some, um, *leverage*. We have a couple of guys on staff who are real good at making . . . inquiries.

Well, we did that with you, Bob, and we have to admit, we were impressed with what we found (and we're not all that easily impressed!). We won't go into everything we came up with, just that little incident outside of Amarillo, Texas a couple of years ago. You know, in that Motel 6, with those two bikers and, let's see, we have your file right here, oh yeah, *a cocker spaniel* (YOU SICK FUCK!!). Our sources tell us that there were some controlled substances involved, and that the motel mysteriously burnt down later that night. To the ground. The law there never did find out exactly what happened.

We think that the Amarillo sheriff's department would be *real* interested in what our "Bob Vickery" file has to say. We even have their fax number in our Rolodex. Do you know how much time the average arsonist does in the Texas prison system?

Now maybe that fire was just an accident. And, who knows, maybe you didn't even have anything to do with it. But if things ever did come to a head, we don't think the Texas courts would be too favorably disposed toward *a sleazy homosexual pornographer*. Not to mention what the SPCA and PETA folks would have to say about that poor cocker spaniel!

But, on the bright side, Bob, this could be a whole new mother lode of material for you to mine as a writer. You know, maybe a little jerk-off story about being the special bitch of a 300 pound serial killer? Or how about one about a prison gang rape? We're sure the possibilities would be endless.

So what's it going to be, Bob? Are you going to write that introduction, or are you going to wind up being a "special friend" to some big, hairy, tattooed guy named Pigfucker? It's your call.

Have a nice day  :-)
*Quarter Moon Press*

---

January 28, 20**
From: Quarter Moon Press
To: Bob Vickery

We're still waiting for an answer, Bob. We're calling the Amarillo sheriff's department at close of business today.

*QMP*

January 28, 20**
From: Bob Vickery
To: Quarter Moon Press

You motherfuckers.

Just for the record, that cocker spaniel didn't do anything it didn't want to.
But okay, you win. I'll write your introduction. Here it is:

Hi, this is Bob Vickery. Thanks for buying my new book, "Play Buddies". It's just full of throbbing, spurting, cum-drenched stories. I hope you like reading them as much as I enjoyed writing them. And if you don't, you can kiss my ass.
Okay, there's your fuckin' introduction. Now eat shit and die.

Very sincerely,
*Bob Vickery.*

_____

January 30, 20**
From: Quarter Moon Press
To: Bob Vickery

Dear Bob,

There now. That wasn't so hard, was it?

Best,
*Quarter Moon Press.*

www.bobvickery.com
San Francisco, February 2004

# Stud Poker

"So are all the other guys makin' it tonight?" Vinnie asks. His eyes are glued to the tube, watching the Mets and the Giants go at it. He kills off the last of his Bud, crushes the can, and tosses it into a corner of the room. Counting the two other cans already there, the fucker's making quite a pile.

"Hey, this isn't a garbage dump, man," I grouse. "Pick up after yourself, okay?"

Vinnie waves me away. "Yeah, yeah, I'll do it later." He turns and looks at me. "So is everyone comin' or not?"

I grin. "What you mean is, is Lionel coming?"

Vinnie tries to keep a straight face. If he were that bad at hiding his interest during our poker games, he'd go home broke every Wednesday night. "You don't know shit what I mean," he grumbles.

"Yeah, right." I put the poker chips on the table and don't say nothin' else. I'm enjoying this. *Let him beg*, I think.

Vinnie goes back to watching the game. His arm's lying along the top of the couch, and I watch his fingers tapping on the pillow. The beat gets faster and faster. He looks like he's about to bust a gut. "All right, asshole," he finally growls. "Is Lionel coming?"

"Yeah," I laugh. "As soon as his shift at the warehouse is over."

Vinne shoots me an exasperated look. "Jeez, was that a state secret or something?"

"Naw, I just like giving you a hard time, Vinnie. It helps pass the day."

Vinnie grimaces and flips me off. "Sit on it, Marty."

"Oh, yeah, baby," I grin. "Just name the time and place." I dump a bag of potato chips into the bowl. "Mike and Jerry are coming too. After their workout at the Y."

Vinnie frowns. "Shit, all those guys ever do is work out. They're a couple of muscle heads."

"What do you want them to do?" I laugh. "Chug beer all day and get a belly like yours?" I knew that would get Vinnie's goat. He's as vain as a damn peacock about his looks.

"Hey, screw you," Vinnie says. He stands up and lifts his shirt. "My belly's as flat as a fuckin' ironing board. And as hard, too."

And he's right. Underneath the hair, his abs are lean and cut. But I just grin. "I don't know, Vinnie," I say. "Looks like you're getting some love handles there."

Vinnie gives me a disgusted look and goes back to watching the game. Vinnie and me go back a long way. We grew up on the same block, got in fights with each other, and later became buddies. He was always a looker: black curly hair, dark eyes that could melt stone, a face that could break your heart, and a hot muscular body that got my dick thumping every time I saw him. Even when we were kids duking it out, all I could think about was how fucking beautiful he was. I never said anything about it, figuring it was a lost cause. That is, until years later when, cruising the docks, I ran into him with his 501s around his ankles and some dude swinging on his dick. Vinnie and me stared at each other for a couple of seconds and then busted out laughing. We've gotten it on a couple of times since then, but there's too much history between us. We're just buddies now. Though I gotta admit, that fucker can still get me hard at a drop of a hat.

About a half hour later, the bell rings, and I buzz Mike and Jerry in. Mike is Vinnie's cousin, but you'd be hard put to tell they were related. He's not good-looking, like Vinnie. His face is broad, his mouth too wide, his nose crooked from being broke God knows how many times from back when he used to box. He's also shorter than Vinnie but more muscular, with huge arms and a chest like a brick wall. He looks like about the meanest ass kicker ever to walk down this city's streets. Which is a hoot and a half, 'cause Mike is about the sweetest, most easygoing guy I ever met. Jerry is his latest boyfriend, and like most of the others, he's lean, well-built, and blond. He walks into the room ahead of Mike, and

Mike's eyes follow him around like there was a string tying Jerry's body to Mike's head.

I toss them each a beer. Jerry tosses it back at me. "You got an Evian?" he asks. "Or Perrier?" I remember now that Mike told me that Jerry was a health-food nut. Behind him, I see Vinnie sneer.

" 'Fraid not," I say. "How 'bout some orange juice?"

Jerry smiles, and for a second I can see why Mike is so gaga over him. "Yeah," he says. "That'll do in a pinch."

Vinnie goes back to his game, and the rest of us make small talk. The doorbell rings again, and the way Vinnie jumps, I can tell he's just been sitting there waiting for it. I keep on talking with Mike and Jerry.

"Hey, you deaf or something?" Vinnie asks. "Didn't you hear the doorbell?"

"I don't think I'm going to answer it," I say, keeping my face straight. "It's probably just some Jehovah's Witnesses. They've been bugging me a lot lately."

Vinnie gets up. "Then I'll get it," he says. "You could use a little religion, you sick, depraved motherfucker." I laugh. He buzzes the street door open.

A couple of minutes later, there's a knock on the door. Vinnie yanks it open, and there's Lionel, standing out in the hall. He's wearing his security guard outfit, and the way he looks, if I was a robber, I'd think twice before trying to break into any warehouse where he works. He's one big dude, at least four inches taller than me, and I'm six feet. Right now, he completely fills the doorframe. You could build a fuckin' condo on his shoulders. He looks at us from behind a pair of lightly tinted shades, copping his stony-face attitude. Lionel's an all-right dude, but he likes to push people's buttons at first, just to see how they react.

"Hey, man, how ya doin'? Come on in," Vinnie says eagerly. A couple of minutes ago, he was watching the tube, ignoring us. Now he's Mr. Fuckin' Congeniality. It's a trip watching him. Vinnie ain't exactly what you'd call "enlightened". As a kid, he and the other local Italian boys used to tangle with the brothers over around Pierce Street, where the two neighborhoods come together. But Lionel's being black hasn't kept Vinnie from getting a major hard-on for the guy. In fact, Vinnie's like a puppy now, wagging his tail. Lionel and me (and sometimes Vinnie) shoot pool over at a leather bar on Harrison Street, and this is the first time Lionel's come over for one of our poker games.

Lionel don't say anything; he just walks in, his thumbs hooked in his pockets. I introduce Mike and Jerry to him, and he nods. "Hey, Marty," Vinnie says. "Get Lionel a beer."

I'm about to tell Vinnie to go fuck himself, but I control the urge. I turn to Lionel. "You thirsty?"

"Yeah," Lionel says. "A beer would be all right." I toss one to him. He pops it open and takes a big gulp. Vinnie helps himself to another beer. We all talk a while longer. Lionel don't say much, but he don't tune us out either. I can feel him checking us out behind those shades. After a while, he takes them off, folds them, and puts them in his shirt pocket. I feel weird talking to him tonight; his eyes fuckin' drill through me, like what's goin' on between us has nothing to do with what I'm saying. Lionel's always been a hard guy to read. After a couple of minutes of this, I suggest we get a game going.

We all sit at the table. "What kind of stakes do you guys play for?" Lionel asks.

"It's just a friendly game," I say. "We keep the pot to about ten dollars."

Lionel shots me another long, hard look. "Sh-e-e-eit, if I'd known this was such a penny-ante operation, I wouldn't have bothered coming by."

"Hey, don't do us any favors," Mike snorts.

"We're just a bunch of working stiffs, Lionel," I say. "We don't have a lot of money to throw around."

Nobody says nothing for a while. Things feel kind of strained. I look at Lionel. "So should I deal you in or what?"

Lionel shakes his head. "I don't know, Marty. I'd just like to make the stakes more interesting."

"Hey, man," Mike says. "Then you ought to start hanging out with the money crowd. It sure as hell ain't here."

Lionel shifts his gaze to Mike. "So who said anything about money?" he asks calmly.

That shuts us all up for a few seconds. "What are you talking about, man?" Vinnie finally asks.

Lionel flashes us a slow, easy smile. I can see why Vinnie's got such a hard-on for this guy.

Lionel leans back in his chair, his hands behind his head. "Let's make this game interesting, guys," he says. "Let's play for sex."

Another silence. Vinnie leans forward. "You want to run that by us again, Lionel?" Ol' Lionel has Vinnie's attention on this one.

Lionel laughs. "What's the matter? You guys never heard of strip poker before? Every time you lose, you take something off. If you fold, you don't do nothing. After you lose four times, you ain't got nothing on but the radio."

"Yeah," Vinnie says quietly. "And then what?" I almost laugh. He looks like a kid being told about Santa Claus.

Lionel fakes a disgusted look. "What do you think, man? Next time you lose, you gotta do what the guy who beats you tells you to do. And if the guy's got imagination, then that's when the game starts getting fun."

"Sh-e-e-eit," Mike says. "No way."

But Vinnie looks interested. It's obvious he's thinking what he could do with Lionel if he wins. I glance at Jerry, and to my surprise he's looking back at me. *Yeah,* I think. *I could get up for this myself.*

Lionel looks around the table. "So what about it, guys?"

Vinnie takes a long pull from his beer. "I'm in."

Lionel turns to me. "Marty?"

I shrug, trying to look cool. But I feel my heart pounding hard. "Sure. Why not?"

Lionel looks at Jerry and Mike. "How 'bout you guys?"

Mike slowly shakes his head. "Jeez, I dunno."

"It sounds hot," Jerry says. "Count me in."

Mike gives him a long look. "You guys are fuckin' crazy," he finally says. "But all right. I'll go along."

"All right!" Lionel grins. "Deal those cards, Marty!"

The game is five-card stud. I got shit in my hand, and I draw three cards. I wind up with more nothing. A piss-poor beginning.

The betting begins. I fold, and so does Jerry. The others start seeing and raising each other a couple of times around, throwing chips on the table just to make it look like a regular game. Mike finally calls, and they lay their cards on the table. Vinnie's got a pair of kings; Mike, two pairs: sevens and tens. But Lionel's got two pairs too, aces high. He grins.

"All right, you fuckers. Take something off!" Both Vinnie and Mike peel off their shirts.

The next hand I win, with three eights. Everyone stayed in this time, so the rest of the guys start peeling again. Lionel pulls his shirt and T-shirt off, giving us an eyeful of a smooth black chest with nicely chiseled pecs. His arms are fuckin' huge, with biceps like polished cannonballs. He's sitting next to Mike, who's just thrown his shoes and socks into the growing pile of clothes. Mike is into heavy-duty bodybuilding, and though he's shorter than Lionel, his shoulders are just as wide and his torso at least as muscular. Jerry's a lot leaner, with a hairless, compact body and a pair of dark, pink nipples begging to be chewed on. He's got a set of abs so sharply cut that you could grate cheese on them.

I lose the next two times, first to Jerry, then to Mike. Vinnie and Lionel are down to their shorts, and me and the others are not far behind. The sexual energy is hanging as thick and heavy as the basket I see bulging out of Lionel's bikini briefs.

I win the next hand with three jacks; no one has folded. "Well, well," I grin, looking at Vinnie and Lionel. "Looks like it's time for you boys to drop your shorts."

Vinnie stands up. Grinning, he slowly pulls his Jockeys down. His dick, half-hard, sways from side to side as he steps out of them. He's got a good thick cock—a nice mouthful, as I remember—and uncut like the rest of us Italian boys. He looks at Lionel. "Your turn, fucker."

Lionel pulls down his bikini briefs. Even half-erect, he's impressive; I bet his dick's a good eight, nine inches when hard. It sure is a tube steak now: black, fat, meaty, with a big ol' head peeping out from under his foreskin. His balls hang low and fleshy, and they fill his nut sac nicely.

"If you lose again, man," Lionel says to Vinnie. "You gotta do what the winner tells you to."

Vinnie stretches and leans back in his chair. "I know the rules. Just deal the fuckin' cards." I don't think he's too bothered about losing.

Lionel wins the next hand, with a straight, nine-high. "Well, how about that?" He grins, leaning back in his chair, his legs spread apart. "This is where the game gets interesting." That thick dick meat of his begins stiffening, flopping against his thigh. Looks like he's getting some ideas. He glances at Vinnie. "I'll deal with you later," he says and turns his eyes on the rest of us. "Okay, guys, it's time for you to get naked."

Which is okay by me. I stand up and kick off my briefs, and after a moment, Mike and Jerry do the same. Mike still looks a little uneasy about all of this, but Jerry seems to be having a good time. He already has a hard-on, and when he pulls his Jockeys down, his dick slaps up against his belly. He's got one of those boners that bend to the right.

"I bet you can fuck around corners," I laugh.

"I manage," Jerry says, grinning. He makes no effort to hide his gaze as he checks me out. I feel my cock give an extra throb.

Lionel turns back to Vinnie. "Now, it's your turn. You gotta do what I tell you." His grin widens, flashing white teeth. "I want you to get up on that table for starters."

Vinnie offers no objections. He crawls on top of the table and lies spread-eagle on it. His dick is rock-hard now, flat against his belly, and his balls hang low and heavy. I'm between the V of his legs, and I look up the length of his body. It's been a long time since I've seen Vinnie naked, and he looks as hot as ever. Memories of how nice it felt to have his dick meat pumping jizz down my throat flash through my head. He props himself up on his elbows and watches me taking him all in.

"You gettin' an eyeful?" he asks. I don't say nothing, but I can't take my eyes off that fat salami of his.

Lionel stands up. "We'll start with something easy," he says. "I'm going to drop my balls in your mouth, Vinnie, and I want you to give them a good five-minute washing. Any questions?"

Vinnie grins. "Just quit with the chatter and get on with it, dude."

Lionel climbs onto the table and squats above Vinnie. We all watch as he lowers himself, his nut sac hanging loose until it's right above Vinnie's mouth. Vinnie sticks out his tongue and begins licking Lionel's balls.

"Yeah," Lionel growls. "That's right." His ass crack is right above Vinnie's head now. Vinnie takes both his balls in his mouth and slurps noisily on them, rolling them around with his tongue. Lionel begins slapping Vinnie with his stiff dick, rubbing it all over his face. Vinnie reaches down and starts stroking his own dick. This is one hot show to watch, and I make sure not to miss any of it. In fact, I begin pounding my own pud as I watch Vinnie's balls bounce above his ass crack.

Lionel stands up and gets off the table. "I think we're ready for another hand," he says.

Vinnie doesn't move. "Shit, man," he grouses. "I was just gettin' warmed up. You didn't even give me a chance to taste that big, black fuck pole of yours."

Lionel gives a slow smile. "It's not like the game is over, Vinnie." He turns to Jerry. "Deal the cards." Vinnie reluctantly rolls off the table.

After watching that little scene, the last thing any of us has got on his mind is playing cards, but Jerry deals them out. Damn if I don't win again with nothing better than a pair of kings. Nobody's bothering to drop out anymore, and they're all watchin' me now, waiting for me to call the shots.

I stand up and look at the four hot, naked men in front of me who have to do what I tell them to. The possibilities are endless. I walk out of the room into my bedroom and come back with an armful of rubbers, lube, dildos, and other toys. "Okay, men," I say. "It's time we get serious."

Ten minutes later, I'm shoving my dick down Jerry's willing throat as Mike eats out my ass. Me and Lionel are kissing hard now, our tongues thrust deep into each other's mouth, while my hand is wrapped around his thick cock, stroking it. My fingers barely touch around it. Vinnie drops to his knees, pushes my hand aside, and eagerly swallows Lionel's beefy cock.

"Hey, man," I growl. "I didn't tell you that you could do that."

Vinnie pulls Lionel's dick out of his mouth and looks up at me. "So call a cop," he says. He goes back to deep-throating Lionel. Lionel holds on to both sides of his head and starts pumping his hips. I cup Lionel's hefty balls in my hand and gently squeeze them. They feel like they're holding a couple of quarts of jism.

Jerry's tongue, wrapped around my dick, is sending hot sparks through my entire body. I watch his head bob back and forth and thrust my dick down deep every time he takes it in again. Mike's tongue is probing into my asshole, now. I look at Vinnie go at it with Lionel's cock. I've never seen the fucker go so crazy. Usually, he plays it cool, letting some other horny bastard do all the work, but he's in a frenzy now, eating dick like his life depended on it.

I'm curious to see how far Vinnie is willing to go. "Hey, Vinnie," I say. "Since I get to call the shots, how about you getting back on that table and letting Lionel plow that ass of yours?"

Vinnie does not look unhappy with this suggestion. For that matter, neither does Lionel.

Vinnie looks at Lionel and grins. "What choice do we have, man? After all, the fucker won the last hand." He climbs on top of the card table again, which sways under his weight. It was a Kmart special, not intended for this kind of abuse. Lionel slips a condom on, takes a handful of lube, and greases Vinnie's ass up good. Vinnie raises his legs in the air, and Lionel slowly eases his thick fuckpole up Vinnie's chute. Vinnie grimaces, but after Lionel begins pumping away, Vinnie relaxes and gets into the swing of things.

Apparently this inspires Mike, 'cause soon I feel his own lube-caked fingers poking against my pucker hole.

"Go for it, Mike," I say, and with this encouragement, his finger slides in up to the third joint. He wiggles it, and a whole new wave of sensations sweeps over me.

"Goddamn!" I groan. I see him reach for a rubber, and after a few seconds, he pulls his finger out, and I feel that stubby dick of his work its way up my ass. He wraps his brawny arms around my chest and begins plowing me good from behind. I can feel his hot breath against my cheek—hear him grunt with each thrust. Jerry, meanwhile, is twisting his head from side to side as his lips slide up and down my dick. He's pulling on my nuts with one hand as he strokes his own wanker with his other.

Lionel is slamming into Vinnie hard now, making that table shake mightily. I watch Lionel's ass clench and unclench with each thrust, Vinnie's legs draped over his shoulders. Vinnie reaches up and twists Lionel's nipples hard, and Lionel lets out a loud groan. The table suddenly collapses, and they both come crashing down to the floor. I laugh, but they're beyond caring, and Lionel keeps slamming that thick meat of his hard up Vinnie's ass as if nothing happened. He bends down, and he and Vinnie kiss hard without Lionel ever once losing his stride.

Mike tightens his grip around me and speeds up his tempo. I feel his hard, muscular body pressed tight against my back, his powerful arms pinning me, his dick impaling me over and over again. I reach back and squeeze his balls just tight enough to make him groan, half in pleasure, half in pain. Then I grab hold of Jerry's head and slam my dick hard down his throat, my balls grinding against his chin. Jerry looks up at me, his mouth full of dick, and I meet his gaze and grin. Mike sticks his tongue into my ear and digs in deep.

Vinnie and Lionel have rolled over so that Lionel is on his back with Vinnie on top, his back to Lionel. I get a clear shot of that thick, black fuckmeat of Lionel's plowing in and out of Vinnie's ass, of Vinnie beating his own meat, his balls bouncing up and down. Lionel's hands are around

Vinnie's waist, holding him steady as he skewers him. They move across Vinnie's muscular torso, stroking and kneading the hard flesh, pinching his nipples. Vinnie leans back against him, his eyes closed, his mouth hanging open. He turns his head, and the two men french each other hard. But my eyes keep returning to that dark cock plowing into Vinnie. It's about the hottest sight I've ever seen. I don't know which I'd rather be at this moment, Vinnie or Lionel or both of them at the same time.

Mike's breathing is getting mighty heavy now. I feel it on my face and neck with every thrust of his dick up my ass. I clench my ass tight against his dick inside, and he lets out a long groan. I tug on his balls again; they're pulled up tight now, and I know it won't be long before he pops his cork. I'm getting pretty close myself, watching Lionel and Vinnie, feeling Jerry's skillful tongue wrapped around my crank and Mike's thick dick shoved up my ass.

All of a sudden, Mike starts shuddering, and his arms around me tighten even more. He cries out, and I feel that dick of his pumping its load into the condom. Mike grinds his hips tight against my ass, groaning loudly, his mouth on my neck and shoulders. That's enough to push me over the edge. My load gushes out, one squirt after another, splattering against the roof of Jerry's mouth. He takes it all in, sucking hard, gulping down my jism, squeezing my balls as if to drain every drop out of them. I look down to see cum ooze between his fingers as he shoots into his hand.

Mike's shudderings finally stop. He still holds me tightly, moving his large, calloused hands across my torso, his softening dick still up my ass. He slowly pulls out. Jerry stands up, and the three of us kiss gently on our mouths, our faces, our necks. I'm sandwiched between the two men, and I feel their hard, naked flesh rub against me tightly.

Lionel and Vinnie are still going at it, and the three of us watch with appreciation. Lionel is slamming Vinnie's ass hard and fast now, shoving that fat cock of his all the way up to his balls and then pulling out to the very tip each time. Both of their bodies gleam with sweat; trickles of it stream down their faces. Lionel's breathing hard now, and his face is all twisted up with the feelings shooting through his body. He groans softly, and after a moment the groans get louder and louder.

"Come on, Lionel," I growl. "We want to see your load shoot out of that monster dick of yours."

"All right, fucker," Lionel gasps. "Then take a look!" He pulls out of Vinnie's ass, rips off the rubber, and one load after another of sweet, creamy jizz spews out of his dick, icing his and Vinnie's torsos. Vinnie groans loudly as cum squirts out of his dick as well, joining Lionel's in spermy puddles on his skin. After the last of the load flies out, Vinnie rolls over and kisses Lionel, their come-slicked bodies pressed tight together.

"Yeah!" I laugh. "That was a really hot show, guys!"

Later, we clean up and get dressed. None of us says much of anything. Lionel puts on the cap of his uniform, straightening the brim while looking in the hall mirror. He looks at us and laughs. "Well, what's it going to be, guys? Are we meeting next week?"

The rest of us glance at each other. Everbody's got a shit-eatin' grin on his face. "Yeah," I say. "I think that can be arranged."

Vinnie's grin widens, flashing white teeth. His eyes take in the full length of Lionel's body. "I'm already thinking about the things I'm going to make you do, fucker, after I win the final hand."

Lionel laughs again. "We'll just have to see, fucker. We'll just have to see."

# Rocker Bruce

Joe twists his body around and glances at the back seat. "Okay, folks," he says. "What'll it be, two rooms or one?"

The two girls look at each other and giggle. I know this is the moment of truth. "One room, of course, Joe," I say, my mouth dry. "You know that's all we can afford." *If they all insist on two rooms, I'm backing out,* I think. *The only reason I've gone this far is to see Joe naked.*

Joe gives a comic leer and waggles his eyebrows. "Uh, oh, orgy time, huh?" He laughs. His glance shifts from Carla to Angela. "How about it, ladies? You don't care that much about privacy, do you?"

The two of them exchange glances again. Carla raises her eyebrows and Angela shrugs. "It's okay by me," Carla finally says. "It'll give us a chance to see which one of you guys got the most to brag about."

Joe looks at me in mock shock. "Jesus, Dan!" he says. "We got a couple of live ones tonight!" They all laugh, and I force myself to join in. My heart's beating like a goddamn piston.

Joe climbs out of the front seat and walks into the motel lobby. There's a sign above the door, in red neon, reading "The Seaview Motel." I can see Joe through the glass door, talking to the night clerk. They both glance toward the car, and Joe shrugs and gives the clerk an easy grin, pouring on the charm like only he can do. Carla turns the rearview mirror in her direction and combs her hair. I glance out the window over toward the beach and the darkness of the Atlantic Ocean. I can just barely hear the music of the Asbury Park carousel over the thud of the surf. It was less than two hours ago that Joe and I met the girls there, riding the lacquered horses and giving us the eye. The bumper-car rides and Ferris wheel softened them up, but it was only after we all took a ride down into the Tunnel of Love that the girls agreed to the motel.

Angela nestles against me, and I absently put my arm around her. She reaches up and turns my face toward her. I look down at her. She's halfway between plain and kind of pretty. I close my eyes and kiss her, pretending that it's Joe I'm kissing, that it's his tongue I feel pushing into my mouth. I think of Joe naked, and my dick stiffens. Angela reaches down and puts her hands between my legs. "Oh, baby," she coos. "You're ready for *bear*, aren't you?"

A couple of minutes later, Joe comes up, whistling. He dangles the key in front of him. "Party time!" he grins.

Angela and I are stretched out on one of the two beds, our mouths fused together, our hands fumbling with buttons and snaps. I unhook her bra and toss it to the floor. I glance over toward Joe and Carla. He's got his shirt unbuttoned and his jeans and boxer shorts down around his ankles. His face is nuzzling between Carla's breasts, his back turned toward me. I take in his smooth, pale ass, the way it dimples as he grinds his hips against Carla. He pushes away long enough to kick off his shoes and pull his pants off. His dick is stiff and ready for action. It's the first time I've seen Joe's dick hard, and I drink in the sight: the thick, veined shaft, the flared head, the orange pubic bush. Joe has the pale, freckled skin of the typical redhead, and his torso looks like it was carved out of ivory. My eyes slide up his body. Christ, he's so fuckin' beautiful. And this probably is as close to having sex with him as I'm ever going to get. He glances over toward me, and our eyes meet. "You having a good time, Dan?" he asks, laughing.

"Yeah, Joe," I say, putting enthusiasm in my voice. "Just swell."

Joe reaches over to the nightstand to turn off the light.

"No," I say, my tone sharper than I intend. "Leave it on."

Joe shoots me a quizzical look but pulls his hand back. I turn my attention back to Angela, stroking her breasts, kissing her, flicking her nipples with my thumbs and forefingers. She moans softly. I pull off the rest of my clothes and stretch out besides her. My dick is only half hard. I wrap my arms around her, and turn her so that I get clear view of Joe. He's on his back, eating pussy as Carla sucks his dick. His muscular body writhes under hers, and he thrusts his hips up, shoving his dick deep down her throat. *What would it feel like to have Joe's dick in my mouth?* I wonder. *Does Carla realize how lucky she is?* As I watch, my dick stiffens to full hardness. I turn back to Angela. Her eyes are hard and her mouth is pulled down into a small scowl. I slide my hand down between her legs, and after a few seconds she relents and opens up for me. I remove my hand and enter her, fucking her in long, slow strokes, my eyes fixed on Joe.

Joe is fucking Carla now, his hips pumping away, his mouth open, his eyebrows pulled down in concentration. I watch his dick plow into her, his balls slamming up against her with each stroke. It makes for an incredibly hot show. I time my thrusts with Joe's, pumping Angela in synch with each piston stroke of his. In my mind I'm plowing his ass, and then the fantasy shifts and he's fucking me, shoving his thick dick hard up my chute. It's hard to tell which part of Joe's body excites me the most: the lean torso, his face, his thick, veined cock, that beautiful pale ass. . . .

"Get off me, you son of a bitch!" Angela snarls.

I look down at her, startled. "What?" She pushes me, and I topple off her, barely keeping from falling onto the floor. "What's your problem?" I ask, more surprised than angry.

Angela doesn't say anything. She starts grabbing her clothes and putting them on furiously. Her face looks like a fist. For a second, her eyes meet mine, and I see pure hate. Joe and Carla have stopped fucking and are looking at us. "What's wrong?" Carla asks. She turns her eyes on me like laser fire. "What did you do to Angela?" she snaps.

"I didn't do anything!" I protest. Now I'm getting nervous. *How much did I give away?* I wonder.

Angela ignores us all. She's dressed now and flings open the door. She slams it behind her like she's trying to obliterate us all.

I pull on my jeans and run after her. I catch up to her half a block down the street. "Will you tell me what's wrong?" I ask.

"Fuck off!" She doesn't look at me or break her stride.

"Angela," I plead. I grab her arm.

She swings around and hits me. Not a slap, but an honest-to-God punch in the face. I stagger back, just barely managing not to fall on my ass. "You think I'm stupid!?" she yells at me. "You think I don't know what you're up to?"

My heart skips a beat. "What are you talking about?" I ask, trying to sound angry. I feel blood running down my nose, and I hold my hand up to block it.

She looks me right in the face. "I saw you staring at Carla. You were pretending you were screwing *her*." She's crying now. "That was the only way you could keep your prick hard, you son of a bitch!"

I don't say anything. I mean, what can I say? *No, Angela, I wasn't looking at Carla, I was looking at Joe. He was the one that was keeping my dick stiff.* After a while I shrug. "I'm sorry."

"Yeah, well, you can shove 'sorry' up your ass." Angela storms down the street. I stand there watching her until she turns a corner and is out of sight. My nose has stopped bleeding. Because I can't think of anything else to do, I go back to the motel.

Joe and Carla are at it again when I walk in. They break away, and Joe glances at me impatiently. Without Angela, I'm definitely a crowd. "I'll be out of here in a second," I mutter, pulling on the rest of my clothes. They don't even wait till I'm out of the room before they're at it again. I leave after sneaking one last glance at Joe's sweet, dimpled ass.

The amusement park has shut down, and all the rides are dark. The main video arcade is padlocked closed, and the booths selling seashells, taffy, and candy apples are empty. Except for a few stragglers and the homeless guys stretched out sleeping on the benches, I've got the boardwalk to myself. I don't have enough money for another room, and it looks like I'm going to have to spend the night out here, walking, until it's time for Joe and me to catch our bus back to Fort Dix. I couldn't be more depressed.

I hear the *thump, thump* of the bass beat before I can make out the actual music. It threads its way through the warm summer night like a heartbeat, sometimes weak, sometimes strong and steady. Eventually I distinguish other instruments: guitars, the bleat of a saxophone. Having nothing better to do, I follow the sound until I come upon a beat-up, cinder block building squatting in the middle of a near-empty parking lot. A flickering neon sign bolted above the door hisses and sputters the words "The Hullabaloo Club." I pull open the door and walk in.

The place is small: a bar along the left wall, a cluster of tables and chairs, a tiny stage up front. There can't be more than a dozen customers scattered throughout the room, clumped together in ones and twos. They sit sprawled in their chairs, drinks in hand, shouting at each other over the music or slouched down and staring glumly at the stage. A smoggy haze of cigarette smoke hangs over everybody's head. *What a dive,* I think.

And yet the band is . . . not bad. It consists of a drum set, a saxophone, and two electric guitars. They're pumping out some kind of rock 'n roll riff now, the beat fast, the music lively. The two guitars take turns running up and down the scales, improvising around one string of chords that keeps making itself heard through all the variations it gets put through. One of the guitar players steps up to the mike and starts singing. I stand there at the door watching him. The song he's singing is pretty down stuff: loneliness, broken hearts, sexual longing, and yet he sings it all with this *exuberance,* standing up there on that cramped stage, his head thrown back, his hips thrust out, whalin' away on the guitar chords. I can't keep my eyes off him. He's dressed in tight black chinos and a black T-shirt that fits him like a second skin. His body is lean and tight, and he moves it with an easy confidence that is a beautiful thing to witness. With his black hair greased back and his sideburns, he looks like a street hood. Yet there's nothing menacing about him, he's almost laughing as he belts out those lyrics about heartache and loss.

I grab a nearby table. A waitress comes over and I order a beer. The band finishes its song and before the echoes of the last note die down, it launches into another. The guy's still glued to the mike, his voice shooting up the scales to a falsetto, and then sliding back down to a clear, steady tenor. His eyes sweep the room, and when his gaze meets mine, he grins and winks at me. By the time the band's wrapped up its set, four or five songs later, I'm actually feeling pretty good.

The band leaves the stage and a few minutes later the house lights turn on. I glance at my watch. It's almost two, closing time. My good spirits come crashing down. *Where am I going to go now?* I wonder.

I walk out into the parking lot and stand there with my thumbs hooked into my jeans' front pockets. I have absolutely nowhere to go. People brush by me, climb into their cars and drive off. I just stand there and watch as the parking lot empties.

"You are one lonely lookin' dude," a voice behind me says.

I turn and see the singer leaning against the wall of the bar, a lit joint between the thumb and forefinger of his right hand. He takes a hit and then holds it out to me. I take the joint, hold it to my lips and inhale deeply. I return it to him. "Where's the rest of your band?" I ask.

"They split in the van," he says. He regards me with half lidded, sleepy eyes. His gaze flickers for a second on my hair. "Nobody has hair that short. You a soldier or something?"

I nod. "I'm stationed at Fort Dix." He doesn't say anything; just stands there, leaning against the wall, his eyes fixed on me. "I'm on a three-day pass," I add lamely. He still doesn't say anything. "I like your music," I say.

He laughs good-naturedly. "We're not exactly packing the place." He hands me the joint and I take another toke. "Where're you staying?" he asks.

I look out across the parking lot and then back at him. "Well, it's kind of a long story, but I'm not staying anywhere, actually. I'm just killing time until my bus leaves for Fort Dix tomorrow morning."

A cop car cruises slowly by, a searchlight mounted outside the passenger window. The singer hides the hand holding the joint behind his body, shifting his weight to his other foot. The beam sweeps over us, and for a second I'm blinded by the light. The cruiser rolls slowly by.

"Listen," the singer says, turning his face back toward me. "You want to help me finish this joint in my car?"

"Yeah," I say. "Sure." I hold out my hand. "My name's Dan."

We shake hands. "Bruce," he says. He nods to some old Cadillac parked in the corner of the lot, the only car there now. It's an improbable shade of pink. "That's my car, over there." He walks over to it, and I follow right behind. He unlocks the front passenger door, and I slide in. Bruce climbs in behind the steering wheel.

"Christ," I laugh. "This car is a *tank!*"

Bruce grins. "I fuckin' love Cads, the goddamn, gas-guzzling monsters. I even wrote a couple of songs about them." He passes the joint to me again. "It's gone out," he says. He pulls out a lighter and clicks the flame on. He wraps his hands around mine as he lights the joint, but even after it glows, he keeps his hands closed around mine. We look into each other's eyes. My dick starts growing hard. He lets go and leans against the car door, his level gaze still fixed on me.

"I bet I could write a song about you," he says. "Lonely soldier wandering down the Asbury Park boardwalk at two a.m., no place to stay.

Handsome and melancholy. Probably lovestruck." He laughs softly. "Oh, the song I could make of you!"

I laugh along with him. There's a long silence. Bruce reaches over and pulls me to him and kisses me, first lightly, and then with greater heat. I return the kiss eagerly, and it's only a couple of beats before our tongues are pushing deep into each other's mouths. Bruce slides his hand underneath my T-shirt and runs his fingers across my torso. He grips my left nipple between his thumb and forefinger and squeezes. My body tingles with sensation. I push against Bruce, pinning him against the door, grinding my body against his. He wraps his arms around me, and thrusts his body up to meet mine. He jams his elbow against the steering wheel, and the horn gives off a loud blast.

"Jeez," he grins. "It's time we moved this party to the back seat!" We scramble over the front seats into the dim cavern behind us. I stretch out onto the back seat, and Bruce sprawls out on top of me. "Christ, I love Cadillacs!" he laughs. "They're like motels on wheels." His hand slides down my jeans and clutches my hard cock pushing against the rough fabric. A street lamp half a block away bathes Bruce's face in its dim light. He's wearing the same exhilarated look he had when he was on stage pumping out his songs. "How about you and me getting naked, Dan?" he growls.

We pull each other's clothes off, and it just takes a couple of minutes before I feel Bruce's bare skin against mine, his hard dick dry-humping my belly as he covers my face and neck with kisses. I slide my hands down his back and cup his ass cheeks, squeezing them as they pump up and down. I wrap my other hand around both our dicks, pressing the dick flesh together, feeling the warmth of Bruce's cock flow into mine. His dick feels thick and meaty inside my palm. I slide my thumb across his cockhead and feel a slippery drop of pre-cum. I milk another drop out of his dick and slide my jizz-slicked hand up and down the two shafts of flesh. Bruce gives a sigh a hair's breadth shy of a groan. "Oh, baby, that feels so *good!*" he whispers.

Bruce kisses me as I jack us both off, pressing his lips against my eyes, my cheeks, down my neck. His mouth works its way south, his tongue flicking my nipples, swirling around them. He lifts my right arm and burrows his face into my pit; I feel his tongue tickle the hairs as he laps my sweat up like some thirsty cat. I bend my neck down and stick my tongue in his ear, probing deep inside the fleshy hole.

Bruce sits up so that he's on his knees staring down at me. "Shift your body a little," he whispers. "Move into the light so that I can look at you."

I slide across the seat out of shadow into the faint illumination. Bruce stares at me, his eyes tracing a path down my body. "Fuckin' beautiful," he croons. He gives a low laugh. "I am so happy I got this handsome, naked soldier in the back seat of my Cad." He bends down and, starting with my balls, slides his tongue up the shaft of my hard dick, swirling it around my cockhead. He does it again.

"You suck cock like you're eating an ice cream cone," I laugh.

"That's what you are." Bruce grins. "One big dessert." He pushes the tip of his tongue into my piss slit, and then takes my whole cock in his mouth, sliding his lips down the shaft until his chin presses down against my balls. He begins bobbing his head up and down, sucking my dick with long, slow strokes. I thrust my hips up, matching the downward slide of his lips. Bruce wraps his hands around my balls and tugs on them gently. I groan softly.

"Turn around," I urge. "Let's get a little '69' action going."

Without taking my dick out of his mouth, Bruce pivots his body around. I crane my neck up and suck Bruce's balls into my mouth, rolling them around with my tongue, gauging their heft and weight by how they fill my mouth, breathing in their strong, musky odor. I stroke his dick slowly, nuzzling my face into that warm, secret place behind his balls. My tongue slides down the hairy path that ends in his asshole. The picture flashes through my head of when I first saw Bruce, looking so hot on that stage, all that pumpin' energy, the lean body arched back, the face full of wild joy. *And now I'm eating his ass out!* I think.

We roll around in the back seat of Bruce's Cad, bouncing off of ashtrays and armrests, sometimes me on top, sometimes Bruce, grunting and eating dick or balls like there's hell to pay. The summer night is warm, and our bodies soon are slippery with sweat. We slide off of each other like otters in rut, our bodies making wet, slapping noises. The windows are fogging up, and what light there is comes through in a pearly glow.

Bruce breaks away and crawls over the front seat, his legs dangling down behind. I hear him rummaging around in the glove compartment. He comes back waving a pack of condoms and a small jar of lube. "Okay, Dan," he grins. "I think it's time we moved on to some serious ass fucking."

I lean back, raising my legs and Bruce proceeds to grease up my asshole. He slips a finger up my chute, and then another. I push my hips up as he slides in to the third knuckle. I close my eyes, feeling Bruce's fingers playing my ass as skillfully as they did his guitar an hour ago.

Bruce pulls his fingers out. He hoists my legs around his hips, and slowly, patiently skewers my ass with his thick dick. When he's full in, he grinds his hips in slow circles, his balls pressed hard against me, his face hovering over mine. His forehead is beaded with sweat, and his dark eyes burn. He slowly pulls his dick out, teasing me, grinning but with his eyebrows pulled down. When the tip of his dick is just barely inside me, he plunges his hips down, and his cock slides in deep. I cry out. Bruce pumps his hips, his fuck strokes hard and fast. I push up to meet him, and we soon fall into synch, me thrusting up in time with each downward plunge of his.

Bruce wraps his arms around me and, without skipping a beat, pivots me over so that he's now on his back. I reach down and twist Bruce's nipples, and he gives a sharp outrush of breath that trails off into a whimper. I bend down and kiss him, our mouths working together, our tongues pushing against each other. Bruce quickens his thrusts, grunting each time his dick slams hard up my chute. I reach back and tug on his balls, feeling their hairiness, their heft, how they fill my hand in such a satisfying way. I think about the load churning away inside them, waiting for the moment when it can spurt out. "When you finally shoot, baby," I growl, "I want to see it! You understand?"

Bruce's eyes are glazed now, his mouth open. He nods 'yes' but says nothing, focusing his attention on the serious business of fucking me good. His hands are gripping my torso tightly; they slide up across my belly and over my chest. He curls his hands into fists and punches me lightly on the pecs. "Fuckin' hot, naked soldier boy," he growls, "with that thick, hard dick and that handsome face and that pretty ass. Sweet Jesus, but your ass is sweet, I could plow it all night!" He cups the back of my neck with his hand and pulls me down into another long, wet kiss. He plunges his dick in with a deep, hard thrust and his body shudders violently.

"Okay, fucker," he moans, "You want to see it? Well, here goes!"

He pulls his dick out and whips off the rubber. His load spurts out, splattering hard against my face, raining down in thick, white drops. Bruce throws his head back and cries out as his body continues to tremble. He looks down at my cum-drenched face and laughs. "It looks like I shot you point blank, buddy. Right between the eyes!"

He slides his hand across my face and then wraps his cum-smeared palm around my dick and starts jacking me off, slowly, lovingly. I arch my back up, and Bruce watches me with gleaming eyes. My load spurts out, caking my chest. I groan loudly, and Bruce laughs his appreciation. He falls down on top of me, our naked bodies pressed tightly together, our mouths fused to each other.

We lay there for a long time. I can just barely hear the sound of the surf, one block down and across the Jersey beach. I drift into sleep, then out, then in again. Bruce finally gently shakes me awake. "I gotta go, Dan," he whispers. "It's a long drive home."

At my request, Bruce drives me back to The Seaview Motel. It's almost four and everything's dark except for a night light by the registration desk. Bruce parks in the driveway and turns off the engine. He bends over and kisses me, sliding his tongue in my mouth one last time. "Thanks," he says. "Catch my act again some time. I'll be playing at the Hullaballoo till the end of the month."

"Yeah," I say. "I will." I climb out of Bruce's monster Cad, and stand there, in the driveway, watching as he drives off. I don't turn away until his taillights are out of sight.

I slip inside the motel room. I don't care if Carla is still there or not, I've got to sleep in a bed for a couple of hours. The moon is up, and its light streams through the open window. Joe is sleeping on his back, his forearm over his eyes. To my relief, he's alone.

I quickly strip and slip under the blankets of the other bed. Once again, I can hear the dull roar of the surf, louder now than when I was in the back seat of Bruce's Cad. Joe is snoring gently. I grin in the darkness. *Well, it looks like we both got laid this weekend after all!* I think. I close my eyes and think of Bruce, up on the stage, pumping his hips to a rock 'n roll beat, playing his guitar, belting out his songs in his clear tenor voice.

# Bill's Big Dick

It's late Sunday morning, and Bill and I are still in bed, tangled up in the sheets. I can feel Bill's latest load slowly crust on my belly. I lay nestled in the crook of his arm, staring at the patterns on the ceiling made by the sun shining through the leaves of the maple tree outside. It's a Vermont Indian summer, and the day outside is bright and clear.

Bill bends down and kisses me on the forehead. "So, are we going to get married or what?"

*Here we go again*, I think. I don't say anything for a while. I clear my throat. "Well, there's this problem. . . ."

"Yeah," Bill snorts. "Your asshole dad."

I let a few beats go by. "What can I say? If I marry you, he'll cut me off without a penny." I glance up at him. "He thinks I can do better."

"Reggie Nichols," Bill sighs, and in that sigh is all the resignation of the world. He sits up and reaches for his skivvies.

"Hey, don't be like that," I say. Bill doesn't say anything. "It's Dad's idea, not mine."

"I think your dad's right," Bill shrugs. "Reggie's perfect for you. He's crazy about you. He's smarter than me, he's richer. He sure as hell is better looking. He's the son of your dad's business partner. Fuck, if you marry him, you two will be heirs to the biggest maple syrup processing plant in the county." He turns and looks at me, his face expressionless. "Frankly, I never could figure out why you haven't dumped me for him years ago."

"Haven't you forgotten something, Bill?" I say gently.

31

Bill shoots a sharp glance at me. "What? What have I forgotten?"

I look deep into Bill's eyes. "You've got a huge dick."

Bill gives a shy grin. "Well, yeah, there *is* that."

I wrap my hand around the back of Bill's neck and pull him down to me, planting my mouth on his. "Let me suck it again," I growl. "Let me feed on that big, throbbing, pulsating, red, veined manmeat."

"Fuck you," Bill growls back. "Go suck on Reggie Nichols dick. What there is of it."

"Come on, baby," I say. "Don't be like that."

Bill shrugs but says nothing. "Please, baby," I croon. "I'm begging you. Sit on my chest. At least let me look at it."

"All right," Bill says gruffly. "But no touching." He sits up and swings his leg over so that he's straddling my torso. His dick drapes over his fat ballsac, its knob resting on the little cleft between my pecs. Even soft, it's a monster, a red, thick spongy tube that coils out like some fleshy python. For all the time I've known Bill, I still can't look at his godzilla schlong with anything but awe.

I reach out to stroke it, but Bill slaps my hand away. "I said no touching," he growls.

My eyes trace the blue vein that snakes down the long pink shaft, ending in a knob that is as red and juicy and round as a ripe summer plum. Bill's piss slit is deep and long. I could (and have) buried my pinky in it up to the first joint. "Please, baby," I plead. "Let me stroke it."

"I don't think so," Bill says.

I continue to stare. Bill's balls are enormous: big, fat jizz factories that can pump out truly prodigious quantities of spunk whenever Bill shoots a load. They hang heavily in a fleshy, red pouch, cushioning Bill's tremendous wanker. As I stare at them, I feel saliva pool in my mouth. I love sucking on Bill's balls, even though, try as hard as I can, I can never fit them both in my mouth at the same time. "Come on," I beg piteously. "At least drop your balls in my mouth. Let me give them a good tongue bath."

"Fuck you," Bill growls. He's leaning back, propped up on his elbows, and his dick and balls hang a tantalizing couple of inches from my face. I inhale deeply and get a funky whiff: musk and sweat and ripe sex. Under the naked worship of my gaze, Bill's dick stirs, thickens and grows slowly hard. I stare fascinated as the blood pumps down into the meaty shaft and engorges it.

"Damn!" I whisper.

Bill's salami flops over against his thigh, lengthening and thickening like one of those stop-action films of a fleshy stalk pushing out of the ground and blossoming. Bill squeezes his ass, and his cock twitches. It's almost scary, like some behemoth stirring and coming to life. I watch the fat red head deepen in color and swell to full ripeness. I can't help myself. I grab for the meaty root like my hand has a mind of its own.

Bill seizes me by the wrist. "No!" he snarls. "You're cut off. Permanently."

"Just let me give it a squeeze," I plead.

Bill's eyes narrow. "You gonna marry me?"

I shake my head miserably. "Baby, I can't."

"Sure you can. This is Vermont."

"You know what I mean."

Bill glowers at me. "Then keep your hands to yourself."

Bill's dick is sticking straight up now, pointing to the ceiling, fully hard, twitching with every beat of his heart. It's like some thick, gnarled tree root, veined, pulsing, engorged with blood. I've never seen a dick in real life, or even in any porn magazine or video, that came even close to this, this . . . feast of man flesh. And I know that I never will. *Face it, Curtis*, I tell myself, *dickwise, this is as good as it's ever going to get.* "Okay," I groan. "I'll marry you!"

Bill stares hard into my eyes for a couple of beats. "You on the level?"

"Yeah, goddammit!" I snap, meeting his gaze.

Bill's mouth curls up into a sly smile, leaning back. "Okay," he says. "Then it's all yours."

I have to use both hands to completely encircle Bill's enormous cock. I can feel the warmth of the pulsing shaft spread into my palms, and I give it a hard squeeze. A clear drop of pre-jizz oozes out from the deep well of his piss slit. I squeeze again, and another couple of drops seep out. I coat my palms with Bill's slippery juice and begin sliding my hands up and down the mammoth pole. I feel like I'm wrestling with an anaconda. I swear the fucker must be at least eleven inches.

"Slide forward," I urge. "Stuff it down my throat."

Bill's sly grin widens. "Sure, Curtis. Anything you say." He scoots forward and his dick head pokes against my lips, like some lumbering St. Bernard trying to push in. I lick the red fleshy knob tenderly, running my tongue around it, probing into the piss slit, tasting the little dribbles of pre-cum that keep oozing out. Bill pushes forward with his hips, and his cock slowly slides into my mouth. I feel my lips stretch wide, trying to accommodate the thickness of the shaft. I can only nibble down half of Bill's cock before the cockhead bangs against the back of my throat. Even with his prick filling my mouth, there's still enough of the shaft left to wrap my hands around.

Bill starts pumping his hips, slowly at first, sliding his dick in and out between my lips. He cradles my head in his hand, and I look up into his eyes as he fucks my mouth. I slide my hand over his lean torso, tugging on the muscles, tweaking Bill's nipples, never breaking eye contact with him. Bill gives a long sigh. "Yeah, baby," he murmurs, "that's it, squeeze my titties." He picks up his pace, fucking my mouth faster now, his low hangers slapping against my chin. I can only take this so long before I have to come up for air. Sensing this, Bill pulls his dick out and drops his balls in my face. I burrow my nose into the loose folds of scrotal flesh, and breathe deeply, getting the full hit now of ripe ball stink, the hairs tickling my nose. Christ, I could get drunk sniffing Bill's balls; their musky scent fills my lungs, goes to my head. I start licking them, washing them with my tongue, sucking one into my mouth and then the other, as Bill lightly slaps my face with his father-of-all-wankers. One of my hands slides down Bill's back, between the crack of his ass, and I push a finger up his bung hole, twisting and working it up to the third knuckle. Bill gives a heart-felt groan, and starts whacking off in earnest. My other hand wraps around my own dick, and I whack off too, my strokes falling in synch with Bill's.

Our jack-fest continues on like this for the next few minutes, the only sounds being the little grunts and groans we give out with increasing frequency and the slap of hands on dick flesh. As I suck on Bill's balls, his dick looms above my face like some huge, pink blimp, some phallic Macy's Thanksgiving Day balloon, some great queer shrine of the Western World. I focus my gaze on it worshipfully, feeling my pumping hand drawing my load out from my balls. Bill's balls are pulled up tight now, and his dick twitches with the hardness of steel rebar.

"I could squirt any time now, buddy," Bill gasps. "How about you?"

"Yeah," I pant. "I'm just about there. Let's go for it."

Bill spits in his hand and then slides his saliva-slicked fist full down the length of his foot-long Polish sausage. "Oh, yeah, baby," he groans. "Here

I come." His body spasms, and a wad of hot jizz blasts out of his cockhead, arcs across space and slams hard into my face. This is followed by another blast and then another, Bill's cock a veritable Vesuvius of erupting splooge. A few quick strokes take me over the edge, and I push up, arching my back as my own load spurts out and splatters against Bill's back. We thrash around in the bed, our dicks pumping jizz, our bodies bucking, both of us crying out loud enough to bring the ceiling down on us.

When it's finally over, Bill rolls over and collapses on the bed beside me. We lay there, side by side, staring up at the ceiling, panting. Bill's load sluggishly drips down my face, and he bends over and licks it off. "So when are you going to tell your father about us?" he asks.

*Shit*, I think. "I dunno. Some time."

Bill reaches down besides the bed, picks up my pants and throws them at me. "Get dressed," he says. "We're telling him now."

We find Dad in the back of the maple syrup processing plant, in the warehouse where the main 5,000-gallon syrup tank is stored. Dad is talking to one of the plant engineers when we walk in. When he sees Bill and me together, I can tell by his expression that he is not a happy camper. He ends his conversation with a few terse words and turns to us.

"Hello, Curtis," he says. He manages a curt nod toward Bill.

*Say it quick*, I think. *While you still can.* "I got something to tell you, Dad," I blurt out. "Bill and I are getting married."

Dad looks like he's just taken a huge bite out of a shit sandwich. "I want to talk with you," he growls. He glances at Bill. "Alone."

Bill shrugs. "I'll just go check out that tank," he says.

"You do that," Dad says acidly.

When Bill is out of earshot, Dad turns to me, his eyes blazing. "Are you out of your fucking mind!?"

"I love him, Dad," I say miserably.

Dad looks over toward Bill as if he were examining a cockroach. He turns toward me again. He looks as baffled as he does pissed. "*Why!?*"

I clear my throat. "It's kind of hard to explain."

Dad looks at me with withering patience. "Try."

I run my fingers through my hair. "Well, you see, Bill has a big dick."

Dad continues staring at me. "And . . . ?" he finally prompts.

I wrack my brains for something else to add. "When I say big," I finally say. "I mean *really* big."

Dad just stares at me. "That's it?" he finally asks. "You love Bill because his dick is big?"

I clear my throat. "Well, nothing else really comes to mind right now." Dad's eyes burn holes in me. I shift my weight to my other foot. "Maybe I should clarify something," I say. "When I say 'really big', I mean *enormous.*"

There's this long, awkward silence between us. Dad opens his mouth, closes it, and opens it again. I'm getting really nervous now. It's the first time I've ever seen him at a loss for words. "If you marry that loser," he finally says in a low, murderous voice, "I swear I'll cut you off without a cent."

"Uh, Mr. Henderson," Bill says. Neither one of us noticed his approach.

"What?" Dad snaps.

"I think you better check out your tank." Bill points toward the syrup storage tank. Maple syrup is gushing out a small hole about three feet above the floor.

"Holy shit!" Dad cries out. We all run up to the tank. The syrup is pouring out in a steady jet now, spraying onto the cement floor. The hole has grown to about four inches in diameter. Dad desperately holds his hand against the hole, but the force of the jet is too strong, and the syrup oozes out between his fingers. His face is twisted in despair. "This is going to ruin me," he moans. "I'm going to lose an entire year's production."

Bill turns to me. "Kiss me," he says, his voice urgent.

I stare at him. "Um, Bill, I don't think this is the time for . . ."

"Just kiss me!" Bill says savagely. He grabs me and plants his mouth on mine, pulling my body up against his. I feel his tongue snaking into my mouth, and I instinctively start grinding my pelvis against him. I can feel Bill's dick stir and grow hard under the denim of his jeans.

Bill breaks the embrace and roughly pulls Dad away from the tank. Dad and I are both too startled to protest. Bill unbuckles his belt, pulls down his fly, and drops his jeans down around his ankles. His hard dick juts out in front of him like a Hun battering ram. Bending his knees slightly, he slides his humongous boner full into the hole in the vat. The gush of maple syrup slows down to the merest trickle. "I think I can staunch the flow," he gasps. "At least for a while."

"I'll go get the tech crew," Dad says urgently. He runs out of the room.

"Bill," I whisper. "You're a goddamn hero!"

"Do you have a condom?" Bill gasps.

I stare at him. "Yeah. Here in my back pocket."

"Put it on and fuck my ass," Bill says urgently. "I've got to keep my dick hard or else I'll lose the seal."

Well, what else can I do? I mean we're talking the survival of the entire syrup company. By the time the tech crew finally comes racing in, I'm plowing Bill's ass like there's hell to pay, just the way he likes it, keeping his giant fuckpole nice and hard. The crew pulls Bill free and while they patch the hole, the two of us go around to the back of the tank and finish what we started. Bill's humongous syrup-coated schlong is like a giant stick of candy, and I make sure to lick it clean and wash the sticky syrup down with what feels like about a quart of Bill's creamy load.

Back in Dad's office, Dad shakes Bill's hand. "I don't know how to thank you," he says. "You saved the company, Bill." It's the first time I've seen Dad behave in any manner approaching "humble".

Bill shrugs, obviously embarrassed, but pleased, too. "I'm just glad me and my dick could be of service, sir."

"Don't call me 'sir', Bill." Dad says smiling. "Call me 'Dad.' After all, you're going to be a part of our family soon."

I feel a lump rising in my throat and tears come to my eyes. Happy endings always have this effect on me.

# Family Affair

Nick and Maria ride up front, in Maria's beat-up, '84 Buick convertible, Maria driving like a lunatic, weaving in-and-out of the traffic, me wedged in the back seat with all the beach gear tumbling over me. The radio is turned on full blast, set to an oldies station, belting out a Beach Boys tune. "I wish they all could be California girls," Nick sings along. He buries his face into Maria's neck and makes loud, farting noises. Maria screams with laughter, and it's only by the grace of God that she avoids plowing us all into the highway's concrete median.

"Jesus Christ!" I cry out in terror.

Nick and Maria crack up, Nick wheezing, Maria's shoulders shaking spasmodically. "What the hell is wrong with you guys?" I shout. "You been sniffing airplane glue?"

"No," Nick says. "Drano." Maria breaks up again, laughing until she starts hiccupping.

"You two are fucking crazy," I say, shouting over the wind and the radio. "You're going to kill us all."

Nick turns his head and looks at me grinning. "Lighten up, Robbie," he says. "We're supposed to be having a good time." I glare at him. He turns back to Maria. "I didn't know your little brother was such a tight-ass," he laughs.

"Oh, Robbie's okay," she says. She glances back at me in the rearview mirror and widens her eyes in comic exaggeration. I turn my head away sulkily and stare over toward the ocean, which stretches out on my left as flat and shiny as a metal plate.

We ride together for a few minutes in silence. Nick reaches over and turns down the radio. He turns his head toward me. "So, Robbie," he says affably. "I hear you're gay."

"Jesus, Maria!" I exclaim.

Maria isn't laughing now. At least she has the decency to look embarrassed. "I didn't think you'd mind me telling him, Robbie," she says. But her guilty tone makes it clear she knew damn well I'd mind. She shoots a poisonous look at Nick. "You've got a big mouth," she hisses.

"He's not the only one," I say.

Nick's eyes shift back and forth between Maria and me. "Oops," he says. He laughs, unfazed. "It's no big deal. I'm cool. It's not like I'm a born-again Christian or anything." He looks at me. "So are you just coming out or what?"

"I don't want to talk about it," I say frostily. Maria flashes me an apologetic glance in the mirror, but I just glower back at her. We ride the rest of the distance to the beach in silence.

It's still early, the sun has just started climbing high, and there's only a scattering of cars in the dirt parking lot. We start the trek to the beach, Nick and Maria leading the way, me lagging behind with the cooler. Nick leans over and says something to Maria, and she laughs again, her previous embarrassment all forgotten now, which makes my mood even pissier. At the top of the dunes, the two of them wait for me to catch up. The sea stretches out before us, sparkling in the bright sun, the waves hissing as they break upon the sandy beach.

"Bitching!" Nick says. He reaches over and squeezes the back of my neck. "You having a good time, Robbie?" he asks, smiling. Though I hardly know the guy, I know that this is as close to an apology as I'll ever get. A breeze whips over the dunes, smelling of the sea, the sun beats down benevolently, and I see nothing but good humor in Nick's wide, blue eyes. In spite of myself, I smile. "Attaboy," Nick laughs. "I knew you had it in you!" He lets go and we start climbing down the dunes to find a stretch of beach isolated from everyone else.

After we've laid the blanket out, Maria and Nick start taking off their clothes. I hurriedly pull my bathing suit out of my knapsack. "I'm going to change behind the dune," I say.

Nick has one leg raised, about to pull off a sneaker. "I'll go with you," he says abruptly.

I have mixed feelings about this but don't know how I can dissuade him. We circle the nearest dune, leaving Maria behind on the broad expanse of beach. Nick peels off his shirt, and I can't help noticing the sleek leanness of his torso, the blond dusting of hair that marches across his chest. My throat tightens, and I turn my attention to my fingers fumbling with the buttons of my jeans. Nick kicks off his shoes and shucks his shorts and Calvins. The honey-brown of his skin ends abruptly at his tan line, and his hips are pale cream. Nick turns his back to me and stretches lazily, like a jungle cat, arms bent. His ass is smooth and milky, downed with a light fuzz that gleams gold in the sun's rays. Nick turns around and smiles at me. His dick, half-hard, sways heavily against his thighs.

I turn away and quickly pull my jeans off. When I look back at Nick, he's still standing there, naked, only this time his dick is jutting out fully hard, twitching slightly in the light breeze. He sees my surprise and shrugs helplessly. "Sorry," he grins, his eyes wide and guileless. "Open air always makes me hard."

"This isn't a nude beach," I say, trying to sound casual. "You have to wear a suit."

"In a minute," Nick says. "I like feeling the breeze on my skin." His smile turns sly, and his eyes lose some of their innocence. He wraps his hand around his dick and strokes it slowly. "You like it, Robbie?" he asks. "Maria calls it my love club."

"What the hell are you trying to prove?" I ask.

Nick affects surprise. "I'm not trying to prove anything," he says, his tone all injured innocence. "I'm just making conversation." I quickly pull on my suit and walk back to the blanket. Nick joins us a couple of minutes later.

Nick and Maria race out into the waves. She pushes him into the path of a crashing breaker, laughing as he comes up sputtering. They horseplay in the surfline for a while and then swim out to deeper water. Eventually they're just specks in the shiny, gunmetal blue. I close my eyes and feel the sun beat down on me. Rivulets of sweat begin to trickle down my torso.

Suddenly I'm in shade. I open my eyes and see Nick standing over me, the sun behind him so that I can't make out his features, just an outline of broad shoulders tapering down. He shakes his head and water spills down on me. "Hey!" I protest.

He sits down besides me on the blanket. "The water feels great," he says. "You should go out in it."

"In a little while," I say. "Where's Maria?"

Nick gestures vaguely. "Out there somewhere. She didn't want to come in yet." He stretches out next to me, propped up on his elbows. "So why are you so upset about me knowing you're gay? You think I'll disapprove or something?"

"Jeez, what's with you? Will you just drop the subject?"

"I've gotten it on with guys," Nick goes on, as if he hadn't heard me. "It's no big deal." He grins. "You want to hear about the last time I did?"

"No," I lie.

"It was in Hawaii. Oahu to be exact." Nick turns on his side and faces me, his head on his hand. "I was there on spring break in my junior year of college. I started hanging out with this dude I'd met in a Waikiki bar, a surfer named Joe." He laughs. "Surfer Joe, just like in the song. Ah, sweet Jesus, was he ever beautiful! Part Polynesian, part Japanese, part German. Smooth brown skin, tight, ripped body, and these fuckin' dark, soulful eyes." He smiles. "Like yours, Robbie. Like Maria's too, for that matter," he adds, as if in an afterthought. "Anyway I had a rented car, and we took a drive to the North Shore. Somehow, we wound up lost on this little piss-ass road, nothing but sugar cane fields on either side. It'd been raining but the sun was just breaking out and all of a sudden, wham! This huge, technicolored rainbow comes blazing out, right in front of us." Nick sits up, getting excited. "It was fuckin' awesome! The motherfucker just arced overhead like some kind of neon bridge and ended not far off in this little grassy patch beyond the cane. Well, Joe leaps out of the car. I tell you, he was one crazy bastard, and he races across the field toward the rainbow, and, because I couldn't think of anything better to do, I do the same." Nick's eyes are wide, and he's talking faster now. "Joe makes it to where the rainbow hits the ground, he pulls off his board shorts, and he just stands there naked, his arms stretched out, the colors pouring down on him, blue! green! red! orange! I strip off my shorts, too, and jump right in." Nick laughs, but his eyes drill into me. "It was the strangest damn sensation, standing in that rainbow, my skin tingling like a low-voltage current was passing through me." He blinks. "Joe wrestles me to the ground, one thing leads to another, and we wind up fucking right there, with all the colors washing over us, me plowing Joe's ass, Joe's head red, his chest orange, his belly yellow, his legs green and blue. When I finally came, I pulled out of Joe's ass, raining my jizz down on him, the drops like colored jewels." Nick gazes down at me, his eyes laughing. "Like I said: fucking awesome!"

"You are so full of shit," I say.

Nick adopts an expression of deep hurt. "It's true. I swear it."

"Fuck you. You can't stand in a rainbow, for Christ sakes. It's against the laws of optics."

" 'The laws of optics,' " Nick snorts. "What are you, an optician?"

"You mean a physicist. An optician prescribes glasses. Jesus, you're an ignorant fuck."

But Nick refuses to be insulted. He laughs, and picks up my tube of sunblock. "Here," he says. "Let me oil you up again. You've sweated off your first layer." Nick smears the goop on my chest and starts stroking my torso. His hand wanders down my belly, and lays there motionless. The heat of his hand sinks into my skin. The tips of his fingers slide under the elastic band of my suit. He looks at me, eyebrows raised. When I don't say anything, Nick slips his hand under my suit and wraps it around my dick. "Do the same to me," he urges.

"Maria . . ." I say.

Nick scans the ocean. "She's way out there," he says. "She can't see anything." His hand, still greased with sunblock, starts sliding up and down my dick. I close my eyes. "Come on," he whispers. "Do it to me, too. Please."

My hand seems to have a mind of its own. It slides inside Nick's suit and wraps around his fat, hard dick. His *love club*. "Yeah, Robbie, that's good," Nick sighs. "Now stroke it."

We beat each other off, the sun blasting down on us, the ocean shimmering off in the distance like a desert mirage. After a few moments, we pull our suits down to our knees. Nick smears his hand with a fresh batch of lotion and then slides it down my dick. I groan. "Yeah, baby," he laughs. "You like that, don't you?" I groan again, more loudly, arching my back as the orgasm sweeps over me. Nick takes my dick in his mouth and swallows my load as I pump it down his throat. Even after I'm done, he keeps sucking on my dick, rolling his tongue around it, playing with my balls.

He replaces my hand with his, and with a few quick strokes, brings himself to climax, shuddering as his load splatters against his chest and belly.

Maria staggers out of the surf a few minutes later and races to the blanket, squealing from the heat of the sand on her soles. Nick and I are chastely reading our summer novels under the umbrella. She flings herself down on the blanket, grabs a towel and vigorously rubs her hair. "You guys enjoying yourselves?" she asks

"Yeah, sure," Nick says, his mouth curling up into an easy grin. "Except your degenerate little brother can't keep his hands off me." He winks. Maria laughs, but she shoots me a worried look, checking to see if I'm offended. I shrug and smile back. I feel like shit.

Nick stops by my place a week later. It's the first time I've seen him since the beach. "Is Maria here?" he asks. "I swung by her apartment but she wasn't home." He's dressed in a tank top and cut-offs, and he carries a summer glow with him that makes him shine like a small sun.

"No," I say, my heart beating furiously. "I haven't seen her all day."

Nick peers over my shoulder. "You alone?"

"Yeah," I say. My mouth has suddenly gone desert dry. Nick regards me calmly, waiting. "You want to come in for a while?" I finally ask.

Nick smiles and gives a slight shrug. "Why not?"

As soon as I close the door behind us, he's on me, pushing me against the wall, his hard dick dry-humping me through the denim of his shorts, his mouth pressed against mine. After the initial shock passes, I kiss him back, thrusting my tongue deep into his mouth. Nick's hands are all over me, pulling at my shirt, undoing the buttons, tugging down my zipper. He slides his hands under my jeans and cups my ass, pulling my crotch against his.

I push him away, gasping. "This isn't going to happen," I say.

Nick looks at me with bright eyes, his face flushed, his expression half annoyed-half amused. "Now, Robbie," he says, smiling his old smile. "You're not going to be a cock-tease, are you?"

I zip my pants up again and rebutton my shirt. I feel the anger rising up in me. "You're such an asshole," I say. I push past him and walk into the living room.

Nick remains in the hallway. I sit on the couch, glaring at him. He slowly walks into the room until he's standing in front of me. He looks out the window and then back at me again. "Why am I an asshole?" he asks. "Because I think you're fuckin' beautiful?"

"You may not give a shit," I say, "but Maria's crazy about you."

Nick sits down besides me on the couch. "Ah," he says quietly. A silence hangs between us for a couple of beats. "What if I told you I'm just as crazy about Maria?" he finally asks.

"You have a funny way of showing it."

Nick leans back against the arm of the couch and regards me with his steady, blue gaze. He gives a low laugh. "Now, next on Jerry Springer!" he says. "My sister's boyfriend is putting the moves on me!" I look at him hostilely, not saying anything. He calmly returns my stare. "You know, Robbie," he says, "lately, every time I fuck your sister, I think of you. It's getting to be a real problem."

"Will you knock it off?"

Nick acts like he hasn't heard me. "It's no reflection on Maria, believe me. She's a knockout. Great personality, beautiful . . ." He leaves the sentence hanging in the air, lost in thought. His eyes suddenly focus on me. "But there are things I want that she can't give me."

I wait a while before I finally respond. "What things?" I ask sullenly.

Nick's smile is uncharacteristically wistful. "You, Robbie. That's 'what things'." I don't say anything. Nick lays his hand on my knee. "It's amazing how much you look like Maria, sometimes. The same dark eyes, the same mouth, the same way you tilt your head . . . It's like the excitement of meeting Maria all over again." He leans forward, his eyes bright. "Only you have a man's body, Robby. That's what Maria can't give me." His hand slides up my thigh. "She can't give me a man's muscles, a man's way of walking and talking . . ." His hand slides up and squeezes my crotch. "A man's dick. I swear to God, if I had the two of you in bed together, I wouldn't ask for another thing for the rest of my motherfuckin' life!" He looks at me and laughs. "You should see your face now, Robbie. You look like you just sucked a lemon."

I feel my throat tightening. "You're fucking crazy if you think that's ever going to happen."

"Maybe I *am* crazy," Nick sighs. His eyes dart up to mine. "But I'm not stupid." His fingers begin rubbing the crotch of my jeans, lazily sliding back and forth. He grins slyly. "If I can't have you and Maria together, I'll settle for you both one at a time." He leans his face close to mine, his hand squeezing my dick. "Come on, Robbie, don't tell me I don't turn you on. Not after our little session on the beach." I don't say anything. Nick's other hand begins lightly stroking my chest, fumbling with the buttons of my shirt. "You want monogamy, Robbie?" he croons softly. "I promise I'll stay true to you and Maria. I'll never look at another family."

"Everything's a joke with you," I say. But I feel my dick twitch as his hand slides under my shirt and squeezes my left nipple.

"No, Robbie," Nick says softly. "Not everything." He cups his hand around the back of my neck and pulls me toward him. I resist, but not enough to break his grip, and we kiss, Nick's tongue pushing apart my lips and thrusting deep inside my mouth. He reaches down and squeezes my dick again. "Hard as the proverbial rock!" he laughs.

"Just shut up," I say. We kiss again, and this time I let Nick unbutton my shirt. His hands slide over my bare chest, tugging at the muscles in my torso. He unbuckles my belt and pulls my zipper down. His hand slides under my briefs and wraps around my dick.

"We're going to do it nice and slow this time," Nick says. He tugs my jeans down, and I lift my hips to help him. It doesn't take long before Nick has pulled off all my clothes. He sits back, his eyes slowly sliding down my body. "So beautiful . . ." he murmurs. He stands up and shucks off his shirt and shorts, kicking them away. He falls on top of me, his mouth burrowing against my neck, his body stretched out full against mine.

I kiss him again, gently this time, our mouths barely touching. His lips work their way over my face, pressing lightly against my nose, my eyes. His tongue probes into my ear, and his breath sounds like the sea in a conch shell. His lips move across my skin, down my torso. He gently bites each nipple, swirling his tongue around them, sucking on them. I can only see the top of his head, the shock of blond hair, and I reach down and entwine my fingers in it, twisting his head from side to side. Nick sits up, his legs straddling my hips, his thick cock pointing up toward the ceiling. He wraps his hand around both our dicks and squeezes them together tightly. "Feel that, Robbie," he says. "Dick flesh against dick flesh." He begins stroking them, sliding his hand up and down the twin shafts: his pink and fat, mine dark and veined. A drop of pre-cum leaks from his dick, and Nick slicks our dicks up with it. I breathe deeply, and Nick grins.

Nick bends down, and tongues my bellybutton, his hands sliding under my ass. He lifts my hips up and takes my cock in his mouth, sliding his lips down my shaft, until his nose is pressed against my pubes. He sits motionless like that, my dick full down his throat, his tongue working against the shaft. Slowly, inch by inch, his lips slide back up to my cockhead. He wraps his hand around my dick and strokes it, as he raises his head and his eyes meet mine, laughing. "You like that, Robbie?" he asks. "Does that feel good?"

"Turn around," I say urgently. "Fuck my face while you do that to me."

I don't have to ask Nick twice. He pivots his body around, and his dick thrusts above my face: red, thick, the cockhead pushing out of the foreskin and leaking pre-cum. His balls hang low and heavy, above my mouth, furred with light blonde hairs. I raise my head and bathe them with my tongue, and then suck them into my mouth. I roll my tongue around the meaty pouch. "Ah, yeah," Nick groans. I slide my tongue up the shaft of his dick. Nick shifts his position and plunges his dick deep down my throat. He starts pumping his hips, sliding his dick in and out of my mouth as he continues sucking me off. His torso squirms against mine, skin against skin, the warmth of his flesh pouring into my body. Nick takes my dick out of his mouth, and I feel his tongue slide over my balls and burrow into the warmth beneath them. He pulls apart my ass cheeks and soon I feel his mouth on my asshole, his tongue lapping against the puckered flesh.

"Damn!" I groan.

Nick alternately blows against and licks my asshole. I arch my back and push up with my hips, giving him greater access. No one has ever done this to me before, and it's fucking driving me wild. Nick comes up for air, and soon I feel his finger pushing against my asshole, and then entering me, knuckle by knuckle. I groan again, louder. Nick looks at me over his shoulder as he finger fucks me into a slow frenzy. "Yeah, Robbie," he croons. "Just lay there and let me play you. Let's see what songs I can make you sing." He adds another finger inside me and pushes up in a corkscrew twist. I cry out, and Nick laughs.

He climbs off me and reaches for his shorts. "Okay, Robbie," he says. "Enough with the fuckin' foreplay. Let's get this show on the road." He pulls a condom packet and small jar of lube out of his back pocket, and tosses the shorts back on to the floor.

I feel a twinge of irritation. "You had this all planned out, didn't you?"

Nick straddles my torso again, his stiff cock jutting out inches from my face. I trace one blue vein snaking up the shaft. "Let's just say I was open to the possibility," he grins. He unrolls the condom down his prick, his blue eyes never leaving mine. He smears his hand with lube, reaches back, and liberally greases up my asshole. Nick hooks his arms under my knees and hoists my legs up and around his torso. His gaze still boring into me, he slowly impales me.

I push my head back against the cushion, eyes closed. Nick leans forward, full in. "You okay, baby?" he asks. His eyes are wide and solicitous.

I open my eyes and nod. Slowly, almost imperceptibly, Nick begins pumping his hips, grinding his pelvis against mine. He deepens his thrusts, speeding up the tempo. I reach up and twist his nipples, and Nick grins widely. A wolfish gleam lights up his eyes. He pulls his hips back until his cockhead is just barely in my asshole, and then plunges back in. "Fuckin' A," I groan.

"Fuckin' A is right," Nick laughs. He props himself up with his arms and proceeds to fuck me good and hard, his balls slapping heavily against me with each thrust, his eyes boring into mine, his hot breath against my face. I cup my hand around the back of his neck and pull his face down to mine, frenching him hard as he pounds my ass. Nick leaves his dick full up my ass, grinding his hips against mine in a slow circle before returning to the old in and out. He wraps a hand around my stiff dick and starts beating me off, timing his strokes with each thrust of his hips.

We settle into our rhythm, Nick pounding my ass, his hand sliding up and down my dick as I thrust up to meet him stroke for stroke. There's nothing playful or cocky about Nick now: his breath comes out in ragged gasps through his open mouth, sweat trickles downs his face, and his eyes burn with the hard, bright light of a man working up to shoot a serious load.

I wrap my arms tight around his body and push up, squeezing my asshole around his dick at the same time. I look up at Nick's face and laugh. It's the first time I've ever seen him startled. "Jesus," he gasps. "Did you learn that in college?" I don't say anything, just repeat the motion, squeezing my ass muscles hard as I push up to meet his thrust. Nick's body spasms. He groans loudly. "You ought to talk to Maria," he pants. "She could learn some things from you." The third time I do this pushes Nick over the edge. He groans loudly, and his body trembles violently. He plants his mouth on mine, kissing me hard as he squirts his load into the condom up my ass. I wrap my arms around him in a bear hug, and we thrash around on the couch, finally spilling onto the carpet below, me on top, Nick sprawled with his arms wide out.

After a while he opens his eyes. "Sit on me," he says. "And shoot your load on my face."

I straddle him, dropping my balls into his open mouth. He sucks on them noisily, slurping loudly, as I beat off. Nick reaches up and squeezes my nipple, and that's all it takes for me. I give a deep groan, arching my back as my load splatters in thick drops onto Nick's face, creaming his nose and cheeks, dripping into his open mouth. "Yeah," Nick says, "that's right, baby." When the last spasm passes through me, I bend down and lick Nick's face clean.

I roll over and lie next to Nick on the thick carpet. He slides his arm under me and pulls me to him. I burrow against his body and close my eyes, feeling his chest rise and fall against the side of my head. Without meaning to, I drift off into sleep.

When I wake up, the clock on the mantle says it's almost one in the morning. Nick is gone, but he's covered me with a quilt from my bed. I'm too sleepy to get up, and so I just drift back into sleep again.

Nick, Maria, and I are all sitting on Maria's couch, watching *The Night of the Living Dead* on her TV. Maria sits between us, nestling against Nick. We're at the scene where the little girl has turned into a ghoul and is nibbling on her mother's arm like it was a hoagie sandwich. "Gross!" says Maria.

Nick grins. "You're so damn judgmental, Maria," he says. "I don't put you down when you eat those Spam and mayonnaise sandwiches of yours."

Maria laughs and snuggles deeper against Nick. We continue watching the movie. I feel Nick's fingers playing with my hair, and I brush them away with a brusque jerk that I make sure Maria doesn't notice. After a while, though, he's doing it again. When I don't do anything this time, Nick entwines his fingers in my hair and tugs gently. From where she's sitting, Maria can't see any of this. The ghouls are surrounding the farmhouse, now, closing in on the victims inside. Eventually, I lean back and sink into the feel of Nick's fingers in my hair.

# School Queer

Saturday night is my night to shine. All the guys neck with their dates out at Bass Lake or the drive-in over on Route 27, or maybe at Jackson Lookout, but because the girls here are all "saving themselves," they wind the guys up so tight that these boys could fuck a knotty pine by the time they finally take the little virgins home. So with blue balls aching, they head out to the back of the Bass Lake boathouse, where they know they'll find me waiting. I suck the hard cocks of these Southern Baptist boys, letting them frantically fuck my face, their eyes shut tight, imagining its not my lips wrapped their stiff, urgent dicks, but *pussy*. So they groan, their full-to-bursting balls slapping against my chin, and when they finally shoot, they cry out "Cindy Lou" or "Peggy Beth" as their loads splatter against the back of my throat. When they've finally got the relief they've been denied all evening, they pull up their jeans and walk away, disappearing into the bushes without so much as a "Thanks."

Before I can get too resentful, the next shadowy figure rounds the corner of the boathouse, and the ritual starts up all over again. Sometimes there are actual lines, or else the guys stand side-by-side, and I go down the row and work the stiff dicks that are throbbing in front of me. During the week, I'm shunned by nearly everyone on the campus of this small Baptist school, but on Saturday night, they can't get enough of me. It's a lonely life, being the school queer, but I serve a useful function, and so I'm tolerated.

I don't suck every dick that's offered to me. And for the men I do suck off, I do have my favorites. Bill McPherson tops the list. What a sweet, hot guy. I can tell that he was raised right: well-nourished, muscular body, straight teeth, clear complexion, glossy brown hair, steady blue eyes that meet your gaze with honest conviction. And so *earnest!* That's the charm of these Baptist boys. They're so damn *wholesome*, you just want to eat them up. Bill is well-liked about the campus, an unexceptional student, but still a big fish in this tiny pond: captain of the wrestling team and vice-president of the Kappa Gamma Chi fraternity. And he dates Becky Michaelson, this year's Azalea Princess in the school's Homecoming Parade, who, lucky for me, holds on to her cherry as if it were a piece of the One True Cross. More Saturdays then I can remember, Bill has come around behind the boathouse, frustrated, shy, embarrassed, dropped his pants and offered up his dick to me. And it's such a beautiful dick: thick, meaty, veined, pink and swollen, with a head that flares out like a fleshy, red plum.

I love making love to Bill's dick. I suck it slowly, drag my tongue up the shaft and then around the head, probing into Bill's piss slit, working my lips down the thick tube of flesh, rolling Bill's ballsac around in my mouth as I stroke him, drawing Bill to the brink of shooting, backing off, and then drawing him even closer. Bill gasps and groans, his breathing gets heavy, his body trembles under my hands as I knead and pull on his muscled torso, and when he finally shoots, he cries out "Sweet Jesus in Heaven!" every time, like he's offering his orgasm to God. When I finally climb to my feet, wiping my mouth, damn if Bill doesn't look me in the eye, shake my hand and thank me. It's a small thing, maybe, but he's the only one who does that, and that gives me just one more reason to like him.

Except for his final thanks, Bill has never spoken to me during our cocksucking sessions. So it's something of a surprise when one summer night, while I'm on my knees before him, he clears his throat and asks, "Do . . . do you ever do this to Nick Stavros?"

I take Bill's dick out of my mouth and look up at him, but his face is in shadow and I can't read his expression. I know from seeing the two of them around campus together that Bill and Nick are good friends. "Yeah," I say. "Nick comes around here from time to time. Not nearly as much as you do."

Bill doesn't say anything, and I pick up where I left off. I twist my head as I slide my lips up Bill's cockshaft, because I know Bill likes that. Bill starts pumping his hips, sliding his dick in and out of my mouth. After a minute of this, Bill clears his throat again. "What's Nick's dick like?" he asks. I look up at him again, and Bill, seeing the questioning expression on my face, laughs nervously. "Nick's always kidding me about what a ladies' man he is," he says, "and so I was just curious about how he . . . well, measures up to me."

"You don't have anything to worry about," I say. "Your dick is awesome." I put it back in my mouth.

"Yeah, well, okay," Bill says. "But what's Nick's dick like?"

*This is weird*, I think. "You really want me to describe Nick's dick?"

"Yeah," Bill says. "Do you mind?" By his tone of voice I'm almost sure he's blushing.

"Unlike yours, it's uncut," I say. "And a lot darker. It curves down, which makes it easier for me to suck, though I sometimes wonder if that would make it harder for him to actually fuck someone. It's a mouthful, but not quite as long as yours, though maybe a little thicker. His piss slit is really pronounced."

Bill is listening to me intently, as if there's going to be an after-lecture quiz on all of this. I half expect him to start taking notes. When he doesn't say anything else, I return to blowing him. After a minute of this he clears his throat again. "And his balls, what are they like?"

*Okaaay*, I think. "He's got some low-hangers," I say. "They're a couple of bull-nuts. When he fucks my face, they slap against my chin. I love sucking on them, washing them with my tongue, though they're so big I can only do them one at a time."

Bill says nothing else for the rest of my blowjob. As his dick gets harder, right before he shoots, he runs his fingers through my hair and tugs at it. "Sweet Jesus in Heaven" he murmurs, as usual, and then I feel his dick pulse and soon my mouth is flooded with his load. I stay like that for a long moment, on my knees before Bill, his dick slowly softening in my mouth. Finally, he pulls out and tugs his jeans up. As always, he shakes my hand and thanks me before disappearing into the night.

From that night on, we settle into a new routine whenever I suck Bill off. He peppers me with questions, asking for more details on Nick's cock, or his balls, or what his ass is like, how he acts when he shoots. And I answer every question, describing in detail just what it feels like to have Nick slide his dick in my mouth, how Nick likes to push my face hard against his belly, me choking on his dick, my nose pressed against his crinkly, black pubes. Or what Nick's balls smell like, the sweaty, pungent scent of a male animal in rut. Or the low grunts Nick gives as his load squirts down my throat, and what that load tastes like (salty, with just a faint undertaste of garlic). And I feel Bill's dick stiffen with each description I give of Nick, and I think how strange it is to know Bill's secret: just how queer he is for Nick.

One day Bill catches up to me on the campus green. I try to hide my surprise. Normally nobody as high up on the campus pecking order as Bill would be caught dead talking in public to the school queer.

"Hey, Pete," he says. "How's it going?"

"I'm okay," I say cautiously.

We walk along the brick path in silence. The people we pass stare at us with the same astonishment that I feel. "Look, Pete," Bill says, lowering his voice but keeping his eyes straight ahead. "Can you be at the boathouse tonight? Around eleven?"

I let a couple of beats go by. "It's a weekday night, Bill. I have a chemistry test tomorrow that I have to study for."

Bill stops and looks at me, and I can see the desperation in his eyes. "I'm begging you, man," he says.

This is all *very* weird. "Okay," I finally say. "If it's that big a deal for you, I'll be there."

Bill looks relieved. "Thanks," he says and then turns on his heel and walks off.

The moon is nearly full tonight, and its light bounces off the lake and flickers onto the boathouse walls. I sit on one of the overturned boats, smoking a cigarette, waiting. I glance at my watch. Five after eleven. There's a rustle of bushes, and then Bill steps out into the light.

"Hi, Bill," I say. But Bill is looking behind him, not toward me. The bushes rustle again, and suddenly Nick walks out and stands next to Bill. He looks at me scowling, and then looks away.

Bill takes a couple of steps closer. "Nick and I were double dating tonight," he says, "But our girls just wouldn't put out." He gives a laugh that rings as false as a tin nickel. "And boy do we have a nut to bust! So

54

we just swung by here tonight on the off chance that you'd be here to help us get a little relief."

I look at Nick, but he's still staring at the ground, refusing to meet my eye. My gaze shifts back to Bill. "You guys are in luck," I say drily. "I'm normally not here on a weekday night."

Neither Bill nor Nick say anything. After a couple of beats, I figure that it's up to me to get this ball rolling. "Who wants to go first?" I ask.

"Why don't you go ahead, Nick?" Bill says, turning toward him. "I'll wait."

Nick shrugs, still not saying anything. He's wearing a school T-shirt that hugs his torso, and a pair of cut-offs. Nick can be a surly bastard, and I like Bill way better, but there's no denying he's the handsomer of the two: intense, dark eyes, an expressive mouth, powerful arms, a muscle-packed torso, tight hips. . . . As always, my heart races as he unbuckles his belt. I pull his cut-offs down past his thighs, and his fleshy, half-hard dick swings heavily from side to side.

"You take care of my buddy, Pete," Bill says. "Suck him good!"

I glance at Bill. His lips are parted and there's a manic gleam in his eyes. If he were any more excited, he'd have a stroke. Because I like Bill, I decide to give him the show he so obviously wants. I look up at Nick. "Why don't you take off all your clothes?" I say quietly. "It'll be more fun that way."

Nick glares down at me, scowling. After a brief pause, he hooks his fingers under the edge of his T-shirt and pulls it over his head, revealing his muscularly lean torso. He kicks off his shoes and steps out of his cut-offs. "Okay?" he asks sarcastically. I glance again at Bill. He's looking at Nick's naked body like a starving dog eyeing a T-bone steak.

"Yeah," I say. "That's just fine." I wrap my hand around Nick's dick and give it a squeeze. A clear drop of pre-cum oozes out of his piss slit, and I lean forward and lap it up. I roll my tongue around his cockhead and then slide my lips down his shaft. I can feel the thick tube of flesh harden in my mouth to full stiffness. I begin bobbing my head, turning at an angle to give Bill a maximum view of the show. Nick responds by pressing his palms against both sides of my head and pumping his hips, sliding his dick deep down my throat and then pulling out again. Nick always was an aggressive mouth fucker.

Bill walks up and stands next to Nick. He unzips his jeans and tugs them down, and his dick springs up, fully hard. "Now me," he says hoarsely. I look up into his face, but his eyes are trained on Nick's spit-slicked, fully hard cock. Bill's the big man on campus, and I may be the queer boy with zero status, but tonight the tables are turned. It's clear that ol' Bill would want nothing more than to trade places with me, get down on his knees and work Nick's dick like I'm doing, swallow it, have Nick plow his face. But it'll never happen. The closest he can let himself get to this fantasy is to have me suck his dick with the taste of Nick's dick still in my mouth. I actually pity the guy as I take his dick in my hand and slide my lips down its shaft.

While I work on Bill's dick I reach over and start jacking off Nick. Nick pumps his hips, fucking my fist the same way he fucked my mouth a minute ago. One thrust catches him off balance, and he reaches out and lays his hand on Bill's shoulder to steady himself. Bill reacts as if Nick's touch is a jolt of high-voltage current; his body jerks suddenly, and his muscles spasm. *This poor guy wants it so bad,* I think. With my hand still around Nick's dick, I pull him closer to me until his dick is touching Bill's. I open my lips wider and take both their dicks in my mouth, feeling them rub and thrust against each other. Bill trembles with the feel of Nick's dick against his, and Nick's breath comes out in short grunts. I wrap my hands around their ballsacs and give them a good tug. Bill groans, I feel his dick throb, and my mouth is suddenly flooded with his creamy load. "Sweet Jesus in Heaven!" he gasps. At the same time, Nick thrusts hard down my throat, his breath coming out faster now, his legs trembling. Suddenly his body spasms and his dick squirts too. I suck hard on the two dicks as they pulse in my mouth, their combined loads splattering against the back of my throat. I roll my tongue over the spermy deposits in my mouth, tasting them like a gourmet, mingling the flavors together, savoring them.

Nick and Bill pull away, and there's this brief moment when the three of us are frozen in our positions: me still on my knees, cum dribbling out of the corners of my mouth, Bill and Nick on either side of me, buck naked, their dicks half hard and sinking fast, their eyes not meeting each other.

Bill is the first to break the silence. "Damn," he says, his voice low. I look up into his eyes, and then the strangest thing happens; for an instant there's a spark, a little jolt of, I don't know . . . *connection.* For that brief flicker of time, I'm not the school faggot and he's not the big man on campus. We're both buddies who've shared the pleasure of Nick's flesh.

Nick pulls up his pants, and this sudden movement breaks the spell. He picks up his T-shirt from the ground, and puts it on. "Let's go," he grunts to Bill. He walks back into the bushes and disappears without looking back at either one of us. Bill gets dressed hurriedly and rushes after him. Before he too disappears into the night, he turns and gives me one last look and then plunges into the bushes after Nick.

I get up and smooth my clothes out, take a comb out of my back pocket and comb my hair. I walk in the opposite direction, down where my car is parked. I'm sure I'll see Bill again this Saturday night. With or without Nick. If he's alone, we'll have something to talk about. Either way, it should be fun.

# A Night At *El Gallo*

I wake up with a start, staring up at the inside of the packing crate I've been using as a makeshift coffin. It's something Bela Lugosi wouldn't be caught dead in; I think it once contained fluorescent tubes. But, hey, you use what's available. I crawl out, a little groggy, shaking my head. Vaslo is sitting at the table by the window, reading an American newspaper. He's wearing Bermuda shorts and a shirt with green parrots. "Good evening," he says, with his Old World formality.

I just grunt something as I climb to my feet. I look at his outfit. "What'd you do, mug a Hawaiian tourist?"

Vaslo smiles his ironic smile. He's gained some muscle since my escape from Van Helsing and our flight to Mexico a year ago, and it suits him. During the day, while I sleep in my box, he works out in the beat-up little gym down the street, pumping iron with *los chicos*. "I just thought I'd wear something a little tropical tonight," he says. He leans back in his chair and stretches. I note how his biceps bunch up, how the light accents his finely molded face and gleams on his slicked-back, black hair. He looks at me and grins. "Are you ready for breakfast?"

"You have to ask?"

Vaslo removes his aloha shirt, then stands up, unzips his shorts and lets them drop to the floor. Naked, he walks across the room toward me, slowly, letting me drink in the beauty of his muscular body. I sit on the floor, my back to the wall, waiting, my heart beating hard. His thick, spongy dick sways from side to side with every step he takes. He stands over me, hands on hips. I slide my hands up his thighs, across his hard belly and the furry mounds of his pecs, and I squeeze his nipples, not gently.

Vaslo's grin loses some of its friendliness, and his dark eyes take on a wolfish gleam. His dick slowly lengthens and hardens. My belly growls with hunger, I feel ravenous, but I go slowly, drawing out the moment. I bury my face in the fleshy folds of Vaslo's balls and breathe in their pungent smell. I think of the creamy sperm teeming inside this meaty, red pouch, and saliva pools in my mouth. Vaslo runs his fingers through my hair, and I part my lips. His balls spill into my mouth. I roll my tongue over them, sucking the loose sac as Vaslo rubs his dick against my face. "Are you hungry, Joe?" he murmurs. "Would you like to feed?"

I say nothing, but I look up at him, my mouth open, like a baby bird waiting for the fat worm of Vaslo's cock. He slides it between my lips, and I savor the feel of the tube of flesh filling my mouth, the push of the cockhead against the back of my throat. My eyes stare into Vaslo's, and I probe into his mind, searching for the pleasure center. I find it and give a little mental twist. Vaslo sighs loudly, and his body shudders under my hands. It's a special gift that vampires of my sort have, the sperm eaters, a kind of telepathy that can pulse waves of pleasure into the minds of the men that feed us. Vaslo begins pumping his hips now, slowly at first, and then with a quickening tempo. I fuck his brain like he fucks my mouth, pushing a throb of pleasure into him with each thrust of his cock. Soon Vaslo becomes drunk with pleasure, his eyes wide and crazed, his breath broken with sharp gasps. I play him like a virtuoso plays his instrument, taking him to the brink of orgasm, pulling him back again at the last moment, only to take him even closer to the edge. Finally, I decide it's time, and at the next thrust of his dick, I give a sharp, hard, mental jab to his brain that triggers the orgasm. Vaslo cries out, and his cock pulses in my mouth as I flood his brain with pleasure. The hot sperm squirts across my tongue, and now I join Vaslo in his ecstasy, drinking thirstily, tasting the sweet, pungent flavor of his load. Vaslo whips his head up, and his body squirms in my arms. I continue to suck on his cock, draining out the last few precious drops, like a baby sucking on his mother's tit. Strength pours into my body. I take his dick out of my mouth and look up at Vaslo, grinning. "Damn! Nice and spicy!"

Vaslo grins back. "I wanted to give you something with an extra kick. I've been eating jalapeños all day."

We sit at the table, Vaslo drinking shots of tequila. He tells me how his day went. Music floats in through the open window from the cantina across the street, occasionally punctuated by laughter and shouting. After a few minutes of this, I discretely clear my throat. "We better get going," I say. Sperm-eating vampires need several feedings before their hunger is curbed. Vaslo knows this, and he accepts it without jealousy, as long as I always start with him.

Vaslo takes a sip of tequila, looking at me over the rim of his glass. "I've heard of a place today, from one of the guys in the gym. It sounded . . . promising." He refuses to tell me more. "Let it be a surprise," he says, in response to my questions. "A special treat for dessert."

We start off the evening at the Botanical Gardens. Vaslo waits by the kiosk next to the entrance as I walk down the narrow path among the giant ferns and palms. The men who cruise here know me well, know the body-wracking orgasms I can give them, and they compete eagerly for my attention. I pick one from the crowd whom I haven't tried before, a muscular day-laborer with a broad, peasant's face and a thick, curved dick that fills my mouth like a kielbasa sausage.

In a matter of minutes, I'm kneeling in front of him, my fingers gripping his smooth, hard ass-cheeks as he plows my face with his cock. I probe into him mind, find his pleasure center and push hard. "Santa Maria," he gasps, as his warm, thick load floods into my mouth, and his body trembles under my hands.

Vaslo and I cruise the city, occasionally pausing while I drain the load from some young man we may chance upon in an alley, or along the waterfront, or sitting in an open window on some deserted street. Sometimes Vaslo joins me, kneeling besides me, taking turns sucking the offered cock in front of us, just to keep me company. Other times he stands to the side, watching, or waits further down the street until I'm done. At a little after midnight, Vaslo takes me by the elbow and hails a cab. "Now for something special," he says.

He leans forward and murmurs an address in the cabbie's ear. I lean back in the seat, watching the city speed by. After a long stretch of darkness, we come upon a square that blazes with light. We pay the cabbie and climb out.

We're in some kind of honky-tonk stretch of cantinas and strip joints. Vaslo looks around until he spots a pale blue, cement block building sporting a neon sign that blinks the words *El Gallo*.

"There it is," he says. Loud music pours out from the open door. He walks inside, and after a couple of beats, I follow him.

The place is a single room hazy with cigarette smoke and sporting a small stage in the front, on which a skinny boy with a dick like a garden hose dances slowly, pumping his hips to the rhythm of the rock guitar that is playing over the sound system. Men fill the room, sitting at the tables that ring the stage, shouting to each other over the music and mostly ignoring the dancer. We take a table by the stage. A server comes up, and Vaslo orders a beer for himself. He glances at his watch. "It's almost one," he says. "Time for the headliner." I glance at the boy on the stage. In spite of the size of his dick, he does nothing for me, and I let my mind wander, looking idly around the room. It's a diverse crowd: locals, a few soldiers, some gringo tourists. One table is surrounded by a group of young sailors wearing the uniform of the German navy. After a few minutes, the music stops and the dancer walks off the stage.

I can feel a change in the room, a certain charged attention. The men crowded at the tables have stopped talking and have their eyes trained on the stage. "And now, gentlemen," a voice says in Spanish over the loudspeaker, "please welcome Miguel." Another song starts playing, something slow and bluesy. The lights go out and then a spot is trained on the stage. A man standa there, dressed simply in a loose-fitting white shirt and dark chinos with snaps that run along the length of each leg. He has a powerful body, with broad shoulders and a tightly muscled torso that tapers down to narrow hips. The light makes his crisp, black curls gleam and shines along the planes of his face, accentuating the wide, sensual mouth, the strong nose, the deep-set, dark eyes. Swaying his body, Miguel slowly unbuttons his shirt and then shrugs it off. He bends down and undoes the snaps along his legs, and with a quick tug yanks his pants off and lets them drop. He stands there on the stage, naked except for his socks, his muscled body slick with a light sheen of sweat, his hard dick thrusting out. I stir in my seat, leaning forward to get a better view. Vaslo smiles, but says nothing.

The music suddenly stops, and the house lights go up. Miguel stands there, shoulders back, hands half-curled into fists, his cock jutting straight out. His eyes slowly scan the audience.

"This is where it gets interesting," Vaslo leans forward and whispers. "According to my friend, every night Miguel picks a volunteer from the audience and fucks him on the stage in front of everyone." His grin widens. "It's considered an honor to be the one selected."

Miguel's eyes move from man to man. For a brief moment they lock with mine. He holds my gaze and raises one eyebrow. I smile and shake my head. He glances at Vaslo and then back at me again. I shake my head a second time. Miguel finally picks one of the German sailors, a young blonde man no more than nineteen or twenty, with the face of a choirboy. The sailor shakes his head, blushing furiously, but his buddies won't hear of it; laughing, they pull him out of his chair and push him toward Miguel. Smiling, Miguel takes him by the hand and leads him onto the stage, the audience shouting and clapping their approval.

Madonna's "Erotica" starts playing. Miguel kisses the blonde sailor lightly, playfully, as he pulls the boy's uniform off. Soon they are both standing naked on the stage. The sailor's body is lean and pale under the harsh glow of the spot, his cock juts out candy pink and fully hard, topped by a blonde pubic fuzz. Miguel wraps his hand around both their dicks and strokes them slowly. He turns and grins toward the audience, which claps its approval. The blonde sailor smiles shyly, blushing and embarrassed but clearly enjoying the exhibitionistic thrill of it all. I find the perverse innocence of this scene wildly erotic.

Miguel bends down and pulls a condom packet and a small bottle of lube from his sock. He tears the package open and slowly rolls it down the shaft of his dick. He squirts a heavy dollop of lube onto his hand and smears it into the ass crack of the blonde sailor, who leans forward, hands on knees, to give Miguel easier access. Miguel positions himself behind the boy and slides his hard dick up and down the length of the sailor's ass crack. The sailor's body squirms under Miguel's hands, and he pushes his hips against Miguel's. Miguel grins broadly, his white teeth flashing in his dark face. Dick in hand, he pokes his cockhead against the sailor's asshole and then enters him, with painstaking slowness. The blonde boy groans loudly, and his buddies shout out words of encouragement. When Miguel's dick is full up the sailor's ass, he stops and holds that position, as if presenting a tableau for the audience, the two men joined together, Miguel's dark, muscular body contrasting against the pale skin of the blonde German.

Miguel begins pumping his hips, slowly at first, drawing his dick out almost to the head and then plunging back into the sailor's ass. His tempo gradually quickens, and it doesn't take long before he's giving the German a serious ass pounding, his dick thrusting hard up the boy's ass, his balls slapping against the boy's pink flesh. My table is right up next to the stage, the two men fuck inches away from me, and I can take in every detail: the slide of Miguel's dick in and out of the sailor's asshole, the furious strokes the sailor gives his own cock, the slapping sound of flesh on flesh, the sharp pungent smell of sweat and sex. The sailor is bent over, his face inches from mine, his eyes squeezed shut. Suddenly he opens his eyes, and his gaze meets mine. I stroke his face, and then, without thinking, lean forward, seize his head in both my hands, and kiss him. The sailor's lips meet mine eagerly, his tongue probes into my mouth just as Miguel's dick thrusts hard up his ass. I reach over and twist his nipples, and the sailor cries out, his voice muffled by my mouth on his. Miguel croons to him in Spanish, his eyes feverish, sweat pouring down his face, his body gleaming. Madonna's voice rises high and clear through the room, engulfing us as the sailor's tongue plays with mine and Miguel continues the serious business of giving this boy the ass pounding he so obviously wants. I break away and stare into the boy's eyes, probing his mind. When I find his pleasure center, I push hard.

The blonde sailor's body trembles under my hands, and he gives a long trailing groan. "Are you going to shoot?" I ask him. He nods. "Then give your load to me!" I say fiercely. The boy nods a second time and stands up. I climb out of my chair onto the stage, and slide my lips down his cock just as it throbs out the first squirt of come. The sailor cries out as I suck thirstily, his sweet, young boy's load flooding into my mouth, intoxicating me. His body spasms convulsively, wracked by the orgasm and the pounding Miguel is still giving him.

Miguel pulls out and walks to the edge of the stage. He whips off the condom and shoots his load out into the audience, laughing. I open my mouth and catch a few stray drops, like coins being tossed from a Mardi Gras float.

Vaslo and I don't leave the club until after four in the morning. By the time our taxi deposits us at our doorstep, the eastern sky has lightened to pale gray. We race up the steps. I just have time to crawl inside my box. I give Vaslo a quick kiss. "Thank you, my friend," I murmur. "It was a special night." Vaslo smiles back. His smile is the last thing I see before I pull the box lid over me and sink into dreamless sleep.

# Hunting For Sailors

It's Friday night and the fleet's in. The ships sailed in a couple of days ago to celebrate Fleet Week: destroyers, battleships, and one aircraft carrier, the John F. Kennedy. All day today the Blue Angels have been buzzing downtown San Francisco in formation, just being a general pain in the ass as they snarled up traffic and made everybody's windows rattle. By some weird kind of logic, this is supposed to be good public relations for the Navy.

The sun set a couple of hours ago, and I sit in darkness in my apartment on top of Telegraph Hill, looking down toward the wharf where the ships are docked. Light streams in from the bedroom door, and I hear Laura moving around in the other room, making herself desirable. My throat constricts with excitement, and my stomach is in knots. I desperately want a cigarette, but Laura hates it when I smoke and so I push the urge down as best I can. "Honey," Laura calls out to me. "Have you seen my hairbrush? I can't find it."

"Try the bathroom sink," I call back. I saw it there earlier this evening. Laura has a disorderly mind. Every time I've pointed this out to her, she's laughed and said if I wanted order I should have married a geisha girl.

I hear the click of the wall switch, and the room is bathed in light. Laura stands in the doorway, one hand on the jamb, the other resting on her hip. "How do I look?" she asks.

She's dressed in a black leather miniskirt, with boots to match, and a thin, white cotton blouse, opened down to the third button. It's tucked in tight, and her breasts push up against the fabric. Her dark blonde hair is brushed back like a lion's mane, and her lips are bright red.

"Try the pout," I say. Last week, we went to one of those foreign cinemas that was having a Bridget Bardot festival. Laura's been practicing Bardot's pout ever since.

Laura obliges me and pouts.

"Your eyes are too alert," I say. "Unfocus them, and lower your lids." Laura's eyes take on a dreamy, myopic quality. She's quite bright and always has been a quick learner. "Yeah, that's right," I croon. "You look beautiful. There isn't a man who could resist you."

Laura laughs. "Let's not go overboard, Bobby. This is San Francisco, remember."

I laugh too. "Yeah, well, I meant among the straight crowd." I nod toward the floor lamp. "Turn that damn light off, will you? And come sit here by me."

Laura flips the switch and darkness takes over the room again. She walks over to me and sits on the arm of my chair. I slip my arm around her waist. Together we look out the window down toward the ships, all lit up like floating night clubs. Laura's fingers lightly trace a path along my chest. "You feeling horny, tonight, baby?" she murmurs.

"Yeah," I say, breathing the word out like a sigh. "More than words can describe." We sit in silence for a while. All those sailors, I think. All those young bucks set loose on the town after weeks stuck on board their ships. All those hot men looking for a chance to drop their pants and their loads. I look up at Laura. "You won't let me down, will you?" I croon. "You'll get me what I need, right?"

In the dim illumination from the city outside, I can see Laura's lips curl up into a smile. "Don't I always, Bobby?" she says with a low laugh.

A few minutes later she kisses me and walks out the door. Nobody here but me, now. The air feels stifling and closed. San Francisco is not known for its warm summer nights, so this is a fluke. The mercury's been in the nineties today, almost unheard of around here, and even with the onset of night, it still feels like the high seventies. None of the waterfront bars have air-conditioning in this city, and with the crush of bodies looking for good times, all the night spots will be insufferable. At least they would be for me. But Laura likes heat; she feeds off it. And she finds crowds exhilarating. I don't have to feel sorry for her, or guilty about sending her out into the fray. She wouldn't be doing this if she weren't getting her kicks from it, too.

I open a window, and a slight breeze blows through. I take off my shirt and let the cool air ruffle my chest hairs. The urge for a cigarette wells up again. *Fuck it,* I think. *Laura's not here, and I can do what I please.* I go to the desk and open the top left hand drawer. From underneath a stack of bills and papers I pull out a pack of Marlboros and light one up. I'm pretty sure Laura knows about this private little stash; she has a way of ferreting out all my secrets. But it's a game we both like to play, pretending that this is one little deception I'm getting away with. I sit down again and luxuriate in the heady trip the smoke makes down my throat and into my lungs. The sound of traffic from the Embarcadero freeway wafts up through the open window. Laura's somewhere down there, I think, making the rounds. The lioness on the prowl.

Eventually I get up and shower, in preparation for Laura's return. I look at my reflection in the full-length mirror as I towel myself dry. I like my body. It's muscular and well-proportioned, and I like the darkness and hairiness of it. My dick is my pride and joy, thick and long, with a large, flaring head. It's swelled to half erection, now, red and meaty, swinging heavily from side to side as I dry my back. But my face is a disappointment. It's a thug's face: the chin too strong, the mouth too small, and the cheekbones so high that the eyes are permanently pushed up into a menacing squint. And it doesn't help that I have a broken nose, a souvenir of my college days on the boxing team. I never did like my face. I feel that I have the soul of a poet, and this *dockworker's* face does me little justice. But Laura has told me she loves it. When I asked her if that meant she thought I was good-looking she just laughed. "Of course not," she said. "Handsome men don't do anything for me."

I slip on a pair of tight-fitting, black chinos and a black silk shirt Laura got me last Christmas, knowing that it'll please her to see me wear it. I go back into the living room, pour myself a brandy, and wait, sitting once more in the darkness. There's nothing more left for me to do.

A couple of hours later I hear the street door slam and Laura's voice on the stairwell, loud enough to give me adequate warning of her approach. I slip out of my chair and into the bedroom, leaving the door open a crack. My heart is racing and my throat's constricted with excitement.

I hear the sound of the front door opening, and Laura's laughter fills the living room. It's joined by a man's young, tenor laugh. Then there's silence. I can picture it, the two of them with bodies pressed together, kissing, without having taken more than three steps into the room. Laura is always careful to keep the fires stoked for things to come.

"Would you like a drink?" she finally asks. I can tell by her voice that she's moved over by the window.

"Sure," the man replies. "A beer if you got one."

"No problem." Her voice fades as she moves toward the kitchen. "Sit down. Make yourself comfortable."

I hear the kitchen door swing shut. A spring in the couch creaks. The kitchen door swings open and shut again. "Here you go," Laura says. "Anchor Steam. To celebrate Fleet Week."

The man laughs again. I like the sound of it. There's an excitement in it, like he knows he's on an adventure. There's nothing jaded or crude about it.

"I'll put some music on," Laura murmurs. After a moment I hear The Doors playing 'Riders on the Storm.' I'm not surprised. Laura has a passion for Jim Morrison that borders on the obsessive.

Another creak of the couch springs. Then nothing but music for a long time. Every now and then, in the interlude after one song ends and the next one begins, I can hear sighs, moans, and soft kisses. This is the part that requires the most delicate timing. When I finally decide that the moment is right, I walk into the living room.

The light is dim, but bright enough to take in the two figures stretched out on the couch. The young man is partially dressed in a sailor's uniform, his shirt and cap discarded on the floor, his back to me as he grinds his hips against Laura. His back is well-muscled and his shoulders are broad. Laura looks at me from above his right shoulder and smiles. "Hello, Bobby," she says.

The man whirls around. He sees me, and jumps to his feet. "What the fuck!" he cries out.

I keep my distance, so as not to alarm him. "Take it easy, buddy," I say in a soothing voice. "Nobody's going to hurt you."

"You're damn right!" he says loudly, cocking his fist. But a lot of it's bravado; I can tell he's unsettled. He thinks he's about to be rolled. Still, he's got a tight, muscular physique, and I suspect he would put up a good fight if it came to that. It won't.

"Relax, Tony," Laura says softly, laying a hand on his arm. "Bobby's a friend."

Tony, I think. It figures. I take in the black, curly hair, the dark eyes, the smooth, brown skin. He can't be more than twenty-one. Twenty-two max. God bless you, Laura. You know my weakness for Italians. Who could ask for a better wife?

"I'm sorry I startled you, Tony," I say. "I guess Laura didn't tell you she had a houseguest."

"It's okay," Laura croons to Tony. "Sit down." She pulls on his arm. He resists at first, unsteadily. Tony appears to be a few sheets to the wind. He finally relents and falls rather heavily down beside her. Laura buttons up her blouse again.

"I don't like shit being sprung on me like that," he says, his voice lower now. "I like knowing what the fuck is going on." His tone is more plaintive than pissed. There's just the faintest slurring of words. His torso gleams with a light sheen of perspiration, and his face is flushed. He is truly a beautiful young man; Laura has outdone herself.

"Nothing's going on," I say. "Just relax. You want another beer?" Tony doesn't say anything, so I take this to mean 'yes.' I go into the kitchen and come back with another Anchor Steam. Tony takes it and after a long pull from it, reaches for his shirt.

"Why don't you leave it off?" I say. "It's a warm night. And we don't stand on formality around here." Tony shrugs and lets the shirt drop back to the floor. Laura's hand once more rests on his shoulder, gently kneading the flesh. A minute doesn't go by that she isn't somehow in contact with his body, keeping the urgency there, on the back burner, maybe, but still simmering. And I start talking to him, asking him questions, drawing his stories out of him. This is something I'm good at, because it's not just artifice, empty seduction. The young men that Laura brings up here fascinate me; I want to drink their life histories out of them. Tony resists at first, obviously pissed that I interrupted what looked like a sure thing. But in a surprisingly short period of time, he gets drawn into conversation with me, telling me about the ports he's visited, regaling me with stories. His face becomes animated, and once, while telling me about some exploit that happened in Subic Bay, he throws back his head and laughs his clear tenor laugh. I could easily fall in love with this guy. I notice his beer is empty and I get him another one. After a while, I casually lay a hand on his knee as Laura runs her hand through his hair. Tony's beautiful eyes are dilated and slightly unfocused, but I see the alarm well up inside them. He's a young man, far from home and family, and way out of his element here. I feel a surge of compassion for him, even as my hand moves up his thigh.

"I think I better go," he says thickly.

"No, baby, no," Laura murmurs. Her hand slides across his smooth chest and she nibbles on his ear. "Please stay. For me."

"I don't think so," he says, but without conviction. Laura turns his head toward her and kisses him tenderly, sliding her tongue into his mouth. He responds eagerly. I take this moment to cup his crotch with my hand. I can feel his dick, hard and urgent, straining against the tight, cotton fabric of his uniform. I bend down and bite it gently. Tony moans and thrusts his hips up. He reaches over and begins caressing Laura's breasts.

I pull Tony's shoes off, unbuckle his belt, and begin unzipping his fly. Tony's face, buried between Laura's breasts, turns toward me now. "Cut it out!" he says gruffly. He pushes my hands away.

"Relax, Tony," Laura whispers. "It's okay."

I reach up and continue tugging his zipper down. Tony scowls. "Shhhh," Laura whispers, caressing his face, running her fingers through his hair. "It's all right. Trust me." She pulls his head back down to her breasts and he nuzzles his face between them. I slowly pull his trousers down. Tony offers no resistance this time. He's wearing boxer shorts, of all things, with polka dots. I pull those down too. His dick is rock hard, thick, uncut, and veined, and his balls in this summer's heat hang low and fleshy. *Beautiful,* I think. *Just beautiful.* I catch Laura's eye and nod toward the bedroom.

"Come on, Tony," she says, almost maternally. "Let's all go to bed. We'll be a lot more comfortable there."

And Tony is seemingly compliant, now. He gets up, a little unsteadily, and steps out of the pants and shorts bunched around his ankles.

"Get rid of the socks, too, Tony," I say. I want to see him standing in the middle of my living room completely naked. He pulls them off obediently. Laura begins to lead him away.

"Hold on, a second, Laura," I say, with just the slightest edge to my voice. She stops. "I just want to look at you for a while, all right, Tony?" I ask him softly.

Tony's eyes dart uncertainly. He knows he's in uncharted waters now and there's confusion and doubt on his face. He's got slightly over two decades of lower-class, straight Italian heritage sounding the alarm inside, telling him to smash my face into jelly, or, barring that, to just hightail it out of there *now*, run down the streets of Telegraph Hill, his clothes bundled under his arms and his heterosexual cherry still intact. But he's drunk, and aroused, and confused, and lonely, and flattered by the attention he's been getting, and ready for adventure anyway, I mean, shit, why does a man join the Navy if not to see what's out there in the wide world?

He stays put. But he's not about to capitulate without some token gesture of manly pride. "What the hell is your problem, man?" he snarls. "You some kind of queer?"

"Yeah, you dago greaseball," I laugh. "Of course I'm queer. Isn't that fucking obvious?"

Tony glares at me, and I calmly return his stare, grinning. "Come on, Tony," I finally say. "Just humor me. You're goddamn beautiful. You know it. I know it. Laura knows it. That's why she picked you and brought you back here. Just let me enjoy it, okay? What harm is there in that?" Tony still says nothing. "Tony," I say softly. "Your dick is still hard. Don't tell me you're not getting off on this yourself."

Another thirty seconds go by as we stare each other down. I can see Laura out of the corner of my eye, watching us. Finally, Tony licks his lips and swallows. "What do you want me to do?" he mutters.

"Come closer," I say, my heart racing. "And start beating yourself off."

Tony walks up and stops right in front of me. His dick is jutting straight out, inches from my face, the cockhead, red and flared, pushing out from its fleshy foreskin. I trace one blue vein making its way up the length of the shaft. With a slight smile, he wraps his hand around his dickmeat and begins stroking it, slow and easy.

"Faster," I say. "Really stroke that fucker."

"I'll do it the way I like it," Tony growls, not changing his tempo.

"Sure, Tony," I say soothingly. "Anyway you like. Only, could you lean back a little, arch your back?"

Tony obeys. I watch his heavy ballsac bouncing up and down with each stroke, his hand sliding over that thick Italian salami. My eyes travel up his body, taking in the chiseled belly, the hard, sharply defined pecs, the broad shoulders, the face of a young Roman god. Tony seems suffused with light and I feel something elemental and profound move through the room. "Jesus H. Christ," I groan. I get down on my knees and worship Tony the only way I know how. I take his cock in my mouth and suck voraciously.

Tony's fingers entwine through my hair, and he begins pumping his hips; I twist my head from side to side, bobbing it in time with Tony's thrusts. I reach back and squeeze Tony's firm ass cheeks, feeling their muscles tense and relax every time he shoves his dick down my throat. My hand slides around and grasps his balls; the meaty pouch fills my palm, the two nuts have a weight and heft to them that are truly impressive. They cry out to be sucked, and who am I to refuse them? My tongue slides down Tony's shaft, and I swallow his balls, first one, and then the other, rolling them around with my tongue. I look up at Tony, his nutsac in my mouth; his eyes glitter brightly as he looks back down at me, and he begins slapping my face with his dick.

The three of us retire to the bedroom. Tony continues to plow my face as he goes down on Laura. He varies his thrusts, sometimes fucking my mouth with long, slow strokes, sometimes keeping his cock all the way down my throat and grinding his balls against my chin. By Laura's soft cries, I can tell that Tony is good at giving head; Laura puts on an act for no one. But I'm an equal match. I wrap my tongue around Tony's dick, meet Tony's thrusts with an open throat, and give him the best damn blow-job a man can get. It's a special talent of mine. Tony starts groaning with increasing loudness, and he falls back on the bed, giving in to my hot mouth and skillful tongue, all but abandoning Laura. She bends down and kisses him long and hard, and he passionately responds.

I know if I keep this up, Tony will shoot a load very soon, and I don't want that to happen yet; it's too early. I give up sucking cock for the while and press my mouth against Tony's torso, feeling the ridged bands of his abdominal muscles against my lips. My mouth wanders upwards, across the smooth, defined pectorals, and I take one of Tony's nipples between my teeth and gently bite. Tony groans, his mouth fused to Laura's, his hand buried between her legs. I run my tongue around his other nipple and bite that too, harder this time, and feel Tony's body squirm beneath me. Raising his arm, I bury my face inside his pit, drinking in the taste of fresh sweat, smelling that special man smell. I join the two of them, adding my kisses to theirs. Tony is hesitant at first, and keeps his lips shut against my thrusting tongue. But I persist, and eventually he relents, letting me slide my tongue deep into his mouth. It doesn't take long before he's returning my kisses, frenching Laura and me with the same intensity.

Tony gently pushes Laura on her back, and prepares to mount her. "Just a second, Tony," I say. I reach into the nightstand drawer, pull out a condom, and hand it to him.

"I don't use those," he says.

I sigh. "It's the rule of the house. No condom, no fuck."

Tony grouses but he eventually lets Laura put it on him. Laura gets on her knees, and he mounts her from behind, his hands squeezing her breasts. I watch in fascination as this young man fucks my wife. Laura skillfully meets his every thrust, pumping her hips in a way that lengthens and prolongs every stroke of his. I lean over and twist his nipples and Tony groans loudly. He looks at me with glazed eyes, and I realize that at this moment he's up for any pleasurable sensation, regardless of the source. I kiss him again and he returns my kiss energetically. I stand up on the bed, my stiff dick directly in front of Tony and rub his face with it. When he doesn't resist, I poke his lips with my cockhead. We look into each other's eyes, and I know this is the moment of truth. After a couple of beats, Tony opens his mouth, and I slide my dick down his throat and begin fucking his face as he continues plowing Laura.

It's an exciting sight, watching my dick move in and out of this young, handsome man's virgin mouth. I hold on to the sides of his head, more for guidance than for force, and quicken the pace. It's easy to see that Tony is a first-time cocksucker; he's actually rather clumsy, and there are techniques I would love to teach him. But what he lacks in finesse, he makes up for in enthusiasm and energy.

Laura and Tony try different positions, but each time, Tony willingly continues sucking my cock. The warmth of the evening fills the room, drugs us, and we are all drenched in sweat. I listen to the sounds of flesh slapping against flesh, to Laura's cries and Tony's grunts. It feels like we've been in this bed for days.

Tony's groans, muffled by my dick, start getting louder and more frequent. I know he's about ready to pop his cork. I'm not far myself. I cram my dick deep down his throat and churn my hips. I feel his tongue against it, squirming over it like a live animal. Sensations shoot through my body, and I feel myself pushing rapidly toward climax. I pull out of his mouth and beat off rapidly, my dick slick and slippery with Tony's saliva. Tony's body starts shuddering and he cries out loudly, his head thrown back, and he grinds his dick deep inside Laura. Laura cries out too, holding tightly onto Tony's body, her face twisted in ecstasy. A few more strokes send me over the edge, and cum spurts out of my dick, covering Tony's face and hair in spermy gobs, one pulse after another. I wipe my dickhead across his face, smearing his cheeks and mouth with my jism. We collapse into a pile; Laura and I gently kiss and lick my load off of Tony's face.

Tony spends the night with us. The next morning, we go at it again, and he obligingly fucks us both. After we shower and eat breakfast, he announces he has to go. I call a cab, and when it arrives, I give him cab fare back; I know sailors don't make much money. I offer him more money, but Tony refuses. I do give him our address on a slip of paper. Over breakfast, he has told us that his ship sails out in two days. I tell him to look us up next time he's in port, or to at least send us a post card somewhere along his travels. He says he will, but I'm resigned to the fact that they rarely do.

After he's left, Laura and I sit on the couch and look down at the ships below. I see Tony's cab at the bottom of the hill, heading toward the wharf. *What an amazing experience that was,* I think.

Laura looks up at me. "You happy, Bobby?" she asks.

I smile at her and squeeze her hand. "I guess so," I say. We sit together in silence for a long time.

# The Job On The 23rd Floor

I can tell that the new apprentice, Eddy, is a punk the first time I set eyes on him. I'm willing to let the piercings slide. Looking like a walking pin cushion isn't my idea of a winning fashion statement, but if the kid wants to pierce his eyebrow and put a stud through his tongue, it's no business of mine. And the tattoo of a skull with a mohawk on his left bicep? Give me a fuckin' break! But hey, that's no skin off my ass, either. It's the attitude he cops with me that riles the hell out of me. I give him a simple order, like go out to my truck and get me fifty feet of half-inch conduit, and he shoots me this cool, level look, just standing there with those blue eyes pinning me down, before turning around and doing what I tell him. I've seen that look before. It's the look an alpha dog wannabe gives the pack leader, waiting for the right chance to make his move. What the fuck is a fuckin' *apprentice* doing giving me that look!?

So I decide to take him down a notch. Stan, the job foreman, has me working on the 23rd floor by myself, dropping two-by-four fluorescents in the ceiling grid and running pipe between them. When it's time to break for lunch, I join the rest of the crew on the ground floor. I see Eddy over with his other apprentice buddies, chewing the shit with them while working on a hoagie sandwich.

"Hey, Eddy," I call over to him. "I need some conduit connectors. Run down to my truck and get me a couple of boxes."

Eddy finishes chewing the piece of hoagie he's got in his mouth. "Yeah, sure," he says. "As soon as lunch is over."

"I'm sorry," I say, keeping my voice low and even. "I don't think I heard you."

The other electricians stop talking and train their eyes on me and Eddy.

Eddy senses the shift as well. He straightens up and meets my stare, but I can see the uncertainty in his eyes. "I'm eating now," he says. "I'll go get the connectors as soon as lunch is over."

"No," I say, in the same level tone. "You'll get the connectors when I fuckin' tell you to get them."

The whole room is still as a morgue. Eddy shoots a glance over toward Stan, but Stan stays out of this. I can almost hear the gears turning in Eddy's head as he tries to decide how to play this. I don't say anything; I just stand there staring Eddy down. Eddy is the first to break eye contact. He climbs to his feet. "Okay," he growls. "I'll get the fuckin' connectors." As he walks out the door, one of the electricians snickers. The back of Eddy's neck burns bright red. Eddy comes back a few minutes later with the connector boxes, and I wait to see how he's going to handle this. If he just drops them at my feet, I'll tear him another asshole. But Eddy has enough native wit to hand them to me, though his eyes are shooting murder. I take the boxes from him. "Just remember," I say, "when a master electrician gives an apprentice an order, the apprentice jumps. You got that, son?"

"Yeah," Eddy mutters. "I got that." He turns and walks out the room, leaving the rest of his hoagie uneaten.

The next morning I head off to the 23rd floor again. The project is a major office remodel job, ranging from the 16th to 23rd floors of a downtown high-rise. All eight floors have been gutted, and we're just now beginning to lay out the new work. I've been working by myself on the 23rd floor for the past two days.

There's no power on, but the windows let in enough sunlight to let me see what I'm doing. There are piles of half-inch conduit scattered around and stacks of fluorescent fixtures. I got enough material here to keep me going for days. But I want to check out the Corporate Executive first.

Only a narrow alley separates this building from the one next to it. I go to the window overlooking an office across from where I stand. I can look right into it. The furnishings seem expensive: wood paneling, a massive mahogany desk, an big, fuckin' aquarium built into the opposite wall. The Corporate Executive (or "C.E." as I've been calling him) is there now, looking very dapper in a dark gray Italian suit. But he's on the phone, talking heatedly, waving an arm around. It doesn't look like there's going to be any action for the time being.

I pull my radio out of my toolbox and crank it up, full volume, to a good oldies rock and roll station. I can't stomach the crap the kids listen to nowadays, all this hip hop shit. I set up my ladder and grab several lengths of conduit from the nearest pile. It just takes me a couple of minutes to get into the rhythm, laying the conduit along the ceiling grid, clamping it down to the T-bar at regular intervals. The music bounces off the far walls and echoes back at me. After about an hour of this, I glance out the window. C.E. is alone now, standing by his window, watching me. How long he's been there, I got no idea. He sees me return his stare, and he begins rubbing his crotch. *All right!* I think.

I grin and wave. C.E. grins back. We noticed each other the first day I started working here, but it took a full day of heavy eye-fucking before things progressed to their present level. I climb down the ladder and walk over to the window. We're so close, I can see this guy in every detail. He's got a good face, easy-going, with a strong jaw and friendly brown eyes. His black hair and bushy mustache make him look Italian, or maybe Greek. He looks damn young to have his own office, just a few years older than me, mid-thirties perhaps. He must be a real hot shot where he works.

I start rubbing my crotch too; the feel of rough denim against my dick gets me hard right away. C.E. has already taken off his jacket. He loosens his tie and pulls it off, too, letting it drop to the floor. One by one, he begins undoing the buttons of his shirt. It falls open, revealing a chest covered with dark hair. The man has a beautiful body; even with his fur, I can see that the pecs are nicely developed and the abdominals are chiseled sharply. I get a picture of him working out in some executive gym, doing his presses and stomach crunches faithfully on the Nautilus equipment.

I pull my T-shirt over my head and let it drop. I pinch my nipples, hard, while slowly grinding my hips. I run my hands over my torso, gently squeezing the skin. C.E. has better definition than me, but I got a more powerful build, with broader shoulders and bigger arms. I get a big kick out of stripping for him, slowly, teasing him. The fucker wants it, bad. I can see the hunger in his face.

C.E. unbuckles his belt and lets his pants drop to the floor. I have to grin. He's wearing red bikini briefs; every other time he's had on boxer shorts. C.E.'s wearing them just for me. Maybe he had to go out and buy them just for this occasion. They look really hot. I give him a thumb's up signal, and C.E. grins back.

I let my jeans drop, as well. I'm not wearing anything underneath, and my prick jumps to attention, swelling rapidly now that it's free. I begin to stroke it slowly, still rubbing my body with my other hand. The radio starts playing The Door's "Light My Fire", and I change my rhythm, beating off in time to it, fucking my hand with short, rapid thrusts.

C.E. hooks his thumbs under the elastic of his briefs and pulls them down. His dick springs up eagerly. I love this guy's cock; it's thick, and uncut, just the way I like 'em. His balls are meaty and hang low. I really get off watching that red, fleshy pouch swing back and forth as he whacks off.

I press my pelvis against the window and start fucking the glass. It feels cool and hard against my dick. C.E. is eating this up. His eyes bore in on my crotch while he pumps that heavy salami of his even faster. Suddenly he lets go of his dick and strikes a pose, flexing his arms. His biceps bulge impressively. At the same time he grinds his hips, letting that fuckstick of his flop up and down. I laugh. The guy is such a ham, but I love it! He's having such a fucking great time, just like I am. He turns around and flexes again, showing a really fine pair of lats. I could spend all day just eating his ass. It's surprisingly smooth, considering how hairy his chest is, firm and well rounded. He bends down and backs against his window, giving me a pressed ham. The asshole puckers invitingly, just a few feet away from me.

C.E. straightens up and turns around again. He seizes his cock once more and begins stroking in earnest. All the flirting's over; we're in for the kill now. I quicken my pace now, too. Bruce Springsteen's "Pink Cadillac" comes on the radio, and I let the driving beat take over, control me. C.E. does a small stroll around his office, working his tool, rubbing his torso with his other hand. He's definitely feeling frisky. He climbs on top his desk and stretches out on it, his legs hanging over the side. It's a hot pose. As he strokes his dick, I get a great view of his bouncing nuts and his ass crack. I'm pounding my own meat hard now, sliding my hand up and down my fuck pole, as I watch C.E. strut his stuff. His eyes are glazing over and his nuts are drawn up tight. He can't be far from shooting. I'm pretty close myself. I spit in my hand, making it nice and slippery, and slide it up and down the shaft of my dick. Little jolts of pleasure shoot through my body. I reach up and pinch my nipple hard. I arch my back as I get ready to squirt my load onto the window in front of me.

C.E.'s eyes flicker, and suddenly a look of alarm crosses his face. He starts pointing in my direction, and it takes a couple of seconds for me to realize that he's pointing *behind* me. I turn around and there's Eddy, by the elevator door, staring at me. He doesn't look all that shocked, but he takes in the whole scene with a cool, shrewd look on his face.

I glance at my jeans, heaped on the floor a good ten feet away from me. I'm just standing there buck naked with my dick in my hand. *Oh, shit!* I think. I decide to take the offensive. "What the fuck are you doin' here?" I growl.

Eddy walks slowly toward me. "Stan sent me up here to see if you needed any help," he says, his voice cool and level. He glances at C.E., who's standing by his window watching us, and then back at me again. Eddy takes a couple of more steps toward me. "Whatcha got going here, Carl?" he asks, his expression all exaggerated innocence.

"It's just you and me here, Eddy," I say. "Whatever you tell Stan, I'll deny it. Stan'll believe me over you any day." But my heart is hammering, and I can't help but wonder if Eddy's picking up on that. He may be a punk, but he's not stupid.

Eddy raises an eyebrow. "You sure you want to put that to the test?"

I let a couple of beats go by. "Okay, Eddy," I say. "You got me by the short hairs. What the fuck do you want from me?"

Eddy keeps walking toward me. He doesn't stop until he's standing toe to toe with me. We're both right next to the window, C.E. just five feet and two panes of glass away from us.

Eddy turns his head, looks over at C.E., and waves. He looks back at me. "Who's your little buddy?" he asks. "He's hot."

"I asked you a question."

"Fuck you and your question," Eddy says. He jerks his head toward C.E. "You like struttin' your stuff, Carl?" he asks. "You like showing what you got to an audience?"

I don't say anything, waiting for Eddy to get to the point.

"Drop to your knees," Eddy says quietly.

"Fuck you!" I snarl.

"Do it!" Eddy barks. I stand there, glaring at him. "Do it, asshole," he says, his voice murderous. "Or I'll tell Stan all about this. I got nothing to lose; I'm just a dumb ass apprentice. But are you willing to risk that Stan will believe you over me?"

Eddy and I glare at each other for a few beats. His blue eyes are like icicles stabbing at me. I look for a sign that he's bluffing, but I don't see any. I think that if Stan *does* buy Eddy's story, I'll never work in this town again. I slowly drop down to my knees.

"Yeah," Eddy says softly. "That's more like it." He looks down at me, his eyes bright with malice. "You like putting on shows, motherfucker?" He unzips his fly. "Okay, so let's both put on a show for your friend." He reaches in and pulls out his dick. "Suck it," he says.

I let a couple of beats go by. "So this is payback time, huh, Eddy?" I say quietly. "This is your chance to get back at the big, mean electrician who yelled at you."

"Yeah," Eddy says. "That's exactly what it is." He shakes his dick at me. "I said suck it!" he snarls.

I look at Eddy's dick. Even half-hard, it's impressive: a thick, veined tube of flesh, the flared cockhead just peeping out of its foreskin. It looks like a real mouthful. "Sure, Eddy," I say. "Anything you say."

I lean forward and take the head of Eddy's dick in my mouth. I swirl my tongue around the fleshy knob and then nibble my lips down the shaft, sucking hard as I do so. Eddy's dick swells to full hardness, and Eddy begins pumping his hips. He grips my head in his hands and fucks my mouth with short, savage thrusts. After a few moments, Eddy reaches up, unbuckles his belt, and lets his jeans fall down around his ankles. "Now suck on my balls, fuckface," he rasps.

Eddy's balls lay heavy and swollen in their meaty pouch, dusted by fine brown hair. I position my face under them and begin licking them, first the left nut, then the right. I open my mouth wider and suck his entire ballsac into my mouth, rolling my tongue over them. I look up at Eddy as I give his balls a tongue bath. Our eyes lock together. "Yeah, you fuckin' asshole," he snarls. "You loud-mouthed dickhead, eat those nuts." He slaps my face with his cock, punctuating each word with a sharp *thwack*. He pulls his balls out of my mouth and starts fucking my face again. I reach up and knead his torso, feeling the hard, muscled body, the smooth skin. I give Eddy's nipples a sharp tweak, and hear Eddy give a low grunt. "Yeah," he sighs. "That's right."

My hands slide around to Eddy's ass. His asscheeks feel warm and smooth under my fingertips, the butt muscles as firm as vulcanized rubber. I give them a good squeeze, like melons I'm testing for ripeness. One of my hands slips into the crack of Eddy's ass and massages his bung hole, while my other hand starts stroking my dick. All the while, I'm still hungrily working Eddy's dick with my mouth.

"Hey, you old fuck!" Eddy snarls. "You're not supposed to be enjoying this!"

I take his dick out of my mouth and look up at him. "Yeah, punk," I smirk. "It takes the bite out of your revenge if I'm having a good time, doesn't it?"

Eddy glowers at me for a couple of beats. He pulls off his T-shirt, kicks off his shoes, and steps out of his jeans. Now he's as naked as I am. "Okay, douchebag," Eddy spits out. "Bend over. I'm going to pound your ass hard. Let's see how much you enjoy that."

"I don't care who you tell about me," I say, meeting his eye. "I don't fuck without condoms."

Eddy bends down and pulls his wallet out of his jeans. He fishes a condom out and shakes it in my face. "Don't worry about it, dickhead," he says.

"Fine, Eddy," I say. "You can fuck my ass. But could you just stop calling me names? It's getting a little old."

"Just bend over," Eddy snaps. I obey, bending down and holding onto my calves, but I twist my head to watch him as he rolls the condom down his hard dick. Eddy positions himself behind me and grabs hold of my hips. He spits in his hand and slicks up his dick. I feel his dickhead poke against my asshole, and I relax my ass. Eddy slides his dick in, inch by inch. Spit is a lousy lubricant, and I grit my teeth as Eddy slowly skewers me. I'm facing the window now, with Eddy right behind me. I raise my head, and there's C.E., taking this all in, furiously pounding his pud. I wiggle my eyebrows at him, and C.E. grins broadly.

Eddy has worked his dick full up my ass, and he keeps it there, grinding his hips against mine. I feel like I'm getting the full Roto-Rooter treatment, and I squeeze my ass hard against the thick, fleshy rod inside me. Eddie holds on to my hips and starts fucking me like there's hell to pay, roaring down my ass like so many miles of bad road. I brace myself and push back hard. If the kid thinks my ass can't take this kind of treatment, he's got another thought coming; this is exactly how I like to get fucked, rough and vicious, and I'm more than willing to give as much as I take. Eddy's balls are slamming against me with each hard thrust, and I reach behind and wrap my hand around them. I give them a good tug, not enough to hurt, just enough to get Eddy worried.

Eddy pulls out. "Lie down on the floor," he growls. I sneer at him and then do what he tells me, lying down face up, with my legs in the air and my asshole gaping. Eddie gets down on his knees and pushes his dick up my ass again, propping himself up on his outstretched hands. My eyes lock with Eddy's, and I wrap my thighs around his torso in a scissors squeeze. Eddy attacks me like an avenging angel, slamming into my ass like I'm going to pay for all the sins of the world. Jesus, do I ever love revenge fucks! I'm pounding my pud with each thrust, and with my other hand I punch Eddy repeatedly on his torso, ending each blow with a long caress. Eddy's lips are pulled back into a wordless snarl, and sweat drips down his face, splashing onto me, getting into my eyes and mouth. I turn my head toward the window and see that C.E. is going apeshit; his balls are a bouncing blur as he beats off, his eyes are burning through the glass as he takes in this little show we're putting on for him. I wrap my hand around the back of Eddy's neck and pull his mouth down against mine, snaking my tongue deep down his throat.

Eddy gives a hard thrust, and a little whimper escapes from his lips. He thrusts again, and the whimper rises in volume. The next time he slides his dick full in, I clamp down on my ass muscles *hard*. Eddy gives a low, trailing groan. "Goddamn, but you're a hot piece of tail!" he growls.

I laugh. "Never underestimate the power of a good bottom, Eddy." Eddy looks down at me for a beat, and then, to my surprise, he cracks a grin. He thrusts inside me, and I squeeze my ass again. Eddy's body spasms and he starts groaning loudly.

"If you're going to shoot," I growl. "I want to see it."

"Okay, motherfucker," Eddy gasps. "Then here it is." He pulls out of my ass and tears the condom off. His jizz squirts out of his dickhead, arcing across space and splattering against my face in thick, ropy wads. Eddy's bucking and heaving on top of me, crying out like a damned soul from hell. A couple of quick strokes pushes me over the brink, and I groan loudly, arching my back as my load squirts out and rains down on my chest and face, mingling with Eddy's spermy deposit. I look out the window and watch as C.E. shoots, his jizz splattering against the glass and sliding sluggishly down the window. Triple simultaneous orgasms. Not too fuckin' shabby!

Eddy collapses onto the floor besides me, getting his breath back. "Damn!" he says softly.

I climb to my feet and pick up my jeans. "Get up," I say gruffly. "We got a lot of work to do."

Eddy and I work together on the 23rd floor for the rest of the day. By the end of the day, we're done hanging the fixtures and are well into laying the pipe in the ceiling grid. From time to time, I give Eddy pointers on better ways to do things, and damn if he doesn't stop and listen to me, following up on what I tell him.

I run into Stan in the building lobby at the end of the day, on my way out. "How'd things go with that new apprentice?" Stan asks. "Did you get him straightened out?"

"Yeah, Stan," I say. "I got him towing the line. He's a good worker now. How about sending him up to me for tomorrow as well?"

"Sure," Stan says, looking surprised. "If that's what you want."

I see Eddy in the parking lot, climbing into his car. I wink at him, and he grins back. *Tomorrow should be all sorts of fun*, I think. I start the ignition to my pick up and drive off.

# Cyber Thugs

The suit is kept in its own private closet with a built-in humidifier and degaussing unit, to keep the suit's thousands of tiny sensors free from excessive air moisture and static electricity (the little fuckers can short out at the slightest provocation). I strip naked, and as I pull the suit on, I marvel once more at how *light* it feels—no more than a couple of pounds—and yet woven within its metallic fabric are countless miles of circuitry. The suit immediately contracts to conform to the shape of my body. The greatest density of sensors can be found in the crotch area, but as I activate the suit, I can also feel my asshole, nipples, and lips tingle as a low voltage charge courses through the fabric. I put on the goggles and olfactory plugs.

I sit down in front of the computer console and flip the switch to activate it. The monitor screen, which takes up an entire wall of the room, lights up to a pearly gray. All the sensors in the suit terminate in one plug, which I now insert into an outlet in the side of the computer. A single word pulses on the screen: MENU, and below it, all the letters of the alphabet. I click the mouse on the letter "T", and the screen fills with options: tank commander, taxi driver, telephone repairman, terrorist, thug, trailer trash, traffic cop, trapper, Trekkie, trick, trucker . . . I click on "thug." The screen pulses blank, flickers, and suddenly a bar scene fills the screen. A nod of my head activates the program, giving me the illusion of walking into the bar.

The place is a dump. The floorboards are warped, and the walls are coated with years' worth of grime. What light there is comes from a string of incandescent bulbs dangling from the ceiling. There's a scattering of beat-up tables and chairs, and one long bar that stretches across the length of the room. I take a deep breath and get a whiff of stale cigarette smoke and old piss. Some old Sinatra tune plays on the jukebox; Frankie's voice sounds thin and tinny over the gimcrack speakers.

About a dozen or so men lounge at the tables or lean against the walls, slugging down their drinks. I eye them curiously. They're a bunch of bad-ass motherfuckers, all tattooed flesh, raw chuck faces, and hulking muscle (in reality, these are the computer-generated images of guys who, like me, are sitting in their homes in their sensor suits, plugged into this particular fantasy). I go over to the bar. The bartender is some trog with a sloping forehead and beady eyes that fix on me with weary disgust. The computer program informs me his name is Max.

I order a whiskey, neat. There's a mirror behind the bar, and I take in the reflection that looks back at me. It's a face that could stop a clock: blunt features, thick lips, a squashed nose and cheekbones so high they push my eyes up into a permanent squint. A long, jagged scar, like frozen lightning, zigzags from my left ear to down below my jaw. I'm wearing a T-shirt, which stretches tightly over my body, revealing a heavily muscled torso. There's a tattoo of a grinning skull on my left, hugely bulging bicep. I give a low laugh. I asked for "thug" and the program gave it to me in spades.

"Something funny, Spike?" Max asks.

"Naw, Max," I say. "Nothing at all." I lift my whiskey to him. "Cheers."

Max watches me, saying nothing, his face as expressive as a slab of beef. I down my drink and push the empty glass toward him. "Another," I say.

Max fills it again. He nods toward left. "Your buddies are waiting for you, Spike," he says. I look in the direction he's indicated. There's a heavy metal door, half open, leading into what looks like some kind of back alley.

I quickly drain my glass. "Well, shit," I grin. "Then I better get a move on." I reach into my pocket, feel some paper, and pull out a hundred dollar bill. I drop it on the bar. "Keep the change," I say. Max stuffs the bill in his back pocket as I slide off my stool and walk through the bar's back door.

I find myself in a narrow alley, lined with trash cans and ending in a blank brick wall. The alley is dark except for a pool of light at the far end, coming from a single exposed bulb mounted on the wall. Two men stand together under the harsh light. The program informs me that the black dude with the shaved head and bull-muscled torso is Alfonzo, and the hawk-faced man with the greasy, combed-back blonde hair and lean, hard body is Rocco. They're facing each other with their jeans down around their ankles. Alfonzo has his huge hand wrapped around both their dicks and is jacking them slowly. Rocco pulls Alfonzo close and frenches his mouth.

Alfonzo is the first to notice me. He breaks his liplock with Rocco and grins, his teeth gleaming in his dark face. "Hey, Spike," he says. "We've been waiting for you." He keeps on lazily jacking the two cocks in his fist.

"It sure doesn't look that way," I say, unbuckling my belt.

Alfonzo laughs. "Don't start getting pissy, Spike. We were just warming up."

I unzip my jeans and let them drop to my ankles. I step out of them, kick them aside, and pull off my T-shirt. I strut naked down the alley toward the waiting guys. The computer program has given me a hot body, muscular and beautifully proportioned, with a thick, meaty dick that swings heavily between my thighs as I approach the two men. My torso is covered with tattoos: bloody knives, demon heads, devil chicks with horns and big tits, that kind of shit. Alfonzo and Rocco drink me in, their eyes hard and bright, and my dick quickly stiffens under their collective lust. By the time I reach them, I've got a full boner on.

Alfonzo wraps his hand around my dick and pulls me toward him. We kiss, with heavy tongue action, and the two men press against me, their hands pulling and stroking my flesh. The three of us swap spit, rubbing our bodies together, hard dicks batting hard dicks. I lift Rocco's arm and nuzzle into his armpit, savoring the sharp, acid taste of his sweat, then slide my tongue across his chest and around each nipple. Rocco's fingers pry apart my ass crack and massage the pucker of my bung hole as Alfonzo jacks me off with a spit-slicked hand.

I drop down to my knees and look up at the two cocks twitching in front of my face. I start with Alfonzo's. His uncut dick arcs up, blue-black, thick, roped with veins, ending in the rubbery dome of his cockhead. I skin the foreskin back and swirl my tongue around his cockhead, pushing into the piss slit. The warm tube of flesh pulses in my hand; I squeeze it and lap up the little clear pearl of pre-cum that oozes out. Alfonzo plants a hand on each side of my head and slides his dick deep down my throat. With an effort, I manage to work it all down, my nose buried in his crinkly, black pubes. I hold that pose for a few seconds; I always fuckin' love the sensation of a mouth full of cock. I give Alfonzo's low-hangers a tug. "Baby, that feels so good," he sighs.

I look up, and my gaze locks with Alfonzo's across the length of his muscled torso. I slide my hands over his hard six-pack, across the mounds of his pecs and give both his nipples a good tweak. Alfonzo's mouth curls up into a lazy smile, and he closes his eyes. "Yeah, baby," he murmurs, pumping his hips. "That's right, keep doing that." The night is warm, and Alfonzo's body gleams with a sheen of sweat, like polished ebony. I take his dick out of my mouth and bury my face in his balls, breathing in the ripe, funky smell of a man in rut. I tongue one ball, and then the other, as Alfonzo rubs his dick all over my face, and then suck both balls into my mouth, rolling them around with my tongue. I go back to blowing him, Alfonzo fucking my face in long, measured strokes.

I pull Alfonzo's dick out of my mouth and starting working on Rocco's, whose dick is cut and fat and candy pink, with a pair of plump balls hanging underneath, dusted with light blonde hairs. His cockhead is a cherry gumdrop on a shaft that widens as my lips slide down it. Rocco's ready for bear; he doesn't fuck my mouth slow and easy like Alfonzo did, but pumps it with fast piston thrusts.

I work the two dicks in front of me, feeding off one and then the other, back and forth. Alfonzo and Rocco lean forward and kiss each other, stroke each other's bodies, pull on flesh, squeeze ass, twist nipples, finger fuck assholes. This goes on for a long time, the still, summer night punctuated by the slurping sounds of my cocksucking, and the grunts and groans of the two men standing over me. Alfonzo finally pulls his dick out of my mouth and pushes me on my back. "Enough with the cocksucking," he growls. "I need to fuck some ass." He pulls a small bottle of lube out of his jeans pocket and squirts a dollop on his hand. I lean back, propped on my elbows, and watch him grease up his dick. Alfonzo kneels down on the gritty pavement, grabs my ankles, and spreads my legs wide apart. His cockhead pushes against the pucker of my asshole, and I breathe out and relax as Alfonzo slides into me, inch by inch, his eyes fixed on mine. "You like that, baby?" he croons.

"Fuckin' A," I gasp.

Alfonzo slides in the last four inches with one quick thrust, and I arch my back and groan loudly. He wraps his arms around me and lies on top of me, churning his hips. It feels like I have a couple of feet of dick inside of me. Alfonzo pulls his dick out slowly, until just the tip of its head is in my asshole, holds that position for a couple of beats, and with one quick thrust, slides his whole cock full into me.

"Goddamn!" I groan. Alfonzo laughs. He starts fucking me with a hard urgency, lips bared, eyes fierce, his cock slamming in and out my ass like a pile driver, his balls slapping against me with a soft *thwack* with each thrust. I wrap my legs around his hips and push back, meeting him stroke for stroke. Alfonzo whimpers softly. I plant my mouth on his and shove my tongue deep down his throat. We play dueling tongues for a while, and then Alfonzo breaks away, gasping. "Get on your hands and knees," he gasps. "I want to fuck you like a dog."

Alfonzo starts plowing my ass doggy style, his hands holding on to my hips as his cock tears up my asshole like so many miles of bad road. I look up and watch Rocco beating his pud, his gunmetal blue eyes trained on us. "Come over here," I growl, and Rocco doesn't waste any time. He comes up next to me, squats and shoves his fat dick down my throat. I start making hungry love to it, sucking on it, playing with it with my tongue. Rocco pulls out, grasps my head with both hands, gives me a long, lingering kiss, and then slides his dick back into my mouth.

It is so fuckin' hot to be stuffed with dick at both ends! The two men slam into me, pull out together, leaving me empty and hungry, and then fill me again with their hard, fat dicks. I close my eyes and sink into the sensation of getting my holes plowed. Rocco and Alfonzo lean over me and kiss, never missing a stroke.

Rocco pulls out and turns around. His ass is a very pretty thing, pale cream and downed with fine blonde hairs, the crack a tight line between the muscular half moons of his cheeks. He bends down, and I bury my face into the crack, lapping up the tight, pink pucker of his bung hole. "Ah, fuck, yeah," he growls. I push my tongue into his asshole, feeling the ass flesh press in against my slobber-drenched face. I reach in front of him and slide my hand up and down his spit-slicked cock as I tongue his ass-hole. Alfonzo skewers me with another long thrust and leaves his dick full up my ass, churning his hips, pushing my face even deeper into Rocco's ass crack.

Rocco straightens up and turns around again. He steps back and starts beating off, putting on a show for me, his eyes locked with mine. It's such a fuckin' hot sight. Rocco's body isn't as massively muscular as Alfonzo's, but it's lean and cut, every muscle beautifully defined. He spits in his hand and slides his fist down his fat dick, the gumdrop head winking in and out of sight with each stroke. I watch hungrily, eating this up, while Alfonzo plows my ass like it's springtime in Kansas. "Get the fuck over here," I snarl, and, grinning, Rocco steps forward and stuffs his cock down my throat again.

We go back to the old rhythm of me getting plugged on both ends. I can hear Alfonzo's labored breath, like some draft horse struggling up a steep hill. He's leaning forward, with his arms wrapped around my torso, his dick sliding in and out of my ass in quick, staccato thrusts. "Fuck," he gasps. "I'm going to pop any second now."

Rocco's cock is crammed down my throat, and I can't do anything but grunt in reply. Alfonzo pulls out until only the tip of his boner is in my ass, and as he slides full in me, I clamp my ass muscles tight and push back. Alfonzo gives a long, trailing groan, and his body shudders violently. No condoms are needed in cybersex, and Alfonzo cries out as his cock squirts his spunk deep into my asshole. His body spasms with each pulse of his dick. "Fuckin' A," Rocco growls. Even after he's shot the last of his load, Alfonzo stands behind me, his dick full up my ass, panting. He finally slides off me onto his knees, and collapses onto the pavement. A last few drops of jizz ooze out of his cockhead.

"Get on your back," Rocco orders. I obey him, and Rocco sits on my chest and drops his balls into my mouth. I suck on them as he beats off, interrupting his strokes from time to time to slap my face with his stiff cock. Alfonzo wedges himself between the V of my legs and blows me, his finger sliding in and out of my asshole. I push my hips up and fuck Alfonzo's face as I slurp and suck on Rocco's meaty pouch. Rocco's breath is coming out in quick gasps, and he cranes his head up, eyes closed. "Oh, yeah," he pants, as he beats himself off. "That's right, uh huh. Yeah, okay, yeah, work my balls. Yeah, that's right, suck on them, uh huh. Oh, shit, I'm getting close. Uh huh, oh shit, oh yeah, here I come, here I come, *aw fuuuuuck. . . .*" He groans, and his spunk splatters against my face, one volley after another. Rocco bucks and heaves, knees clamping into my side, and right at the moment, when the last of his load comes blasting out, Alfonzo's wet mouth and busy finger takes me over the edge and I blow my load.

"Goddamn," I groan, as my spunk squirts down his throat. Alfonzo sucks greedily, draining my dick of every drop as I splatter his tonsils. Rocco bends down and kisses me hard while the orgasm sweeps over me. When I'm finally spent, Rocco rolls off me, and the three of us collapse onto the pavement in a tangle of arms and legs. Rocco's load drips sluggishly down my chin, and I wipe my hand across my face and lick my fingers, one by one. I look over at Rocco and grin. "My favorite flavor," I say. Rocco laughs.

The three of us climb unsteadily to our feet. I take Alfonzo's head in my hands and plant a big, wet kiss on his mouth. I taste my load on his tongue. I do the same for Rocco. "So long, guys," I say.

"So long, Spike," Rocco says. Alfonzo just grins. I look up into the night sky. "Abort program," I say loudly.

Rocco, Alfonzo, and the alley around us blink out of existence. I'm back in my chair in front of the blank computer screen. These program aborts are always something of a shock. It takes a couple of moments to adjust to reality. I climb, a little unsteadily, to my feet, unzip the cyber suit and step out of it. My dick is still half-hard, and there are a couple of drops of jizz dribbling out of my cockslit.

I take a shower, shave, pick up the newspaper from the front step. I fix breakfast. *I'll give myself another hour to prime the pump,* I think, as I sip my coffee. *Then I'll try "trailer trash."* I should be through with the T's by Sunday evening. I can't remember exactly when I last set foot outside my apartment. Four days? Five? I glance through the paper. It's all full of murders, war, natural catastrophes, the usual shit. *Thank god for fantasy,* I think. I eat everything on my plate. I've got a busy day ahead of me, and I'll need my energy.

# Playing It Straight

When I wake up, Julian is still asleep, his legs all tangled up in the sheets. I slip out of bed, pull my boxers on and wander out to the kitchen. Sam is sitting at the kitchen table, drinking a cup of coffee and reading the morning paper.

"Morning," he says.

"Morning," I grunt.

I pour a cup of coffee for myself and pick up the paper's front section. I wince and shift in my chair.

Sam peers at me over the paper. "You all right?"

"It's nothing," I say. "Julian gave my ass a real pounding last night, and it's a little tender right now."

Sam grimaces. "You really didn't have to put that picture in my head."

"Yeah, right," I laugh. "Like you never miss a chance to tell me how much you love eating pussy."

"Yeah, well, that's different," Sam grins. "Eating pussy is *normal*."

Sam and I go back a long ways, since college, actually. I needed a roommate a couple of years ago right when Sam's marriage had gone into self-destruct. Sam moved in and has been here ever since.

We hear the shower running. Sam glances toward the bathroom, then at me again. "So what's the story with Julian? Is he the flavor of the week, or something else?"

I shrug. "Julian's great, but this is just a fuck buddy thing we've got going."

Sam shakes his head. "Jesus, I wish it were half as easy for a straight guy to get laid as it is for you gay boys."

I laugh.

Julian comes out, fully dressed a few minutes later. He turns down my offer of a cup of coffee. "I can't," he says. "I gotta get to work." He bends down and gives me a lingering kiss. Sam doesn't look up from his paper. I walk Julian to the door, then head back to the bedroom to get ready for work myself.

Sam intercepts me on my way out. "Can I ask a favor?"

"Sure," I say.

"While you're downtown, will you pick me up a couple of stroke magazines?"

I look at him. "Hell, no," I say. "I'm not going to buy some pussy magazines for you. What if someone I know sees me?"

Sam looks amused. "God forbid somebody should think you're straight."

"I mean it," I say. "How would you feel if I asked you to buy some gay porn for me?"

Sam shrugs. "I'd do it. What's the big deal?"

Sam wheedles me, and eventually I give in. "All right," I say. "I'll get you your damn pussy mags. But you owe me, now. Next time you're downtown, I'll have you pick up a dildo for me."

"It would be a pleasure," Sam says, grinning.

There's a porno bookstore a couple of blocks from where I work. At five, after I leave the office, I duck into it, intending to make this quick. The place is your generic mom-and-pop sex emporium: racks of videos and magazines, with an open doorway leading to the video booths in back.

Some guy's standing by the magazine rack, rifling through one of the gay rags. I do your classic double take, glancing at him briefly and then taking a longer, harder look. He's young, barely out of his twenties, with slicked back, black hair, and a tough, punk face. He's got the body of a bull terrier: compact and muscular, with wide shoulders and narrow hips. He glances up at me as I walk in, and our eyes meet briefly. His eyes are dark and shrewd, and they sweep up and down me in quick appraisal. Apparently he's not buying, because he turns back to his magazine.

*Okayyyy,* I think. I go up to the stand, just a couple of feet from him, and rifle through the straight porn. I don't know what the hell Sam's taste in porno is, and I just pick a couple of magazines at random. As I turn, I see that the guy is looking at me again. He glances down at the pussy magazines in my hand and then back into my face, this time his eyes boring into me.

I take the magazines to the counter, my mind racing. *Fuck,* I think, *is this guy cruising me or not?* The clerk rings up my purchase, and I hand him three tens. "Give me the change in tokens," I say. I turn and head back toward the beaded curtain leading into the arcade. As I pass the guy at the magazine rack, he gives me a classic eye fuck that would rival that of the most experienced bar cruiser.

I push through the curtain and stand outside the row of booths, waiting. After a few seconds, the guy walks into the arcade. His eyes meet mine again. I hold his gaze for a couple of beats and then walk into the nearest booth and close the door behind me. I dump the tokens into the slot, and some of that lesbian porn that straight guys seem to like so much comes on the screen. Before I can change the channel, the door opens, and the guy slides in, closing the door behind him.

"Hi," he says.

"Hello," I reply. The light from the video flickers on him. I take in the dark, hooded eyes, the sensual mouth, the tight, lean body. My dick gives a special throb.

He glances at the video. "You got a good pussy channel on? Something to get your dick nice and hard?"

That wasn't what I expected. Something about the way he asks that makes me wait a couple of beats before answering. I decide to give him the answer that I think he wants to hear. "Yeah," I say slowly. "I just fuckin' can't get enough pussy. I could look at it all day."

"I bet you got a serious nut to bust," the guy says. "Horny straight guy, buying those pussy magazines, taking them home to whack off to." He glances at the video on the screen. "Watching some lesbian porn. . . ."

I'm warming up to this. "Yeah," I say. "I'm hornier than a motherfucker right now."

The guy reaches down and gives my crotch a squeeze. "I can get you off, man," he says. "You just keep watching your lesbian porn and let me work that dick of yours." *This guy's hot for me because he thinks I'm straight,* I think. I have to keep from smiling. Fucking human nature: we always want what we can't have.

I pause, trying to think of the best way of playing this. The guy mistakes my silence for hesitancy. He leans forward. "Let me clue you in," he says. "Nobody can suck a dick like a gay guy. We know what feels good and what doesn't."

*Yeah, tell me something I don't know,* I think. "Oh, yeah?" I say, fixing him in my gaze. "You mean it? You really wanna suck my dick?"

"Fuck, yeah," he growls. He gives my dick another squeeze.

I give a sigh. "It's been such a long since I've gotten head. My wife's just not into the dick-sucking thing anymore." I sigh again. "Sex just hasn't been the same since we had the kid."

The guy is eating this up. "Let me help you, buddy," he says. He pulls down my zipper, reaches in and pulls my dick out. He smiles. "I knew you'd have a big one." He spits into his hand and slides his spit-slicked hand down my shaft. His other hand snakes under my shirt and twists my left nipple. I close my eyes. "You ever have another guy suck you off before?" he croons.

I open my eyes and look at him. *Yeah,* I think. *About a thousand times.* I shake my head. "No," I say. "Never."

"That's cool, buddy," the guy says softly. "I can give you some great relief." He unbuckles my belt, and my slacks slide down to my ankles. The guy tugs my boxers down, and my hard dick springs up and sways gently back and forth. "Fuuuck," he groans. "Your wife doesn't know what she's missing. Your dick is beautiful." He unzips his jeans and pulls his own dick out. I can see by the flickering light of the video that it's thick and uncut, with a fat, bulbous head peeking out from the foreskin.

"I think she's fucking someone else," I say. "Maybe the mailman."

"What a bummer," he says. But I can tell that his mind's on other things. He slides to his knees and starts jacking me off. He looks up at me, grinning. "I love it when a man's balls hang so low that they bounce when you jack him." He opens his mouth and sucks my balls in.

"Oh, yeah," I groan.

The guy looks up at me. "You like that, buddy? I bet it's better than your fuckin' wife can do."

"Hey, easy, man," I say. "I still love her."

"Sorry," he says. He slides his tongue up my wanker, swirls it around my cockhead and then nibbles his lips down my shaft. I thrust forward until I've crammed my dick full into his mouth. I grasp his head with both hands and begin fucking his face with quick, deep strokes. The guy's hand slides down my ass and burrows into my ass crack. His finger finds my bung hole and pushes in. I close my eyes and groan. He works his finger up my ass, knuckle by knuckle. He's got his other hand wrapped around his own dick, jacking himself as he sucks my dick and finger fucks my hole.

"Damn," I sigh. I open my eyes and look down at him. It's such a turn-on seeing my dick slide in and out of this hot guy's mouth, feeling his finger fuck my ass. . . . He twists his head from side to side as his mouth slides down my cock shaft, all the while licking and sucking my dick. I lean back against the wall of the booth and squeeze my nipples as the sensations ripple over me.

He takes my dick out of his mouth and looks up at me. "You feel like fuckin' my ass?" he asks.

*Fuck yeah!* I think. This is just getting more and more interesting. "I don't know," I say, making my tone hesitant. "I mean, what you're doing feels great and all that, but this is all just kind of . . . weird."

He stands up. "Trust me, you'll love it," he says. "An asshole is a lot tighter than snatch." The booth is small and his face is just a couple of inches from mine. He leans forward. "Just let it happen," he says softly. "You won't regret it, I swear." I can tell he's really getting off on playing the role of the gay seducer. "You're just taking a little break from your wife. While she's fucking the milkman."

"Mailman," I say.

"Whatever," he says. He kisses me hard, sliding his tongue deep into my mouth. I kiss him back, pushing my body against his, feeling his hard cock poke against my belly. He reaches into his pocket and pulls out a condom. "Fuck my ass, man," he urges. "Don't make me beg."

"All right," I breathe.

"Then let's get to it," he says. He unbuckles his belt, and his jeans slide down to his ankles. I wrap my hand around his hard, thick dick and stroke it slowly, sliding the silky foreskin up and down the shaft.

"You ever touch a man's hard dick before?" he asks.

I'm the farm boy on his first visit to the wicked city. "No," I say, wide-eyed. "Never." He takes the condom from my hand and rolls it down my dick shaft. He breaks out a little tube of lube and greases me up. "Are you always this prepared?" I laugh.

He doesn't laugh back; he's all seriousness now. "I am when I cruise the porn videos for straight dick," he answers. He turns around, twisting his neck to look at me. "I want you to fuck me hard," he growls. "Close your eyes and pretend you're fucking some big-titted, tight-snatched babe, and really ram my ass."

"Sure," I say. "I'll pretend you're Pamela Anderson."

I wrap my arms around his torso and push my dick against the pucker of his asshole. The adrenalin's pumping through me like a wrecking ball. He leans forward, bracing himself against the booth wall, and pushes back. My dick slowly slides into his tight chute, and he exhales deeply. "Yeah," he breathes. "That's right." When I'm full in, I hold the pose, feeling his ass muscles envelop my dick. I pull out until my cockhead is just barely within the ring of his sphincter.

"I have to warn you," I whisper in his ear. "When I start fucking, there's no stopping me."

"You think I got a problem with that?" he asks.

I slide full in again, pause, and then start pumping my hips, hard, slamming into his ass. I've got my arms wrapped around his torso, my hands under his shirt, pulling and tugging on the muscles of his tight, hard body, as I plow in and out of his ass. He meets me stroke for stroke, pushing up against me every time I thrust in, squeezing his ass tight. I grip his nipples and twist hard, and he groans. He's jacking himself off, stroking his dick in synch with each of my thrusts. The booth is cramped and the ventilation sucks, and I can feel the sweat trickle down my face. The dude's sweating too; his skin is slippery and damp under my hands. The light from the lesbian porn video flickers over his body, and I drink in the sight of his naked, tight flesh.

The guy reaches down behind and gives a tug on my balls. "Fuckin' hot, straight dude plowing my ass," he growls. "Never did it with a gay guy before, pretending it's pussy, yeah, that's right, fuck me hard." He twists his head around and we kiss as I churn my hips. He groans loudly. I start varying my tempo, fucking his ass with long, deep strokes and then slamming hard into him with a burst of rapid thrusts, my balls slapping against the backs of his thighs. The guy is one hot piece of tail; he responds to each stroke, pushing against me, matching my tempo as soon as I change it.

"I'm getting close," I gasp.

"I want to see you squirt," he growls. "I want you to squirt your load all over my face."

"Okay," I groan. "Then here goes."

I pull out of his ass and rip the condom off. The dude drops to his knees and turns his face up to receive my load. The orgasm sweeps over me, and I cry out as my jizz squirts out and splatters against his face, coating his cheeks, his nose, his chin. He groans too, and I look down and see his jizz ooze out between his fingers. "Yeah, fucker," I growl. "That's right. Shoot your load."

We both shudder out the last of our orgasms. The guy wipes his sleeve across his face, then looks up at me and grins. "So how did you like getting off with a guy?"

I grin back. "Well, it was . . . interesting." I pull up my shorts and pants. "I gotta go," I say. "I promised my wife I'd take her out to dinner tonight." I wink at him. "It's our anniversary."

"No shit?" the guy says. He stands up. "I hope you work things out. I mean, what with the mailman and everything."

"We're in counseling," I say, tucking my shirt in. I squeeze the back of his neck and walk out the booth door.

I tell Sam about my experience in the porn shop when I get back home. "Like isn't that pretty twisted?" Sam asks. "A gay guy wanting to get off with another dude just because he thinks the dude is straight? I mean, that's kind of self-oppressive, isn't it?"

I toss the stroke magazines to Sam. "Tell me about it," I say, "while you whack off to your lesbian porn."

Sam grins. "Okay," he says. "You made your point." He takes his magazines and trundles off to his bedroom.

# Seeing Red

I never know when it's going to happen, the next attack that is. Today it's on the bus on the way to the dentist. As with all the other times, everything starts out completely normal: I'm just sitting there, staring out the window, my mind on idle. The bus pulls over to the next stop, people push on board, nothing special. And then I see him.

He climbs up the stairs to the bus like the dawn exploding, his hair as fiery and bright and red as the sun when it first clears the horizon. I'm blinded by it; it takes a few seconds before I can even begin to see beyond the blazing hair, take in the tight body on display beneath the jeans and Muscle System T-shirt, the masculine, not-quite-handsome face (the chin too strong, the nose too prominent, the brown eyes, though bright and expressive, set a little too close together). He pushes through the crowd, his eyes idly scanning the bus. For one brief moment, his gaze locks with mine, and then he looks away. As inevitable as a law of nature, I feel my brain whirr and click, my heart start pounding, and my chest tighten. *No,* I think fiercely. *I will not let this happen!* I aim my gaze down at my shoes, breathing hard, fighting for control. But damn if my head doesn't lift on its own accord, and soon I have my eyes trained on the guy again, burning holes in him. Of course, he's completely oblivious to me.

*Shit, shit shit!* I think, as I fish my cell phone out of my jacket pocket. I punch in my dentist's number. When I get the receptionist on the line, I tell her that I'm sorry but I've suddenly taken sick and I'm going to have to cancel the appointment. She cops an attitude, but eventually we reschedule and I hang up. He's taken a seat across the aisle from me and two rows up. I can only see the back of his neck and a quarter profile of his face, but beneath the fiery hair, his skin is the pale, fair skin of the red-head, splattered with freckles. I wedge myself between the window and my seat, drinking him in. I feel like I'm falling into a pit. *You can still put a stop to this,* I tell myself. But I know the symptoms well enough to real-ize I'm going downhill in a car without any brakes, and all I can do now is sit back and experience the ride.

I pull out my cell phone and call Allen's number. He picks up on the third ring.

"It's me. Josh," I say. "It's happening again, Allen."

"Oh, Christ," Allen groans. "Where are you?"

"I'm on the 32 Geary, heading out toward the avenues. I was going to see my dentist, but I had to call and cancel."

"Josh," Allen says, his voice hard and even. "Get off the bus at the next stop. Then catch the next one and go to the fucking dentist."

"I can't, Allen."

"Yes, you can, you twisted fuck. Just stand up, walk to the door, and when the bus stops, get your fucked-up, neurotic ass off of it."

"You should see this guy, Allen. I've never seen red hair like this, this bright, this . . . blazing. He's magnificent."

"Josh . . ."

"He's wearing a Muscle System T-shirt. That's the gayest gym in town. He's got to be queer."

"Remember the red-headed construction worker, Josh? The one work-ing on the high-rise next to your office window? Remember how he had to get a fuckin' restraining order out on you?"

"You're wasting your breath, Allen."

"And the redheaded Safeway checkout clerk? How you bought stuff there seven, eight times a day for weeks, hitting up on the poor kid every time? How you're now banished permanently from that store?"

The man rises from his seat. "He's getting up, Allen," I say. "I gotta go." I hang up.

The bus stops, and a handful of people get off, including the man. I get off, too, and stand there at the stop, watching him walk down the street, taking in the wide shoulders and tight haunches, the sexy little pivot his butt makes with each step. There's a sudden break in the clouds, and the sun pours down onto the street, igniting his hair into pure fire. I close my eyes and take a deep breath. When he's half a block away, I start following him. After a couple of blocks, he walks into a storefront business with the words "Andrini's Windows" painted in gold and blue over the front window. Next to the two-story office is an asphalt lot with a fleet of trucks, surrounded by a cyclone fence. I cross the street and loiter in the entrance of a Chinese bakery, my eyes trained on the building. A few minutes later, a truck pulls out of the lot and disappears down the street, the redhead behind the wheel.

I know what I have to do. I hail a cab because I don't want to lose time waiting for a bus. As soon as I walk through the door to my apartment, I make a beeline to my back porch, where I keep my tools. I pull a hammer out of one of the drawers and return to the living room. There's a wide, tall window that overlooks the street. I walk over to it, raise my arm, and proceed to shatter it with the hammer. There's a brief music of tinkling glass as shards burst out and rain down on the sidewalk below. I stand at the window, staring out of the jagged hole I made, a breeze blowing through my hair. After a couple of beats, I retrieve the phone book, look up a number, and dial it.

"Andrini's Windows," a woman's voice answers.

"Hi," I say. "I've got something of an emergency here. Someone just threw a rock through my front living room window, and I need to get it replaced."

"I'm afraid we can't get anybody out there until tomorrow, sir."

*Shit*, I think. "Look," I say, forcing my voice to sound calm and reasonable. "This really *is* an emergency. I live on the second floor and anybody can climb in. I really need to have the glass replaced tonight. I'll be willing to pay extra, cover any overtime that's involved."

There's a long silence. I hear the rustling of papers. "All right," the receptionist says. "I'll see what I can do. But you'll have to wait until the end of the day when all the other orders are finished."

"Thank you," I say, relief flooding over me. I pause. "Look," I say. "Just so that I'll recognize him, what does your guy look like?"

"He'll identify himself at the door, sir."

"Yeah, yeah, I know," I say. "But could you just give me a physical description? This whole vandalism thing has got me completely spooked. I just want to make sure I'm letting the right person into my apartment."

There's a brief pause. "It'll most likely be Harvey," she says. "He's mid-twenties, tall, red hair . . ."

"Thanks," I say. I hang up. *Harvey*, I think.

When the doorbell finally rings, my heart begins hammering hard enough to hurt. I squat, put my head between my knees, and breathe deeply. The doorbell rings again. I straighten up, walk to the door, and push the intercom button.

"Who is it?" I ask.

"Andrini's Windows," a voice, Harvey's voice, answers in a rough baritone.

I buzz him in. *Get cool, Brian*, I tell myself. After a minute, I hear Harvey's footsteps as he walks down the hall to my door. There's a knock.

I throw the door open. Harvey stands framed in the doorway, just as I remember him, his face impassive, his brown eyes regarding me calmly. Same jeans, same Muscle System T-shirt, only it's plastered to his chest with sweat. Harvey must have had a busy day. The hall light is dim, and Harvey's red hair gleams dully.

"Come in, come in," I say. I step aside, and Harvey walks into my living room.

"Dispatch told me you got a broken window," he says, his eyes sweeping the room. They rest on the jagged hole of the front window. He looks at me. "Damn! How did that happen?"

"It was the weirdest thing," I say. "I was just sitting here, watching TV, when someone threw a rock through the window." I shake my head. "Probably some street punk."

Harvey walks up to the window and sticks his head out, cautiously avoiding the shards. He pulls back in and looks at me quizzically. "There are glass splinters on the sidewalk down below," he says. "It looks more like the window was broken from the inside."

"Oh, yeah, that," I say. "Well, you see I swept the broken glass up in here and just dumped it out the window."

Harvey gives me a sharp look but doesn't say anything. He unclips a tape measure from his tool belt and quickly takes the window's dimensions. He's got his back to me, and as he lifts his head, I stare at the tangle of orange hair he presents to me. I imagine running my fingers through it, tugging it, curling my hands into fists with fiery strands of hair sprouting between my knuckles. Harvey turns to me, and I quickly compose my face. "This is a standard window size," He says. "I think I have a pane in the truck that will fit."

"Terrific," I say.

Harvey leaves to get the glass from his truck, parked out in front of my apartment. I stand by the window and watch him carefully pull the pane out from the truck's back. In the sunlight, his red hair gleams. *Maybe I could drug him*, I think. *Offer him a beer doped up with something, and then, when he's out cold, tie him to my bedposts and strip him naked.* But that thought is outside the pale of even my craziness, and I push it back down into its dark little hole.

Harvey comes back with the pane of glass and carefully leans it against the wall. He takes a knife and begins digging out the last remnants of glass from the slots in the frame. The window faces west, and the late afternoon sun pours down on him. Harvey is soon drenched in sweat; it trickles down his face and stains his armpits and back. His shirt flutters from a slight breeze that blows in. The sunlight picks up individual strands of hair and makes them gleam like copper wire.

"Would you like a beer?" I ask.

Harvey turns his head and glances at me over his shoulder. He hesitates for the briefest moment. "We're not supposed to drink on the job," he says.

"This is your last gig for the day, right?" I say. "What's the big deal?"

Harvey considers this. "Okay," he says.

I get two Coronas from the refrigerator, walk back to the living room, and hand one to Harvey. "Cheers," I say.

"Cheers," Harvey says. He tilts his head back and takes a deep swig. I watch his Adam's apple rise and fall in his muscular throat as he gulps the beer down. He wipes his hand across his mouth, puts the bottle on the floor, and resumes working.

I pop a Doors CD into the player, and "Crystal Ship" starts playing. I sit on the couch and watch Harvey. His hands are raised to the upper part of the frame, and I mentally trace the V of his lats down to his tight waist. I imagine what his ass must look like. I bet it's a very pretty thing, pale and freckled, firmly molded, downed with a light red fuzz. "Light My Fire" is now playing. After a while, Harvey starts humming along. "Come on, baby, light my fire," he croons. He pauses, picks up his beer, and takes another swig. He glances at me and grins. "Fuckin' 'Doors'," he says. "I fuckin' love that group."

"Yeah," I say, "Me, too. I got all their CDs."

After a couple of minutes, Harvey starts applying putty inside the grooves of the window frame.

"Are you Irish or East Polish?" I finally ask.

Harvey stops work and flashes me a sharp look. "What?" he finally asks.

"I asked if you're Irish or East Polish," I say. "With your red hair, I mean. You're probably one or the other."

"My name's Kowalski," he finally says, as if that's answer enough.

"Like Stanley," I say, grinning. I look at him. "You know . . . 'A Streetcar Named Desire?' "

"I know where it's from," he says, a slight edge to his voice. I guess he gets that comment a lot. But then he grins and throws back his head. "STELLA!!!" he bellows.

I laugh. Harvey picks up his beer and polishes it off. "You want another one?" I ask.

"Okay," Harvey says.

By the time Harvey's done with the window, we've graduated to smoking doobies. The Doors have been replaced by Janis Joplin's "Pearl" album. Harvey tokes up and passes me the joint. "Man," he laughs, smoke bursting out of his mouth. "Don't you ever listen to anything later than the fuckin' sixties?" He's lounging back on my couch now, his legs spread wide apart, his tools left in a pile by the new window. His eyes are just beginning to glaze over, and he's wearing the loopy grin of your typical stoner.

"No," I say. "I'm stuck in a fuckin' time warp."

We sit there in silence for a few beats, Janis wailing away with "Piece of My Heart." I stare at the bulge in Harvey's crotch, and then raise my eyes to his face. Harvey's eyes are trained on me. We still don't say anything for a while. "Can I suck your cock?" I finally ask.

Harvey's grin widens: "It's about time you asked." He starts to unbuckle his belt.

"No, wait," I say. "Let me." I cross the room and drop to my knees in front of him. I unbuckle his belt, forcing my hands not to tremble, and unzip his fly. I glance up at Harvey's face, and he returns my look, his face impassive. I hook my fingers under his belt loops, Harvey raises his hips, and I pull his jeans down. Harvey is wearing cotton briefs, and his hard dick strains against them, a drop of pre-jizz darkening the white cloth. "Jesus," I murmur. My blood is singing in my ears in the high whine of a ripsaw. I take a deep breath, slide my hand under the elastic band, and, with my heart hammering, slowly slide Harvey's briefs down.

A line of pubic hair clears the band: tightly curled, carrot-orange, jungle dense. I keep pulling the shorts, and the base of Harvey's dick appears, wonderfully thick. As the shorts continue to descend, I can see more of Harvey's fat, pink shaft, trace the blue veins that snake their way up the pale column. Harvey's boner pushes up against the elastic band, revealing itself inch by inch. When the cloth finally clears the swollen, flaring head, his dick snaps up and slaps against his belly. I yank the shorts all the way down over his feet and toss them aside.

Harvey sits there on my couch, his legs spread far apart, his feet planted firmly on the floor. I drink him in with my eyes, the fat, pink dick laying on the pale skin of his belly, the balls low-hanging in their fleshy sac, and that glorious explosion of orange pubic hair. I slide my hands under Harvey's T-shirt, stroking and pulling at the hard flesh of his torso, tweaking the nubs of his nipples, as I bury my face in Harvey's balls and breathe deeply. Their ripe, musky scent fills my lungs. "Damn!" I mutter. I open my mouth and suck Harvey's ballsac inside, bathing his nuts with my tongue. Harvey slaps my face with his hard dick. I slide my tongue up the long, thick shaft, and when I get to Harvey's dickhead I roll my tongue around it, nipping it gently, feeling the give and take of the rubbery, red fist of flesh between my teeth and tongue. I slide my mouth down the full length of Harvey's dick, twisting my head, until my throat is crammed full and my nose is pressed hard against Harvey's orange pubes. Harvey gasps, and, for the briefest moment, we hold that pose, my mouth full of cock, Harvey's balls pressing against my chin, Harvey's nipples firmly squeezed between my thumbs and forefingers. Then Harvey pumps his hips, breaking the spell, and begins the serious business of fucking my mouth with slow, deep thrusts.

I proceed to make love to Harvey's dick, opening my throat to it, taking whatever he gives. Harvey's thrusts get faster, pick up a staccato beat, and I wrap my hand around his shaft so that my fist follows my mouth up and down. I break away for a second and let my eyes sweep up

Harvey's muscular torso to his face. Harvey's eyes are bright and fierce and they burn into mine. "You're a good little cocksucker, aren't you?" he growls. "You really know how to work a man's dick."

"Pull off your shirt," I say. "I want to see you naked."

Harvey peels off the sweat-dampened T-shirt and tosses it on the floor. Unlike his pale hips, his torso is lightly tanned and splattered with darker freckles, as if someone had dipped a brush into a can of brown paint and shaken it over him. His nipples are wide and the color of old pennies. I reach down for a half-finished Corona that stands on the floor by the couch, and tilt it over his body, watching the beer foam up and stream down his torso, spilling over the pubes and around his dick. I drag my tongue once again over Harvey's cock and balls, tasting the sour pungency of the beer mingled with the taste of his sweaty flesh.

Harvey pulls me up and plants his mouth on mine. We play dueling tongues for a while as I wrap my hands around Harvey's dick and beat him off. Harvey reaches down and squeezes my crotch. "Get naked," he orders.

We walk back to my bedroom, me dropping my remaining clothes on the floor behind me. By the time we fall into bed together, we're both naked. I climb on top of Harvey's body, kissing him again as I feel the full length of his bare flesh against mine. Harvey wraps his hand around both our dicks and squeezes them tight together. I look down at the two cocks pressed together, encircled by Harvey's fist, and I kiss Harvey again as he beats us off. He slowly drags his tongue down my neck, around my left nipple and then my right, gently nipping them, working them to hardness. I look down at the tousle of fiery hair inches from my face, feeling Harvey's tongue descend along my torso, swirl around my navel, engulf my cock. "Turn around," I pant. "I want to suck your cock while you do that to me."

Harvey grins and pivots his body around, and then we're both fucking face and eating dick. I reach up and run my hands over Harvey's ass, the cheeks firm and muscular, smooth as sun-warmed stone under my fingertips.

Harvey turns his head toward me. "I'd like to plow your ass right now," he growls.

"Shit yeah!" I say. I pull open the drawer of the bedside table and pull out the lube and rubbers. In a matter of seconds, Harvey is sheathed and lubed, and my legs are wrapped around his torso. Harvey's dickhead pokes against my asshole, and I breathe out, relaxing my muscles, accepting Harvey's fat, red dick as it slowly works its way inside me.

"Ah, yeah, baby,' I groan.

"You like that, baby?" Harvey grunts, his eyes bright and savage. "Does it feel good having my dick up your ass?" He doesn't wait for an answer but starts thrusting in and out, churning his hips, squirming his torso against mine. Harvey's face is inches above mine, and his mouth is pulled back into a fierce grin. I reach up, running my fingers through his blazing hair, feeling how wiry it is, like bristles of a brush. I pull Harvey down and kiss him hard, biting his lips. Harvey shoves his dick deep up my ass, slapping his balls against me. I meet him stroke for stroke, thrusting my hips up every time his dick plunges deep inside me, squeezing my ass muscles hard against the shaft of flesh. Harvey's face is dripping with sweat now; it splashes down onto my face, stinging my eyes, filling my open mouth with its salty tang. His body slaps against mine with wet, smacking sounds. He wraps his hand around my dick and beats me off, timing his strokes with each thrust of his hips. We fuck like a well-oiled machine, thrust and counter-thrust, eyes locked together, breaths in synch. Harvey whimpers softly. He thrusts again, and the whimper gets louder, longer, his lips pulled back into a snarl. I reach down and cup Harvey's balls in my hand, tugging on them. They're pulled up tight, and I know it won't be long before he squirts his load. Harvey pulls his dick almost completely out of my ass, its head just barely penetrating me, and then he slides it full in with a slow, hard thrust. I squeeze tight, and Harvey's whimper turns into a long, dragged out groan. I feel his body spasm against me, and I kiss him as the orgasm sweeps over him. Harvey thrashes in my arms, his dick pumping a steady load of jism into the condom up my ass, one pulse after another. Harvey collapses on top of me, spent, his face buried against my neck.

A minute later, I sit on Harvey's chest and jerk off as Harvey tweaks my nipples. When the orgasm finally comes, my dick squirts my load high, above Harvey's face and into the coppery tangle of his hair. I drag my tongue over the red strands, cleaning them, eating my sperm. I stay there like that for a long while, my face buried in Harvey's hair. *So fuckin' beautiful*, I think. Ten minutes later, he's dressed and out the door.

That night I go out with Allen for beers at a corner pub. I tell him everything that happened with Harvey. Allen just shakes his head. "Are you happy being like this, Josh?" he asks. "Being so out of control?"

"Happiness doesn't have anything to do with it," I say. "All I know is that when I suck the cock of a redhead, it's like sucking God's cock. Whenever a redhead squirts a load down my throat, it's God's jizz I'm tasting. It's probably the closest thing to a spiritual experience I'll ever have."

"Jesus H. Christ," Allen mutters. He drains his glass and pushes himself away from the table, his chair legs scraping against the concrete floor. We get up and make our way to the exit. As we push through the door, another man brushes past us and enters the pub. I get a quick impression of a tall, lean body, a clean-cut, freckled face. And hair the color of a Halloween pumpkin.

I hesitate. Allen glances at me and then at the retreating back of the redhead. Without saying anything, he locks his arm around my head and drags me to his car. He doesn't let go until he's got the engine running. I sit back in the seat, rubbing my neck. "I was only looking," I say.

Allen just keeps his eyes trained ahead. "Jesus H. Christ," he mutters. He pulls out onto the road, tires squealing.

# Elephant Men

I'm cruising across the Bay Bridge at 80, really pushing it, because I'm late for my dinner with Roger, and I know how pissy he gets when he has to wait for me. He'll be even more so tonight. The dinner was my idea to cheer him up for getting laid off yesterday, the victim of a corporate downsizing. He's taking it hard and it won't be fun and games trying to roust him out of his depression. Suddenly I see a blinking red light in my rearview mirror. *Shit,* I think. I slow down, with the cop riding my butt, and pull over by the Treasure Island exit. I watch in my mirror as the cop gets out of his car and walks over.

"License, please," he says, his tone all business.

I reach up and hand it to him, looking him full in the face. He blinks and his fingers fumble over my license, almost dropping it. His reaction gives him away as clearly as if he were wearing a rainbow flag pin on his uniform. A gay cop. There are a fair number of them in San Francisco. *Just take the damn ticket from him without trying anything,* I think. But I have the new cap on my front tooth to pay for, and my brakes need to be realigned, and the rent is coming up, and I just can't fit a speeding ticket into my budget right now. I smile at the cop and adopt my friendliest expression. Nothing too flashy or he'll know I'm manipulating him. Just a warm, "aw shucks" grin. It works. The cop smiles back and I get off with just a warning. I drive off relieved, thinking if Roger had witnessed that, I'd never hear the end of it.

\* \* \*

Things got hairy for a second when that cop pulled Mike over. As I passed the two of them parked along the side of the freeway, I was hit by an attack of panic, convinced that I would lose him in the traffic for sure. That just can't happen, because I'll never work up the nerve to pull off this stunt again. It's either tonight or else. *What does "or else" mean?* I ask myself. I don't know, but something drastic. Maybe just swerving my car around and driving off the Bay Bridge, gunning my engine to maximum acceleration, sinking into the oblivion of the Bay. Mike, Mike. Look what you're driving me to. I am a truly desperate man.

I pull into the right hand lane and slow down to 25. It's the only thing I can think of, giving Mike time to get his ticket from that asshole cop, and then catching up and passing me again. The cars behind me are blasting me with their horns. *Fuck you, motherfuckers!* I put on my blinkers so that it looks like I'm having engine trouble. Cars pass me, with the drivers flipping me off and cursing me. *Assholes!* All I want is a little loving tonight, a chance to taste Mike's sweet, sweet body, worship him in the way that he deserves. Is that too much to ask for, for chrissakes?

Mike's red Triumph zips past me, and I start sobbing with relief. *Stop it!* I snarl, and I pull myself together. I fall in behind him, keeping a couple of cars between us so that he won't notice I'm following him.

*     *     *

I'm twenty-five minutes late when I walk into the restaurant. Roger is seated in the corner, well on his way to killing a carafe of wine. He sees me and scowls.

"Don't say anything. I'm sorry," I say, sliding into my seat.

Roger looks like he's going to bitch anyway, but he manages to stifle the impulse. He hands me one of the two menus on the table.

"The food's okay here," he says, "but the service sucks. I practically had to do a flying tackle on the waiter just to get this carafe of wine."

A waiter comes up to our table. "Can I take your order?" he asks. His eyes focus on me alone. I glance at Roger, but his face is expressionless.

"I haven't made up my mind yet," I say. "Could you come back in a couple of minutes, please?"

The waiter doesn't waste any subtlety as his eyes scan my body. "Whatever you like, sir. Just wave when you need me." He walks away, but can't resist turning his head and looking at me one last time.

"The service has sure gotten better since your arrival," Roger says dryly.

I let that one go by and attempt a sympathetic smile. "So how are you doing?"

Roger shrugs. "I've been better. I've spent the entire day trying to over-haul my resumé. It's been a long time since I've had to . . ." His eyes focus on our left. There's a man and a woman at the table next to ours; the man's back is turned to us, but she's staring at me boldly. When I follow Roger's gaze and look at her, she smiles. Roger glares at her until she turns away. He turns his gaze back to me, his expression murderous. He takes a long sip of wine and puts the glass down. "I should have known this would happen," he snaps.

"Roger . . ." I say.

Roger drains his glass, picks up the carafe and fills it again. He looks off into space, breathing deeply. "Just let it drop, Roger," I plead. I know I'm wasting my breath.

Roger fixes me in a hard, savage stare. I brace myself. "Remember that movie, 'The Elephant Man?' " he asks, in a low, furious voice. "About that freak so ugly he had to wear a sack over his head whenever he stepped out in public?" Roger's eyes blaze into mine. "That's what it's like whenever I'm with you in a public place. Eating with the goddamn Elephant Man."

"Thanks."

"No, I mean it." Roger's voice rises in volume. "You're just as big a freak. Nobody looks like you. Nobody's so goddamn *handsome*." He spits out the last word like it's the worst insult he can think of.

"Will you lower your voice?" I say, looking quickly around the room. More people are staring at us, and I'm feeling very self-conscious. I pick up Roger's carafe of wine, fill my glass, and take a long sip. I meet Roger's gaze. "I can't help the way I look, okay?" I say. It's ridiculous but he's actually making me feel defensive.

Roger's left eyebrow rises on that one. "Oh, really? This from a guy who works out at a gym an hour and a half a day six days a week? Hell, you bust your ass to look the way you do."

"So what?" I laugh in exasperation. "What the hell business is it of yours?" I slouch back in my chair. "You're acting like a jealous lover, for Christ's sake."

"It's not jealousy," Roger says. He takes a gulp of wine. "Sure, I'd love to jump your bones, just like everybody else in the fuckin' world would. I just get sick of you getting away with murder all the time." He glowers at me. "I bet you have a big dick, too, don't you?"

"Roger, will you knock it off?"

But Roger is just getting started. "How big, Michael? Seven inches? Eight? Nine?"

I give him a long, level look. "Eight and a half, if you really want to know. And it's thick, too."

Roger throws his napkin on the table. "Shit," he mutters.

\*　　\*　　\*

Mike is having dinner with some old guy, mid-forties at least. There can't be anything going on romantically between them, the other guy is so *ordinary* looking. Still, I can't help feeling a sharp stab of jealousy. I order another beer from the bartender, a slick, tanned guy with too much hair and biceps. Some might consider him good-looking, but next to Mike, he's dreck. He keeps snatching looks at my face, and then flicking his eyes away when I catch him at it. But not before I can see the disgust in them. I'm used to it, and after a while I just ignore him. I got a good view of the dining room from my barstool, and I can watch Mike and the other guy openly. It looks like they're fighting. Mike is leaning back in his chair and frowning. The other guy leans forward and says something, and Mike rolls his eyes and looks away. I can't help smiling. *Good, good,* I think.

The restaurant is perched on Telegraph Hill in a remote cul-de-sac, a stroke of good fortune for me. I had no idea that Mike would end up here when I followed him. I wonder briefly if he goes by "Mike". His mailbox says "Michael Barry", and maybe he prefers "Michael." But I like "Mike." It's masculine and to the point. Anyway, Mike has parked his car in a nearby alley, dark and lonely. I take that as a good sign, a sort of cosmic blessing on my plans. I pat the bottle in my coat pocket and feel reassured, though I have an adrenalin pump going for me like you wouldn't believe. My heart is pounding hard enough to crack a rib. I have a feeling Mike won't be spending too much more time with that creep, and I slip off my stool head outside to wait for him.

It's starting to rain. I go back to where Mike's red Triumph is parked, and take shelter in the doorway of a nearby apartment. There's a porch light on overhead. I take my shoe off and smash it, stepping aside to avoid the shower of glass. I wait for Mike in the darkness.

\*　　\*　　\*

Dinner with Roger is about as much fun as having a root canal. I try to humor him out of his mood, but he's having too much fun acting like a jerk. It's just one crack after another about how easy I've got it because of my looks, how he has more character in his little finger than I have in my whole body, and how one day when I'm gumming farina in some nursing home and with my looks all shot to hell, I'll see that life isn't such a picnic, after all. And so on. Finally I drop my fork on my plate and glare at him. "You know, Roger," I say, "This is really getting boring." I push my chair back. "I'm sorry you got laid off, but I don't want to hang out with you anymore tonight."

Roger shrugs. "Why don't you at least stay until our waiter gets off duty? He looks good for a quick tumble."

I grimace and drop enough money on the table to cover my meal. "Give me a call when you're willing to knock off the bullshit," I say. Roger just looks away. As I walk toward the door, I pass our waiter. He winks at me. "Kiss my ass," I tell him.

"Any time!" he calls out after me, laughing.

A cloud bank has rolled in since I entered the restaurant, whipping up a brisk breeze from the Pacific. I button up my coat against the damp, chilly air. A raindrop pelts me and then another, and then suddenly I'm caught in a downpour. Christ, I hate the weather in this city. I race down the deserted street to where my car is parked, my keys clutched in my hand. The nearest street light is a block away, too damn far for me to see anything and I try to find the keyhole to my car door by touch alone. I only succeed in dropping my keys somewhere in the gutter. Cursing, I squat down and fumble my fingers against the pavement searching for them. This night couldn't get any worse.

\*　　\*　　\*

This is almost too easy to believe. Mike is down on his knees with his back to me, trying to find something he dropped. I can hear him cursing under his breath. I take the bottle of ether out of my pocket, soak my handkerchief with it, and creep up from behind. The sound of the rain drumming against the pavement covers any noise I might be making. Mike hasn't a clue what's in store for him. Just as he begins to straighten up, I rush up, grab him in a headlock and shove the ether-soaked rag into his face. He puts up one hell of a fight, and it's all I can do to hang on. I'm a pretty big guy myself, but Mike is powerful and muscular. He wrenches himself free, and I think *aw shit, I'm in for it now*. But he staggers and then drops to his knees, like Al Jolson singing *Mammy*. I'm on him in a flash, with the cloth stuffed against his nose and mouth, and after a brief struggle he slumps to the sidewalk. I drag Mike's body toward my car, parked across the street. He's nothing but dead weight, and we're not even halfway there before I'm panting heavily. I'm terrified that some car will turn the corner and pin us in its beams, but my luck continues to hold out, and the street remains deserted. We make it to my car. I take a few deep breaths, yank open the car door, and manage to shove Mike onto the back seat.

I slip into the front seat behind the steering wheel. I feel like I'm flying and the blood is singing in my ears. All this is going too smoothly; I'm not used to having things work out for me. My dick is hard enough to split my fly open. I turn on the ignition and drive down the dark streets to the freeway entrance. The rain beats on my car roof and splatters against my windshield. Even with the wipers on full, visibility sucks. As I cross the Golden Gate Bridge, sheets of rain sweep across the highway. What cars that are out on the road this night creep along at a crazy-making snail's pace. I gun the motor and pick my way through the traffic, making what time I can.

I glance in my rear-view mirror at Mike. He's slumped in the back seat, a dark, formless shape. The headlights of an oncoming car sweep inside and I get a quick glimpse of his face: the closed eyes, the slack, open jaw. It's hard to imagine just how *completely* he's under my control, how I can do anything to him that I want. My throat tightens with excitement, and my dick throbs again. Once, he stirs and groans; I briefly consider pulling over onto the highway shoulder and hitting him with another dose of ether. However, he sinks back into unconsciousness, and so I just keep driving. I keep my eyes on the highway. On a normal night, I'd only have about another hour more of driving ahead of me. In this rain, I probably won't even make it to Jenner until after midnight, and it'll be another half hour at least before I reach the cabin. The rag in my pocket is beginning to stink up the car with the smell of ether, and I feel myself getting drowsy. I roll down the window and toss it out.

It's well past one before I pull in to the unlit driveway. I've only been here once before, in daylight, when I was scouting the area out, but I remember how the gravel road snakes across the field for about half a mile, passes behind a clump of pines, and ends at the back doorstep of the cabin. *What if the owners are there?* I wonder, and the thought makes me sick with anxiety. It's off-season, and the place should be empty until next spring, but who knows what the owners use the cabin for? When I pass the pines, I see that the place is dark and there's no car parked in the driveway. My shoulder muscles sag with relief. I pull up behind the house, by the back door.

It's a cinch breaking into the place: just a rock through one of the back door panes, then a reach inside to undo the bolt. The cabin is too remote and small for a security system. The rain is pelting me at gale force now; I'm completely drenched just from the short walk to the door. I go back to the car and fetch Mike. It's not an easy task, slinging him over my shoulders and carrying him in, his feet dragging in the mud. Mike stirs suddenly, and, caught off-guard, I stumble, falling face down in the mud, the weight of Mike's body pressing down on me. I roll him off me, struggle to my feet, and, hooking my hands under his armpits, drag him through the back door entrance. Mike gets heavier with every step I take, and the rain pelts us in drenching slabs of water. I trudge through the kitchen and into the cabin's one bedroom, and with my last ounce of strength, heave Mike onto the bed, barely visible in the darkness. Panting, I turn on the lamp on a nearby night table. The bed has a brass headboard and two brass bedposts at the foot. *Perfect,* I think. Mike stirs again. His eyelids flutter and then his eyes open, staring right at me. "What?" he asks, as if I had just said something. I stumble into the bathroom, find a washcloth, and douse it liberally from the bottle in my pocket. When I return to the bedroom, Mike is propped up on one elbow, rubbing his eyes. I cram the washcloth against his face until he's out cold again, and then go back to the car. I unlock the trunk, but before I can open it, I start heaving. I stand there in the rain, bent over, my hands on my thighs, puking out everything in my stomach. When I'm finished, I open the trunk, pull out the rope inside, and head back to the cabin.

It's an easy job tying Mike's wrists to the brass tubing that makes up the headboard, and his ankles to the two bottom bedposts. I make the knots secure, but not too tight; I don't want to cause Mike any unnecessary discomfort. When he's lying on his back, spread-eagle on the bed, I pull up a chair next to him. Other than removing his shoes, I've left him fully clothed, even though his shirt and slacks are soaked and plastered against his skin. The top button has popped off his shirt during the struggle, and a few dark blonde chest hairs poke through his open shirt. I had no idea his chest was so hairy. I'm learning other things about Mike as well, such as that he has a tiny mole behind his left ear, and a faint scar shaped like a crescent moon above his right eye. There's a hole in the toe of his left foot, and the nail of his big toe needs clipping. I'm fascinated by these little flaws I'm discovering; Mike is becoming more human to me every second now. I wonder what other discoveries lie beneath his clothes; my dick throbs at the thought. But I will not touch him again until he's awake, even to brush the lock of dark blonde hair from his forehead.

For the first time, I notice how chilly it is in this room, and I'm flooded with concern about Mike catching cold. There's a small, wood-burning stove in the corner, with a cord of firewood stacked next to it and a pile of newspapers. I find matches in the kitchen, and it only takes a couple of minutes before I've got a fire going. I find a comforter in the closet (but no clothes) and I tuck Mike in, like a mother would her child.

The room slowly warms up, and, with the rain lashing against the window and drumming on the roof, I'm beginning to feel snug and sheltered. I reach over and switch off the lamp by the bed. The only illumination now comes from the stove, which fills the room with a dim, ruddy light. There's an upholstered chair in a corner, and I pull it up to the bed, with the stove to my back. I sit in it, contemplating Mike's handsome, perfect face lit by the flickering, red light, and wait.

\*       \*       \*

The first thing I'm aware of is that I'm in bed. The second thing is the sound of rain hammering on the roof. *How can that be?* I wonder. *There are four more floors above my apartment.* I feel awful: groggy, headachy, nauseated, like I have a major hangover. I try rubbing my eyes but something is keeping me from moving my arm. I try again, harder, and it's only then that I feel rope dig into my wrists. I open my eyes. All I can see is a raftered ceiling above me. I struggle to get up, but now realize that both my hands and feet are securely tied. *What the fuck . . . !* I think. I thrash about, trying to get free.

"Take it easy," I hear a voice say. "You're just going to give yourself rope burns."

I turn in the direction of the voice, and see the dark shape of an armchair beside the bed, and inside it the darker form of a man. The only light in the room is from a small stove behind him, and his face is lost in shadow.

"WHAT THE FUCK IS GOING ON HERE?" I yell.

"Nothing you have any control over," the man says calmly. "Are you comfortable? Would you like another pillow, some water?"

I struggle against the ropes until my wrists and ankles burn from the chafing. It doesn't do any good. "UNTIE ME, YOU SON OF A BITCH!" I scream.

But the man just sits there, watching me. "I tied the knots real good," he finally says. "You're not going to be able to untie yourself. Trust me." There's a strange, slurred quality to his speech. His voice sounds young.

"Who the fuck are you!?" I ask, panting. Panic rises up in me, and I try to push it down.

The man just sits silently in the shadow of the chair for a couple of beats. He seems to be weighing his options. Finally, he reaches over and switches on a table lamp by the bed. Light floods the room, spilling onto his face. I flinch. His upper lip is split in two as far up as his nose. I wonder if I'm having a nightmare.

He smiles slightly, the split in his face widening. I look away. "It's called a harelip," he says. I struggle again against the ropes, but the knots remain secure. "You know, you're just going to hurt yourself," he says. There's a thread of anxiety in his voice now.

I ignore him and thrash around on the mattress, tugging at the ropes until I can't take the pain anymore. A thin trickle of blood drips down from my right wrist and both wrists feel like they're on fire. I lunge at the man as far as the ropes will let me. "UNTIE ME, YOU GODDAMN FREAK!" I scream at him.

He flinches, and the blood rushes to his face, turning it bright pink. But then his eyes narrow, and a mean, red light shines out of them. "You better watch your mouth, Mike," he snaps. "Or you're going to be fuckin' sorry. And that's a promise."

I let my muscles sag and I take a few deep breaths. "How do you know my name?" I finally ask him.

The man grins. "You'd be surprised the things I know about you".

My rage comes boiling up again, but I stifle it quickly. I'm taking his earlier threat very seriously. "Where am I?" I ask, trying to make my voice calmer.

The man shrugs. "You're eight miles north of Jenner, in a cabin by the Russian River." He pauses, and then adds as if in afterthought, "I don't own this place. I'm just borrowing it for a while."

I raise my head and glare at him. "What the fuck. . . ." I see that light in his eyes turn on again, and I stop. I take another deep breath. "What do you want from me?" I ask, trying to keep my tone reasonable.

The man looks at me in silence for a long time. "I want to talk with you," he finally says. "I want us to get to know each other. And then we'll take things from there."

I'm calming down a bit. I look at the guy again, more closely. Once you get past the harelip, he really doesn't look particularly frightful. He's young, real young, maybe nineteen or twenty. No more than a kid. His eyes are slate gray and long-lashed, his hair, sandy brown and shaggy. He's wearing a T-shirt plastered to his body from the rain; the torso underneath is tight and lean. "What's your name?" I ask him.

His face softens, and I allow myself a little twinge of hope. It's the first indication I've seen that I just might have some power in this situation. "Danny," he says.

I flash Danny the same smile I flashed the traffic cop this morning. "Look, Danny," I say, making my voice warm and friendly. "If you want to talk, fine, we'll talk. About anything you want. Only why don't you untie me first?" I give a little aw-shucks laugh. "Believe me, I'll be a much better listener without all these ropes tied around my wrists and ankles."

But Danny just shakes his head. "Sorry, Mike," he says, his voice a parody of mine, all concerned friendliness. "I like things just the way they are." He winks at me and gives me back my smile, made grotesque by his harelip.

"You motherfucker!" I snarl.

Danny just laughs and leans back in his chair. He gives me an apprising look. "No, really, Mike, are you comfortable? I mean, besides the ropes. I could get you another pillow if you want."

I close my eyes and then open them again. "Would you take this fucking blanket off me?" I ask. "I'm burning up."

"Sure, Mike," Danny says, all solicitous now. He tugs the blanket off and drops it on the floor beside the bed. "I guess the room has really warmed up. You wouldn't believe how chilly it was, though, when we first got here."

I can't believe how . . . *conversational* his tone is. Like we're old friends chewing the fat over a beer. I fix my gaze on him. "Why are you doing this?" I ask. "I don't even know you."

Danny gives a low laugh. "Well, that's a long story, Mike. And I really want to tell it to you. In fact, that's why I brought you up here." I glare at him without saying anything. Danny crosses his arms against his chest and stretches out his legs. "I guess it's best to start at the beginning. How we met. Which I guess you don't remember." He looks over at me for confirmation. I keep a stony face. "I'm not really surprised," he says. "It was only for a few seconds, except," his smile goes thin, "I do have a face that's hard to forget." He reaches down, picks his jacket off the floor, and fishes out a pack of cigarettes from an inside pocket. He shakes a cigarette out, places it in his mouth.

"You don't mind if I smoke, do you, Mike?" he asks.

"Fuck you," I say, but without any real spirit to it.

"Yeah, well, maybe later," Danny says, with a small laugh. He lights up, inhales deeply and exhales a cloud of smoke. "Would you like a cigarette, Mike?" he asks. "I could hold it up to your mouth so that you could inhale."

I glare at him, saying nothing.

Danny shrugs. "I guess that means 'no'." He takes another puff and exhales again. "You're right; it *is* a dirty habit." He extends his arms and stretches deeply. "Okay. How we met." Danny straightens up in his chair, as if preparing for a recitation. "We met three and a half weeks ago, on a bus," he says. "The 22 Fillmore. My day was *not* going good." He leans forward so that his face is just inches from mine. "You see, Mike, I get frustrated a lot of times. And depressed. And horny. I walk around this city, or ride the bus, or eat somewhere and I keep seeing these fuckin' hot looking men. Christ, they're all over this city. You can stand on any street corner and throw a rock, and it'll most likely hit one of them on the head. I mean, have you ever noticed that?"

He stares at me expectantly. "Not particularly," I mutter.

Danny takes another drag from his cigarette and exhales. He gives slight laugh and shakes his head. "Yeah, well, I can understand that. I guess what I'd consider good-looking would be pretty ordinary to you." He puts the cigarette down on the edge of the night table and claps his hands. "Okay, well, on with the story." He has a manic cheerfulness about him that is making me increasingly anxious. I don't know what this guy is capable of.

"Now, I've been queer long before I even knew what the word meant," Danny continues in his same story-telling voice. "I love men's bodies, their muscles, their tight bodies. But you know what I love most about them?" He looks at me expectantly. I glare back at him, saying nothing. "I bet you thought I was going to say 'their dicks', but you'd be wrong." He keeps his eyes trained on me. "It's their faces, Mike." He shakes his head. "I tell you, Mike, a handsome man can just about always break my heart. I collect pictures of men; I got a trunk full of porno under my bed, magazines and videos that I jerk off to all the time. Four, five times a day, actually. And yet, damn, even after I squirt a load, I'm *still* horny. Even when my dick's drained dry and limp, and there's no way it'll get stiff for the moment, I still can't stop thinking about handsome naked men having sex. And, Mike, you know what I think when I watch those videos?" He pauses. I still don"t say anything. "You know," he says with some exasperation, "this would be a lot more interesting if this conversation weren't so one-sided."

"Eat shit," I say.

Danny shakes his head. "You *do* have a mouth on you, Mike. Anyway, what I think is 'What must it feel like to look like those guys look? To have faces like those guys have. What would it feel like to have sex with men that looked like that?' "

I don't like the way this monologue is going. I lick my lips nervously. "Danny," I say quietly. "Untie me. Please. You don't know what you're getting yourself into."

Danny gives a breezy laugh. "I know what I'm getting myself into," he says. "I just don't fuckin' care." He shakes his head. "So anyway," he continues. "I'm on the 22 Fillmore, thinking these thoughts, and you get on board." Danny laughs again, and the folds of his harelip flutter out. "Christ, Mike, it was like the clouds parted, and this fuckin' *god* just walked in on the scene. It was a goddamn religious experience. As soon as I saw you I wanted to get down on my knees before you." Danny leers. "But not to pray." He pauses, wrapped up in the memory. His eyes burn into mine. "You got on the seat, right across from me, and I was just eating you up! I had never in my life seen such a fuckin' beautiful man. And you know what I was feeling, Mike?"

The question hangs in the air. "What?" I finally ask, in my most surly tone.

Danny stands up. "I was feeling PISSED," he shouts. I flinch. He starts pacing back and forth. All his cheerfulness is suddenly gone, replaced by rage. "I mean, enough is fuckin' enough! How much more bullshit am I supposed to take?" His gestures become increasingly agitated. "How many more hot guys am I supposed to look at and think about the great sex they're all getting, how they can get all the dick they want? Wondering what their bodies would feel like next to mine and knowing I don't have a snowball's chance in HELL of that ever happening?" Danny turns to me, his eyes burning. "And there you were, and I bet you'd just been laid, you looked so smug. Someone had just swung on your dick, you'd just squirted a load on somebody's face—another hot, beautiful man like yourself—and it was all just fuckin' ROUTINE for you." Little specks of spit were flying out of his mouth now.

I swallow. "Danny," I say. "Just calm down. Take it easy."

"DON'T YOU TELL ME WHAT TO DO!" Danny screams. I shut up fast. He glares at me for a long time, panting. Finally, he sits back in the chair again, and takes a long puff from his neglected cigarette. The ash falls on the floor. He looks at me coldly. "So when you got off, I got off, too. Even though my stop was eight blocks later. And I followed you to your apartment." To my relief, he seems to be calming down. "I saw you take out your mail, and after you went inside I got your name off the mail box. And from that day on, I started tracking you. I'd hang out in that café across the street from your apartment, waiting for you to leave and then following you when you did. I followed you to work, to your friends' places, to the clubs you like to dance at, everywhere. For three and a half fuckin' weeks."

*This guy's a goddamn lunatic,* I think. "Why?" I asked.

Danny shrugs. "You know, Mike, I didn't really know at the time. I just did it for the hell of it." He taps his forehead and grins. "But after a while a plan started forming." His grin widens and he makes a sweeping gesture. "And here we are!"

I stare him. "This is your *plan?*" I feel my own rage well up again. I tug at the ropes. "THIS?!" I shout.

Danny shrugs again. "More or less. There are some details I haven't worked out yet."

Neither one of us speaks for a long time. The rain beating on the roof doesn't seem to be letting up any. I wonder if the Russian River is going to flood, and I almost laugh at that thought. Christ, that's all I need. "Danny," I finally say, keeping my voice low and even. "You had your fun. Now just untie me and let me go home."

Danny grimaces. "You're sounding like a broken record, Mike." He picks up his jacket. "Anyway, I *haven't* had my fun. All this is just the set-up for my fun." He pulls out a hunting knife from a jacket pocket and unsheathes it. "*Now,* I'm going to have my fun."

"Oh, Jesus," I whisper.

"Oh, relax, Mike," Danny says impatiently. "I'm not going to gut you, if that's what you're thinking."

But all I see is that six inch blade glinting in the light of the bedside lamp. "Danny, please," I beg.

He stands up and leans over toward me. I close my eyes and turn my head away from him.

*       *       *

I can tell I'm scaring the hell out of Mike with my knife. He must think I'm a real psycho, but then again, I guess I can't blame him. "Easy, Mike, easy," I croon. I slide the blade under the bottom button of his shirt and pop it off. I do the same to all the rest of the buttons until his shirt falls open. Mike's torso lives up to all my fantasies: packed with muscle, cut, powerful, lightly furred. His nipples are wide, the nubs dark brown and rubbery. I slide the flat of the blade across them and the cold steel prods them to full erection. Mike shudders. Moving the knife across his shoulders, I cut down the length of each sleeve, until nothing remains of his shirt but ribbons. I pull them away and run my hands across his torso. His eyes never leave my face, and I can see the fear in them. His skin is warm to my touch, and the heartbeat under his left, furry pectoral is rapid and strong. The adrenalin must be pumping through his body now, cranking the fight-or-flight alarm up to screaming volume. But ol' Mike can't do either. He can only just lie there and take what I dish out.

I unbuckle his belt and pull down his zipper. "Don't do this, Danny," Mike pleads softly. But I ignore him, piercing the cloth of his slacks with my knife. I work my fingers into the holes I just made and rip the seams apart. His thighs underneath are hard and muscular, smooth against my hand. I look up into his face. "I see you've been doing your squats," I say. I pull the ruins of his slacks from under him and toss them aside.

Now all he's wearing is his briefs. I figured Calvin Klein, but they're just white cotton Fruit-of-the-Loom, something you'd buy at Kmart. For some reason I find this funny. I slit them apart, too, and toss them away.

Mike lies naked before me, spread-eagle, his ankles and wrists tightly bound to the bedposts. His body lives up to the fantasy: tight, muscle-packed, perfectly proportioned. His face is flawless, the mouth generous and firm, the eyes the color of a noonday sky. They watch me now anxiously, tracking me as I move around the room. By its thickness, his dick promises to be impressive, but right now it lies limp against his thigh, his balls pulled up tight in fear. I put the knife back in its sheath and see the relief flood into his face. "Did you really think I was going to do something to you?" I ask.

"I don't know what the fuck you're capable of," Mike says, his voice free of all that bullshit charm he was laying on me earlier. Things seem to be working their way down to the kernel. I like that. I stand at the foot of the bed and strip. Mike watches me, his face expressionless. I can just imagine the men in the past who have taken off their clothes for him: the tall, rangy athletes, the firm boys with angel faces, the tattooed street punks, the strutting machos, the big-dicked body builders. Models, actors, porn stars, high priced callboys (only for Mike, they give it away for free). Men with broad shoulders, narrow hips, biceps like grapefruit, dicks that sway heavily between muscular thighs, asses so smooth and pale they look more like polished stone than flesh. And the faces! Christ, think of the faces of these men! Faces seen only on magazine covers or movie screens, faces that make heads turn and throats constrict in long-ing. How many dicks has Mike sucked that were attached to men I couldn't even dream of getting close to? How many beautifully formed mouths have slid down his own shaft or sucked on his balls? This exclusive club of hot, handsome men, this elite army of sex buddies. . . . My body is wiry and tight, not "ripped," but muscular enough. However, I'm afraid I'm not Mike's usual caliber of bed partner. But then, that's something he's just going to have to get over.

I bend down and run my tongue across his left nipple, flicking it, teasing it with my teeth. It stands to full attention, and I do the same to the other nipple. I straddle Mike's torso, tweaking his nipple nubs between the thumbs and forefingers of each hand. Mike's lips part, and he begins breathing heavier. I bend down and bury my nose in his armpit, smelling his sweat, sniffing deeply the acid stink of the fear underneath the musk. I lick the hairy pit, dragging my tongue across it, rolling the taste of pit sweat around in my mouth. Mike's head is turned away, and I drag my tongue up his neck and into his left ear. I probe deep inside. There's a vein fluttering in his neck and I lay my hand on it, feeling Mike's pulse underneath my fingertips. His body is rigid under my hands, the tendons in his neck knotted like cords with his face turned to the wall. The fucker is totally freaked that I might try to kiss him; I guess the image of my harelip on his mouth is more than he can stand. A jolt of rage shoots through me, and I pinch his nipples hard. Mike groans and his body shifts under me. I look down, and see that his dick is stirring, lengthening out. Well, what do you know! I pinch the nipples again, and again he groans.

My own hard dick lies on top of Mike's belly like a beached whale. I reach down and twist his nipples again as I slowly rotate my hips, rubbing my dick against his torso. The nipple play is getting to Mike; his dick is fully hard now, pumped full of blood, the head flared out and red. It's beautiful: smooth, sleek, thick, and long. I wrap my hand around both our dicks, squeezing them together, feeling all that dick flesh within the circle of my fingers. I squirm so that my balls press against Mike's.

I want my body to feel every inch of his naked skin. I lay out full length on top of Mike, dry humping his hard belly, the warmth of his body flooding into me. My face is buried against his neck and my arms wrap around his torso. I run my hands down his back and cup his ass cheeks. They feel smooth and hard beneath my fingertips. I probe his ass crack with my finger, brushing against the pucker of his bung hole. Mike sighs and I feel the echo of a groan in it. *Is he enjoying this or just enduring it?* I wonder.

I slide down his torso until my head is beneath the "V" of his legs. His nuts are just an inch from my mouth; they seem to be hanging a little lower from his body now. I start tonguing the fleshy ballsac and then suck it into my mouth, rolling his scrotum meat around with my tongue. I look up, his balls still in my mouth; my eyes meet his across the length of his muscled torso. His expression is unreadable, but his mouth is open now, his eyes half-lidded. His dick is still at full attention, and when I wrap my hand around it, it throbs against my fingers.

I work my tongue up the length of the shaft and then swirl it around the cherry red knob of his dickhead. Mike shudders, and when I slide my mouth all the way down, he groans loudly. I begin sucking him off, and it isn't long before he's pumping his hips up and down, shoving his dick deep down my throat. He's doing it savagely enough that it's clear he's trying to hurt me, the only way he can, trussed like he is. *That's okay, Mike,* I think. *If you want to use your dick as a battering ram, that just makes everything all the hotter.*

I suck cock like my life depends on it, wrapping my tongue against the dick shaft, sliding my lips up and down its length, the back of my throat getting fuckin' *bruised* by the force of Mike's thrusts. Mike thrashes around on the bed, the muscles of his shoulders bunched tightly by the upward splay of his bound arms. "Christ!" he groans, but I don't know if it's through pleasure or rage. His dick is hammering my throat like it's knocking on Heaven's door.

I stand up tall and look down at him. Mike returns my stare, panting. Along with the rage, the unspoken question burns in his eyes: *What next?* I'm stroking his spit-slicked dick slowly now, just enough to keep it hard. I bend down and fish a condom out of my jacket pocket. "One of us is going to get fucked now, Mike," I say. "You get to choose. I could go either way on this."

"Then let me fuck you," Mike says quickly.

The speed of his response is an interesting revelation. *So, Mike,* I think. *You're afraid of getting fucked, huh?* It wasn't my original aim to torment the guy, but I feel a devilish urge to play with this fear. A quick exploratory trip to the bathroom yields a jar of skin lotion. I straddle Mike's torso and smear the grease all over my hand. His eyes widen with alarm, and a nasty little spasm of pleasure shoots through me. I reach behind me and burrow my hand into Mike's ass crack, pushing past the muscular cheeks until my fingers are massaging his bung hole. I thrust a finger in all the way up to the third knuckle. The muscles of Mike's ass clamp down around it in protest of this violation. A lot of good that'll do him. I finger fuck Mike at a slow, leisurely pace, pushing hard against his prostate with each inward thrust. Mike groans and his body stirs under me. I slip in another finger. Mike trembles violently, and his eyes flash their outrage. "What do you say, Mike?" I smile. "Should I go for three?"

"You gave me a choice!" he snarls. "You said *I* could do the fucking!"

I grin. "I did, didn't I?" I pull my fingers out and wipe them across Mike's beautiful face, leaving a trail of grease on his cheeks and chin. I'm surprised, even a little shocked, by my own nastiness. "All right, Mike," I sneer. "If you're so hot to fuck me, let's get to it." I slide the condom down Mike's shaft, and then smear it with lube.

"I can fuck better untied, Danny," Mike whispers. "I can give you the ride of your life if you set me free."

I actually ponder this for a second. But then I shake my head. "I don't think so, Mike," I say. I straddle his torso and, reaching behind, grab his dick. "And don't ask me again, because it pisses me off." I guide Mike's dick to my bung hole and then just ease it on in. The shaft works its way in until I feel like I have about two feet of dick up my ass. I close my eyes, letting the sensations sweep over me. This is what I've been wanting all along, to be fucked by a beautiful man, to have his dick pound my ass. I start thrusting myself up and down, sliding along that slippery pole.

I open my eyes again and look down at Mike. His face and torso gleam with sweat; his forehead is beaded with it, and his skin is slippery under my hands. His beauty is like a fuckin' knife in my heart; I want to scream curses at him and grovel before him at the same time. He's lying still, with eyes closed, but as I slide up and down his dick, he starts matching my rhythm, thrusting his hips up with each descent of my ass. I twist his nipples again, hard, the way he seems to like it, and he lets out a mighty groan. He pumps his dick faster, shoving it deep up my chute and then grinding his hips against me. I squeeze my ass muscles tight and as he pulls out, Mike groans again. He opens his eyes, and the excited gleam in them is unmistakable. *He's actually getting off on this!* I think with a thrill. I started jacking off, fucking my lube-greased hand.

Mike's mouth is half-open and I can see his pink tongue between the double row of his even, white teeth. It's such a fuckin' beautiful mouth, the lips full and generous. Out of the blue, I feel a sharp stab of envy, an ache so deep that my eyes fill up with tears. I tightly squeeze them shut. When I open them again, Mike is staring at me. Instead of the pity that I dread, or the contempt, I see only curiosity and confusion in his face. Impulsively, I bend down and kiss him. Mike's lips part and I slide my tongue in, pushing it as deep into his mouth as I can. Mike's tongue pushes apart the flaps of my harelip, and for a second I freeze, waiting for him to stiffen with revulsion. But his tongue just forges on into my mouth and probes to the back of my throat.

I sit up again and lean back, giving Mike a chance to plow me from another angle. His lip is curled up into a snarl, and his hair is matted against his forehead. His eyes still watch me carefully. It's amazing how many different ways Mike can plow my ass: grinding, circular motions; short, fast jabs; long and deep thrusts that set my prostate tingling. And this with his arms and legs tied down!

Mike is beginning to groan steadily now, first low and then with increasing volume. I reach behind and feel his balls; they're pulled up tight again, but this time not from fear. The fucker's about ready to shoot! I pinch his nipples viciously, and his whole body shudders. He cries out and his dick spasms in my ass, squirting load after pulsing load into the condom, as he thrashes around beneath me. The rope tying his left ankle snaps and his leg kicks up, twitching. I ride him out, holding on to keep from being bucked off, until he collapses into the bed, panting.

I shift my body and drop my balls into his mouth as I pull hard on my dick. Mike sucks on the fleshy sac, rolling my nuts around with his tongue. Our eyes meet, and I see the exhaustion in his gaze, but something else too: a look of wonder. Mike's been taken to places he's never seen before, he's had his face shoved into things he never knew existed. And I'm the sonuvabitch who gave him this gift, whether he wanted it or not. A few more strokes take me over the edge. I groan loudly and let the orgasm sweep over me; my jizz squirts out, splattering Mike's face, coating him, dribbling down his cheeks and chin. After the last shudder, I collapse beside him. A few seconds later, I lean over and lick my load off of his perfect face

We lie next to each other. The storm seems to be letting up some; the rain still drums against the roof, but not as loud and furiously as before. Mike turns his head toward me. "Now what?" he asks quietly. I can see the anxiety in his eyes.

I don't say anything. I climb out of bed and pick up the ether-soaked washcloth from the floor. "No, don't, Danny, please!" Mike begs. "It isn't necessary!" He thrashes around again, trying to kick me with his one free leg. But it's pretty hopeless for him. I have the cloth over his face in no time, and it just takes a few more seconds before he's out cold again.

I look down at Mike's naked body for a long time. His dick is still half hard, encased in the condom. I peel the condom off, tie it in a knot, and slip it into my jacket pocket. Something to jack off to the next time the screaming blue devils hit me. A drop of cum dribbles from his cockhead; I bend and lick it up, then softly kiss his dick. I stand up again and stare for a long time at his beautiful face, now calm in his unconsciousness. *Thanks, Mike,* I think. *For once, the reality matched the fantasy.* I pick my knife up off the floor and pull it out of its sheath.

\*　　\*　　\*

I wake up again to the same brutal hangover: the pounding head, the nausea, the dizziness. Christ, I feel like hell. It just takes me a second to see that I'm free now, the ropes cut off from my wrists and ankles, now bruised and chafed raw. I look around for Danny, but the room is empty. I stagger out of bed into the bathroom and turn on the sink faucet. The cool water stings my wrists. The face that looks back at me in the bathroom mirror is a shock: white, gaunt, the eyes wild, their pupils dilated. My legs start shaking. I sit down on the closed toilet seat and put my head between my knees until I feel steadier. Afterwards, I fill my cupped hands with water and splash my face.

A quick check shows that Danny's nowhere in the cabin; there's no car parked outside, only muddy tire tracks in the road. I want more than anything else to get home, but I don't know where the fuck I am, other than in some cabin north of Jenner. That is, if Danny was telling the truth. My clothes are in ribbons and there's nothing else to wear in the cabin. I'm not crazy about the idea of trekking out into the rainy night wrapped only in a sheet.

I pick up the phone, expecting it to be dead. To my surprise, I get a dial tone. I get a second surprise. Danny has carefully written directions to this place and has left them by the phone.

After I roust Roger out of bed, it takes a full thirty minutes before I can convince him that I'm telling him the truth about my abduction, that this isn't just some kind of weird prank I'm playing. I read the directions to him over the phone. By the time he finally makes it to the cabin, it's already daylight, and the rain has lightened to a drizzle. Roger stares at me bug-eyed, but I'm too tired to care. I do notice him checking me out when I drop the sheet to put on the clothes he brought with him. The picture goes through my mind of Roger picking up the ether-soaked cloth and repeating the whole scene all over again. I'm beginning to envy Danny his harelip.

We don't say anything for a long time during the ride back. "Why won't you let me call the police?" Roger finally asks.

I think about spending hours in a police station answering questions, trying to get suspicious cops to believe my wild story. All I want to do is crawl into bed. *My* bed. I shake my head. "Not now," I say. "Maybe later."

Roger gives me a look, his eyes narrowed with suspicion. I know he suspects this was a little sex adventure I consented to that just got out of hand. Frankly, I don't give a fuck what he thinks. I flip on the radio; the Stones are singing *Tumblin' Dice*. Outside, the rush hour traffic on Highway 101 is just beginning to pick up. I lean back and close my eyes, listening to the Stones and the steady click of the windshield wipers.

# Tim's Dad

It's a running joke between Tim and me about Tim's dad being gay, all those "like father, like son" cracks I make that Tim (sort of) laughs at. Tim has snapshots of his dad in an old photo album: birthday parties, family outings, that kind of thing. On a whim, we're flipping through the album, taking a brief trip through Tim's childhood. We come across pictures of his family's Arizona vacation: there's Tim, a skinny adolescent squinting at the camera and flanked by his dad and mom, the Grand Canyon behind them.

Tim keeps his eyes trained on the photo. "Two months after our trip, Dad dropped the bombshell that he was gay," he says. "He moved out a couple of weeks later."

"Damn," I say. "That must have been pretty heavy for you and your mom."

Tim shrugs. "More for her than me. Actually, I thought it was kind of cool when Dad fessed up to being gay. I already knew that I was."

I take a closer look. In the photo, Tim's dad stares cooly back at us. He has Tim's dark, intense eyes, but his jaw's squarer and his build's more muscular. He's got his arms crossed, and I note how his biceps bunch up.

"Why was he staring like that at the camera?" I ask.

"A park ranger took the picture," Tim laughs. "I think Dad was cruising him."

I know from past conversations that Tim's dad lives just across the bay in San Francisco. "We ought to invite him over for dinner," I say. "I'd like to meet him."

Tim closes the album and stands up. "Yeah," he says, his voice bland. "We'll have to do that some time." I glance at him, but he doesn't meet my eye. Somehow, I know that dinner with Tim's dad is not a likely prospect.

Later that night, after we go to bed, one thing leads to another, and we wind up fucking. I plow Tim's ass with deep, steady strokes; Tim on his back, me sprawled on top. I bend down and kiss him hard, then break away and stare into his eyes. Tim gives me back a look that gives away nothing. I plunge into his ass and churn my hips, and then start fucking him with quick thrusts. My orgasm slowly builds up in me, and I squeeze my eyes shut and keep pumping away. Without any warning, the image of Tim's dad flashes in my mind, that dark, level gaze, that arrogant mouth. I squirt my load in the condom up Tim's ass, groaning loudly.

Three months later Tim tells me he wants out of the relationship. This totally blindsides me. As far as I'm concerned, things were going fine between us. Well, at least "okay."

"What the fuck?" I say. "Is there somebody else?"

"No," Tim says. "This just isn't going anywhere, that's all."

"You know," I say, "it'd be nice if you looked at least a *little* sad."

"I'm willing to let you keep the apartment," Tim says. "I'll go find a place of my own."

"Hey, don't do me any favors."

Tim gives me a level look. "You don't have to get sarcastic. These things happen."

He goes into the bedroom and packs a suitcase while I stand in the middle of the living room. I'm not feeling a damn thing, but I at least have enough native wit to realize that that won't last long. By the time he comes out again, lugging his Tourister behind him, I'm feeling the first tremors of what promises to be an emotional meltdown.

"I'll be staying at Rick and Bob's place," Tim says. "Until I can find something more permanent. I'll come back Saturday for the rest of my things." He locks eyes with me. "It might be less awkward for both of us if you weren't here then."

"All right," I say, because I can't think of anything else. Tim walks out the door, closing it behind him.

*Holy, fucking shit,* I think.

Tim turns suddenly, and I duck into a doorway. But not fast enough. Tim retraces his steps until he's standing right in front of me. "Look," he says. "Do I have to take out a restraining order?"

"Hey," I say. "This is a public street. I have a right to walk down it."

Tim looks away and then back at me again. "I'm getting sick of this shit," he says. "Just what do you hope to accomplish by fuckin' stalking me?" I don't say anything. "That wasn't a rhetorical question," Tim says.

I start crying. "I don't know," I say. "It's something I can't seem to help."

Tim gives me a long, hard stare. "Jesus, this is all so pathetic," he finally says.

I wipe the back of my hand across my eyes. "No argument here."

"Just knock it off," Tim says. He walks off.

It's Saturday night, and I'm in a San Francisco bar with a couple of friends, slamming down beers and talking bullshit. The place is packed, and I'm wedged between the wall and the cigarette machine, shouting over the din of voices and the music, which is nearly loud enough to make a person's ears bleed. It's been months since I last saw Tim. I don't stalk him anymore, though sometimes, at night, I do drive by his apartment and glance up to see if there's a light in the window. If there is, I wonder who he's fucking up there. If it's dark, I wonder where else he's doing his fucking. Then I drive on. Incredible as it may seem, this is an improvement.

My friend Jamie is shouting in my ear about this hot fuck buddy he's met from an Internet chat room. I turn my ear to his mouth to hear him better, and my eyes idly scan the rest of the bar. My glance gets snagged by a man leaning against the bar and pulling on a Corona. He looks like he's in his mid forties, well-built, dark, thinning hair, powerful arms, intense brown eyes. *I've seen that guy before,* I think.

"Are you listening to me?" Jamie shouts.

I turn to him and nod my head. "Yeah, sure," I shout back. "As much as I can over all this damn noise." I glance back at the man at the bar. He's folded his arms across his chest, and that's when I make the connection. His hair's a little thinner, and his face is craggier than when the photo was taken at the Grand Canyon, but it's Tim's dad, all right.

Jamie follows the direction of my gaze. He looks back at me. "What, you into daddies now?"

I turn to Jamie. "Interesting choice of words," I say. I push away from the cigarette machine. "I'll call you tomorrow."

"Happy hunting," Jamie says.

I thread my way through the crowd. When I'm just a couple of feet away from Tim's dad, I can see that he's almost done with his beer. "Hi," I say. "Can I buy you another?"

Tim's dad turns toward me. His eyes flick rapidly up and down my body without the slightest attempt at subtlety. "Okay," he says.

I fight my way to the bar, buy two Coronas, and fight my way back. "Thanks," he says. He holds the bottle up to me in toast and then takes a long pull. He looks at me again. "What's your name?"

"Carl," I say. "How about you?"

"Jack," he says. "You having a good time tonight, Carl?"

"Yeah, I guess," I say. "It's a lot noisier than I like."

"There's a yard out back," Jack says. "You want to go out there? It'll be quieter."

"Yeah," I say. "Sure."

Jack and I lean against the railing of the deck behind the bar, talking the standard bar bullshit. We start getting personal. I ask Jack if he's ever been in a relationship.

"Yeah," he says. "I was once married, if you can believe it."

"Oh, yeah?" I say, my heart hammering. "Any kids?"

"Yeah," Jack says. "A son." He takes another pull. "He's grown up now. I don't see much of him."

We don't say anything for a couple of beats, just stand there, leaning against the porch railing, listening to the voices and music pouring out from the bar behind us. "Look," Jack finally says. "Do you want to go back with me to my place?"

"Fuck, yeah."

Jack drains the last of his beer and tosses the bottle into the weeds. "Let's go," he says.

Jack opens the door to his apartment and flicks on the switch. We walk in. There are clothes strewn on the floor and furniture. "Sorry," he says. "I wasn't expecting company tonight." He snatches a couple of shirts off the couch and tosses them onto the floor. "Have a seat," he urges.

I sit down.

"You want something? A beer maybe?"

"Yeah," I say. "A beer sounds fine."

Jack disappears into the kitchen and comes back with a couple of bottles. He hands me one. "To good times," he says, clinking his bottle against mine.

"A-fuckin'-men," I agree.

Jack sits down beside me. Neither one of us says anything. I put my hand on Jack's knee, he turns to me, and I feel like Tim is watching me through his father's eyes. My throat tightens with excitement. I lean over and kiss him gently. Jack's lips part, and I slip my tongue into his mouth as I roll over on top of him. Jack wraps his powerful arms around me and presses his body against mine as our tongues snake around each other. "Fuckin' A," he murmurs.

I reach down and squeeze his dick. "You got something for me there?" I murmur.

"Yeah," Jack growls. "Wanna see?"

I slide down between Jack's knees and tug his jeans down to his ankles. His eyes burn into mine. His hard dick is outlined against the white cotton of his briefs, a small, dark stain of pre-cum at the tip. I drag my tongue up the length of the bulge, hook my fingers under the elastic band and pull the briefs down, too. Jack's dick snaps up against his belly; thick, uncut, roped with veins. I bury my face in his balls, breathing in the musky scent, feeling the soft scrotal flesh press against my nose and mouth. *This is where Tim came from,* I think. *Twenty-four years ago he was a sperm cell swimming around in this fleshy pouch.* I find the thought almost unbearably erotic. I open my mouth, and suck Jack's balls inside, rolling them around with my tongue, as I reach up and twist Jack's nipples. Jack gives a long, drawn-out sigh, and his body shifts under me. I look up at him, his balls in my mouth, and our eyes lock together. I wrap my hand around his dick and stroke it slowly. It's a beautiful dick, thick and meaty, and I love the feel of its warmth spreading into my hand. I think about how the Tim-sperm once swam up this shaft as Jack's body shuddered in orgasm.

"Let's go back to the bedroom," Jack says.

"Okay."

Jack hikes up his jeans to mid-thigh and leads me down a narrow corridor to the bedroom in the back. His ass is great, the crack a tight, thin line between two solid, half-moons of flesh. I reach down, grab a handful of ass-cheek and squeeze hard. Jack laughs.

When we get to the bedroom, Jack wraps his arms around me again, and we fall onto the bed. We pull off our clothes as we kiss, and when we're naked, Jack straddles me, dry humping my belly. I wrap my hand around both our dicks, cockflesh against cockflesh, balls against balls. Jack buries his face into my armpit. His mouth lightly moves down my body, his kisses feathery against my skin. When he gets to my chest, he twirls his tongue around each nipple, biting them gently. I run my fingers through his hair, tugging at it as I feel his lips on my belly, then my pubes. He rolls his tongue around my cockhead, probing it into my piss slit, then slides his lips around the shaft and nibbles down to the base. I push up with my hips and start fucking his face in slow, measured strokes.

"Pivot your body around," I say. Jack obeys, and it isn't long before we're both eating dick and fucking mouth. Jack thrusts up hard, sliding his dick deep down my throat until my nose is pressed against his balls. I pause, loving the feeling of my mouth completely filled with dick. Tim's dad's dick. Jack reaches down and presses a finger against my asshole and then pushes on in.

"God . . . damn!" I groan.

Jack looks up at me and grins. "You like that?"

"Yeah," I say. "I'd like it even better if it were your dick."

Jack's eyes are hard and fierce now. "That's just what I had in mind," he says. He reaches into a drawer of the bedside nightstand and pulls out a condom packet and a jar of lube. I close my eyes as he slowly skewers me. "Damn," I groan.

Jack holds that position for a moment, his body pressing against me, his dick full inside my ass, his face inches above mine. He draws his dick out with excruciating slowness until just the tip of his cockhead is in me, and then plunges hard inside me with one swift, sure stroke. I groan loudly as he begins pumping his hips hard and fast. It takes me a second to catch the rhythm, but I push up, matching him thrust for thrust, wrapping my legs around his thighs. Jack is a wild man. He slams his dick in and out of me with a punishing energy, his balls slapping hard against me with each slam. I reach up and pull his face down onto mine, kissing him hard, biting his lips. I wrap my arms around him and flip him onto his back, never breaking the rhythm of our thrusts. I sit on his dick, my hands squeezing his nipples hard, as he continues to plow me. He wraps his lube-smeared hand around my cock and strokes it rapidly. I drink him in with my eyes, his muscular torso, his rugged, dark face (*Tim in twenty years,* I think). I think about his dick sliding in and out of my ass, how it slid in and out of Tim's mother twenty four years ago, building up to the final squirt that would wind up creating Tim. I kiss Jack again, shoving my tongue in his mouth.

Jack is breathing hard now, and drops of sweat trickle down his face. He thrusts up and gives a little whimper. With the next thrust, the whimper becomes a trailing groan. I reach back and tug on his balls. They're pulled up now, ready to shoot. "I'm getting close, buddy," he gasps.

"Go for it," I growl. He gives another sharp, upward thrust, and I squeeze my ass muscles tight.

"Ah, jeez," he groans, and I feel his body shudder. He arches his back, and his body thrashes and bucks under me. He finally collapses onto the bed. "Hot damn," he says, laughing.

I stroke my dick as Jack tongues my balls, and when I come, my load splatters his face in one pulse after another. I lick it off and slide down next to him, into his arms. We lay in the darkness for a while. After a few minutes, I sit up. "I have to go," I say.

"Okay," Jack's voice says. It's too dark to read his expression.

After I'm dressed, he slides his jeans on and walks me to his front door. He kisses me lightly. "I'd like to see you again," he says.

"Yeah," I say. "Sure."

Jack takes a scrap of paper from the hallway stand and writes his number down. He thrusts it in my hand. "Call me," he says. "I mean it."

"All right," I reply, slipping the paper into my shirt pocket.

As we kiss good night, Jack reaches down and gropes my dick. "You're a sexy motherfucker. You know that?"

"Thanks," I say. I walk out the door.

I cruise by Tim's place before driving home. His window is dark, which is not surprising, since it's after two in the morning. I think about how it would fuck Tim's head up in a major way if I started something up with his dad. I sit in the car, savoring this thought like a hungry man gnawing on a chicken leg. After a while I start not liking how much I'm enjoying this. I roll down the window and toss out the scrap of paper with Jack's number on it. The wind picks it up, and it flutters down the street. I start up the car engine and drive down the dark streets toward home.

# Uncle Ted's Big Send-Off

By the time the third joint is passed around, I feel like I'm floating in a warm, blissed-out fog, no body part touching the ground. It's such a bitchin' day; the sky like a pure blue bowl, the sunlight sparkling on the Pacific. I close my eyes as a breeze passes over me, and let myself drift. One of the guys is sitting off to the side beating on one of those small East Indian drums, and the drumbeats thread through my skull like fuzzy worms. Snatches of conversation float around me from Uncle Ted's old friends. I don't really know anybody here all that well, except for Uncle Ted of course, or what's left of him, his ashes firmly sealed in the Folger's coffee can that occupies a place of honor in the middle of a blanket stretched out on the beach.

Two of the guys (I think their names are Mark and Al) are off to the side, talking heatedly. They're keeping their voices low, but since I'm at the edge of the group, I can still hear every word.

"Are you sure you gave him the right directions?" Mark asks.

"Yeah, I'm sure," Al says. "Will you just relax? He'll be here."

"He fuckin' better. Without him, the whole ceremony will be ruined."

"Jesus, will you calm down? This guy's very reliable. I've worked with him before."

"Yeah," Mark snorts. "I'll just bet you have." He rejoins the group, intercepts the circulating joint and takes a hit.

"Look," Al says, pointing behind us. "What did I tell you?"

And sure enough, we see the figure of a man crest the nearest sand dune.

"Hey, Casey," Al shouts, waving. "Over here!"

Casey turns toward the sound of Al's voice and waves back. Mark visibly relaxes. The sun is behind Casey's back, so all I see is his silhouette: broad shoulders, the V of a well-muscled torso, the bulge of biceps, narrow hips. Everyone else draws a bead on Casey as well, and the mood of the group noticeably shifts, becomes more alert. Casey reaches us, and Al puts his hand on his shoulder and pulls him into the circle of friends.

"Everybody," Al says, "This is Casey." And all of us stand there drinking Casey in with our eyes while pretending not to. The words "golden boy" flit through my mind, from the honey gold of his smooth skin, the sun-bleached, shaggy hair, the easy smile of a man who gets to go through life being heartbreakingly handsome. Casey is wearing a tie-dye tank top and board shorts, and it's impossible to imagine him in any other setting than on a California beach on a warm summer's day.

"Hey, guys," Casey says, regarding each of us with friendly blue eyes.

"Did Al explain the . . . ceremony we had in mind?" Mark asks.

Casey shrugs. "Sure. Piece of cake." He turns to the latest guy toking. "Hey, can I have a hit?" he asks, and the guy hands him the joint. Casey inhales deeply and passes the joint on.

Mark glances around at all of us. "Let's get in a circle around Casey," he says. We climb to our feet and form a ragged ring around Casey, except for the guy with the drum, who is still beating out a steady tattoo. Mark bends down, picks up the Folger's can, and peels off the plastic lid. "Hold out your hands," he instructs us, and we obey. Mark slowly walks around the inner perimeter of the circle, stops in front of each of us, pouring a handful of ashes into our outstretched, cupped hands. All except for Casey, who stands with his arms at his side, watching us. Mark reaches me last and turns the coffee can completely upside down, thumping it lightly on the bottom. A pile of fine ash forms a heap in my hands. I stare at it, trying to grasp that this is Uncle Ted I'm holding.

Mark nods to Casey, and Casey lazily hooks his thumbs under the edge of his tank top and pulls it over his head, revealing a torso packed with muscle, his nipples two wide, pink circles set on tawny flesh. Casey yanks off the Velcro snap of his shorts and lets them drop to his ankles. He steps out of them, kicking them aside, and stands naked in the center of our circle. Sunlight pours down on his body, and his skin gleams with a sheen of sweat. I'm still totally stoned with the killer weed we've all been smoking; there's a high buzzing in my ears that mingles with the soft whoosh of the waves behind me and the rapid beat of the drum, and none of this seems real.

"Okay, guys," Mark says. "You all know what Ted's last wish was, how he wanted his ashes scattered. Let's get to it." His voice is matter-of-fact, but there are tears in his eyes. He steps forward and sprinkles the ashes on Casey's body. They cling to the sweaty surface of Casey's skin and quickly form a gray paste.

Al steps forward, and then the others join him, and soon we are all smearing Uncle Ted's ashes all over Casey's naked skin, across the mounds of his pecs, the rounded curves of his biceps, down the hard, chiseled stretch of belly, over the smooth, twin globes of Casey's perfect ass. Casey is our canvas, Uncle Ted the medium. I take my own handful of ashes and fling them against Casey's torso, and then slide my hands down his belly. The strokes of our hands are clearly arousing Casey. His dick slowly lengthens and thickens, the head pushes out from the uncut foreskin. I wrap my sooty hand around his shaft and stroke it slowly, then tug on Casey's low-hanging balls, coating them with ash as well. I cup them in my hand, rolling them around. Casey watches me calmly, and there's this moment when our gaze meets, and, stoned as I am, I fall into those blue, blue eyes. I reach behind, slide my hand into the crack of Casey's ass, and massage his asshole. I push a finger inside, and Casey's dick gives an extra twitch.

We all step back and regard our handiwork. Casey's body is no longer golden-brown, but dull gray, with long smear marks running over his torso and face, and ashy clots in his hair. His dick juts out thick and hard, pointing up toward the sky. His eyes are closed, and his mouth is curved up in a lazy smile. I sway, trying not to lose my balance. I am so fuckin' stoned. Mark pulls a piece of paper from his back pocket and starts reading a poem by Rumi, Uncle Ted's favorite poet. We all just stand there, listening to the soft drone of his voice.

When he's done, there's a moment of silence, broken only by the waves and the beating drum. Casey opens his eyes and looks around. When his gaze meets mine, he winks. The circle breaks, leaving an opening that leads out toward the softly crashing waves. Casey calmly walks toward the sea. A wave breaks on the beach and water swirls around his ankles. Casey wades deeper into the Pacific. When he's thigh-deep, he plunges headfirst into the next swell of the wave and swims out further in strong, sure strokes. He circles around and comes back toward us again, staggering out of the waves that are sucking on his legs, trying to pull him back in. He looks like a sea god emerging from the ocean depths. His skin gleams gold again, and whatever is left of Uncle Ted is now being swept out into the wide blue of the ocean.

Casey walks up to us. "Well," he says. "Is that the end of it?"

Mark's eyes are still moist. He nods, saying nothing. Casey bends down and picks up his clothes, and the sense of ritual is suddenly gone. When Casey's done dressing, Mark takes him aside and discreetly slips some folded bills into Casey's hand. Casey calmly puts the money in his back pocket without counting it. He and Mark shake hands, Casey waves at us, climbs the dune, and soon disappears behind its crest.

Al is standing next to me. "Where did you find Casey?" I ask him.

Al turns his head and regards me for a couple of beats as if he's trying to remember who I am. "On an escort Web site," he says absently. He walks over to Mark and puts his arm around Mark's shoulder. There's nothing else for me to do here. I pick up my stuff and head back to the beach lot where my car is parked.

I pull out onto the main road that flanks the beach. There's a bus stop a couple of hundred feet down. Casey is standing there, waiting.

I pull up next to him. "You need a ride?" I ask.

Casey smiles his easy smile. "Sure," he says. "If you don't mind. I live over in the upper Haight."

"No problem," I say. I lean over and unlock the door, and Casey climbs in.

Casey glances over toward me. "I didn't catch your name," he says.

My eyes meet his. "It's Paul."

We cruise down the Great Highway, the Pacific spread out on our left like a plane of sheet metal. "What a bitchin' day," Casey says.

"Yeah," I agree. I glance at Casey. "That whole thing we did with Uncle Ted's ashes didn't creep you out?"

"Naw," Casey says. He stretches, looks out toward the ocean then back at me. He's grinning. "Bizarre requests come with the territory in my line of work." We drive together in silence. "So were you pretty tight with your uncle?" Casey finally asks.

"Yeah," I say. "We had a bond. You know, the only gay members in the family, that kind of thing. A couple of years ago, when I came out, my folks freaked. I stayed with Uncle Ted for a while until things cooled down." I turn onto Geary Avenue. "He was a good guy. I'm going to miss him."

We don't say anything else for the rest of the ride. Casey's got his knees spread apart, and my hand keeps brushing his thigh whenever I shift gears. The first couple of times are accidental. After that, I make a point of sliding my knuckles against the length of his thigh each time I shift. The memory of Casey's hard, ash-coated dick flashes through my mind, how it felt in my hand when I stroked it, and I feel my own dick stir. Casey makes no effort to pull away when my hand touches his leg. This is turning into a very strange day.

We pull up to Casey's apartment. "Well," I say lamely. "It was nice meeting you."

"Look," Casey says. "Would you like to come up for a while?"

"Fuck, yeah," I say.

Casey's place is a small studio on the third floor. It faces west, and the early afternoon sun pours in through the one window. The furnishings are sparse, and the only decoration on the wall is a surfing poster. Casey puts a CD on the player and Chris Isaak's voice fills the room, singing "Wicked Game." Casey goes into the kitchen and comes back with two Coronas, handing me one. We sit on Casey's threadbare couch. I clink my bottle against his. "To sex and death," I say.

"You can't get any more basic than that," Casey grins. He holds up his bottle. "Sex and death," he says and takes a swig. We sit together for a moment. I still have a buzz on, and Isaak's voice makes my brain tingle like a low voltage current is passing through it. After a couple of beats, Casey hooks a hand around my neck and pulls me toward him. He kisses me softly, his tongue snaking into my mouth. I wrap my arms around him and pull him down onto the couch, squeezing him tightly. Our kisses become hungry, our hands slip under each other's clothes, fumbling with buttons, tugging on zippers. Casey pulls away. "Let's get naked," he says.

We strip quickly. Casey pushes me down and straddles me, wrapping his hand around both our dicks. He gives them a good squeeze and starts stroking them slowly. A bead of pre-cum leaks out of my piss slit, and Casey uses it to lube up my shaft. I look down at our dicks pressed together, his fat and pink, the head a rubbery dome of flesh, mine dark and veined. "Fuckin' beautiful," I growl, and Casey laughs.

I run my thumbs over the pink nubs of Casey's nipples and then take them between my thumbs and forefingers and squeeze. Casey slides his hands down my torso, pulling on my flesh, kneading it. His eyebrows are pulled down in concentration, and his gaze follows his hands intently as they stroke my body. A ray of sunlight, laced with dust motes, angles in and falls full on us, and Casey's skin glows like polished teak. Traffic noises from the street below float up through the window, and the heat of the day presses down on us, making our movements feel slow and lazy, like we're having sex under a pool of warm water. Casey bends down and gives me a lingering kiss.

I break free and roll my tongue around Casey's nipples, first the right one, then the left, nipping the tender flesh with my teeth, sucking on them, feeling them stiffen in my mouth. Casey entwines his fingers through my hair and gently tugs on it, as I deliver a series of butterfly kisses down his chiseled, flat belly, across the forest of his pubes, and into the fleshy folds of his ballsac. I inhale deeply, breathing in the musky scent, feeling the tiny hairs tickle my nose. I open my mouth and suck his balls in, rolling my tongue over them, tasting the salt of the Pacific on them. My eyes lock with Casey's, and his mouth slides up into an easy smile as he rubs his hard cock over my face, pre-cum smearing my cheeks.

I hook my hands under Casey's knees and raise his legs up, exposing the pink bud of his asshole. I push my face into Casey's ass crack and rim him, running my tongue over the puckered flesh. Casey gives a drawn out sigh. I retrace the path to his balls, and slide my tongue along the length of Casey's fat cock. I roll my tongue around Casey's cockhead, pushing into the piss slit, and then nibble my lips down the shaft. Casey pushes up with his hips, and his cock slides full into my mouth, until my nose is pushed hard against his pubes. I hold that pose for a couple of beats, savoring my mouthful of dick. Casey begins pumping his hips. I suck on the fleshy tube hungrily, twisting my head from side to side, wrapping my tongue around the shaft.

Casey twists around and takes my dick into his mouth. We fuck each other's mouths, eat each other's dicks, our bodies squirming together. I worm a finger into Casey's asshole and twist it slowly. Casey groans. I start fingerfucking Casey, bending my finger, pushing it up, as I go back to working his dick with my mouth. "You gonna let me fuck that sweet asshole?" I growl.

Casey laughs. "Go for it." He opens a drawer of the table next to the couch, pulls out lube and a condom, and hands them to me. I slide the condom down my dick shaft, and grease it up liberally as Casey watches, stroking his dick. I wrap my hands around Casey's calves and pull him toward me. Casey arches his back, exposing his asshole to me, his eyes trained on me. As I slowly impale him, Casey squeezes his ass tight around my dick, and I close my eyes, groaning.

"Open your eyes," Casey says. "Don't break the contact."

I open my eyes and keep my gaze locked with Casey's as I pull out and slide into his ass again. "Yeah," Casey murmurs. "That's right." He reaches up and pushes a lock of hair from my forehead, keeping his hand resting on the side of my head. I pump my hips, plowing in and out of Casey's ass. Everything I do to Casey's body, every sensation, is reflected back in Casey's gaze. Casey's lids are pulled back, and his blue eyes burn into mine. I quicken my thrusts, slamming into Casey's ass so hard that my balls slap against him. I've never fucked like this before, so . . . *aware* of everything. I feel once again like I'm falling into Casey's eyes, like I felt earlier today at the beach, with the sun pouring down on me, and the drum beating and Uncle Ted's ashes smeared all over Casey's naked body. We fuck with bodies thrusting and pulling away in a rhythm that comes together more smoothly with each stroke. I reach up and run my hands over his torso, now slippery with sweat.

Casey's breathing becomes faster, more ragged. Beads of sweat dot his forehead, a drop of it trickles down the side of his face, and his lips are pulled back into a soundless snarl. But his gaze never wavers from mine. By the hardness of his cock in my hand, I know he could come any moment now, and I can feel the load being pulled up from my balls as well. It would be easy for me to shoot, but I manage to hold on, to wait for Casey; it feels like I have more control over my body than I've ever had before. He groans. I twist his nipple, and that's all it takes to push him over the edge. I thrust deep and hard one final time, and just as the first volley of spunk shoots out of his cock, my orgasm sweeps over me, and I squirt my load into the condom up his ass. We thrash around together on the couch, bodies squirming together, our cocks pulsing out our loads. He cries out, and I bend down and plant my mouth over his as the last spasm passes over me.

Even after I've shot my load, I stay inside Casey, my face buried in his neck, feeling his naked skin against mine. A breeze blows through the open window across my back. I finally roll off Casey, sliding down onto the carpet. "Fuuuck," I say. I look up, my glance meets his, and we both laugh. I sit there on the floor, resting my head against his torso, feeling the warmth of his skin against the side of my face. After a while, I get to my feet. "It's getting late," I say. "I gotta go."

"Okay," Casey says.

I pull on my clothes as Casey lays naked on the couch, watching me. When I'm dressed, I go over to him and kiss him lightly on the mouth. "You are one hot motherfucker," I say.

Casey grins. "So are you, buddy."

There's this little moment of tension as Casey and I look at each other. I'm wondering where I can go with this, if I should ask if there's going to be a repeat performance. Casey seems to sense this. "Goodbye, Paul," he says, and that says it all.

"So long, Casey," I say. I give him a last kiss and walk out the door.

Instead of going home, I drive through Golden Gate Park, past the green meadows and flowerbeds, until I'm back on the Great Highway again. I pull into the Ocean Beach parking lot, get out of my car, and sit on the sea wall. The sun sits low in the sky, its rays slanting across the sand, casting long shadows. I stay there a long time, staring out at the Pacific. *Uncle Ted's out there,* I think. *He must be halfway to Hawaii by now.* I watch the kids playing frisbee, the lovers, the old men and women soaking up what heat they can. I don't leave until after the sun dips below the horizon and the lights that flank the Great Highway blink on.

# Carnal Tuesday

King Neptune's float sways jerkily down Canal Street, sequined waves sparkling, a sunken ship with treasure chests bolted to its slanting deck, painted seahorses, sharks, coral reefs. Mermaids sit perched inside giant clamshells, tossing out glass beads and doubloons to the crowds below. "Over here!" people scream. "Over here!" and the mermaids fling more strands into the sea of waving arms. I'm right up front, squashed against the barricades, the float barreling down toward me like a runaway Disney ride. Only I'm not looking at the treasure chests or the smiling mermaids or the seahorses. My eyes are locked onto King Neptune himself, perched on top of the float, his throne decorated with painted fish and sea shells and encrusted with glass jewels. He's stripped to the waist, his smooth, muscular torso sweat-drenched and gleaming, a trident in his left hand, which he waves majestically at the screaming mob. He clutches beads in his right hand, but unlike the mermaids, he doesn't just toss them promiscuously into the crowd. His eyes scan for faces and then, when he finds a worthy target, he throws them to the person he's deliberately singled out.

I watch the play of muscles across his torso as his arm arcs out and the beads fly off into the night, and I wonder what it must feel like to have that powerful chest squirming against mine, those hard, pumped biceps wrapped around me, those muscular thighs, revealed beneath his tunic, gripping me tight as he skewers me with his fat, sea-god cock. The float rumbles up, the speakers attached to its flatbed blasting out a bunch of retro disco shit, and everyone surges against the barricades, arms thrust out, taking up the chant of "Over here!" I push forward too—I don't have any choice in the matter—but while all the others are scrambling and fighting for the doubloons and beads the mermaids are tossing out, I just stand there, in the front of the crowd, staring up at King Neptune, my eyes drilling into him, willing him to notice me.

"Over here!" I shout, and damn if his head doesn't slowly turn toward me and our eyes meet! There's this *moment*, I can't describe it, when time stands still. I don't hear the screams or the music; it's just me and King Neptune, eyes locked, attention riveted. Then he reaches into his bag, pulls out a string of beads, and looking right at me, grinning, tosses it to me. The glass beads arc out into the night, glittering and spinning, and fly right into my outstretched hand. Just as I wrap my fingers around them, another hand grabs hold of the other end and tugs hard. Startled, I turn and see some pimply-faced goon on my left giving me the evil eye. He tugs again, snarling "Let go, asshole!"

I don't even think. I swing my free arm around and slam my fist into his face. He falls back, loosening his grip just enough for me to yank the beads out of his fist. Now I don't normally do that kind of shit. I'm a peaceable guy, but those beads were meant for *me*, dammit! Someone grabs my arm and I swing around with my fist still cocked, but I see that it's Jack, and he's looking righteously pissed. The guy I punched is on his feet again and pushing through the crowd toward me with murder in his eyes.

"Come on, move it!" Jack snarls, and the two of us hightail it away from the barricades, Jack's hand yanking me by my armpit.

"Hey, easy!" I cry out, but Jack ignores me, locked into this role of big-brother-saving-little-brother's-ass. It's a role he loves to play.

We duck into a doorway. Jack slams me against the wall, and shoves his face into mine. "What the *hell* do you think you were doing back there, Trevor?" he yells.

I try to push him away, but he's got his arm pinned against my chest, and I can't move. "Let go of me!" I yell back, and after a moment, Jack backs off. I see I've still got Neptune's beads clenched in my fist, and I stuff them in my jeans' pocket.

"You trying to get us killed?" Jack rages on. "Punching some guy for a bunch of stupid beads! Did you see the size of him! He could have ripped your goddamn head off!"

"Hell, Jack," I say, grinning. "I don't think I've ever heard you say 'god-damn' before." Which is true. Jack never swears. He'll have some powerful explaining to do at the next Bible study class of the Tulsa First Baptist Church.

Jack just glares at me. "I should never have agreed to take you along with me to Mardi Gras," he mutters. "I got better things to do than keep you out of trouble."

"Yeah, well who the hell made you my babysitter?" I say, glaring back at him. "I'm eighteen. I can look out for myself." I push past him and plunge back into the mob. Jack doesn't have any choice but to follow me.

There's a knot of people ahead of us, all looking up. I look up, too, and see five or six girls leaning over the edge of a wrought-iron balcony waving at the crowd below.

"Show us your tits!" someone yells out, and the girls, laughing, pull up their blouses and flash us. The crowd below whistles and yells, pelting the girls with beads.

"Sweet Jesus," Jack mutters. He looks like he's just sucked a lemon.

*What a sad, Baptist hick,* I think, looking at him. I almost feel sorry for him.

He turns his head toward me, scowling. "We're going back to Canal Street," he says. "Now."

"I like it here," I say. "I want to stay."

Jack's eyes stare icily into mine. "I'm not asking you, Trevor," he says. "I'm *telling* you."

We stand still in the shoving crowd, glaring at each other. I'm the first to blink. I make myself smile. "Okay, you win," I say. "Lead the way."

Jack gives me his standard Big Brother smile, the one that always makes me want to punch his face. "That's better. Now let's go." He turns and starts threading through the crowd in the direction of Canal Street.

I watch his retreating back for a couple of seconds and then I just walk off in the opposite direction. In a matter of moments I'm completely swallowed up by the crowd. Losing him is as easy as that. I turn onto Bourbon Street and let myself get carried along with the surge of the bodies: the clowns, the vampires, the gypsies, the cowboys, the Southern belles, the riverboat gamblers, the voodoo witch doctors, and every drag queen that ever lived. The mob pours over the borders of the street, spilling into the bars and nightclubs, overflowing the wrought iron balconies. People thrust drinks in my hands, or I buy whatever the bartender of the moment is giving out, or I just pick up whatever unguarded drink I stumble upon. A woman, topless except for the strings of beads around her neck, lunges at me and plants her mouth over mine, tonguing me fiercely. A Dixieland jazz band belts out ragtime from one of the bars, while speakers from the club next door blare out a Sheena Easton tune. Somewhere a ways back, I've lost my T-shirt, someone ripped it off my back, I think, or maybe I pulled it off and tossed it into the crowd. The beads that King Neptune tossed me hang around my neck, and I'm wearing a Huck Finn straw hat that someone planted on my head a few bars back.

I see them leaning in an alcove of a wall as the surge of the crowd sweeps me past: a red devil with horns glued to his forehead and a pirate wearing an eye patch and a red bandana. The devil reaches over and, grabbing my arm, pulls me out of the crowd as someone would snatch a drowning man from a raging river. "Hi," he says, grinning. "It's about time you showed up!"

"You made a mistake, man," I say, laughing. "I don't know you."

The devil's grin widens, becomes sly. His eyes are a light, clear blue made startling by the red of his face. "No mistake." He's holding a half-full Hurricane glass that he thrusts into my hand. "Here, have a drink. Party with us." He's wearing a vest with red-sequined flames stitched on it. His torso, painted red as well, is hairy and powerfully muscled. The image of King Neptune flashes through my mind, the massive chest, his bicep bunched as he hurled the beads right at me. I hold the devil's glass to my mouth and let the icy cold liquid pour down my throat. I begin to lower the glass, but the pirate reaches over and tilts it up again. Rum spills out the corners of my mouth and down my neck and chest.

"There you go," the pirate laughs. "Drink it all." He lifts his eye patch and winks at me. He looks Creole: dark eyes and crisp black hair, his skin teak brown and gleaming with sweat. He's wearing a loose, white Buccaneer's shirt with rolled up sleeves. His forearms are muscular, the hands huge. I think about the line, *big hands, big dick,* and wonder how true it is.

I'm at that point of drunkenness where a person blurts out any stray thought that's in his head. I look at the two men in front of me. "Goddamn, but you guys are beautiful!" I grin. I shake my head. "I'm sorry, I'm kinda drunk."

The devil reaches over and curls his hand around the back of my neck. "Don't sweat it," he says, his blue eyes focused hard into mine. "We think you're beautiful too. Why do you think we picked you out of the crowd?" The pirate is behind me now, his strong arms wrapped casually around my torso. I lean back against him. The mob lurches by, just a foot from us, roaring and screaming, threatening to sweep us up into its currents again. "I am sooooo drunk, guys," I laugh.

"I know, baby, I know," the devil croons, his face floating right before me. "It's okay, we'll take care of you." He embraces me lightly, and I find myself pressed between the two men. They sway back and forth, and we dance without moving our feet, the devil's eyes piercing mine, the pirate's breath hot on the back of my neck. The devil bends his neck and kisses me lightly on the lips. He begins to pull away, but I reach up and pull his face down against mine, opening my lips and pushing my tongue deep into his mouth. We french each other enthusiastically while the pirate grinds his crotch against my ass, his stiff dick pushing hard up against my crack. His hands slide over my chest and find my nipples, squeezing them, flicking them, rubbing them between his thumbs and forefingers.

The devil's hard dick bulges against his red tights, and he rubs it slowly back and forth against mine. The pirate has slipped his hand inside my jeans and is squeezing my ass. The three of us play-fuck each other, our bodies pressed tight together, grinding and dry humping. Hundreds of people sweep past us, and every now and then a disembodied hand reaches out from the crowd and gropes me, before moving on. I think about how Jack would react if he were to see this little scene, and the picture of his outrage is so vivid I throw back my head and laugh.

"Are you enjoying yourself, buddy?" the pirate murmurs in my ear.

"This is . . . amazing!" I say, still laughing.

The devil leans forward until his lips are at my ear. "It can get even wilder, if you want," he whispers. "I got a place on Royal Street a couple of blocks away. We can do some serious partying there." Sweat trickles down his face, smearing the red paint. The hunger in his blue gaze is hard and clear, mirrored by the dark, intense stare of the pirate. For a second, the fog in my head lifts, at least enough to see just where all this is leading. A simple 'yes' and their naked bodies will be squirming against mine in a matter of minutes.

"Hell, yeah!" I say, laughing. I straighten up and hitch my pants up.

"All right," the pirate grins.

The devil grips my arm. "Okay, then. Let's go for it."

We poise ourselves to dive into the screaming mob. I pull back. "I just want you guys to know," I say, shifting my gaze from face to face. "I'm not doing this because I'm shitfaced. I'd do the same thing stone, cold sober."

"Thanks," the devil laughs, his eyes mocking. "That's nice to know." I take a deep breath, and we plunge into the crowd.

The devil kicks open his door and flicks on a wall switch. "Well, here we are," he says, sweeping his arm in a grand gesture. "Welcome to Hell."

The place is small, only a studio, and messy. Clothes are strewn around, and the bed is unmade. "So this is what Hell looks like!" I say laughing. "I always thought it'd be neater."

The devil laughs along with me. "Sorry. I wasn't expecting any Lost Souls tonight."

We stumble in, and the pirate drops into a chair. He fixes his one, unpatched eye on me. His white shirt is half-unbuttoned, and one nut-brown nipple peeks out. His dark eyes are playful, and he wears the happy expression of a man who knows he's about to get laid. "Look what you do to me, baby" he says, unbuttoning his breeches. "See how hard you make my dick." He pulls out a long, brown dick, thick and hard, and begins to stroke it slowly in his giant hand.

"What do you want me to do?" I ask, grinning.

"Strip," says the devil. "Take everything off. Except the beads." He sits down on the floor, next to the pirate. One of his horns is lopsided, and his eyes burn with a hard blue light.

I can hear the crowds outside on Royal Street, the spillover from the French Quarter, screaming and laughing, music blaring out from the bars below. My drunkenness makes me feel feather light, floating, like I could just drift out through the open windows into the warm, New Orleans night. I kick off my shoes, and unbuckle my belt. "I usually do this to music," I laugh.

The pirate grins, but the devil is all seriousness now, his eyes burning holes in me. I slowly pull down my zipper, revealing my pubes and the base of my cock. The pirate is beating off faster now, his hand a blur, his breeches down around his knees. His heavy balls bounce with each rapid stroke. He's pulled his eye patch off, and his dark eyes gleam. He's got his shirt hiked up around his chest, and he plays with his nipples with his free hand, pinching one and then the other. The devil is rubbing the front of his red tights. I can see his hard cock outlined under them, bulging against the tight spandex.

"Yeah, baby," he croons, "Don't tease us. Show us what you got." I pull my jeans and briefs all the way down and step out of them. A light, warm breeze blows in from the open window across my naked skin. The devil and the pirate sit there, staring at me, the hunger stamped across their faces, and under their eyes my cock swells from half-mast to full woody. "Stroke it," the devil whispers. "Put on a show for us."

I spit in my hand and slide it down my cock. I gotta say, I've got an *awesome* dick: red, thick, fuckin' *meaty*. I wrap both hands around it, proud that there's still an inch and a half more showing. The devil has kicked off his tights and joins the pirate in beating off. It's both sexy and comical how the pale skin of his lower body contrasts with his red painted torso. He's more massively muscular than the pirate, the pecs nicely defined under his chest fur, his biceps bulging impressively. The pirate's dark body is smooth, leaner, wirier. His abs are *cut,* each muscle sharply defined. It's fuckin' hot watching the two of them side by side, looking at their naked bodies, their cocks (the devil's pink and fat, cut, blue-veined; the pirate's not as thick but longer, uncut, brown, with a dark, flaring head.) I pull down on my dick and let it slap against my belly with a loud *thwack.*

"Come over here," the devil growls. I strut toward them, my hard dick swaying from side to side, and stand before them, hands on hips. Both men are staring hard at my dick. The devil reaches over and wraps his hand around it. "Beautiful," he murmurs. "Just fuckin' beautiful." He nuzzles against it, rubbing my cock against his cheeks, his eyes, over his nose and forehead, smearing his red makeup against the shaft. He sticks out his tongue and twirls it slowly around my cockhead.

The pirate gets on his knees and, ducking under the devil, takes my balls in his mouth. He rolls them around with his tongue as the devil slides his warm, wet mouth down my shaft. I start pumping my hips, fucking the devil's face in slow, easy strokes. The pirate grabs my ass cheeks and squeezes them as he tongues my balls. I close my eyes and let the sensations sweep over me, the warm electricity of the two mouths on my cock and balls, the breeze from the open window, the cries and laughter below from the crazy-drunk crowd. The room spins when my eyes are shut, and I open them again, focusing on the blond and dark heads bobbing below me. I suddenly pull away. "Stand up," I say.

Both men climb to their feet. I pull the pirate's shirt over his head, and toss it away. We're all naked now, our bodies slowly swaying together in the dimly lit room. We wrap our arms around each other, and the mouths of the two men press against mine. I run my hands down their backs and over the swell of their asses. The devil's ass is heavily muscled, like the rest of his body; the pirate's is more compact, leaner. I slowly lower myself, dragging my tongue down one torso and then another, the furry chest of the devil, the smooth, dark torso of the pirate. When I'm finally on my knees, I pause and look at the two hard dicks that bob before me. I wrap my hands around them both, the pirate's in my right, the devil's in my left, and start stroking, making their balls bounce. I bend over and run my tongue lightly around the devil's cockhead, probing it into the piss slit.

"Yeah, buddy," the devil croons. "That's right. Lick my dick."

I squeeze the pirate's dick, and a clear drop of pre-jizz oozes out. I lap it up, rolling the sticky, salty drop around on my tongue, and then work my mouth down his shaft until my nose is buried deep against his black, crinkly pubes. I break away, and do the same to the devil's, holding the balls of both men in my two hands, squeezing them gently, weighing their heft. The pirate's balls hang loose and heavy in their dark brown sac. The devil's, plumper and pink, ride high, hugging the shaft of his thick dick. The two ballsacs are meaty handfuls, and I drag my tongue over them, licking and sucking.

The devil and the pirate are kissing now as I suck them off; I look up, their dicks in my mouth, and watch as they work their mouths together, tonguing each other, pinching each other's nipples. I start whacking off, bringing myself just to the brink of shooting and then backing off. The devil pulls me to my feet. "It's time we go to bed," he says gruffly.

The three of us collapse onto the unmade bed, wrestling, stroking, and kissing. The pirate's face is smeared red by the devil's paint, and my body is streaked with it wherever the devil has nuzzled against me. We form a twisted daisy chain, the pirate's dark dick in my mouth, the devil sucking me off, the pirate giving the devil head. The air lies warm and heavy around us, and our bodies are slippery with sweat. I love the pirate's dick, how thick and hard it feels in my mouth as he fucks my face, how his low hanging balls slap against my chin. I could spend all night just swinging on his dark dick.

The devil disentangles himself from us and reaches over to a bedside table. He opens a drawer and pulls out a jar of lube and a fistful of condoms. He greases up his index finger, slides his hand down my ass crack and pushes his finger up my bung hole. I instinctively clamp my ass muscles around it. "Oh, you feel tight, baby," he croons. "You going to let me plow that sweet ass of yours?"

I take the pirate's dick out of my mouth. "Fuck yeah," I growl.

The devil positions himself behind me, and I feel his dick slide up and down my ass crack. I give a low groan when he impales me, and he starts plowing me with slow, lazy strokes, while the pirate continues to fuck my face. This is the first time I've taken dick at both ends at once, and I work the moment, sucking on the pirate's dick as the devil skewers me from behind.

The three of us move into a sort of dance; the pirate and the devil are not only fucking me, but each other as well, using my body, my mouth, and asshole. They lean over and kiss as they plow my holes, stroking my dick with lube-greased hands, playing with my balls, twisting my nipples. The heat pours into the room from the night outside, and this whole little fuck fest feels like it's happening underwater, in slow, dream-like thrusts and strokes.

The devil flips me on my back and fucks me that way, his strokes faster and more urgent now. The pirate squats over my head and drops his balls in my mouth. I tongue the meaty, dark sac, sucking on it as he beats off. The devil wraps his lube-smeared hand around my dick and jacks me, his blue eyes burning into mine, his eyebrows pulled together in concentration, his mouth open as his breath comes out in ragged gasps. He gives a little whimper, and I know he's getting close to shooting. He pulls his cock out, right to the head, and then plunges it full in to the balls. The whimper turns into a trailing groan. He does it again, and this time, as he slides that fat, red dick up my chute, I squeeze my ass muscles tight. The devil's body shudders, and he throws back his head and groans loudly. He pulls out and rips the condom off his dick, and his jizz blasts out, splattering against my belly and chest in one pulsing load after another. The pirate moans, and I reach up and twist his nipples as he blows his load, the cum raining down on me in thick, white drops, mixing with the devil's spermy puddles. His balls are still in my mouth, and I roll them around with my tongue. I smear my hand across my belly, coating it with devil/pirate cum, and start fucking my jizz-slimed fist. The devil presses his finger hard between my balls, and that's all it takes to trigger my load. The orgasm sweeps over me, and I arch my back, my groans muffled by pirate ballmeat. "Fuckin' A," the pirate laughs, and the devil grins too, his blue eyes shining in his paint-streaked face.

The pirate and the devil lay down beside me, kissing me and each other softly, our arms and legs entwined together. The crowd continues to roar outside, like some river in flood. Every now and then a particularly high scream or wild laugh separates itself from the clamor of voices. The booze and the spent sex catch up to me, and I drift off to sleep in the tangle of bodies and not-so-distant cries.

I wake up still drunk, with the room spinning around in slow, swooping circles. The pirate and the devil are asleep, the devil snoring, the sheet twisted around the pirate's legs. It's still dark outside, but there's a streak of light over in the eastern sky. The clock on the night table says it's 5:27. I want to get out of this room, get back onto the streets again. There are no crowd sounds, but someone outside is singing drunkenly. I pull my clothes out from the heap of discarded costumes piled on the floor, and quickly dress. By the thin light that straggles in through the window, I can make out the naked bodies of the two sleeping men: the devil's muscularity, the pirate's lean tightness. Their bodies are the last thing I see before I close the door behind me.

By the time I make it back to Bourbon Street, the whole sky has turned from black to washed-out gray. The street is ankle deep in trash: beer cans, bottles, stray bits of costumes. The partying hasn't really stopped yet, but it seems to have moved inside the buildings on either side of me. People move back and forth behind the lighted windows or spill out onto the wrought iron balconies.

I pass a corner where a wide terrace overlooks the street. It's packed with people, all men. A line of them hang over the railing. "Hey, hot stuff," one of them calls out to me. "Show us your dick!" Others around him laugh. I stop and look up at them, grinning. More of them take up the chant: "Show us your dick! Show us your dick!"

I kick off my shoes and socks and then drop my jeans. More men join the others by the railing, whooping and whistling. I pull my briefs down with killing slowness, showing my pubes, then inch by inch of my cock. The men cheer again, and some of them begin tossing beads at me. I lie down naked in the middle of Bourbon Street, grinning, my arms flung back, my legs spread open. Men from other rooms, other buildings, crowd the balconies or hang out of open windows, pelting me with beads. The beads rain down on me, catching the light of the rising sun, all the colors of the rainbow. Even when my entire body is covered with beads, they still rain down, the men cheering, my naked body spread-eagle against the gritty asphalt of the street.

# Helping Rufus

When I told Daddy I was going out for the high school wrestling team, I could tell he wasn't pleased. He just stood there, chopping onions, the knife whacking into the cutting board so hard I thought he'd lose a finger for sure. Finally, he looked up at me, his eyes red and angry from all those onion fumes. "Who's goin' to help me out in the diner, Rufus, if you're spending all you're time wrestling with your buddies after school?"

"I'll help you out after practice, Daddy. I'll still have time." Cora and Tammy were making a big deal about cleaning the counter and setting out the forks and knives. But I could tell they was listening to every word. It was too early for customers, and they didn't seem to have nothin' better to do with their time.

Daddy just shook his head and started in on the green peppers. "I don't know. It just don't seem like a good idea." He put the knife down and looked at me again. "How d'you know you'll be any good at it anyway?"

"Hell, Daddy," I say. "I'm the biggest kid in the senior class." And I am. I'm six foot four and weigh two hundred twenty three pounds, stripped naked. And it's all solid, too; there ain't a butcher's ounce of fat on me. I know that sounds like bragging, but it ain't. I'm just stating a fact.

Daddy snorted. "Yeah, you're the biggest kid all right. Staying back two years sure took care of that." I felt my face burn on that one, but I didn't say nothing. I just stood there watchin' Daddy have at those peppers with the cleaver like they was his worst enemy in all the world. I could tell he was ashamed for what he said by the way his mouth got all tight and his eyes squinty. That warn't no help for me, though, 'cause when Daddy gets shamed, he just gets meaner. "You're big, all right, Rufus, but you're slow and clumsy. You need to be quick to be a good wrestler."

"Oh, hell, George," Cora said. "If Bigfoot wants to join the wrestling team, why don't you just let him? It's only natural for a boy to want to participate in high school sports." People call me Bigfoot because I wear a size fourteen shoe and there was once a story in one of the supermarket papers about some hunters tracking Bigfoot in California. Some of the guys in school started joking about calling those hunters up and tellin' them to hightail it over here to Enid, Oklahoma, if they really want to bag Bigfoot, and the name just sorta took.

"Yeah," Tammy laughed. "And he can practice his holds on us anytime." Cora giggled. Cora and Tammy are always making little jokes like that about me. I wish they wouldn't; it's embarrassing.

Daddy glowered at them. "I got three things to tell you ladies. No, make that four. One, I don't recall asking for your opinion in this private conversation between me and my son. Two, the boy's name is Rufus. Three, I don't like you making those dirty remarks about Rufus, and four, if you can't find something better to do with your time than cackle like a couple of hens, then what the hell am I paying you for?" But Cora and Tammy just rolled their eyes and went back to wiping the counter.

Daddy threw the cleaver down on the cutting board and walked away. "Hell, Rufus, join the damn team, if that's what you want," he grunted. "You're going to anyway, whether I say so or not." And he stomped out of the kitchen and up the stairs.

Tammy came around the counter and next to me. "Bigfoot, would you hand me those dishes on the top shelf?" she asked me. When I reached up for them, she pressed her body tight against mine. "Just don't let those boys mess up that pretty face of yours, Bigfoot," she growled. "You're the best-looking thing this podunk town's got going for it." I didn't know what to do but just hand the plates to her. Tammy laughed. "What the hell do I want those for?" she said and walked off.

So that's how I wound up going to Coach Garibaldi and telling him I wanted to join the team. Coach just looked me over slowly, nodded, and said, "Okay, Rufus. I'll give you a try. Practice starts today after school."

I went to practice every day, and I tried real hard to learn the moves. At first, nobody wanted to wrestle me because of my size, but then some of the bigger boys took me on. And they found they could win, more often than not. I hate to say it, but Daddy was right; I am slow. And clumsy. Sometimes if I could just get a good grip on the guy, I could hold on and pin him to the mat. But if he slipped out of my hands and started his moves on me, I was a goner. I went to a few meets and usually wound up "eating mat." I was just glad that Daddy never went and saw it. I'd never hear the end of it.

Every afternoon, after practice, we all would shower up before going home. More often than not, Coach Garibaldi just stood at the doorway, sometimes talking to the other boys, giving them pointers, sometimes just watching us. Coach never much talked to me, but lately I began catching him looking at me more and more. Probably just wonderin' what to do with such a pitiful wrestler. One day, as we were all walking out of the shower back toward the locker, he grunted and said, "I guess it's true what they say about guys with big feet." And he walked back to his office. A couple of other guys nearby laughed.

"What did Coach mean by that?" I asked.

One of the guys shook his head. "Nuthin', Bigfoot."

Another guy grinned. "It's just Mother Nature's way of evening the score. You may have been behind the door when she gave out the brains, Bigfoot, but good God almighty, you sure were first in line on other days." And they laughed again and walked off. *Damn fools,* I thought. But it always bothers me when people won't explain a joke to me. It's not my fault I'm dumb.

I got dressed and started walking out the locker room. When I passed Coach's office, I could see that his door was open. I heard him call my name out, and I stuck my head in. "Yeah, Coach?"

Coach was sitting behind his desk. "Come in here, Rufus," he said. Except for Daddy, Coach was the only person who called me by my Christian name. I walked in.

"Close the door," he said.

*I'm in for it now,* I thought. When Coach asks you to close the door, you know he means business. I 'magined I was going to get a chewing out for being such a poor wrestler.

But Coach didn't look mad. In fact, he didn't look much of anything. He just sat there, leaning back on his chair, looking at me with a blank face. He finally sighed. "Rufus," he said. "I just don't know what to do with you."

I felt my face turning red. I wish that wouldn't happen all the time, but I ain't got no control over it. Daddy likes to say, laughin' "It don't take much more than a fart or a hiccup to get that boy's face as red as a baboon's ass," and he's right. Anyway, I just stood there, shiftin' from one foot to the other, feeling my face get all heated up. Coach didn't say nothing more for a while, making it worse. He just sat there, his fingertips tapping together, looking straight at me. I felt like one of them bugs my cousin Olaf used to pin to a roof shingle, not enough to kill, just to get it squirming. Finally, Coach cleared his throat.

"How old are you, Rufus?" he asked.

"Eighteen, Coach."

"Eighteen," Coach repeated this like it was a remarkable thing. "I'm thirty-three." He laughed. "I know to you that must sound older than dirt, but believe it or not, it just seems like yesterday that I was your age."

"Yes, Coach," I mumbled. Hell, I didn't know what else to say.

"I've been giving your case a lot of thought," Coach said. "You know what I think your problem is?"

I looked at him. "No, sir."

"It's sexual tension, Rufus. Do you know what that means?" I shook my head. "Rufus," Coach said. "Didn't your Daddy ever tell you about sex?"

Well, I just liked to die right there! I knew that by the way my face felt, it must've been redder than a damn fire engine. I shook my head, but couldn't say nothin'.

Coach smiled. "There's no reason for you to be embarrassed, son. Sex is a natural, God-given gift. But it can cause problems, too, especially for young men. Now I don't mean any disrespect to your father, but he should have explained this all to you. If a young man can't find some kind of release for his sexual tension, it can affect the quality of his athletic performance. Do you understand what I'm saying, Rufus?"

I shook my head again. "Not really, Coach."

Coach sighed. "Well, it looks like I got no choice but to show you, Rufus. Lock the door."

I looked at him all surprised-like, but finally did as he said.

Coach smiled. "You're a good boy, Rufus. And believe it or not, I think you've got the makings of a damn fine athlete. But we just got to lick this sexual tension problem of yours. Now drop your pants."

Well, you could have hit me on the head with a two-by-four! "Wh-what, Coach?" I stammered.

"I said, drop your pants." When I didn't do nothin', Coach made a face. "Rufus," he said, his voice all exasperated. "I've seen you in the shower dozens of times. It's not like you're showing me anything new, you know. I just want to prove a point to you." I still didn't do nothin'. "Drop 'em, Rufus!" Coach barked, and I knew there was no arguing the matter. I pulled down my blue jeans. "The shorts, too," Coach said. I pulled them down too, all the way to my ankles.

Coach just leaned back in his chair and looked at me. Or rather, at my dick. He was wearing the funniest look I ever saw on another man's face. "Sweet Jesus in Heaven," he said, all low like. I didn't have a Chinaman's clue as to what he was thinkin', but something in his look made my stomach flutter, like it did last summer on the Winotchka Bridge, when all the guys were daring me to jump off, and I was looking straight down into the water, trying to work up the nerve. To my embarrassment, I felt my dick start getting hard. I put my hands over it to hide this from Coach.

"Leave your hands at your sides," Coach said quietly.

I did like he told me. My dick just kept on getting harder and harder. Soon it was sticking straight out. I snuck a quick peek down at it. Sure enough, it was just as red as I knew my face must be.

Coach looked in my eyes now, all triumphant. "Do you see what I mean, Rufus?" he asked. "This proves my point exactly!"

"No, Coach. I can't say that I do."

Coach got up and walked around the desk. He stood right in front of me. I was a good three inches taller than him, so he had to look up into my face. "Rufus," he said. "You've got the biggest cock I've ever seen. Hell, it must be at least eleven, maybe twelve inches long." He reached down and grabbed it. "Look, I can hardly put my hand around it. With a cock like that, a man's just got to be full of sexual tension. He can't help but think of nothing but where to put his pecker. And look how easy it was for you to get hard. No wonder you can't put your mind on your athletic performance!"

Well, I just felt lower than a snake's belly in a wagon rut hearing this. 'Cause I knew Coach was right. Even now, pert near all I could think of was how good Coach's hand felt wrapped around my dick. And here Coach was just trying to prove a point. Coach was so wrapped up in makin' his point, though, that he must not have noticed that his hand was slowly stroking my dick up and down. But I sure knew it. And what's worse, I didn't want him to stop. "I'm sorry, Coach," I said, all low and sadlike.

Coach smiled. He reached up and squeezed my shoulder. He also squeezed my dick in the same friendly way. "Hell, Rufus," he said. "It's nothing to apologize for. Lots of young men suffer from sexual tension. Some of my most promising athletes. I see it as part of my job as a coach to help walk them through the problem."

I'll be darned if my eyes didn't start watering up when he said that. Coach was taking such an open-hearted concern in helping me through this "sexual tension" problem, that it just choked me up. "What are we going to do, Coach?" I asked.

Coach smiled again, and it was such a friendly, encouraging smile, that I couldn't help but take heart. "Well, Rufus," he said, "we're just going to have to explore the problem, find out just what causes this sexual tension to flare up, and then work it through. Now take off the rest of your clothes.

Coach's way was so friendly and helpful that I could feel my embarrassment just sort of slide off and sink into the ground. In fact, I was kind of liking this. I didn't even think my face was red anymore. I pulled my shirt off, kicked off my shoes, and stepped out of my jeans. When I turned back to the Coach, I saw him pulling off his pants, too. That kind of got me confused again. "What gives, Coach?" I asked.

Coach tossed his pants aside and started unbuttoning his shirt. "Well, Rufus, some things can best be taught by comparison. Each man's body responds to sexual tension in a different way. And that's what I'm trying to show you. Normally, I'd just have one of the other boys come in to demonstrate, but since they've all gone home, I guess it'll have to be me."

Well, I'd never seen Coach's body before. In fact, I'd never seen the body of any man except the other guys in the wrestling team, and I have to confess that I was finding this all mighty interesting. Like I said earlier, Coach was shorter than me, but he was just as broad in the shoulders. I never realized before what a good body he had, how big his muscles were. His chest was covered with black, curly hair that trailed down his belly and then got all bushy again right above his dick. And his dick was just as stiff as mine now, just sticking straight out for the whole world to see. I'd never seen another man's boner before, and I looked at Coach's with some powerful curiosity. It wasn't pink, like mine, but dark, with a big ol' head. And his balls hung down real low, one lower than the other, where mine are a lot tighter.

Coach saw me staring down at his dick and he smiled kind of regretful-like. "I'm afraid it's not as big as yours, Rufus."

I just said the first thing that came to mind. "It's beautiful, Coach. It's just the right size for you." And then I got a little scared for making such a personal remark to Coach.

But he just smiled. "You're a good boy, Rufus," he said. His face got serious again. "But we've got to explore this problem of yours some more. Now let's just see what causes this sexual tension of yours to flare up." He reached up and squeezed my nipples, gently at first, and then harder. "What does that do for you, Rufus?" he asked.

Well, I couldn't begin to describe the feeling to him. "It feels real good, Coach," I finally sighed. "In fact, if you want to squeeze harder, that's all right by me."

Coach squeezed harder. "Like this?" he asked.

"Oh, yeah," I groaned. Then, realizing that wasn't really a respectful way to talk to Coach, I cleared my throat. "I mean, yes, sir."

Coach looked thoughtful. "Hmmmmm," he said. "And what about this?" He leaned forward and began licking my nipples, biting them gently with his teeth and flicking them with his tongue.

"Ahhhhh, jeez," I moaned.

Coach pulled back again. "Interesting," he said. He dropped down to his knees so that his face was right in front of my dick. He took ahold of my dick and began stroking it slowly, pulling the skin over the head and back again. "And what about that, Rufus?"

"Yeah, Coach, yeah," I groaned. "I'm definitely feeling somethin'."

Coach looked satisfied. "Very good." He looked up at me again and grinned. "Now my mouth is going to be full for a while, so I won't be able to talk to you, Rufus. It'll be up to you to give me feedback."

"Okay, Coach," I gasped. "I'll try."

Coach put his mouth around my balls and began sucking on them hard, still stroking my dick. He worked his tongue around each nut, giving them a good washing.

"Oh, God, Coach, I think we're onto something here," I moaned. Coach slid his tongue up the shaft of my dick, back to my balls again, and then back up my dick. He flicked my dickhead with his tongue, pushing it down into the piss slit, sliding it all over the head. Suddenly he plunged down and took my dick in his mouth. Well, my knees just about gave out with that. "Sweet Jesus!" I cried out. And I'm ashamed to admit this, but I lost control and did a very disrespectful thing. I grabbed Coach's head and began pumping my dick back and forth inside his mouth, as deep as I could get it. Which was still three or four inches shy from being all the way.

Coach broke away. "Slow down, Rufus," he gasped. "You're too big to just go plowing my mouth like a bull in heat." I was about to apologize, but he made an impatient wave with his hand. "Just shut up and let me do this my own way. Believe me, I know what I'm doing." He took hold of my dick again and swallowed it. Slowly, he worked it down his throat, inch by inch, until his nose was buried in my pubes. I never would have thought it possible, but Coach is a man who knows how to do things right. His head began bobbing back and forth, and each time he came back he managed to take my cock in all the way. I held on to his head again, but gently this time, just running my fingers through his hair, slowly moving my hips back and forth in time to his sucking. I have to admit, we was goin' over this sexual tension business with a fine-tooth comb.

Well, the Coach started twisting his head from side to side now, wrapping his tongue around my dick in a manner that would have pert near lifted me out of my socks if I had still been wearing them. I looked down, and dang if I didn't see Coach strokin' his hard dick too, while suckin' on mine. And a thought just kind of lit up in my head.

"Coach!" I said. "You got sexual tension, too, don't you?"

Coach took my dick out of his mouth, looked up at me and grinned. "Well, yes, Rufus, I have to confess that I do."

And I realized that I'd not been minding my manners. Here Coach was working so hard to help me get over my sexual tension, and dang if I'd so much as lifted a finger to help him with his. "Well, shoot, Coach," I said. "It just don't seem right that I don't help you out, too."

Well, I tell you, Coach's face just lit up like it was Christmas morning and he was ten years old. It made my heart glad just to see it. "Rufus," he said. "You are a true gentleman. And don't let anybody tell you otherwise."

He stood up and, without giving it a thought, I just dropped down to my knees the way the Coach had done. Coach's dick shot out in front of my face, long and hard, and I looked it over with curiosity, following the veins along it, watching how the head flared out.

"You can touch it, Rufus, it won't bite," Coach said. And I reached out, put my hand around Coach's dick and squeezed.

It seemed like an awful familiar thing to do to a member of the Enid High School faculty, but after all, Coach had said it was all right. Damn if Coach's dick didn't just throb in my hand like something with a mind of its own, and a little drop of pre-cum oozed on out. I took a deep breath. I never sniffed a man's dick and balls before; Coach's had a smell of fresh sweat, but something else too, a smell something like when Daddy took me out hunting: the smell of a stag in rut. Damn if that didn't just set my own dick a-twitching something fierce. I sniffed again, and that ol' smell just got me drunker than moonshine. I leaned forward and ran my tongue around Coach's dickhead and then slid the whole thing down my throat. At that moment, it felt like my mouth was just the most natural place in the world for Coach's dick to be, like they was specially made for each other. Coach gave a mighty groan. "Goddamn, but that feels good!" he gasped, and he commenced to pumping his hips, sliding his dick back and forth between my lips.

Well, we went on like that for a while, me just licking and sucking on Coach's dick. All of a sudden, Coach pulled out. "Lie down, Rufus," he said, his voice urgent. I lied on the linoleum, and Coach sat on my chest. He dropped his balls into my mouth and I began licking them hard, rolling them around with my tongue, putting them both into my mouth and sucking on them. Coach started jerking off with me doing this. That surprised the hell out of me. I never realized men as old as Coach jerked off, too! I remembered how good it felt when Coach pinched my nipples, so I reached up and pinched his too.

"Oh, yeah!" Coach groaned. "That's right, son." He spit in his hand, reached back and began stroking my dick again. Well, damn if that didn't just get me a-squirming and a-twisting all over the linoleum.

Coach twisted around so that he could get at my dick as well, and we both commenced to sucking each other off, Coach doin' pushups above me like it was a pre-practice warm-up. I swear, I can't remember doing anything that was so much fun!

Coach was real good about getting all of my dick down his throat. We rolled around on the floor, and this time I wound up on top. He grabbed hold of my ass with both hands and just pushed me to him. I could feel my big, ol' dick just slide through his mouth and down his throat like butter on a hot skillet. I did my best on Coach's meat, as well. I may not have had as much practice as Coach, but I was having one hell of a good time, and I think that was registering on him. "Yeah, son," he said, laughing as he pumped his meat into my mouth. "If you were only as good at wrestling as you are at sucking cock, we'd be up for the interstate championship by now."

Well, it wasn't much longer before I had to cry out, "Coach, I'm fixing to shoot any second now!" I felt like it was only polite that I inform him.

Coach pulled my dick out of his mouth and yelled "Hang on, Rufus! I'm almost there myself, and we might as well come together!" He pumped his dick a couple of times hard into my mouth, and I could feel his body commence to shuddering. He quickly started sucking my cock again hard, squeezing my balls, and that was what pushed me over the edge. I felt what must have been a couple of quarts of cum just pump on out of my dick into Coach's mouth, just as he squirted his own load down my throat. Well, we just rolled around on the floor, happier than two pigs in shit, with each other's dicks in our mouths, gruntin' and snortin', eatin' cum like we was starving and it was manna from heaven. Then we just collapsed on the floor.

Coach looked over at me and grinned. "And that, Rufus, is how you relieve sexual tension." I didn't say nothing, just squeezed his hand in gratitude.

Well, Coach has made it a particular point of his to keep on helping me out with my sexual tension problem. We meet for sessions just about every day after practice. Coach is a stickler for trying new methods. And I think we've pert near got the problem licked. I ain't never felt so relaxed and easy as I do now. And my wrestling's improved a whole lot, too. But Coach says we got to keep on with the practices, just in case, and how next time he's in Tulsa he's gonna pick up a few "toys" as he puts it, to add a little more spice to our sessions. Hell, I'm game, Coach. Anything for the good of the wrestling team.

# The Grave Digger

The minute I see the landlady's face, I know I'm in for a rough time. I've seen friendlier faces on America's Most Wanted.

"I came to see about the furnished apartment you got for rent," I say.

Her eyes slide up and down my body quicker than a gate man's at a high priced night club. I just got off my shift at my cousin Vinnie's garage and I'm wearing my old, greasy coveralls. Five seconds after we meet, she's got me pigeon-holed good, and I know it isn't under the heading "Likely Prospects."

"First and last month's rent, plus a $200 deposit," she says flatly.

I feel a little flicker of anger flare up at her attitude, but I quench it quick. I'm new in town and need a place bad. I can't hold up much longer sleeping in that rattrap motel, not with what Vinnie's paying me. "Can I see the apartment?" I ask politely.

She gives me another poisonous look and pulls a ring of keys from off a nail by the door. "Follow me," she mutters.

I tag after her as we climb three flights of stairs. By the time we're at the third floor, she's wheezing bad. Maybe that's why she's so pissed off at having to show the place. She staggers over to a door, unlocks it, and opens it, without saying a word. I walk in. The place is a studio, bigger than your average steamer trunk, but not by much. The carpeting is torn to hell and stained, and whatever color the walls were painted originally, I'm sure they hadn't started out as the puke yellow they are now. The apartment has only one thing going for it: it looks affordable.

I walk across the room and look out the window, beyond the fire escape. There's a tiny yard covered with brown, beaten-down grass, and a board fence. On the other side is a cemetery. It's pretty small, just a couple of hills covered with tombstones that seem to come right down to the property line. Near the top of the closer hill, a man is standing knee deep digging a grave, a pile of damp dirt beside him. I wonder about what it'd be like seeing a bunch of graves every time I look out the window. *Hell,* I tell myself, *it's just a park with tombstones and it's better this than facing a noisy city street.*

I turn to the landlady. "What's the rent?" I ask.

She looks at me as if trying to decide whether or not to take me seriously. "$550 a month," she says. "Utilities not included."

"Okay, it's a deal," I say. "I want to move in tonight."

She blinks in surprise. "First and last month's rent, plus a $200 deposit," is all she manages to come up with.

"Yeah, you already told me," I reply. I sit on the bed and write her a check, hoping I can hit Vinnie up for an advance on my pay to make it good. I hand it to her. The mattress I'm sitting on feels like a sack of rocks. "Any chance you can come up with another mattress?" I ask.

"Anything extra will cost you extra," she says. She hands me a set of keys and walks out the door. I can tell we're going to get on like gangbusters. Still, it's a relief to have a place. I can't get out of that damn motel soon enough.

I walk over to the window and look out at the cemetery again. The grave digger is now up to his thighs in the hole. I watch him stab the ground with his shovel, swing his arms high and let the dirt fly. He's giving himself a good workout; his pits are stained with sweat, and his T-shirt is plastered to his back. He pauses for a second and peels his shirt off. His chest is matted with black hair, but that doesn't hide the cut of the pecs or how hard his belly is. His biceps bunch nicely with each thrust of the shovel, and when he twists his torso to toss the dirt, the muscles in his back ripple in a way that tightens my throat up. With his thick black hair and moustache, and his dark skin, he looks like a Greek sailor, or maybe an Italian gondolier. He looks fuckin' beautiful.

A few minutes later he's done with the hole. He grabs his T-shirt, slings his shovel over his shoulder like a soldier's rifle, and strolls up the hill, disappearing over the crest. I stand there staring at the open grave for a few seconds, my hands jammed in my pockets.

I move in that afternoon. It doesn't take long, just going over to the motel and piling my clothes and Jim's weight set into my car. I still think of the weight set as Jim's; it's the only thing of his I've kept. I spend my first night out on the fire escape, smoking cigarettes. The moon's almost full tonight. I know graveyards are supposed to be spooky in moonlight, but I don't feel that way at all. Actually, it's nice and peaceful; the tombstones look like buildings in a small city, and I fantasize about taking a walk among them, like Godzilla on a stroll. Only the open grave makes me feel a little creepy. All I see in it is black, and from the fire escape it looks like the hole could go on down for miles. I imagine dropping into the grave and falling down into the blackness, never hitting bottom. After a while, I climb through the window back into my apartment and go to bed.

When I come home from work the next day, there's a funeral going on. The mourners are gathered around the newly dug grave. The hole doesn't seem bottomless anymore; in fact I can see the top of the coffin lying in it, with what looks like a wreath of roses and lilies on top of it. I open the refrigerator for a beer; that plus my vials of AZT are the only things in there. I really got to do some shopping.

I'm curious about the ceremony. After a couple of minutes I climb out on to the fire escape, a beer in hand, to get a better view. The grave is close enough that I have something of a ringside seat. A hefty lady with legs like a linebacker's stands on the edge of the grave sobbing. A young man (her son?) stands next to her, his hands clasped together in front, his face as stony as the marble angel's on the tomb a few plots away. There's a gust of wind, and a lock of dark hair falls against his forehead. He impatiently brushes it away. His dark suit is cut nicely, showing off the broad shoulders and the tall, lean body to good advantage. As the priest drones on, the young man looks around, obviously bored. For a second our eyes meet. His mouth pulls down into a scowl and he gives me the evil eye. I guess I can't blame him; I must look like some kind of rubbernecker sitting up on the fire escape, watching them all between sips of beer. I look away, but I don't go back inside until after the last of the mourners has walked away.

I strip off my greasy overalls and step into the shower. I feel in a weird mood: restless, edgy, like the idle of my choke is set too high. Maybe it's because of the funeral. The last funeral I went to was Jim's, and some sleeping dogs are threatening to rise now. I stand under the shower head and let the hot water beat against my face, keeping my mind blank. Unexpectedly, the image of the young mourner flashes into my head, and with it a surge of lust as violent and unexpected as a bolt of lightening. My dick swells to full erection and I wrap my soapy hand around it, stroking it slowly. I stop short of shooting. I turn the water off and walk out of the bathroom, toweling myself off. The light from outside is dimming as the late afternoon fades into evening. I flip the wall switch on. I'm aware that I'm buck naked in a room with no curtains, but who's out there to see me—the stiffs in their graves?

I put the towel behind my back and rub, feeling my still half-hard dick swing heavily from side to side. *When's the last time I got laid?* I think. *Too long. I got to meet some guys in this town, get a sex life going for myself again. Maybe tonight I'll hit a couple of bars and see if I get lucky.*

A movement outside in the cemetery catches my eye. It's the grave digger, filling in the grave. I wrap the towel around my waist and walk up to the window to watch. He stands on the edge of the hole, shoveling the dirt in with quick, easy swings of his arms. With the setting of the sun, the day has cooled down; he's got a red flannel shirt on this time, but it's unbuttoned, and I grab the opportunity to check out his fine body again. I take in the hairy chest, the torn, mud-smeared jeans, the muscular forearms that extend down from the rolled-up sleeves, and my dick makes a little tent against the terry-cloth of my towel. *Where is all this horniness coming from?* I wonder. Yesterday the grave digger reminded me of an Italian gondolier. Today, the impression is darker, even a little menacing. Watching him toss the dirt inside the hole, I can't imagine him doing any other line of work than what he's doing now: burying bodies.

He puts the shovel down to rest for a while, and when he raises his head, our eyes meet. We look at each other for a few beats; in the dimming light it's impossible to read his expression. Eventually, he goes back to his shovel and continues filling in the grave. But a few seconds later he looks back up at me again. I stand there without moving, my left arm raised and pressed against the side of the window, my weight leaning against it. He goes on shoveling, but always, every few seconds, he raises his head and glances up at me. I feel my heart pounding. After a few more minutes, the hole is filled and he tamps the dirt down with the blade of his shovel. He looks back at me one last time and then disappears beyond the crest of the hill.

*That night I dream I'm in a coffin that must be made of glass, because I can see through it. I'm in a grave, surrounded by high banks of dirt. A figure stands at the edge of the hole, looking down at me. It's the mourner I saw yesterday; except for a black armband around his left bicep, he's naked. At first his face is as expressionless as it was at yesterday's funeral, but when he sees me staring at him, his lips curve up into an easy smile. He wraps his hand around his dick and starts jerking off with slow, regular strokes.*

*The grave digger walks up to the other side of the grave, equally naked. His dick juts straight out, and his balls hang loose and heavy, just above the crack of his ass. I've never seen a naked male body from this perspective before, and it excites the hell out of me. He carries his shovel over his shoulder in his usual way. Like the mourner, he starts stroking his dickmeat, and his balls swing in tempo to his beating off. The two of them lean over the grave and kiss, their mouths fused together in a long, wet liplock. I stare up at the two torsos bent over me, struck by the contrast: the mourner's smooth, pale body against the grave digger's dark hairiness. As if on cue, they both quicken the speed of their strokes. Their bodies are soaked with sweat; drops of it splash against the top of my coffin. After a while, the mourner's body begins to shudder. He throws back his head and cries out, as he squirts a load into the grave. The grave digger is soon doing the same, his knees buckled and his hairy chest heaving. He roars like a bull in pain. The jizz from both men comes splattering down on top of my coffin in thick, spermy gobs. The grave digger shakes the last few drops out of his dick and winks at the mourner. He shifts his shovel to both hands and, with slow, precise thrusts, begins filling in the grave. In a matter of seconds, I'm completely buried.*

I wake up with my heart hammering. After a while, when it's obvious I'm not going to fall back to sleep, I get up and walk around the room. Looking out the window, I can just barely make out the new grave in the moonlight. I feel my belly turn over. I spend the next couple of hours working out at Jim's weight set so hard that by the time I finally crawl back to bed, I can barely lift my arms.

The next day, after I get home from work, I see that the grave digger is working on a new hole. He looks up immediately as I approach the window. I get the feeling he's been waiting for me. Once again, I feel my throat constrict. I move away from the window, out of his line of sight. I try to think about the best way of handling this. Eventually I go into the kitchen and get a couple of beers from the refrigerator. I climb out onto the fire escape. The grave digger is staring at me without any pretense of subtlety.

"Howdy," I call out to him.

The grave digger leans on his shovel. "Hi," he calls back in a deep baritone. Just like the first time I saw him, he's shirtless, and his muscular torso is streaked with sweat and dirt.

I hold a can of beer out to him. "You look thirsty. Wanna beer?"

He keeps looking at me but says nothing for a couple of beats. Finally he grins, and the white of his teeth flashes in sharp contrast against his dark face. "Sure," he calls.

"Come down by the fence," I shout.

The grave digger drops his shovel and descends the small hill. When he's almost at the bottom, I pull my arm back and toss the beer with a snap. The can arcs through the air, glinting in the light of the sun, and just clears the fence. The grave digger runs down the rest of the hill and catches it skillfully. He pulls back the tab, and a spray of foam spews out onto his face and torso. We both laugh. He toasts me with the can and chugs down what's left. I watch as the beer foam drips through his chest hairs and runs down onto his belly. When he's done, he tosses the can and climbs back up the hill. He continues with his digging, but a minute doesn't go by without his looking up at me. I lean against the wall of the building, warmed from the afternoon sun, and watch him with a deceptive laziness. After about half an hour he's done. He slings his shovel over his shoulder, but before he walks off, he turns again toward me. "What's your name?" he calls out to me.

"Tim," I call back.

"I'll come back later tonight. Around ten. If you want it, meet me here." He climbs to the top of the hill and disappears over the edge.

I can't quite believe that I heard him right. I play the scene back in my mind. *If you want it, meet me here.* Is that really the proposition that it sounds like? I tell myself that there's no way I'm going to be lurking in a graveyard in the dark, like some damn ghoul. But for the rest of the evening I can't take my eyes off the window for more than a couple of minutes. A few minutes before ten I'm clambering down the fire escape and over the board wall as if I'd been planning this all along.

There's a cloud hiding the moon, and I have to grope my way between the tombstones. It's a warm night tonight, with a slight breeze. I can hear the sounds of traffic off in the distance, but here it's quiet and still. With what light there is, the marble tombstones gleam faintly. After a while, I sit on a granite headstone adjacent to the open grave and wait. I close my eyes and breathe deeply, trying to calm down.

"Hello, Tim," a voice says behind me. I jump up, with a sharp intake of breath. The gravedigger steps out of the shadow of a cypress tree.

"Jeez," I say. "How long have you been standing there?"

The grave digger walks up to me. "Not long." He smiles. "I didn't know if you'd make it or not."

His smile isn't altogether reassuring. There's something more than a little wolfish about it. "I didn't know either," I say. "It just sort of happened." I give a nervous laugh. "I wasn't sure whether or not you'd come either."

The cloud covering the moon passes away, and the grave digger's face is suddenly bathed in light. His smile broadens and his teeth gleam. "Oh, I'm going to come tonight," he says. "You can bet your life on it." He pulls me over to him and plants his mouth on mine. His tongue works its way into my mouth and thrusts deep inside. I suck on it greedily, my hands slipping under his T-shirt and across the bare skin of his torso. I pinch his nipples hard, and he gives out a long, trailing groan. He cups my ass with his hands and pulls my body against his. We grind our torsos together, dry fucking each other with slow, circular thrusts of our hips. I can feel the hardness of his dick against the rough fabric of his jeans.

He raises his arms as I peel his shirt off, and I get a whiff of fresh sweat. I bury my face in the nearest pit, inhaling deeply. The acrid/sweet smell fills my head, and I slide my tongue down his torso, till my mouth engulfs his left nipple. I run my tongue over it, feeling it harden. Taking it between my teeth I nip it gently. He gives out a long sigh, just shy of a groan. I trail my tongue across the hairs of his chest and work over the right nipple as well. His hands slide down my back and slip under my jeans. I feel the calluses of his palms rub roughly against the skin of my ass.

I step into the open grave so that my face is level with his crotch. I run my tongue across the front of his jeans, tasting the dried mud and grit accumulated from the day's digging. I can feel his dick push up against the fabric, and I work my mouth against it, wetting the cloth with my saliva. He unbuckles his belt; I open his fly and pull his jeans down around his ankles. His dick springs out at full attention. It gleams in the moonlight, the head red and flared. The balls hang low and fleshly, swollen like ripe fruit. I bury my face in them and inhale deeply, breathing in their sharp, musky odor.

I wrap my hand around the grave digger's cock and squeeze gently. A spermy pearl oozes out and I lap it up. The warmth of his dick spreads across my palm. I run my tongue along the shaft teasingly, flicking it lightly as my hands continue to move across his torso. I take his dick into my mouth and nibble my lips down its length. His body trembles beneath my fingertips, and his breath takes on a harsh, rasping quality, like some large animal struggling.

He places his hands alongside my head and begins pumping his hips. I twist my head from side to side to increase the sensation of my lips sliding along his dick, and he groans his appreciation. With both hands, I grab his ass cheeks and squeeze. I can feel them clench and relax with each thrust of his dick down my throat.

I work a finger into the crack of his ass and rub it against his bung hole. I look up at his face, washed in moonlight, as I slowly penetrate his sphincter with my index finger. He returns my gaze with feverish eyes, and another groan escapes from his open mouth. I work my finger up his ass to the third knuckle and begin finger-fucking him in a slow, steady tempo that matches the way he fucks my mouth. His legs tremble against my body like trees in a stiff wind.

He pulls his dick out of my mouth. "Get naked," he orders, his voice urgent. I kick off my shoes and pull off my shirt and pants. "The socks, too," he says. "I don't want any clothes on you." I pull them off too. There's a gust of breeze and I shiver slightly. The grave digger stands naked above me, legs apart, his dick jutting sharply over me. Last night's dream comes back to me with a sudden vividness. He squats down until his nut sac dangles above my face. "Eat my balls," he orders.

I place my mouth on them and kiss them lightly, the tiny hairs tickling my face. I bathe his nuts with my tongue, and then open my mouth wide, sucking them in. I reach up and run my hands over his torso. He slaps my face with his dick with a sharp *thwack* and then rubs it over my cheeks, my eyes, my nose.

He pulls away and steps into the grave with me. He wraps his arms around me tight and lowers me onto my back. As if in a trance, I let him determine the actions. Grabbing my jeans, he stuffs them behind my head to make a rough pillow, and then stretches out full on top of me, his mouth planted on mine. His body writhes against me with a slow, heavy sensuality. I raise my arm and accidentally brush against the side of the grave. Dirt sprinkles my face and the back of his head.

He lifts his hips and his dick begins poking in the crack of my ass. "Wait a second," I whisper. I reach behind me and fish out a condom from my jeans pocket. He watches silently as I roll it down the length of his shaft. He slicks his dick up with spit and then with excruciating slowness impales my ass. I gasp and close my eyes, feeling the fullness of his dick slide into me.

He begins to pump his hips, fucking me in a grinding, hypnotic rhythm that is as stately as a waltz. Each thrust drives me deeper into the dirt; I can feel the gravel and gritty mud rake my back, work their way up into the crack of my ass. His body presses down on me like all the weight of the world, and his hot breath rasps across my face. The sides of the grave seem to close in on me and I'm suddenly swept up by a wave of claustrophobia. I look up and see the full moon caught in the branches of the cypress tree. I breathe deep and focus on the moon. Eventually the panic passes. The grave digger has his strong arms wrapped around me as he plows my ass, and I slide into the warmth of his embrace. I thrust my hips up and match the rhythm of his strokes. He groans his gratitude, and my dick throbs with the knowledge of the pleasure I'm giving him.

The grave digger's groans become louder, more ragged. Little whimpers escape from him. I reach down and feel his balls; they're pulled up tight against his body, ready to shoot. He pumps his hips faster now, with a more driving force and I match him thrust for thrust. I reach up and twist his nipples hard and his body shudders convulsively. He raises his head and bellows. I can feel his throbbing dick squirt out load after load of jizz into the condom up my ass. I pull him down and kiss him hard, biting his lips. As our bodies rock together against the grave walls, dirt rains down on us. I'm stroking my own dick furiously and it's just seconds later before my own load pulses out of me, gushing onto my belly. The grave digger gives one last, trailing groan and then collapses on me. We lay there in the grave for God knows how long. The moon has passed out of sight, beyond the grave walls, and everything is dark.

The grave digger eventually stirs and rises to his feet. He climbs out of the grave and squats down, offering me his hand. I take it, and he pulls me out back into the night air. A breeze blows through, and I shiver. "Put your clothes back on," he says softly. "It's getting cold."

We dress in silence. When we're done, he pulls me to him and kisses me again. "I'll be back" he murmurs. "This is just a taste of things to come."

"I know," I whisper.

He turns and walks away and after a few steps disappears behind the hill. I stand there alone in the cemetery and breathe in the night air, grateful for the open space around me. The breeze blows again, brisker this time, and I shiver once more. I climb over the board fence and up the fire escape back to the warmth and security of my apartment. In bed I think about the next time, when I'll feel the grave digger's callused hands on my body again, his hot breath on my face. I close my eyes and sleep the sleep of the dead.

# Chef's Surprise

You know that old Shangri-Las rock and roll song, "Leader of the Pack", about dating a guy from the wrong side of the tracks? All that fuckin' class warfare and teenage angst? That's what my thing with Luigi was: a bad rock and roll song.

I knew Luigi from high school, back when I was taking the college prep courses while Luigi was in auto shop. I'd see him out in the school-yard, smoking with the rest of the hoods, looking like an extra from "Grease", the slicked back, blue-black hair, the cigarette pack rolled in the sleeve of his grimy T-shirt, a smart-ass sneer plastered on his face.

Of course, I had a total hard-on for the guy. He was in my gym class, the only class we shared, and the looks I sneaked at Luigi naked in the showers gave me all the fodder I needed for my nightly jack-off sessions. All I had to do as I lay in bed, pumping my fist, was conjure up the image of Luigi soaping himself, the lather washing down his tightly muscled body, over his pubes and his thick, meaty dick, and I was repainting my bedroom ceiling with my load.

Jump ahead a few years. I'm on spring break, bored and horny, and pissed off at my dad for all the shit he's been giving me about my grades at college. I drive out to Big Sally's, a beat up bar with a bad (read "gay") reputation, a few miles out of town. The first person I see when I walk in is Luigi; I recognize him instantly. He's standing by the cigarette machine, pulling on a beer and looking sexier than anyone has a right to in his tight black chinos and wife beater shirt. The tattoo on his left bicep is new: a snarling bulldog with *U.S.M.C.* written underneath. *What the hell is Luigi doing* here? is my first thought. *Damn, that fucker's hotter than ever!* is my second.

I go to the cigarette machine and buy a pack of Marlboros. Luigi glances over toward me, his expression bored. "Hey, Luigi," I say.

"Hey, Roy," Luigi says.

*At least he remembers me,* I think. "It's been a while," I say. "Two, three years, maybe?"

"I guess." Luigi takes a long pull from his beer, finishing it. I watch how his bicep curves as he brings the bottle to his mouth. Luigi has packed on some muscle since high school. His head is like a stallion's, the neck muscular, the hair thick, black and glossy. *Fuck, he looks good,* I think.

"I'm going to get a beer," I say. "You want a refill?"

Luigi turns his head and for the first time, he really looks at me. His gaze sweeps down my body and then back to my face again, his eyes shrewd. He lets a couple of beats go by. "Yeah," he says. "Sure."

We talk the meaningless bullshit two guys talk who hardly know each other and have nothing in common. I tell Luigi I'm going to University of Virginia, majoring in business. Luigi is vague about what he's been doing. I point to the bulldog tattoo and ask what that's all about.

"I hitched up with the Marines right after high school," Luigi says.

"Oh, yeah? How did that turn out?"

"I got kicked out," Luigi says, his voice flat. I don't say anything, but Luigi catches the inquisitive look I shoot him. He shrugs impatiently. "I don't want to talk about it," he says.

There's an uncomfortable silence. We start talking about the kids we knew in high school and where they are now, a subject that dies quickly since we had no friends in common. We fall into silence again and just stand there listening to the music from the juke box, drinking our beers. The place is a morgue: some guys shooting pool in the back, a couple of relics playing liar's dice at the bar. I think about going home.

"I've got some weed in the glove compartment of my van," Luigi says. "In case you're interested."

"Sure," I say.

We share a couple of joints while listening to the Red Hot Chili Peppers on Luigi's tape deck. The night is warm and the windows are rolled down. We don't say anything. Luigi's wedged in the corner made by the front seat and the door. Every time I glance at him, he's got his eyes trained on me. I've got enough of a buzz on to get my marijuana paranoia kicked into high gear. "Why are you looking at me like that?" I finally blurt out.

Luigi doesn't say anything at first. He takes another hit on the joint, his dark eyes burning holes in me. I can hear the crickets chirping in the weeds outside. "You feel like sucking my cock?" he finally asks, as he hands the joint back to me.

I take another toke and flick the butt out the window. "Okay," I say.

Sucking Luigi's dick isn't anything like my high school jack-off fantasies. Luigi doesn't just lie there and let me blow him, he aggressively fucks my face. He straddles my torso, holding my head clamped tight between his hands, and thrusts his dick in and out of my mouth with punishing force, his balls slapping against my chin. "Yeah, college boy," he growls. "Take it, choke on it. That's right, rich kid." We lock our eyes together the whole time. Even when he comes, Luigi's dark eyes burn into mine, watching me intently as his dick throbs in my mouth and his load splatters against the back of my throat. He leans back, propping himself on his elbows, as I suck on his fleshy balls and get my own nut off.

Afterwards, Luigi lights up another joint, and we smoke it, watching the fireflies blink on and off in the warm night. I turn toward him. "What was that 'college boy' 'rich kid' stuff all about?" I ask.

Luigi shrugs. "Just my way of getting off," he says.

We get together the next night. This time Luigi fucks me in his van, wrapping his arms tight around me, churning his hips as his dick thrusts in and out of my ass. Like the night before, his eyes bore into mine, not searching for anything, but more like pinning me down like an insect in a specimen tray. Luigi has beautiful eyes, dark and liquid, but they give nothing away. He comes without making a sound, squirting his load in the condom up my ass, all the time holding my gaze.

We see each other every night for the rest of my break. An hour after I'm on the train headed back to school, I start missing him like an amputated limb.

So now I've got this *thing* with Luigi. It's so fucked. I call him from school, he tells me he's fuckin' some waitress from Denny's, I call him a lying sack of shit and slam the phone down and then go through hell until I see him at the next school break. I know nothing about Luigi's life outside of our times together. He doesn't even tell me how he supports himself. Basically, all we do is fuck. We've moved up to fucking in the no-tell motel behind the railroad tracks, Luigi dropping quarters in the vibrating bed and plowing my ass with deep, hard thrusts as the bed shimmies and shakes like a prop from *The Exorcist*. "Do you love me, baby?" I ask, as Luigi rips through my ass like a tornado slamming into a trailer park, and he just laughs. "Fuck no," he says. "You're just some piece of tail I know."

In July, my folks give me a used MG sports car for my twenty-first birthday. It's six years old, the upholstery's torn, and I have to pay for the insurance out of my own pocket, but that doesn't stop Luigi from making sneering comments about "the spoiled rich kid." But he eyes the car with a cold lust that gives me twinges of jealousy. Sometimes I let him drive it, with me sitting in the passenger seat beside him, Luigi tearing down the country roads, working the stick shift like this was what he was born for. His face takes on this blissed-out look; it's the only time I've actually seen Luigi look *happy*, and when he finally has to give the keys back to me, he looks at me with an expression approaching hate.

At the end of the summer Luigi tells me that he's going back to pussy. "I'm tired of fags," he says, looking at me with half-lidded eyes.

"Fine," I say. " 'Cause I'm tired of dead-end greaseballs." That doesn't stop us from fucking one last time in that shit-hole motel, me squirting my load while tears are running down my face. Luigi gets out of bed, gets dressed and walks out the door without looking back or saying goodbye. I mean, how fuckin' clichéd can you get? Like I said, it's all just bad rock 'n roll.

My first days back at school are consumed with revenge fantasies. I want to kill the motherfucker, but not before I've hurt him so bad he's begging me to finish him off. After a while, hating Luigi gets too exhausting, and I think of him less and less. But whenever I do, the rage flares up with the same intensity as before, like a bad tooth suddenly exposed to cold.

On my second day of Christmas break, Dad takes me out to his country club for lunch. Just the two of us, some kind of "guy thing", I guess. There's a dress code, and I put on a jacket and tie. The dining area is a wide, high-ceilinged room that overlooks the golf course, now covered in snow. We get a table by the window. I look up from the menu, and to my astonishment, Luigi is standing next to the table. It takes a second before I notice the apron and white shirt. *I'll be damned!* I think. *He's a busboy here!*

The big mystery of how Luigi supports himself is finally solved. The little man in my head that controls my personality turns the dial hard to "shit."

I pick up my glass and look at it. "This is dirty," I say. "Could I have a clean glass, please?" Luigi's face is expressionless as he takes the glass and comes back moments later with another one. I pull the same stunt with the silverware. Luigi glares at me, and I give him back my best *fuck you* look.

The waiter comes, and Dad and I both order the roast chicken dish. I can see the kitchen door from where I sit, and a few minutes later I see Luigi come out with a tray of food. This is *not* a busboy's job, and right away I get suspicious. Instead of bringing the food to the dining hall, Luigi goes into the club's men's room. *What the fuck!?* I think. A few minutes Luigi comes out and places the plates on our table.

"What's that?" Dad asks, looking down on my plate. I look down as well. Something white and sticky is smeared all over my chicken. It takes a couple of seconds before I realize that Luigi has just jacked off on my food.

"It's a new sauce the chef is trying out," Luigi says, his face deadpan. "The Chef's Surprise."

Dad looks at his plate. "How come I didn't get any?" he asks.

Luigi regards him blandly. "There was only enough left for one more order," he says. He walks away.

I look at Luigi's spunk splattered all over my chicken. *That motherfucker!* I think.

"Let me have a bite," Dad says. I can tell he's put off that he didn't get any of the "Chef's Surprise."

I'm not about to watch my father eat my ex-boyfriend's spunk. "I don't think so," I say. I pick up my knife and fork and start eating the chicken, just to keep it away from him.

"I'm just talking about one bite," Dad says.

"You wouldn't like it," I say, stuffing more jizz-covered chicken in my mouth. "Besides, I thought you were trying to keep your chloresterol intake down."

Dad gives me a hard look. "Hey, who made you my guardian?" He tries to sound like he's joking, but I can tell he's pissed. Off on the other side of the room, Luigi's smirking at me. He disappears into the kitchen.

Every bite I take of Luigi's "Chef's Surprise" pushes me into greater rage. I don't dare leave any of it on my plate in case Dad makes another bid for it. Dad tries to make conversation, but I'm too pissed to do more than give an occasional grunt in reply. Later, when Dad and I are out in the front of the club, and the valet has pulled the car up, I clear my throat. "Listen," I say. "There's some business I've got to take care of here. I'll just catch a cab home later."

Dad gives me an exasperated look. "Whatever, Roy," he says, his voice tinged with disgust. He climbs into the car and drives off without another look at me. I stand at the club entrance, gripping and ungripping my fists, obsessing on Luigi. *I'm going to kill that motherfucker*, I think. I turn and stalk back into the club, through the dining hall, into the kitchen. Cooks and waiters and busboys look at me curiously as I scan the room. I don't see Luigi anywhere. I push through outside the kitchen's back door.

I find Luigi out back, standing on a ledge overlooking an open dumpster, emptying a garbage can. His back is to me. I sneak up onto the ledge behind him and tap him on the shoulder. Luigi turns, and I slug him in the face as hard as I can. Luigi drops the garbage can, which comes crashing down, and he staggers and falls into the dumpster. I jump in after him, fists flying. We slug it out, snarling, on a bed of potato peels, egg shells and coffee grounds. The bin offers little purchase room, and we can do little more than wrestle and claw at each other, spitting out curses.

Luigi pivots on tops of me and pins my arms down. There's this moment where we glare at each other, panting. Without warning, Luigi plants his mouth on mine. There's a couple of beats where I'm too startled to do anything, but then I kiss him back, thrusting my tongue deep into his mouth. With our mouths still fused together, Luigi lets go of my arms and starts tearing my clothes off. I pull at his belt buckle, his shirt buttons, and in a couple of minutes we're both naked. We roll around in the garbage, kissing and stroking. Luigi lifts my arm and buries his face in my armpit. I reach down and twist his nipple viciously. Luigi lifts his head and stares at me. His eyes gleam fiercely. He plants his mouth on mine again, reaches down and wraps his hand around my hard dick and strokes it.

"Pivot around," I gasp, and Luigi does so, swinging his dick next to my face. I bury my face in Luigi's crotch, his dick full down my throat, his balls pressed hard against my nose. I inhale deeply, and even surrounded by the stench of the garbage, I can catch that special ripe man-smell of Luigi's ball flesh.

Luigi's tonguing my balls, and then he burrows down deeper and starts eating my ass out. I feel his wet tongue push against my asshole, and I go fuckin' apeshit, bucking and heaving my body, Luigi's dick still deep down my throat.

Luigi comes up for air, panting. "I'm going to pound your ass into raw meat," he growls.

"Talk is cheap," I growl back.

Luigi picks up his jeans and fumbles a condom package out of the pocket. He rolls the rubber down his hard cock, grabs my ankles and pulls me toward him. I push my hips up, exposing my asshole to him. Luigi slicks up his cock with spit and slowly skewers me. I push my head back onto a bed of rotting lettuce and groan as Luigi drives his dick hard up my ass. Luigi holds that pose for a beat, his face inches above mine, our eyes locked, and then he starts pumping his hips. He slams my ass hard, driving his cock in and out of me like a fuckin' diesel piston. I wrap my hand around the back of his neck and pull his mouth down on mine. We roll around in the garbage, our bodies straining together, slippery with sweat and slime, Luigi plowing my ass, me stroking my dick. I reach down and tug on Luigi's balls, and Luigi grunts his appreciation. He grinds his hips against me, rotating them, driving his dick even deeper inside, churning my ass with it. I squeeze my ass muscles tight and push up against him. Luigi gives a long, trailing groan. He pulls his dick out until the head is just pushing against my asshole and then thrusts full in. I squeeze again as I push my hips up to meet him.

"Ah, shit," Luigi gasps. "I'm going to pop!"

He pulls out and tears the condom off. His load arcs across space and slams onto my face. I open my lips wide to receive it, the white rain of spunk splattering my eyes and cheeks and into my mouth. A couple of quick strokes are enough to push me over the edge, and my groans mingle with Luigi's, as I thrust my hips up and shoot. Luigi takes my cock in his mouth and sucks hard, swallowing the jizz that my cock pumps down his throat. We thrash together in the bin, our bodies spasming as our loads pump out. Luigi's body gives a final shake, and he collapses on top of me. We lay like that for what seems like a long time, Luigi stretched out full length on me, his body pressing against mine. He finally pushes himself up.

"Fuck," he says. "It stinks in here."

We climb out of the bin, retrieving our reeking clothes. I don't know how Luigi's going to explain the state of his busboy's uniform to the club manager, and as for me, it's going to be a smelly ride in the cab back home. Without the warmth of skin-on-skin and rotting garbage, I feel the December cold slice through me. We stand by the dumpster, looking at each other, our breaths fogging the air. It's a moment that could go in any direction. Even smeared with garbage, Luigi is a sexy, hot-looking fucker. My asshole still throbs from the pounding he gave it, and it feels empty without Luigi's dick crammed up it. I start wondering if maybe we *could* patch things up. . . .

My gut immediately clenches at the thought. *Fuck no!* I think. *Enough is enough!*

I hold out my hand. "So long, Luigi," I say.

Luigi looks at my hand with flat, hard eyes. After a couple of beats he takes it and shakes. "Yeah," he says. "See you around." He turns and goes back into the kitchen, lugging the empty garbage can behind him. I watch until the metal door closes behind him and then head out to the front of the club where I can get somebody to call me a cab. It's beginning to snow again, and through the dining room window I can see the flakes drift down onto the empty field outside.

# Gamblers

There's an empty seat at the blackjack table where Sam's dealing, and I quickly slide into it. I push two five-dollar chips in front of me as he deals out the cards. Sam nods at me and smiles. "Hello, Al," he says, in his friendly baritone. "Nice to see you again."

"Hi, Sam," I say. "Thanks. It's good to be back." This is the casino that feels most like home for me on my frequent trips to Reno, and by now I've got a nodding acquaintance with just about all of the staff. Sam's my favorite dealer, big-boned and easy-going, with a handy smile that flashes white in his tanned face.

I glance around quickly at my table mates: a middle-aged couple with matching aloha shirts, a leather faced cowboy, an old woman with gimlet eyes and a permanently bitter mouth, and a kid with a Grateful Dead T-shirt and torn, faded Levis.

Sam's done dealing, and my face card is the queen of diamonds. I sneak a look at my down card. Two of clubs. Damn.

"Hit me," I say, and Sam hits me with a nine of hearts. Things are looking up. "I'll stick," I say. Sam goes around the table, ending with the kid, who stays with what he has. Sam flips over his cards. Two jacks.

"Fuck!" the kid mutters.

"Hey, watch the language," Sam says, fixing him with a look as he takes the kid's chips.

The kid just shrugs in disgust. I give him a closer look. He's young, barely out of his teens, and he looks like a punk: black hair greased and combed back, a surly, baby face, eyes dark and contemptuous. The torso under his tight shirt is lean and muscled, and his bicep curls to a nice pump when he raises his cigarette to his mouth. I catch Sam's eye, nod toward the kid and raise an eyebrow. Sam rolls his eyes and shakes his head. *The kid's bad news* is his silent message.

The kid takes what's left of his chips and pushes them in front of him. "Okay," he says. "Enough dicking around. I'm going for broke." I put out my standard ten dollar bet.

Sam deals the cards again. He deals himself an ace and a queen. "Blackjack," he says.

The kid slaps his hand on the table. "Motherfuck!" he snarls.

"I warned you about the language," Sam says. "Keep it up, and you're going to have to leave the table."

The kid gives a bitter laugh. "Big fuckin' deal. I'm broke anyway." He stands up, and his chair tips over and crashes to the floor. He stalks away from the table and gets lost among the slots.

The old woman shakes her head. "Loser," she mutters. The others at the table nod in agreement. Still, I can't help feeling a little sorry for the kid. Some folks just don't know when to quit.

Later that night, out in the parking lot, I notice an old, beat up Pinto parked next to my car, badly dinged and mottled with primer paint. I glance inside it as I unlock my door. The kid's curled up in the back, asleep. *Jesus Christ,* I think, shaking my head. I climb into my car and drive off.

Sunday morning, I check out of my hotel and head for home. I did all right this weekend, winning enough to cover my expenses and even walk away with a hundred or so extra dollars. As I approach the Highway 80 on-ramp, I notice a hitchhiker standing at the side with his thumb out. It's the kid who lost at Sam's table.

I don't normally pick up hitchhikers, but, I dunno, maybe because I have a little history with the kid I make an impulse decision and pull over. He grabs his duffel bag and hops in.

"Thanks, man," he says.

"Where you headed?" I ask.

"Bakersfield."

"I'm going to Modesto. That'll get you part of the way at least."

"Cool."

We make the introductions, and the kid tells me his name is Billy. We drive down the highway in silence for a couple of minutes. "What happened to your Pinto?" I finally ask.

Billy shoots me a sharp glance. "How did you . . . ?"

"I saw you asleep in it a couple of nights ago in the casino parking lot."

"Oh," he says. He looks out his window and then back at me. "I sold it at a used car lot." He snorted. "The sonovabitch only gave me a couple hundred bucks for it."

*Which you pissed away at the blackjack tables,* I think. It's not even worth asking him about. He's looking out the window, and I sneak a glance at him. I take in the quarter profile he's offering me: the left jawline, the tip of his nose, the young, strong neck. . . . He turns suddenly to face me, and I glance away.

We travel down the highway for a long time without saying anything. After a while, Billy slouches down into his seat and closes his eyes. He starts snoring lightly. I look at him again. He's a handsome kid, his face boyish but just beginning to take on the shape of a man's. His mouth, half open now, is wide and sensual. My eyes slide down his tight, muscular torso and settle on the bulge beneath the crotch of his tattered jeans. I glance back at his face again and see his eyes staring back, fixing me with a sharp, knowing look. Neither of us says anything as I direct my eyes back to the road.

Traffic comes to a dead halt just outside of Elk Grove. The highway's a fuckin' parking lot, nothing but cars, bumper to bumper, for as far as the eye can see. I turn on the radio and find a traffic report, which tells us there's a five car pile-up just north of Stockton that has traffic backed up for twenty miles. After two hours, we creep no further than half a mile. "Screw this," I say. "I'm going to get a motel room, and finish this trip tomorrow." Billy says nothing.

We inch up to the next exit and pull off the highway. There's a Holiday Inn just down the road, and I pull into the parking lot. The sun is beginning to set, and the shadows from the motel buildings fall across the asphalt paving. I turn off the ignition and turn toward Billy. "Okay, Billy," I say. "This is where we part company."

Billy just looks at me. "Can I sleep in the back of your car?"

"I don't think that's good idea," I say. "I'm sorry." Billy doesn't say anything. I don't bother asking if he's got money for a room. "You need to get out, now, Billy," I say, putting an edge to my voice. Billy still doesn't say anything. "Billy . . ." I say.

Billy turns to me. "I got nowhere to go, man," he says.

I give Billy a long, level look. "All right," I finally say. "Just don't scuff up the upholstery with your shoes, okay?"

"Sure," Billy says. "No problem."

I check in and secure a room. I grab dinner in the motel restaurant, deliberately pushing Billy out of my mind. As I walk back to my room, I notice how cold the night has gotten. Once inside, I stretch out on the double bed and turn on the TV. After about an hour of this, I turn it off. *Fuck*, I think savagely. I put on my coat and walk out to the parking lot. There's a pole fixture nearby, and by its light I can see Billy curled up in the back seat.

I open the door, and Billy raises his head and looks at me. "Okay," I snap. "There's a couch in my room. You can sleep there. Or the floor, if you prefer."

Billy's face is in shadow, so I can't see his expression. "Just let me get my duffle bag," he says.

Inside, the first thing Billy does is head for the bathroom. "I'm going to take a shower, okay?" he says.

"Fine," I say. He's probably long overdue. God knows when he's last slept in an actual room with a bath.

I lie back in my bed and go back to watching the television, half-listening to the hiss of the shower. After a few minutes, Billy comes out, a towel wrapped around his waist. He sits in a chair that faces the bed, grinning. "I fuckin' needed that," he says.

I grunt something, trying not to stare at how the muscles of his torso are cut, the stomach lean and chiseled. I turn my attention back to the television, but I keep sneaking glances in Billy's direction. Billy returns my stare calmly. Each time I look at him, his legs are spread a little wider, until I finally get to see that he's got half a hard-on flopped against his thigh. My dick is straining against the fabric of my slacks like there's hell to pay.

I give Billy a hard stare. He smiles. His dick is fully stiff now. "Look," I say. "You don't have to do this. I wasn't attaching any strings when I said you could sleep here."

Billy undoes his towel and lets it fall beside him. He's slouching in the chair, and his stiff dick lolls lazily against his belly. It's a beauty, fat and veined, the head a red, shiny knob. He twitches it, and gives me a sly look to gauge my reaction. "I'm not doing anything I don't want to," he says. His balls hang heavily between his legs, furred by a dusting of fine, dark hairs. I imagine them slapping against my chin as he fucks my mouth.

"Christ," I mutter. I climb out of the bed and bury my face in his red, wrinkled sac, tonguing it, inhaling deeply. In spite of Billy's shower, his balls have a faint, musky scent to them. I open my mouth and suck them inside, rolling my tongue over them. "Yeah," Billy murmurs. "That's right." I look up and lock eyes with him, his ball sac still in my mouth. Billy's mouth curls up into a slow grin. "Why don't you get naked, Al?" he says.

"Yeah," I say, standing up. "Good idea." I unbutton my shirt while Billy unbuckles my belt and pulls my zipper down. My slacks slither down to my ankles, and with a quick yank, Billy tugs down my boxers. My dick springs up and sways heavily from side to side.

Billy looks up at me, grinning. "Jesus, Al," he says. "What a big dick you have!"

"Who the fuck are you?" I ask. "Little Red Riding Hood?" Billy laughs. I pull him to his feet, and we kiss, our bodies squirming together, flesh on flesh. Billy's tongue snakes into my mouth as he grinds his hips against me. I wrap my arms around him in a bear hug and topple us onto the bed.

We wrestle on top of the bedspread, our mouths fused together. "Scoot up my chest," I say, "and drop those balls in my mouth."

"Sure, Al," Billy says. He straddles my torso, his dick and balls looming above my face. I crane my neck and start washing his low-hangers with my tongue. I suck the meaty, red pouch into my mouth, and reach up and tweak Billy's nipples.

"Yeah, that's right," Billy breathes. "Squeeze them hard." I lock my gaze with Billy's as I roll my tongue around his balls and give his nipples an extra twist. Billy's eyes burn into mine with the look of a man with a serious nut to bust. He rubs his cock over my face, smearing my cheeks with pre-cum, and then shifts his position and pokes the fleshy knob against my lips. I open my mouth, and Billy slides his cock full in until his balls are pressing against my chin and my nose is buried in his crinkly pubes. He holds that position for a few beats. "You like that, Al?" he croons. "You like having your mouth stuffed with dick?"

I grunt my assent. Billy begins pumping his hips, fucking my face with slow, measured thrusts. He reaches behind and wraps his hand around my dick. "You got such a nice, fat dick, Al," he says. "I'm just going to have to suck it for a while." He pivots around. I feel his mouth slide down my shaft, and I groan appreciatively, my mouth still filled with his dick. We fuck face and suck dick, our bodies pressed tightly together. I slide my hand down Billy's back, across the smooth, tight mound of his ass, and into his ass crack. I find his asshole and massage it. Billy gives a muffled groan, and I push in, working my finger up his chute knuckle by knuckle.

Billy takes my dick out of his mouth. "Jesus," he groans.

"You want me to stop?" I ask.

"Fuck no!" he says.

I slide my finger in and out of his hole. Billy's got a spit-slicked hand wrapped around my dick and is jacking me with quick, urgent strokes.

I add a second finger to my first, and Billy squirms. "You like that, baby?" I grunt.

"I'd like it better if it were your dick," he says. I hesitate. "I have a condom in my back pocket," Billy says, reading my thoughts. He jumps out of bed, picks up his jeans and fishes out the condom and a small bottle of lube. "Here," he says, tossing it to me.

I toss the condom back. "You do the honors," I say.

Billy gives my dick a few last sucks and then rolls the condom down my shaft, greasing it liberally. He rolls over onto his belly.

"No," I say. "Turn around. I like to look into a man's eyes when I shove my dick up his ass."

"Sure, Al," Billy says, grinning. "No problem." He flips onto his back, I seize his calves and wrap his legs around my torso. I probe against his ass crack and pop the head of my dick in his hole. "Fuck yeah!" Billy groans. I thrust my dick full up his ass, pumping my hips, slowly at first, my cockshaft sliding out of Billy's ass to the very tip and then plunging full in again. I pick up speed, pumping my hips faster now, and Billy pushes up to meet me, squeezing his ass muscles tight, clamping down on my cock with a velvet grip. I bend down, and we kiss, with lots of tongue and squirming flesh on flesh. I wrap a lube-smeared hand around Billy's dick and jack him off as I thrust in and out of his ass.

Billy closes his eyes and pushes his head against the pillow, arching his back up to meet me thrust for thrust. He opens his eyes again, and I pin him down with my gaze as I skewer his ass with a series of quick, deep strokes. Our bodies are slippery with sweat, and they come together in wet, slapping sounds. I twist Billy's nipples. Billy reaches behind and pulls hard on my balls.

"Yeah," I snarl. "That's right. Give my balls a good tug." My orgasm rises up inside me, ratcheting to the trigger point. Billy tugs my balls again just as I plunge deep into his ass, and that's all it takes to push me over the edge. I groan loudly, thrusting deep into Billy, my load pulsing out into the condom up Billy's ass.

I start jacking Billy faster, and just when my dick gives its last throb he cries out. His spunk squirts out and splatters against his belly. I quickly bend down and take his dick in my mouth, catching the last of his load as it pulses out. I give Billy's dick a few good sucks, and then fall on the bed besides him. I slip my arm under Billy and pull him toward me, giving him a lingering kiss. "Goodnight, baby," I say.

Billy smiles. "G'night."

When I wake up the next morning, Billy's not in bed. I think that he might be in the bathroom until I notice that his clothes are no longer strewn on the floor. Then I notice that his duffel bag is gone and that my pants, which had been lying at the foot of the bed last night, are now on the floor by the door. My belly clenches. I jump out of bed and grab my pants, praying that I'm jumping to conclusions. A quick check reveals that my wallet and car keys are missing. "GODDAMN, FUCK, SHIT, PISS," I snarl, slamming my fist against the wall. I walk the length of the room and then come back and slam the wall a few more times.

Out in the parking lot, I stare at the empty space where my car had been. Rage slams into me like a gale force wind, pure, blind rage like I've never felt before. "BILLY, YOU MOTHERFUCKER!" I scream. I stand in the middle of the lot panting.

After a few minutes I calm down enough to weigh my options. The whole day stretches out ahead of me like some field of shit I'm going to have to slog through: getting hold of the local police, calling the credit card companies, somehow arranging to get back home. . . . It's all just too fuckin' much. *What the fuck possessed you to pick that little hoodlum up?* I think furiously. *Everything was going fine until then.* As I walk across the parking lot to the motel lobby, I think that that's one thing that punk and I had in common. Neither one of us knew when to quit while we were ahead.

# Vitamin V

I have no problem finding Dad in the airport. He's wearing Bermuda shorts, a blue aloha shirt with green and red parrots, and a Panama straw hat with a yellow-and-green-striped band.

"Couldn't you have worn something a little flashier?" I ask. "I think there's still a couple of people at the other end of the terminal who haven't been struck blind by your outfit."

Dad grimaces. "Thanks, Dan. It's nice to see you, too."

I wrestle Dad's beat-up suitcase out of the baggage carousel and carry it out to the parking lot, Dad walking briskly beside me. There's a steady wind blowing from the direction of the bay, damp and laced with fog. Dad hugs his arms across his chest, and I glance at him. "I warned you to dress warmly," I say.

"It's August," Dad says. "This is California." His tone suggests there's no further room for discussion.

"All California isn't Los Angeles," I say. "Summer is San Francisco's coldest season."

"Jesus," Dad mutters. "Is there anything about this city that isn't abnormal?"

I glare at him. "What's *that* supposed to mean?"

"Nothing, nothing," Dad answers quickly, all injured innocence.

When we're on the freeway, I try to get things back on a better footing. "So what do you want to do during your visit, Dad? You want to see Muir Woods? The Wine Country? Maybe visit Fisherman's Wharf?"

Dad clears his throat. "Actually," he says, "what I most want to do is pick up women." He glances at me. "That is, if there are any straight women left in this city."

"No, Dad," I say. "They're all lesbians. Though there are plenty of drag queens I could hook you up with. I'm sure they'd be glad to give you a tumble."

Dad grimaces and looks out the window. We drive for a couple of blocks in silence, Dad staring at the passing cityscape. He turns his head toward me again. "I was serious. I really want to meet some women while I'm here. I was hoping you'd turn me on to some places where that could happen."

"Jesus, Dad," I laugh. "I'd be the last person who could help you in that department."

Dad shrugs. "Just 'cause you play in a different league doesn't mean you don't know where the other team's ballpark is."

We stop at a red light. I meet his gaze. "I'll ask my friends if any of their mothers are available."

"You're a regular riot," Dad says.

I oversleep the next morning, and by the time I pull myself out of bed I have only half an hour to get ready before my bus arrives. As I stumble to the bathroom, I hear Dad snoring behind the closed door of the guestroom. I jump in the shower, towel down, grab my vitamins and herbal pills from the medicine cabinet and gulp them down, all in ten minutes.

I'm in the kitchen pouring myself a quick cup of coffee when I hear Dad make his way to the bathroom. A moment later, he sticks his head through the kitchen door. "What's the big idea, messing with my Viagra?" he asks.

I raise my head and look at him. "What are you talking about?"

"My Viagra," he says, holding out a pill bottle. "I put it in the medicine cabinet last night, and it was on the bathroom sink when I walked in just now."

I stare at the bottle in his hand. "You're crazy. That bottle says 'Vitamin C'."

Dad makes an impatient gesture. "Yeah, well, that's just to keep prying eyes from knowing my business. This is where I store my Viagra."

I let the implications sink in. "Shit!" I say softly.

Dad looks at me sharply. "How many did you take?" he asks.

"Two, I think. I was in kind of a rush."

Dad rolls his eyes. He looks at me with an expression half-exasperated, half-amused. "Half a pill will give you a woody that won't quit." He laughs. "In about an hour's time, you're going to get a hard-on the size of Florida. And you'll be sporting it until sometime around Thanksgiving."

"Oh, jeez," I say, running my hands through my hair. "This is just great. I've got a presentation to make first thing this morning."

"Well, you better concentrate on baseball scores while you talk," Dad says, still laughing, "or else everybody's going to think you've stuffed a zucchini down your pants."

The bus ride to work is pure hell. *As long as I don't get a hard-on, I'll be okay,* I tell myself. All of a sudden, every guy on my bus looks like he's just stepped out of a Tom of Finland sketchbook—from the junior executives decked out in their tailored gray suits to the construction workers in their jeans and flannel shirts. I spend the entire ride leaning forward, my eyes trained on the floor of the bus.

When I reach my stop and get off, I keep staring down at the sidewalk, not risking a glance toward any passerby. It's not until I finally push through the office door that I begin to let my guard down. My cubicle's only a short walk away, and once there, I can stay put, surrounded by my unerotic beige cloth walls until it's time to give this presentation.

My relief makes me careless. I look up, forgetting that I'm passing the glass door to the company fitness center, and I spot Eddie inside, dismounting from one of the StairMasters. *Oh, shit!* I think. He sees me, waves, and pushes open the door, grinning. "Hey, Dan," he calls out. "You all set for your little talk this morning?"

I try not to notice how tightly his gym shorts hug his hips or how his sweat-dampened T-shirt clings to his leanly muscled torso. "Yeah, sure," I grunt. Eddie can get me hard in a flash, even without a gram of Viagra pumping through my bloodstream. In the state I'm in now, one good look at him and I'll be a walking towel rack for the rest of the day. I mumble something about being late and push past him with my head turned away.

"Hey, nice talking to you," Eddie calls after me. I can tell by the edge to his voice that I've hurt his feelings. This makes me feel bad because Eddie's a sweet guy, but it can't be helped. Today, he's poison.

I'm a complete basket case by the time I'm setting up the PowerPoint projector in the conference room. I can just feel my dick stirring in my pants, like some stalking beast, and every time it twitches I have to stop and conjure up images of the most repulsive people I can think of, buck-naked. I've already worked through images of my elderly sixth-grade teacher, Mrs. Franklin, the fat, warty newspaper vendor at the corner kiosk, and just about every Republican politician ever elected.

Nine o'clock rolls around, and the company staff starts wandering in. Eddie is the last to make it, and he swings into the only remaining empty chair, in the front and no more than a couple of feet away from me. This is casual Friday, and he's dressed in a pair of tight jeans and an open-collared blue-checked cotton shirt with the top two buttons undone. His dark blonde hair is still damp from his shower, and he looks young and boyish, as if he just stepped out of a green meadow by a sun-dappled lake. My dick springs to life, and I have to close my eyes and conjure up the image of Newt Gingrich nude and spread out on a bearskin rug, blowing kisses at me. My dick reluctantly lowers itself again.

I start talking about the company's earnings during the last quarter, how our domestic and foreign markets have been doing. Eddie sits back in his chair, his arms draped over the back, his left ankle crossed over his right knee. I can see a few stray chest hairs peeking out through the V of his open shirt, and I find myself wondering what it would feel like to run my fingers lightly over his furry pectorals. My dick stirs rapidly. I tear my eyes away. "While our domestic sales have been strong," I say, my heart beating hard, "our efforts in the foreign markets have been sporadic." Eddie runs his fingers through his thick, blonde hair and yawns. I watch his Adam's apple rise in his muscular throat and wonder what it'd feel like to nuzzle my face against the nape of his neck. My dick stirs against the thin fabric of my slacks, pushing them out into a gray flannel tent. Someone snickers in the back of the room.

"Many companies in our manufacturing sector are making inroads into our European markets," I continue, trying to fight down a wave of panic. "In the next quarter we can expect our competition to be stiff." The snicker is louder now, joined by another. Eddie stirs in his seat, spreading his legs apart. Images run through my mind of me sliding my hands slowly up those fleshy thighs, massaging them, stroking the muscles . . . My dick throbs with a slow, heavy pulse, making my pants flutter. "We will have to redouble our efforts to recapture these markets," I continue blindly. "But the road to profitability may prove long and hard."

The snickers have spread across the room like brush fire. My mind is flooded with images of me stripping Eddie naked, swallowing his thick dick, plowing his sweet, tight ass. I risk a glance down. Dad was right; it does look like a zucchini's been stuffed down my pants. The entire length of my fully erect dick is clearly outlined under the thin fabric for everyone in the room to see. And right where the head can be made out, there's a dark stain of pre-jizz against the light gray of my slacks. My eyes sweep the room, and I can see faces red with the effort to keep from bursting out in laughter. If there were a window in the room, I'd kick it out and jump.

I make it to the end of my presentation, mumble a wrap-up, and walk out of the room, my boner leading the way. I can feel my face burn and can only imagine how red it must be. *Maybe not,* I think, *considering that all my blood is in my DICK right now.*

Back in my cubicle, I can feel the Viagra pulsing through my body, keeping my dick as stiff as a friggin' iron pipe. I wouldn't step out of my cubicle right now if the goddamn building were on fire.

I reconsider this as my morning coffee works its way through my system, and the need to piss grows. My dick is still as stiff as ever. I could drill through steel with my cock, batter down thick, oaken doors, pry boulders loose and roll them down hillsides.

I pick up the phone and dial home. Dad picks up on the third ring. "Tell me again," I ask. "When does this stuff wear off?"

"What day of the week is it again?" Dad asks.

I hang up cursing. Dad is having way too much fun over this.

The urge to piss has now reached crisis proportions. I can just imagine all the snickers and whispers I'd get walking past the secretarial pool with Dickzilla thrusting out in front of me. I consider pissing in my coffee cup.

Noon finally comes around, and the place empties as everyone heads out for lunch. I peek over the cubicle walls; the place looks deserted and I race to the bathroom. I pull down the zipper to my pants, and my dick springs out, proud and stiff, pointing up toward the ceiling. I push down on it, but it resists every effort I make to aim it toward the urinal. If I piss now, I'll look like a fountain in the Tivoli Gardens.

I hear the bathroom door open. I try to shove my dick back inside my pants, but it refuses to bend and be forced through my fly. Eddie walks up to the urinal next to me, unzips, hauls out his cock and starts pissing. He glances down at my stiff dick in my hand and then at my face, his expression startled. "Jeez, Dan," he says. "You really are a horny bastard today. But jerking off in the john . . . ?"

"I'm not jerking off!" I say angrily, still struggling to force my dick inside my pants. I give it up and look at Eddie, my face burning. "I just have a little problem I'm trying to handle, *okay?*"

Eddie smiles, his eyes intent on my dick. "It doesn't look so little to me," he says as his eyes meet mine. He raises his eyebrows. "Anything I can do to help?"

"I don't know," I say cautiously. "What do you do about a dick that gets hard but refuses to go down again?"

"Well," Eddie says, his face deadpan. "I guess you just gotta take the problem in hand." He reaches over and wraps his hand around my dick, giving it a squeeze.

"Eddie," I say, "that's not going to make my dick any softer."

"I certainly hope not," Eddie says. His hand starts sliding up and down my shaft. He sees me glance toward the door. "Relax," he says softly. His hand picks up speed, sliding my foreskin up and down my shaft. "Everyone's out to lunch. We've got the place to ourselves." He spits in his hand and then continues stroking. I close my eyes and sigh and then pull Eddie toward me. I plant my mouth on his and kiss him hard, pushing my tongue toward the back of his throat. Eddie eagerly responds, and I reach over and start stroking Eddie's dick. It feels great in my hand: thick, flushed with blood, warm and throbbing.

"Let's go inside one of the stalls," Eddie murmurs. "We don't have to push our luck."

We shuffle inside the nearest stall and shut the door behind us. Eddie pushes me against the door and sticks his tongue into my mouth. We kiss enthusiastically, Eddie pressing his body tight against me, his hard, fat dick dry-humping my belly. I fumble impatiently with the buttons of Eddie's shirt. When I finally get them undone, I run my hands along his furry chest and give his nipples a good tweak. Eddie sighs. I bend down and run my tongue over those twin brown nubs as my hands continue their slide down his firm flesh, across the ripples of his abs, down his flanks. I tug his jeans down and run my fingers over his smooth ass, squeezing the cheeks, feeling the warmth and sleekness of the sweet flesh. Eddie's asshole is tightly closed, and I push against it gently with my fingertip, not penetrating him, just massaging the pucker of flesh. The way Eddie squirms, I can tell he likes that.

Eddie pushes away and sits down on the toilet seat. His eyes are level with my dick, and he looks at it intently. "Fuckin' beautiful," he murmurs. He wraps his fist around it, pulling the foreskin over my cockhead, until the loose flesh forms a tiny rosebud. He bends my dick down, then releases it. It slaps hard against my belly and then sways from side to side. "Just fuckin' beautiful." He squeezes the fleshy shaft, and it leaks a drop of pre-jizz. Eddie leans forward and laps it up. His tongue continues to swirl around my dick head, and then his lips nibble their way down the shaft, while his other hand tugs at my balls. I lean against the stall door and close my eyes, letting the sensations pulled up from Eddie's warm, wet mouth tingle through my body. "Damn, that feels good," I groan. I begin pumping my hips, sliding my dick in and out of Eddie's mouth, fucking his face with long, deep plunges. Eddie can't get enough of it, and he makes hungry love to my dick, twisting his head from side to side as his lips slide up and down the shaft.

Eddie drags his tongue over my balls, burying his face in them, nuzzling them, swallowing them in his mouth as his hand starts stroking my dick again. He looks up at me, his mouth full of ballmeat, his hand full of cock. I reach down and run my hand through his hair, then clench my fist around it and tug his head from side to side. "Yeah," Eddie growls, "that's right."

I plant my hands under his armpits and pull him to his feet again. I reach down and wrap my hand around both our dicks, feeling the heat of his flow into mine, the two cockheads pressed together, his like a dark plum, mine pink and flaring. They're both leaking pre-jizz, and I use the slippery fluid to slick up the twin meaty shafts. We kiss again, my mouth traveling over Eddie's eyes, his nose, his throat, always returning to his lips. Eddie sighs softly

"Jesus, I wish I had a condom," I say. "I'd love to plow your ass."

Eddie bends down and fishes one out of his back pants pocket. He grins. "I always carry one with me. You never know when the little fuckers will come in handy."

I laugh. I push open the stall door a crack and take a peek. Nobody's out there, and I make a quick dash to the sink, yank the soap dispenser off its rack, and return to the stall. "Put your palms against the wall," I say.

Eddie obeys, leaning against the wall, arms outstretched, legs spread apart, like a street punk waiting to get frisked. I put a generous dollop of soap on my hand and slide it between Eddie's ass cheeks, greasing up his asshole good, sliding a finger inside him. Eddie groans, and I slide in another, feeling them both encased in the warm, velvet flesh. I roll the condom down my dick and then slide my boner up and down the length of his ass crack. Eddie leans against me, and I wrap my arms around his torso, burying my face into his neck. I push my dick head against the pucker of his asshole and slowly impale him. Eddie moans as I work my dick up inside him. When I'm fully in, we just hold our position, unmoving, except for the rise and fall of Eddie's chest underneath my arms.

I start pumping my hips, my strokes short and slow at first, but deeper with each thrust of my hips. Eddie turns his head, and we kiss, our tongues pushing hard against each other. I slide my hand down the tight muscles of Eddie's body and wrap it around his hard dick, beating him off in synch with my thrusting dick. I pick up the faint scent of soap from Eddie's body, from his morning workout shower, and the newer smell of fresh sweat. I feel like I'm sinking into his body, my flesh absorbing his, my skin melting into his.

I pull out of Eddie's ass and sit on the toilet seat, my dick pointing to the ceiling. "Turn around and sit on my dick," I say. "I want to watch your face as I fuck your ass."

Eddie looks at me, grinning. "Sure, Dan. Anything you say." He steps out of his jeans and straddles me. I love the feel of his warm asshole sliding down my cock. Eddie wraps his arms around my neck and leans his torso back, squeezing his ass muscles as I churn my dick deep inside him. Our eyes lock together as we fuck, and I feel Eddie's hot breath on my face. He unbuttons my shirt, and then slides his hands over my torso, pulling on the flesh, squeezing my nipples. I do the same to him, and then pull Eddie toward me, kissing him as our bodies rock together, flesh on flesh. I spit in my hand and slide my saliva-slicked hand down his thick shaft. Eddie groans as I work his dick over, the sound muffled by our mouths fused together. "Yeah," he whispers. "That's right." He leans back and slides his gaze down my body. "Fuckin' hot dude plowing my ass," he growls. "Fuckin' hot, sexy man." He laughs low.

"What?" I ask, grinning.

Eddie grins back. "I was just thinking of your presentation this morning. With your big, stiff dick waving in all our faces."

"Please," I say. "Don't remind me. I'll never live that down."

Eddie kisses me lightly and pulls back to look at me again. "Fuck, Dan. You have no idea how hot you were, all embarrassed and sexy. It was all I could do to keep from dropping to my knees right there and working your dick."

I give a hard thrust up Eddie's ass, and he lets out a soft groan. "And now here we are," I growl. "Fucking in the company john." I thrust up again, churning my hips. Eddie closes his eyes briefly and then looks at me again. We lock gazes as I pump a series of rapid fire thrusts. Eddie's mouth is open, and he's panting hard. He's a great fuck; he works his ass beautifully, squeezing the muscles around my dick as I thrust up, rocking his body smoothly, drawing my orgasm out with a slow inevitability. Eddie's forehead is beaded with sweat, and I watch a drop of it trickle down the side of his face. I feel the warmth of his cock in my hand as I stroke it, and by the little groans and whimpers that Eddie is giving off, I can tell that he's getting close to shooting.

"I could pop any second now," I pant. "Are you ready to go for it?"

"Fuck, yeah," Eddie says softly.

"Twist my nipples," I say. "Hard."

Eddie gives them a good tug just as I thrust up, and that's all it takes to push me over the edge. I groan loudly, and my body spasms as my dick pumps my load into the condom up Eddie's ass. "Ah, yeah," Eddie sighs, and his body shudders against me as his own jizz squirts out and splatters my chest. We kiss, our bodies rocking tightly together as our dicks pump out our loads. We ride out our orgasms, shuddering, holding on to each other. It's such a fuckin' sweet moment, sexy Eddie's flesh pressed against mine, his mouth all over my face. Afterwards, we just sit there, locked in our embrace, my softening dick still up Eddie's ass, our bodies sweaty and caked with Eddie's load.

I kiss Eddie lightly. "Eddie, Eddie," I say softly. "That was so fuckin' nice."

Eddie squeezes the back of my neck. "For me too, babe," he says. He gives a low laugh. "Next time, though, let's do this on an honest-to-God bed, okay?"

"Yeah," I laugh. "Okay."

That evening, Dad is all over me about what happened.

"Nothing," I say. "The presentation went fine."

Dad looks at me suspiciously. "But what about the Viagra?" he asks.

"I took care of the problem," I say. Dad opens his mouth to say something. "I said I took care of the problem," I repeat, looking straight at him. Dad gets the message and backs off. When I ask him how his day went, he shows me a book he bought at a neighborhood bookstore: *The Single Man's Guide to San Francisco*. Later, after dinner, he tells me he's stepping out to check out the night scene. After he leaves, I look in the bathroom medicine cabinet. Dad's taken his Viagra with him. I decide not to wait up for him.

# Pumping

The night sky is cloudless, and the full moon bathes the desert in a pale, pearly light. Looking east from the gas pumps, all I see is a flat terrain cut by a two lane highway that runs straight as a plumb line out to the horizon. Except for a rise of hills off in the distance, the view to the west is just more of the same.

The town of Henderson lies behind the western hills, and most of the traffic that comes down this godforsaken highway consists of local residents going about their business. During the day there's a steady flow of cars and trucks, but on night shift I'm lucky if I see half a dozen vehicles, usually trucks filled with iron ingots and scrap metal for the foundry in Henderson, the town's major business. In the middle of the night, with the winds whipping across the sand and the coyotes howling in the distance, I get to feeling like I'm the last man on the planet. As feelings go, this one sucks.

I'm out by the pumps, smoking a joint, when I see the dot of light swerve around the western hills and point its beam toward me. I wait and watch as the dot gets bigger, separates into two points of light, and finally resolves itself into the headlights of an approaching car. I glance at my watch. It's a little after two in the morning. *Who's coming out of Henderson at this time of night?* I wonder.

The car is a beat up piece of shit, an old Pinto with a crumpled hood and enough dings to make the body look like a moonscape. I can hear the engine knocking a hundred yards away. I lick my thumb and forefinger, snuff the joint out, and put it into my jacket pocket as the car pulls up.

The driver stares at me blearily. "You want to fill 'er up?" he asks, his voice rasping like sandpaper. I give him a sharp look. The muscles in his face are sagging with exhaustion and he looks like he can barely keep his eyes open. I remove the nozzle, open the gas tank cap, and start pumping. I glance at the driver again. He's older than me, mid-thirties maybe. In spite of his obvious fatigue, I can see that he's a handsome man: the stubbled jaw square, the nose slightly hooked, the eyes, dark and expressive. His hair is jet black and pulled back into a pony tail. *Part Navajo, most likely,* I think.

"Where you headed?" I ask him.

He looks at me and blinks his eyes, as if I've asked him a tough math question. The fucker really is burnt out. "Chenle," he finally says.

I shake my head. "That's one long-ass drive. You sure you're up for it?"

The man shrugs. "I'll be all right." He runs his hand through his hair. "It's my first day at work at the foundry, and I just put in two shifts." He looks out his windshield at the long highway that stretches in front of him. "Jesus fuck," he says softly. He rubs his eyes.

The gas stops pumping and I pull the nozzle out. "That'll be nineteen dollars and sixty two cents," I say.

The man pulls a twenty out of his pocket and hands it to me. His forearm is brawny, and his bicep bulges against the sleeve of his T-shirt. "Keep the change," he says. He starts his engine.

"Hold on a second," I say. I go into the office and come back with my thermos. I hand it to him. "It's coffee. You can return the thermos the next time you pass through."

The man trains his eyes on me, and for the first time I get the feeling that he's actually looking at me. After a couple of beats, he holds out his hand and takes the thermos. "Thanks," he says. He puts it on the seat besides him. He holds out his hand again. "I'm Sam," he says. We shake. "I'm George." Sam's grip is strong, and his hand is large and rough with calluses. He pulls away and drives off down the long stretch of highway.

The next night, a few minutes after two, Sam pulls up to the gas pumps again. The wind has kicked up some since last night, and the sand whips around the corner of the station, the fine particles caught in the beams of Sam's headlight. Sam opens the window and tosses the thermos to me. "I filled it for you," he says. "All I had was instant coffee."

"You driving back to Chenle again?" I ask.

Sam shrugs. "That's where I live, man."

I look down the long, lonesome strip of highway. "Fuck, why don't you just move to Henderson if you're going to work there?"

Sam shrugs again. "All my family live in Chenle. That's where I grew up."

I pull a joint out of my pocket and light up. I take a toke and exhale a cloud of smoke. "It hardly seems worth the effort, just for a lousy job."

Sam pointedly looks at the rundown shit hole of a gas station behind me and then back at me. He grins. "Not all of us have the career opportunities that you have, my friend." He reaches over, takes the joint out of my hand and takes a long hit. He hands the joint back. "See you tomorrow, George." He drives off and disappears into the clouds of sand.

I pack it in a few minutes later, shutting down the pumps and switching the lights off. I go back to my room behind the office, strip and lay down on my cot, listening to the wind howling outside. I think about Sam's dark, knowing eyes, the way his muscles strain against the cotton of his shirt. My dick stirs to full hardness, and I stroke it lazily as I fantasize about Sam fucking my ass with slow, measured thrusts, talking dirty to me in his raspy baritone. After I squirt, I just lay there, staring up at the darkness and feeling my load crust on my belly. After a while I drift off into sleep.

The next night, Sam shows up like clockwork, right after two. He pulls up to the pumps. "Hey, George," he grins. "How's life in the fast lane?"

I laugh. "It just doesn't get any better than this." I stick the pump nozzle in his gas tank. "How's the job working out?"

Sam hesitates, and then shrugs. "It puts food on the table."

After the tank is filled, I take the nozzle out, and Sam pays me. I expect him to start his engine, but he just stays there, looking at me. He seems to be weighing his options. "I got a pint of Johnny Walker in the glove compartment," he says. "You feel like sharing a snort with me?"

"Sure," I say.

I have a couple of glasses in the desk drawer in the office, which I rinse out and hand to Sam. He fills each one with about three fingers worth of whiskey, and hands one back to me. "Here's to ports in the storm," he says, clinking his glass against mine.

I laugh. "Is that what this is? A port in the storm?"

Sam takes a long gulp from his glass and wipes his hand across his mouth. "It's as close to one as I'll ever hope to find." Off in the distance, a coyote gives a long, trailing howl. Sam shakes his head and looks at me. "Jesus, George, how did you ever end up in this godforsaken place?"

I tilt my head back and drain my glass. I put it on the table and run my fingers through my hair. "Fuck if I know," I finally say. Sam fills my glass again, and I pick it up and look at the brown liquid inside. "Things just happened, and I wound up here." I drain the glass, and Sam fills it a third time. I'm getting a real buzz on now. Sam shifts in his seat, and his knee bumps against mine under the table. Neither one of us make an effort to break the contact.

We sit there in silence, working on Sam's pint, listening to the wind and the coyotes outside. My eyes meet Sam's. We hold the gaze. After a couple of beats, Sam reaches over, cups his hand around the back of my neck, and pulls my face against his. We give each other a long, wet kiss, Sam's tongue snaking deep into my mouth. When we finally break, Sam leans back against his chair and gives me a level look. His mouth curls up into a slow grin. "I've been wantin' to do that since the first time I saw you."

"I got a cot in the back," I say.

Sam's grin widens. "Fuckin' A," he says. "Let's go."

We stretch out full length on the cot, fully clothed, kissing each other, our fingers working buttons and zippers. Our clothes fall off, piece by piece, until after a couple of minutes we're both naked. Sam's body is hard and packed with muscle, his skin as brown as polished oak. He runs his large, callused hands over my body, pulling on my muscles, stroking my skin, his mouth fused to mine. "Jesus," he sighs. "It's been such a fuckin' long time since I've been in bed with a man."

"It's been such a fuckin' long time since I've been in bed with *anybody*," I reply.

Sam gives a low laugh. "We've both got some lost time to make up for."

I kiss Sam's face lightly and then work down, along the crook of his neck, finally nuzzling under his armpit, drinking in the sweet/bitter taste of his sweat. I swing my head around and suck on his nipple, biting it gently between my teeth, rolling my tongue around it. Sam sighs deeply, and I repeat this with his other nipple. My tongue slides across Sam's smooth pecs, then down his hard belly and into the thicket of his pubes.

I hold his hard dick in my hand and gaze at it for a couple of seconds, feeling its warmth spread into my palm. It's a beauty, all right, thick and long, uncut, the head flared, veins snaking up the shaft. I pull the foreskin back and work my lips down the shaft. Sam begins pumping his hips, and I match his movements, bobbing my head with each thrust of his hips. I close my eyes, concentrating on the sensation of having a mouth full of *dick*. Sam's dick.

As I suck Sam off, I cradle his balls in my palm, feeling their heft. They fill my hand nicely, the fleshy pouch spilling over my fingers. I bury my face in Sam's ballsac, breathing in the thick, pungent odor of ripe ballmeat. I part my lips and suck the fleshy pouch into my mouth. I roll my tongue over his balls, tasting their sweat, as Sam rubs his thick cock over my face. I slide my tongue once more up the shaft of Sam's cock and swirl it around the dark knob. I give it a squeeze, and a drop of clear pre-cum oozes out. I lap it up and go back to sucking Sam off.

"Look at me while you blow me," Sam growls.

I raise my eyes and lock my gaze with Sam's as he fucks my mouth. "I can't begin to tell you how fuckin' hot it is watching you suck my dick," Sam murmurs. I reach up and twist Sam's nipples, not gently. "Fuuuck," Sam groans, closing his eyes. He opens them again. "Pivot around," he says. "Let's get a little 69 action going."

I don't need any persuading. I shift my body around, and now we're both fucking face and eating dick. The small room is filled with the sounds of our slurping mouths and sighs and groans, of flesh slapping against flesh. I wrap my arms around Sam's torso, feeling his body squirm against mine, his skin slippery with sweat. Sam moves his body like a dancer, grinding his hips in slow, circular motions, twisting his head back and forth as his mouth slides up and down my dick shaft. His hand slides down my back, across my ass, and burrows into my ass crack. I feel his finger push against my asshole and worm its way inside, knuckle by knuckle, and my whole body shudders.

"Fuck," I groan. I raise my head and look at Sam. "You feel like fucking my ass?" I ask.

"I thought you'd never ask," Sam replies, grinning.

I get a pack of condoms from the machine in the station's men's room and toss it over to Sam. He rolls the condom down his stiff dick. A sudden blast of wind outside makes the building shake and groan, but the air inside the room hangs thick and heavy. A bead of sweat trickles down my back. I get back into bed. Sam slings my legs around his torso and slowly impales my asshole, until his dick is full in me. He holds that position for a couple of beats, his face inches above me, his dark eyes burning into mine. He bends down and gives me a lingering kiss as he begins pumping his hips with deep, slow thrusts.

I breathe in with each stroke, focusing my eyes on his, arching my back, pushing up to receive each downward plunge of his dick. Sam picks up his pace, and soon his dick is slamming into my ass, his balls slapping against me. I wrap my legs around him and meet him thrust for thrust, squeezing my ass tight. Sam groans and then laughs from the sheer pleasure of it. He plunges all the way in my ass and grinds his hips. His cock roots into me like he's digging for gold, and my own groans bounce off the ceiling of the small, enclosed room. I wrap my hand around my cock and beat off like there's hell to pay.

We settle into a steady rhythm, Sam plowing my ass, me fucking my hand, our bodies pressed together. My breath rasps in and out of my lungs, I can feel the sweat trickle down my face, and each thrust of Sam's dick up my ass sends a thrill of sensation through my body. Sam gives a low whimper. With his next thrust, I push up and squeeze my ass muscles, *hard,* and Sam's whimper turns into a long trailing groan. I reach down and cup his balls in my hand; they're tight against his body, ready to pump a load. I give them a squeeze with Sam's next thrust, and Sam's body spasms in my arms. "Ah, jeez, I'm coming," he groans, and he kisses me fiercely as his dick pumps his jizz into the condom up my ass, one pulse after another.

I speed up the tempo of my own strokes, feeling my load being pulled out from my balls. Sam reaches down and twists my nipple. I give a loud groan as I squirt out the first volley of spunk onto my belly. "Yeah," Sam growls. "That's right." I arch my back, still pumping my fist. Sam reaches down and tugs on my balls as the last of my orgasm shudders through me.

Sam collapses down onto the cot beside me, and wraps his arm around me. We lay there in the dark, sweaty flesh against sweaty flesh, as the wind continues to howl outside and the coyotes answer in a higher register. After a while, Sam stirs and props himself up on his elbow. He kisses me lightly on the mouth.

"I gotta go," he says. "It's a long drive back to Chenle."

"You can spend the night here if you want," I say, trying to sound casual. But Sam just smiles and shakes his head. "I can't, George. I got things to do."

He gets up and picks up his boxers.

"Just a second," I say. I take his dick in my hand and kiss it softly, running my tongue around the dark fleshy head. "I just wanted one last taste," I say.

Sam smiles but says nothing. He hitches his boxers up over his hips, and I get dressed as well.

I walk him out to his car, the wind whipping sand around us. Sam climbs in and rolls his window down. He grabs me by my T-shirt and pulls me down for a long kiss.

"I'll see you tomorrow, right?" I ask.

Sam looks me full in the face. "No," he says. He glances straight ahead at the highway, and then back at me again. "I quit my job at the foundry. I just couldn't take all this fuckin' driving. I'm going to work in my brother-in-law's hardware store in Chenle." I don't say anything. Sam reaches up, takes me by the scruff of the neck and shakes me gently. "Let me give you some advice, George. Get the fuck out of here. From where I'm looking, you don't have anything going on here that seems worth keeping."

I break free of Sam's grip and stand up. "I don't plan to stay here forever," I say coolly.

Sam chuckles softly. "Just don't wait too long, George. Or one day you'll wake up thirty seven years old and a fuckin' hardware store clerk." He turns on his ignition, waves and takes off. In spite of the sand storm, I stand out there in the middle of the road, watching his taillights dwindle until they disappear into the night. The wind carries another coyote howl from off in the distance. I cover my eyes from the swirling sand and hurry back inside the station.

# Driving

Iinch slowly down the street, trying to read the house numbers and keep my eye on the road at the same time. *Why is it,* I think, *that the higher the income bracket, the harder it is to find an address? Just another way to discourage the riffraff.* I pass by the same stretch of street three times before I finally spot the number "62", half-buried under a clump of ivy above the front door of a sprawling Tudor mansion. I park the limo, a little nervously, at the curb. I'm not used to driving such a tank; the last thing I need is to put a dent in the damn thing. Benny, the dispatcher, would shit a brick.

The house has a million-dollar view of the San Francisco Bay. There's still enough light to watch the wind surfers skimming across the water one last time before they have to call it a day. The front yard is small, immaculate. A breeze blows, and a leaf from a large magnolia tree drifts lazily to the ground. I half expect somebody in a blue blazer to run out and sweep it up.

I ring the bell. A middle-aged Hispanic woman answers the door and regards me coolly. "Hello," I say. "Would you please tell Mr. Bigelow that his driver is here?"

She ushers me into a hallway twice as big as my apartment. "Mr. Bigelow will be down shortly," she says.

I stand there waiting, killing time by counting the pendants on the crystal chandelier above me. I lose count after 71 and give it up. I hear footsteps on the stone staircase and turn.

Bigelow looks to be in his early forties. He's dressed in a tuxedo, and it looks good on him, setting off his trim body nicely. His hair is short-clipped, brown, with gray at the temples, and his face is clean-shaven and rugged. He wears an expression of calm that only the supremely confident can muster.

He extends his hand. "I'm Lloyd Bigelow."

"Good evening, Mr. Bigelow. I'm Tom, your driver." We shake hands.

Bigelow smiles, but his eyes are thoughtful. "Did the limo agency tell you where we're going?"

"Yes, sir. The Burlingame Country Club."

"Good. Sorry I made you wait, but I'm running a little late. We better get going."

"Yes, sir."

He doesn't speak again until we're on the highway. "I don't remember seeing you before. Are you new to the agency?"

"Yes, sir. My first week."

"Oh, really? Were you a driver somewhere else before this?"

"No, sir." I pause, wondering how much of my personal history I'm supposed to get into. Finally I add, "I was a carpenter before this. Working for a general contractor for commercial buildings. But the construction industry's taken a nose dive lately in this town, and I was laid off. I haven't been able to find any work in construction since."

Bigelow sighs. "We're living in tough times, that's for sure."

I glance in the rearview mirror at him to see if he's mocking me. But his expression is bland. *Yeah,* I think. *It looks like you're really suffering.* We don't say anything for the rest of the drive out there.

Something's cooking at the country club, because the parking lot in front of the clubhouse is packed with cars: Mercedes, Cadillacs, Porsches, with a few Beemers thrown in for good measure. Music pours out of the building's lighted windows. I drive up in front of the main entrance, and a doorman rushes over and opens the door for Bigelow.

I park the limo alongside the clubhouse, where I can get a view of the front entrance but not block the driveway. Two parking valets are sharing a joint in the nearby bushes, apparently clueless that they can be seen from my part of the parking lot. I wonder how the members here would feel knowing that their $80,000 cars are being parked by a couple of stoned teenagers.

Hours go by. I share cigarettes with some of the other drivers, talking trash with them, but always keeping the country club entrance in my line of sight. Bigelow finally comes out of the front door, onto the terrace, scanning the parking lot. I stub my cigarette out with my toe, jump in the front seat and pull up in front of him. I jump out and open the door, and Bigelow climbs in. A couple of minutes later, we're driving once more down the quiet, well-heeled streets of Burlingame.

"Did you have a good time, Mr. Bigelow?" I ask.

"Hell, no," Bigelow snorts. "I just went there to close a damn business deal. I wasn't even able to do that. The son-of-a-bitch Jacobson is playing cagey with me." He gives a short laugh. "You've got the right idea, Tom. Just drive cars and keep it simple."

"Yes, sir," I say. "That's why I decided not to be a corporate executive after I got laid off from my last job."

Silence from the backseat. I guess I sounded more sarcastic than I had intended. I glance in the mirror and see that the expression on Bigelow's face is stony. But then he laughs. "I suppose I was a little patronizing there, wasn't I?"

"Not at all, sir."

"I'm sorry."

"No offense taken."

We pull onto the highway. "How long were you out of work before this job?" he finally asks.

"Eight months."

"It must have been hard on you. A strong young man like yourself being inactive all that time."

"I found ways to kill time."

"Oh, yeah? Doing what?"

*Is this normal?* I wonder. *Do clients usually talk this much to their drivers?* For the first time, I realize that Bigelow is a few sheets to the wind. "I worked out at a gym. Jogged. Went to the movies. Bargain matinees, that is."

"No girlfriends?"

"No, sir."

"That's surprising. A good-looking guy like yourself." A minute of silence passes. "How are you making out financially?" he finally asks.

*Jesus,* I think. *A little booze under the belt really makes this guy nosy.* "I manage," I say.

We drive in silence for the rest of the way back. I pull up in front of his house and turn the engine off.

Bigelow makes no effort to leave. "Tom, can I ask you another question?" he asks.

"Sure."

"How much money do you make doing this?"

I look at Bigelow through the rear view mirror and he returns my stare calmly. "Nine-fifty an hour," I finally say. "Plus whatever you decide to tip me."

Bigelow continues to hold my stare. "How would you like to make a quick two hundred bucks?"

This time I let a full thirty seconds go by. "Doing what, Mr. Bigelow?" I ask slowly.

"Call me Lloyd."

"Okay. Doing what, Lloyd?" I keep my voice flat and neutral.

"Well, it's very simple, Tom. You're a very handsome guy. And I like you. I want you to come up with me, let me strip you naked and throw you in bed, and we could just have a little party. It's a big bed. King-size. Plenty of room for fun and games."

I keep staring at him through the rear view mirror. Bigelow gazes back, a look of unshakable calm on his face. The look he must wear whenever he closes some minor deal in the boardroom. I sit there, clutching the steering wheel, and think about the long months of unemployment, the humiliation of taking this shit ass job. And now this. Rage rises up in me, hot and thick.

I turn around and face Bigelow, doing my best to keep my face expressionless. "Gee, I don't know, Lloyd," I say slowly. "I'll have to think about this."

"I'll make it three hundred bucks."

I put on an expression like I'm mulling it over. Finally, I smile. "Let me ask a favor of you first, okay?"

"Shoot."

"Pull out your cock."

Bigelow's composure wavers for a second. I fight an impulse to laugh. "I beg your pardon?"

"Pull out your cock, Lloyd. Let me see it. Since we're negotiating a deal, I want to check out the merchandise first."

After a couple of beats, Bigelow's mouth curls up into an easy smile. "Sure, Tom. It's a reasonable request, I guess." He unzips his fly, reaches inside and pulls his dick out. It's already half erect, and exposed to the great outdoors, it quickly hardens. I pretend to examine it closely. Actually, as far as cocks go, it's a nice one: thick, long enough, with a dark red bulbous head. I trace one long blue vein running up the length of the shaft. My eyes meet his again. That look of smug confidence is all over his face.

"I'll pass," I say.

That sure as hell wipes the smugness off. Bigelow blinks. "What?"

I smile. "I said I'll pass, Lloyd. I'm not interested."

The blood drains from Bigelow's face. Then it rushes back up again. His expression grows murderous. "Why, you son-of-a-bitch!" he snarls.

"Go fuck your houseboy, if you feel like slumming."

Bigelow fumbles with his dick, pushing it back inside his trousers, and zips up his fly. His eyes shoot venom at me. "I could get you fired for this, you little prick."

This time I do laugh. "Go ahead. I just told you what I make. Do you think I care?" I stare back at him. "As for me being 'little', I would guess that I'm three inches taller than you and outweigh you by thirty pounds. I could mop up the street with you if it came to that." Pause. "Lloyd."

Bigelow opens the car door and pulls himself out of the backseat, slamming the door behind him. He stalks up the walk toward his house.

I roll down the window. "Does this mean I don't get a tip?" I call out after him, laughing.

I drive away, still grinning. But there's a sour feeling in my belly. I don't feel amused at all. If anything, I just feel depressed.

The next day I get a call from Benny, the dispatcher. "I got a call from your Mr. Bigelow today," he says.

"Oh, yeah?" I grunt. I wonder why the agency is making Benny fire me. Normally it would have been the agency manager.

"You must have made quite an impression on him. He's got another engagement tonight, and he asked specifically for you as the driver."

I purse my lips in a noiseless whistle. So Bigelow hadn't complained. "Get somebody else," I say.

Silence. "Why?" Benny finally asks. "You busy tonight?"

"No, I just don't want to deal with Bigelow again. You got other drivers. Get one of them."

Benny sighs. "Tommy, Tommy. We can't afford to be prima donnas in this business. It's too competitive. Bigelow's a big client of ours, and he asked for you. Now don't make me lean on you, all right?"

"Oh, yeah, Benny? And just what does that mean?"

"It means," Benny says, putting an edge to his voice, "that either you take this gig, or else I'll see to it that the agency fires your ass."

I let a few seconds go by. "You'd do that, huh, Benny?"

"Yeah. If I have to." Benny's voice becomes cajoling. "Come on, Tom. It's just a gig. Let's not turn this into giant pissing contest, all right?"

"Fuck you, Benny."

"Yeah, fuck me. So is that your final answer?"

I tighten my grip on the telephone. *That motherfucker Bigelow,* I think. "No," I say quietly. "I'll do it."

"Great, Tom. I knew you wouldn't let me down." Benny's all affability again. "Bigelow's expecting you at eight o'clock tonight."

"You're a real asshole, Benny."

"Tell me something I don't know." Benny hangs up.

I shake a cigarette out of my pack and smoke it. All I can think about is how quickly I caved in to Benny. I stub the butt out, pick up the receiver again, and punch out numbers. Joe Ortega answers on the third ring.

"Hey, Joe," I say. "It's Tom. You working tonight?"

"No," Joe answers. "What's up?"

"Would you like to do a gig?"

"Sure."

"Benny's got me lined up with this client, but I got a hot date tonight I don't want to break. Can you cover for me?"

Joe clears his throat. "I dunno, Tom. Benny might not like it. You know what a stickler he is for going by the book."

"Hey, Joe, I'll take full responsibility, okay?" Joe doesn't say anything. "Don't tell me you can't use the extra cash, Joe."

Another silence. "Okay," Joe finally says. "But if Benny starts squawking when I turn in my time card, I want you to tell him this was your idea."

"Sure, Joe. Don't sweat it." I give him Bigelow's address and hang up grinning. Joe is sixty-three years old, balding, with a beer paunch so big he has trouble squeezing it behind the steering wheel. Let Bigelow play "fun and games" with *him.*

The end of the week, after all the time cards are turned in, Benny calls me up and fires me.

I run into Bigelow two weeks later, quite by accident, two o'clock Sunday morning. I'm walking out of a Folsom Street bar and almost crash into him as he's going through the door. He's dressed in a tony brown leather jacket and a pair of scruffy jeans. There's an awkward silence as we stare at each other.

I'm the first to break it. "Hello, Lloyd," I say.

Bigelow's face is unreadable. "This is sure a hell of a surprise."

"Yeah, well, it's a small world." I start to walk away.

Bigelow catches my arm, and I turn around to face him, frowning. "The only reason I called the agency and asked for you again," Bigelow says, "was so that I could apologize. I was drunk that night, and I behaved like a jerk."

I pull my arm from his grasp. "It's no big deal."

Bigelow motions his head toward the door. "Look, can I buy you a drink?"

I shake my head. "It's late, and my last bus leaves in fifteen minutes."

"Let me give you a ride then."

I give a short laugh. "You just got here."

"I don't mind. Look at it as a sort of peace offering."

*Is this another mindfuck game?* I wonder. "Naw," I say. "I prefer the bus." I walk out the door.

Damn if Bigelow doesn't follow me. He falls into step besides me, and we walk in silence for a few seconds. "I'm just parked down the street," Bigelow says. "Why won't you let me give you a ride?"

*Fuck it,* I think. I stop abruptly and turn toward him. "Okay," I say. "Fine."

Bigelow blinks. "Well, all right then," he says.

When we get to Bigelow's Mercedes, he unlocks the front passenger door for me.

No," I say. "I want to sit in the back."

Bigelow shoots a look at me. "What the hell is this, some kind of a game?"

I stare hard back at him. "Yeah. That's exactly what it is. A game. You can either play it with me, or I'll take the fucking bus."

Bigelow regards me speculatively. After a while he smiles. "All right." He unlocks the back door and opens it. "Hop in." I climb in, and he closes the door after me. He gets in behind the wheel. "Where do you want me to drive you?"

"I'll give you directions. For the time being, just go straight."

He pulls away from the curb. There's no conversation between us except for an occasional direction on my part. I reach into my pocket and count my change. I have sixty-seven cents.

"Tell me, Lloyd," I ask. "How much money do you make? On an hourly basis."

Bigelow's eyes meet mine in the rear view mirror. "I don't get paid by the hour, so I wouldn't know."

"Just give me an estimate."

Bigelow's silent as he thinks about it. "Assuming a forty hour work week, I'd guess around $500 to $600 an hour. Of course it varies, depending on how my investments are doing."

"Pull over," I snap. We're in a dark, isolated warehouse district. Bigelow pulls alongside the curb without a question. "I'll give you sixty-seven cents for a blowjob."

Bigelow turns around and looks at me. "Why don't we just go back to my place?"

"I don't fuck the servants in their quarters. That would be degrading."

Bigelow says nothing. I can almost hear the gears inside his head spinning, as he goes over his options. "All right," he finally says. He gets out from behind the wheel and opens the back door. We're parked by a street lamp, and its light floods the backseat. He climbs in.

I lean back, with my hands behind my head. "Go ahead. You do all the work."

Bigelow smiles. "I want my money first."

"I'll pay you after you've earned it." I make my voice harsher. "Now get going, punk!"

Bigelow begins unbuckling my belt. His hands are trembling slightly, and I know now that I control this situation completely. It's an exhilarating feeling. Bigelow slowly pulls down my pants and my shorts. I'm rock hard, and my cock springs to attention.

"Beautiful," he murmurs. He takes my cock in his hand, bends down, and kisses it gently. He runs his tongue along the length of the shaft and then down along my balls. He puts one ball in his mouth and sucks it, and then the other, as he begins stroking my spit-slicked dick. His mouth returns to my fat, red cockshaft, and this time he swallows it completely, until his nose is buried in my pubes.

I grab his head with both hands and begin pumping his mouth hard. "That's it, fucker," I growl. "Take it all in. Service your master."

I quickly pivoted around so that he's lying on the car seat as I sit on his chest, fucking his face. I reach back, unzip his jeans, and pull out his dick. Spitting hard in my hand, I begin stroking it. Bigelow groans, his voice muffled by a mouthful of dick.

I pull my cock out of his mouth and drop my balls in. I begin beating his face with my hard-on. "That's good prole meat, Bigelow," I growl. "Strictly blue-collar. Just the way you like it." He looks up at me, still tonguing my nut sac. His hands move up my torso, over my hard belly, and across my chest. His fingers grip my nipples and squeeze hard.

"Yeah, that's right, fucker," I rasp. "Play with my nipples."

I push myself off him and pull off my pants and shirt. "Get naked," I say. Bigelow hesitates and looks nervously out the window. I think about how embarrassing it would be for him if we get caught by a passing patrol car and smile. I look down at him, my dick sticking straight out, my balls hanging just above his mouth. "What's the matter, Bigelow?" I growl. "You want me to stop? Put my clothes back on?" He shakes his head and pulls off his clothes.

I lie down on top of him, feeling the length of his naked body against mine as we kiss, our tongues pushing into each other's mouth. I begin dry-humping him, poking his belly with my cock. Bigelow reaches down and grabs both our cocks together, fusing them into one giant fuck muscle. I wrap my arms around him in a bear hug, and we roll all over the backseat, the two of us crashing into ashtrays, armrests, door handles. Our bodies are damp with sweat, our flesh comes together and separates in great, wet, slapping noises.

Bigelow breaks away and swoops down on my cock again, cramming it down his throat. I swivel and descend on his dick as well, gorging on it. I breathe in deeply, taking in the sweaty odor of balls. Bigelow sucks cock like a pro, twisting his head from side to side, nibbling on my cockhead, sliding his tongue down the shaft in long, wet slurps. I feel him work a finger up my ass, past the second knuckle, and twist it, and whole new sensations tingle through me. I go fuckin' wild, bucking and heaving like a bronco, working over Bigelow's fat dick like I'm on some kind of feeding frenzy. I can feel Bigelow's skillful tongue pulling my load out of my balls, sucking me into climax. I'm almost at the brink. A couple of deep thrusts with my hips push me over. I sit up and cry out, still pumping Bigelow's mouth hard, squirting what feels like a couple of quarts of jism down that rich bastard's million-dollar throat.

I start to pull out, but Bigelow will have none of that. He keeps sucking hungrily on my dick as he pummels his own cock with his hand. I watch his balls bounce up and down, still panting from the load I've just dropped. I reach down and squeeze his nipples hard. That does the trick. Bigelow begins moaning; the moans become cries, and he arches his back as thick gobs of cum spurt out of his dick. Even after he's stopped shooting, he keeps on sucking my now softening cock. "You can't get enough of that, can you, fucker?" I growl. He doesn't answer, but just keeps on sucking.

Bigelow eventually drives me home. As I climb out of the car, he hands me a card from his wallet. It has his telephone number on it. "That's my private number. I want to see you again," he says. "You can dictate the circumstances. Just make it happen."

I put the card in my shirt pocket. "I'll think about it," I say. Then I grin. "And I got something for you, too." I hand him the sixty-seven cents. "Next time, if there is a next time, I might bump it up to a full dollar."

As I climb the stairs to my place, I find myself grinning. Being born with a silver spoon in your mouth is okay, I think. But when it gets down to the bottom line, a nice stiff cock is always better.

# Risky Sex

It's a little after eleven o'clock, late enough to draw a decent bar crowd, but early enough, if I'm lucky, to score and still catch a few hours sleep. I have to be in the hiring hall by eight o'clock sharp tomorrow morning if I'm to get a crack at a job. It's crazy to be cruising on a weekday night, but I haven't been laid since I moved out here, and my cock is giving me a hard time about it. Springsteen is playing on the juke box, and the boys are lined up against the walls, checking out any new action that walks through the door. I feel their eyes draw a bead on me, and it's gratifying to see how they track me as I push my way through the crowd. I need a little tender loving tonight; I'm feeling lonely and more than a little depressed about not finding work.

I make my way to the bar and order the cheapest beer they got, which is still four goddamn dollars. As I pull the bills from my wallet, I realize that I'm going to have to nurse this sucker for the rest of the night. That is, unless I can get someone to buy me another. This is very possible. I'm muscular and hairy, with the face of a back alley thug, perfect fodder for all those guys out there with fantasies of getting it on with a knuckle-dragger. And they *are* out there. I found out long ago that by just leaning against a wall and looking stupid, I can usually draw in someone looking for a little walk on the wild side.

Within half an hour I've hooked up with a couple of boyfriends who have a place in the Village. One's a humpy little dago with a tight, compact body and dark soulful eyes. He tells me his name is Lou, short for Luigi. His buddy is lighter, with blond hair, a kid's face, and the tall, lean body of a competitive swimmer. They both fall into the "sex candy" category, and I'm quite happy to be their stray mutt for the night. We talk the usual barroom bullshit, and I answer their questions as politely as I'm capable of, waiting for them to make up their minds. When the blonde guy, whose name is Charley, asks me what I do for a living, I tell him I'm an iron man. Well, that tips the scales in my balance fast enough; I can see they're about creaming in their jeans at the thought of making it with *a construction worker*. They exchange glances, raise their eyebrows and give each other a silent nod, with all the subtlety of a two-by-four between the eyes. It's funny, but they seem to think I'm too clueless to notice any of this. Or else they just don't care. They finally ask if I want to go home with them and I say "sure."

Riding in their car, I pick up signals that these guys want someone mean and stupid. I think about calling this off, but decide to just go ahead and play the game. When we get back to their place, I throw them around the bedroom, rough them up a bit, rip their clothes off, and then make them strip me naked. Lou pulls my pants down; when my dick springs out to full attention he looks like a kid who just got a new bike for Christmas. I grab his head and start fucking his face hard while Charley eats out my ass. Lou is no slouch at giving head. I close my eyes and let the sensations sweep over me of having my dick *finally* in some place warm and wet. We play out all the expected riffs on the theme of the big, bad construction worker. I call them "faggots" and "cocksuckers" and knock them around some more. But later on, I let them turn the tables on me. Charley "pins" me down as Lou slowly works a greased dildo up my ass. I snarl and spit, cursing threats at them, with all of us just having a grand old time. I end up fucking them both in retaliation; first Lou, then Charley, then Lou again, because I find him the hotter of the two. I shoot my load while plowing him, and as I squirt it deep into the condom up his ass, I throw back my head and bellow like a bull. A neighbor pounds on the wall and shouts at us to shut the fuck up. I lay back while Lou and Charley kneel over me and shoot on my face. They beg me to spend the night, but I tell them no, I got plans tomorrow morning. When they don't give it up, I kick over an end table and tell them to go fuck themselves. They love it.

On the subway back, I think about how easy it was to give them what they wanted. Hell, if things get desperate enough, I could always try hustling. Christ, I hope it doesn't come to that.

I luck out. The next morning I finally land a job up on Lexington Avenue. One of the iron men there took a flop yesterday and fell two stories, breaking his leg. Tough luck for him. Lucky break for me. Oh, does that sound callous? Excuse me, I'll be more sensitive when I have more than fifty-seven bucks in my checking account.

I show up the next day right at eight o'clock, like I was told to; I'm not about to do anything to blow this gig. The building's a big motherfucker all right—already fifty-four stories worth of iron up, with another twenty-two to go. I take the lift up to where the crew is punching in. By force of habit, I zero in on the humpiest guy there, some Irish piece of tail with a red crewcut, alert blue eyes, and a tight, sexy body that's just screaming for a serious plowing. I ask him what the foreman's name is and where I can find him.

He gives me a quick look-over. "His name's Jackson," he says. "Last I saw him, he was over by the derrick bullwheel."

"What does he look like?"

He gives a hint of a smile. "Think pit bull on steroids." He buckles on his tool belt and hoists a coil of cable on his shoulder. "Just go over there. You can't miss him."

It doesn't take long to find Jackson. The guy was right. He does have the small bloodshot eyes and sloped head of an attack dog. I report in, and he looks me over, his eyes pausing for a second on the four gold rings pierced in my left ear. He doesn't look too happy with what the cat drug in. We're standing just a few feet away from the bullwheel and have to shout to hear each other. "The hall tells me you're a connector," he growls. "Is that for real?"

I nod. "For five years. Out in L.A."

Jackson squints his eyes, a third rate Clint Eastwood. "Oh, yeah? Why'd you come out here?"

*What,* I think. *I need a passport?* But I know how crews guard their turfs like junkyard dogs. I give my best shit-eating smile. "Construction's gone to hell out west. All the trades are scrambling for work. I thought I'd try east for a change."

Jackson's squint doesn't lighten up any. Then again, maybe that's how he always looks. He points up to a figure balanced on an eight-inch beam overhead, guiding down a twenty-foot I-beam hung from a derrick cable. Even from this distance, I can see that's it's the red-headed guy I talked to earlier. "That's Mike O'Reilly. You're going to be working with him bolting those headers." I start climbing up the column next to Mike's, but Jackson grabs me by the arm and pulls me back. By instinct my hand clenches into a fist, and I unclench it just as quick. I don't think slugging the boss would be such a good idea.

"I'll be keeping my eye on you," he says, giving me the fisheye. "If you can't cut it, your ass will be off the crew by tomorrow."

*Thanks for the pep talk,* I think. I shimmy up the column with my eyes trained on Mike. He's perched on the beam, wrestling a header into place. I take a few seconds to take in the sight: his shirt off, his body packed with muscles, his powerful arms lifted up and struggling with all that steel against the backdrop of clear blue sky. Pure poetry. Enough to set my dick thumping. God, I love construction!

Mike is still humping the header when I finally get level with him, though with twenty feet of empty air still between us. "Howdy!" I call out to him.

He glances my way and then back at the header. He gives it a mighty whack with his spud wrench and then looks back at me again, his gaze bold as brass. His mouth curls up into an easy smile. "I wondered if you were Pete's replacement. How ya doing? Did Jackson chew a chunk out of your ass?"

"I still got most of it left." I grabbed my end of the header. "You need some help with that?"

"Yeah, if you feel so inclined."

I get the header lined up just so, slip a few bolts in, and tighten the nuts. I glance over to Mike. "You secure?" I call out. He nods. I hoist myself up onto the beam, trot out to the center and cut the choker loose. A gust of wind blasts me and I sway to compensate, nothing to fall back on but empty air. Girder surfing, we call it back in L.A. The building foundation pit is a tiny patch of blackness fifty-four stories below. Far enough down that if I took a dive, parts of me would splatter into Brooklyn. This doesn't bother me any. If it did, I'd be selling shoes for a living.

Mike and I pace ourselves like dancers, matching our rhythms and moves as we line up the headers and start bolting them down. I can see Mike knows what he's doing. He works the iron good, moving the beams easily where he wants them, and bolting them down quick and skillful. It doesn't take long before we get a good heat up and are snapping those beams into the columns like they're from a kid's erector set.

I find myself sneaking glances at Mike from time to time. He isn't exactly cocky, but he handles himself like a man who knows he's good and just lets his body take over and do what has to be done. It's late in the morning, now, and the sun is getting hot. Streams of sweat trickle down his torso, making it fuckin' *gleam;* drops of it bead around his nipples, which are as big as quarters and the color of old pennies. I think about what it'd be like chewing on them, flicking them with my tongue, nipping them with my teeth as Mike's muscular body squirms under me. His torso is nut brown but when he leans down to spin in a low bolt, I see his tan line and a strip of creamy skin beneath it. His ass must be a very pretty thing, pale and smooth like polished ivory. The fun and games a couple of nights ago haven't taken the edge off my hunger; if anything I'm stoked for more of the same.

We're on our fifth header by the time the lunch whistle blows. Mike pulls off his hardhat and wipes his forehead with the back of his hand; I watch as his biceps bulge up and dance. He stands there for a few seconds, his left knee bent, his weight on his right hip, that muscle-packed torso so nicely slicked. I feel my throat squeeze tight just looking at him. He's a slab of prime beef, all right, and my brain goes overtime thinking of all the dirty things I'd like to do to him. He suddenly turns and looks at me, and there's this second when my face is still naked, my thoughts written on it for anyone to see. I couldn't have been more obvious if I'd reached out and grabbed his basket. Mike's eyes burn into me, and it's clear he *knows* what's on my mind. But he turns his head and gazes out toward the Jersey shore, like he's searching for something. Slowly, carelessly, he reaches up and scratches his balls, giving them a little extra tug. The signal is so fuckin' blatant that my brain buzzes with confusion. I'm surprised smoke isn't coming out of my ears.

Mike and I eat lunch together sitting on a girder with our legs dangling over 800 feet of nothing. Mike is relaxed and friendly, so open and at ease that I begin to wonder if I misread what was going on between us just a few minutes ago. I ask Mike how Pete, the guy whose place I'm taking, happened to fall.

Mike shrugs. "We were working a little late. I guess he was tired and just got sloppy. It happens."

After a while, we run out of conversation. I lay on my back and close my eyes, feeling the sun beat down on me. I think about what Mike looks like naked, and I give him a dick that's meaty and thick, just to keep the fantasy interesting. My dick gives a hard thrust against my jeans, but I don't do nothing to hide it.

"Thinking about pussy?" Mike asks. I half open my eyes and see him looking down at me, grinning. "I was just wondering. It looks like your dick's about to split your pants open."

"It's been a problem lately," I say, keeping my voice casual. "I seem to be horny all the time."

Mike's grin widens. "Well, maybe you'll get lucky soon." He winks his eye at me, and again I get that weird feeling he's sending me some kind of message. He stands up and dusts himself off. "Time to get back to work."

For the rest of the afternoon it's like that, Mike joking around, giving me these looks that may mean something, but then again maybe not. He's got me wound tighter than a clock, and I don't like it. For one thing, it's affecting my work now. A couple of times I fumble the bolts, stupidly watching them slip between my fingers and drop down all that space beneath us. I almost lose my spud wrench the same way, just grabbing it in the last half second before it's gone for good. I glance toward Mike, and he's watching me, grinning. "Uh, oh," he says. "You almost killed a businessman that time." His smile is good-natured enough, but his eyes gleam with a bold light that misses nothing. He's just having a good ol' time at my expense. I feel like pushing him off his beam.

At 4:45, Jackson signals for us to start wrapping it up. Mike cups his mouth with his hands. "Send another beam up!" he shouts. Jackson shakes his head and points to his watch. "We can do it!" Mike shouts back. "Al and I don't mind working a little late." Jackson shrugs and signals for the crane operator to hoist another beam up.

I glare at Mike. "What the hell's got into you?" I call over to him. "I want to go home."

Mike just grins. "The way you been fucking up this afternoon, I figure you owe the company a few minutes extra work." The beam swings down overhead, and he guides it into place. Pissed, I help line up the holes and slide a few bolts in. By the time he cuts the choker loose, the rest of the crew has taken off, leaving us alone. I spend a few more minutes bent over my end of the beam, slipping in the remaining bolts and tightening the nuts. I'm working as fast as I can so that I can just get the hell out of here and put an end to this day. I turn to see how Mike's doing with his end. He's still out there on the middle of the beam, only now his pants are down among his ankles. He's slowly stroking his stiff cock, his face as calm as if this is the most natural thing he could be doing. I almost drop my wrench for the second time that day.

"You ought to tie that thing around your wrist," Mike says, "before you kill someone."

I just stare at him. "What the fuck are you doing?"

Mike laughs. "What does it look like?"

I watch him standing there on the beam, beating off. My own dick starts beating against my zipper, yelling to be let out. "Come on down to where there's some floor beneath us," I say. My throat's so tight I can barely get the words out.

Mike shakes his head. "No. I got a better idea. Come up here and join me."

The beam he's standing on juts out over the side of the building. I look down at the fifty-four stories worth of empty air beneath us. If we fell, I just might be able to shoot a load before hitting bottom, but there'd be hell to pay afterwards. I shake my head. "No way, Mike. I only practice safe sex."

But Mike just stands there grinning, stroking his dick. He stops for a minute and peels off his T-shirt. His sweaty torso gleams in the late afternoon sun, cut and chiseled in such a way that every muscle stands out. He tosses the shirt into the wind, and I watch as it floats down into oblivion. The street below is deep in the shadow of early evening, but up here it's still bright day. I spend a couple of seconds watching Mike standing there buck naked except for his hard hat, and I know I'm going to get it on with him or die trying. I jump up on the beam.

"Hold on," Mike calls out. "I want you to get naked first."

*What the hell,* I shrug. I'm ready for anything now. I do a careful strip, draping my clothes over the column head. Seconds later, I'm bare-ass naked. A slight breeze plays over my body and I can feel the last rays of the sun on my skin. The steel's cool and smooth under my bare feet; everything else around me feels like miles of empty air.

Mike's lips curl up into a slow smile. "You look fuckin' great, Al," he says. He kicks off his shoes, and I watch as they disappear into the darkness below. He steps out of his pants, leaving them piled on the girder behind him.

I walk across the girder toward him like a man crossing pond ice on a sunny day. I've been walking for years on narrow beams above open space, and I feel my body automatically make the tiny adjustments that keep me from losing my balance. When I reach Mike, I run my hands over his chest and torso, as much to steady myself as to feel his naked body. He leans forward and kisses me lightly, then not so lightly. We play dueling tongues for a while, and then Mike reaches down and wraps his palm around my dick. He glances at it and then back at me. "Jeez, you got a beautiful dick, Al."

"Yeah, I get a lot of compliments on it."

Mike grins. "I bet. Look how thick it is. And long, too. And how big and red the cockhead is." He laughs. "Not many men have a dick this pretty, Al. I hope you appreciate what you got." He glances down again. "Your balls have a nice size to them too, even though they're pulled up a little tight."

I smile stiffly. "Being scared shitless has a way of doing that to me, Mike. Maybe we should just skip the commentary and move on to what's next."

Mike looks amused. He carefully bends down and picks up his jeans. He pulls a condom out of the back pocket. "All right, let's get to it. How 'bout plugging my butt hard?"

I have to laugh. "Well, I'm glad you practice safe sex," I say, as I slip the condom on. Mike turns around and bends over, hands on knees.

I have never fucked with such concentration before. My mind is alert to every movement we make, and my body is as tuned as if each nerve ending has a mind of its own. I begin pumping my hips, first with a slow, grinding tempo, then faster and deeper. Everything is reduced down to one word: *balance*. Mike knows this too and he meets me stroke for stroke, his body reacting to the thrusts and pulls of mine like we're both well-oiled parts of one moving machine. I hold on to his torso, not roughly, but with a touch light and cautious enough to just barely feel the squirm of his muscles beneath my fingertips. We fuck like we're defusing a bomb, in carefully controlled terror. I have never had sex that felt so goddamn exciting.

I spit in my hand and begin stroking Mike off. Mike groans loudly and squirms against me, a move I wasn't expecting. For a second, we sway to one side and I feel the beam slip from under my feet. Mike and I both quickly shift our weight and regain our balance. "Sweet Jesus," I mutter. But I never miss a stroke.

The lights are beginning to go on in the buildings below us. The city spreads out beneath us to the horizon and I feel like I'm fuckin' flying. Even this far up, I can still faintly hear the sounds of traffic from below. I plunge deep into Mike again. Mike's groan trails off into a long whimper. His balls are pulled up tight, and his dick in my hand is as stiff as dicks get. I know he's not far from squirting his load. Each time I pump my hips, Mike's groans get louder and more heartfelt. I pull my dick out just to the head and then slide in with a long, deep thrust. Mike cries out, and his body spasms against me. His dick pulses in my hand, his load gushing between my fingers and dripping down into the darkness below. I hold on tight as his body shudders in my arms, keeping the control and balance for both of us. When he quiets down, I give my hips a few quick thrusts. That's all I need to get me off. I ride the orgasm out like a surfer on a killer wave, getting off on the thrill but concentrating on my balance all at the same time.

When the last shudder is over, I carefully pull out. Mike turns around and we kiss each other lightly, our bodies pressed tightly together. Mike makes a sudden jerking movement to the side, and I feel a half-second of pure terror before I regain my balance. Mike laughs.

I glare at him. "You dickhead."

But Mike just keeps on grinning. He picks up his pants. "Come on, let's get off this damn beam."

Back by the foreman's shack, I give Mike my undershirt to replace the one he tossed over the side. But he's going to have to take the subway home barefooted. He just shrugs this off. As I get dressed I start thinking about what a fuckin' insane thing it was we just did. To my annoyance, my hands begin to tremble as I tie my shoes. I make sure Mike doesn't see this.

I look up at him. "Did you ever do anything this crazy before?"

The muscles in Mike's face twitch, like he's trying to decide whether or not to say something. Finally he breaks into a slow, easy smile. "Sure. How do you think the guy you replaced, Pete, fell?" He sees the expression in my face and laughs. "Hey, I was *joking*, okay? I've never done this before."

We ride down in the lift in silence. Mike is idly looking out toward the city skyline. I stare at his face, trying to figure out just exactly how Pete did fall off that girder.

Down on the street, Mike kisses me lightly. "See you tomorrow, Al. You're great to work with." I watch as he walks barefoot down the sidewalk to the subway station on the corner, his arms swinging jauntily by his side. I shake my head. Jamming my hands in my jeans pockets, I thread through the crowds of people. When I get to the first street corner, I wait for the light to turn green, looking both ways carefully before crossing.

# Calcutta

At five in the morning, I usually don't expect to run into anybody on the streets. Which is fine with me. This is the time of day that I like the best, when most people are still in bed and the city is quiet. The streets take on a whole new feeling: peaceful, empty, the stores and coffee shops shut down, the yellow blinking traffic lights providing the only distraction. It's also my favorite time to work out. I belong to one of those 24-hour fitness centers, and at this time of day the place is almost empty: no lines for the weights, no guys waiting impatiently for you to wrap up your set.

So, I'm just walking down the street toward the gym, enjoying the quiet, not thinking of anything in particular, when I notice this guy in a wheelchair on the corner ahead. I size him up in an eye blink: the torn Metallica T-shirt, the long, ratty hair, the powerful arms, and . . . no legs, just jeans pinned against the stumps of his thighs. When I pass him, I avoid eye contact, hoping to escape getting caught up in some little street encounter. Dream on. He reaches out and lightly touches my arm. "Hey, buddy," he says, "can you give me a minute to help me out?"

*Shit,* I think. I turn to him. "Sure. What's up?"

The guy points up the block, which rises before us in a long, sloping hill. "I got to catch a bus at the next street over," he says. "Can you give me a push up this hill?"

Well, what am I going to do, leave him stranded there? "All right," I say. I get behind his wheelchair and start pushing. The guy twists around so that he's half facing me. "My name's Jerry," he says. He holds out a hand to me that is large and none too clean.

I shake it reluctantly, wedging my knee against the chair to keep it from rolling back. "I'm Paul," I say. Jerry's grip is powerful, and I can feel a ridge of calluses rub against my palm. Looking at him more closely now, I can see how broad his shoulders are, how much his muscles bunch up beneath his T-shirt. I resume pushing Jerry's chair, bending down and leaning forward, my face right above him. I get a whiff of something that isn't exactly roses, and I start breathing through my mouth. Pushing Jerry is turning out to be a harder job than I expected: there's something wrong with the chair; it keeps swerving over to the right, and the wheels keep getting stuck. Now I see how Jerry got his biceps.

"This chair's a piece of shit, isn't it?" Jerry says, as if reading my mind.

"It's pretty beat up," I agree.

"I got it from the VA hospital. I get to go there because I'm a Gulf War veteran. That's how I lost my legs: stepping on a fuckin' land mine two weeks before my tour of duty was over." Jerry's tone of voice is conversational, almost cheerful.

"That's a tough break," I say, because I can't think of anything else to say.

Jerry gives a laugh without any bitterness. "No shit!" He jerks his thumb in the direction we're coming from. "You know that Highway 80 overpass, a few blocks away?"

"Yeah. What about it?"

"I slept under there last night. I'll probably sleep under there tonight, too."

*Why is he telling me all this stuff?* I wonder. But it's pretty fucking obvious. I can smell a touch coming on a mile away. "Why don't you just sleep in one of the shelters?" I ask.

Jerry snorts. "Those fleabags. I never go to those places. Only bums hang out there."

I keep a diplomatic silence. After a little while, we finally make it to the top. I wheel Jerry next to the bus stop. "Here you go," I say.

"Thanks, man," Jerry says. He holds out his hand again, and, again, reluctantly, I shake it. Only he doesn't let go when I try to pull away. "Listen, Paul," he says, his voice suddenly low and urgent, his words coming out fast. "I wonder if you could help me out with a little contribution. I'm trying to make it to the Y so that I can get a room and clean up. I smell like shit, I know that. Do you think I like being this dirty? Only they charge sixty bucks for a room and I'm kind of low on cash. My disability check isn't due for another week. Do you think you could spare a few bucks?"

I pull my hand out of Jerry's grasp and clear my throat. "Look," I say. "I have a standing policy not to give money to panhandlers." Jerry doesn't say anything, he just looks at me, his gray eyes narrowed. "I mean, I give to charities," I say, talking faster. "I belong to the United Way, I'm a member of the Sierra Club. It's just that I get hit up for money all the time, so I decided that I just wouldn't give any more money on the streets . . ." *Jesus, will you stop babbling!* I think. I take a breath and look Jerry in the face. "I'm sorry."

Jerry shrugs. "Don't be." He spins his chair around and wheels down the street. "Thanks for the push," he says, over his shoulder. I watch his retreating back for a few moments and then turn and go to the gym.

The place is almost deserted, just me and a couple of other guys in the weight room. I go through my routine quickly and efficiently, keeping my mind blank. There's some guy there I haven't seen before, a kid in early twenties: blond, milk-fed, downy-skinned, his body smooth and beautifully defined. I think of Jerry, and the contrast between the two is grotesque. The guy asks me to spot him when he does his presses, and I lean over him, ready to catch the weight if I have to. His T-shirt is hiked up to his chest, and I check out the hard torso, the cut of the abs. A little later, he returns the favor as I do my bench presses, and I catch a glimpse of the bulge in his jock strap under his gym shorts. We talk briefly; he tells me that his name is Jeff and that he's a student at U.C. San Francisco.

When I'm done with my workout, I go back to the locker room, strip, and enter the steam room. Except for me, the place is empty. I lean against the tile wall and close my eyes, listening to the hiss of the steam, feeling the rush of heat pour over my body. I hear the click of the steam room door open and close. After a couple of beats, I open my eyes again. Jeff is sitting on the bench across from me, naked, knees spread apart. He watches me intently as his dick slowly gets hard. After a pause, I reach over and slide my hand over his torso, feeling the hard muscles beneath my fingertips. Jeff hooks his hand around my neck and pulls my mouth against his; we kiss for a few seconds. I drop to my knees and slide my lips down his dick, until my nose is mashed against his dark blond pubes.

Jeff lays his hands on either side of my head and starts pumping his dick in and out of my mouth. I suck on it greedily, my hands still exploring his torso. I find his nipples and twist them, not gently. Jeff groans.

He pushes me back. "Stand up," he says, his voice urgent. I climb to my feet, and stand before him, my arms at my side. My dick is as hard as dicks get. Jeff wraps his hand around it and starts stroking, his fist sliding rapidly up and down the shaft. He replaces his hand with his mouth, and I close my eyes, letting the sensations sweep over me. The steam hisses out of the vents and pours over my body, and my sweat trickles down my face, my torso, my back. Jeff tugs gently on my balls as he deep-throats me; his hand wanders to my ass, squeezing the cheeks, burrowing into the crack, massaging my asshole. I feel my load get pulled up by his mouth, and one sharp thrust of my hips sends me over the edge. My body spasms, and I groan loudly. Jeff pulls my dick out of his mouth and jacks me off as I shoot, my load raining down onto his upturned face. And right at that moment, while the orgasm sweeps over me, the image of Jerry's face floods my brain. *What the fuck . . . ?* I think. All I see is Jerry, his narrowed eyes, his weather-beaten face, the stumps of his legs. I try to shake the image out of my head. Jeff is jerking off, and then he cries out as the sperm pulses out of his dick. I reach down and twist his nipple until he's done.

We're silent for a few beats. "That was hot!" Jeff finally says, grinning.

"Yeah," I say absently. "Real hot."

When I'm out on the street again, I walk back to the bus stop. If by some chance Jerry is still there, I'll give him a couple of bucks. But the place is deserted.

For the whole morning at work, I can't get Jerry's face out of my mind. After a while this gets annoying. *What the fuck is this?* I wonder. *Some spasm of liberal guilt?* At lunch, I leave the office to run a few errands; for some reason I notice the street beggars more than I usually do. They're on every corner, squatting down in doorways or against newspaper racks or street lamps, their Styrofoam cups in front of them, along with their cardboard signs, hand-printed with their hard-luck stories. Nobody gives these guys a dime. I don't either.

I still think of Jerry that evening, while I wait in line to see a movie with my friend Tony. Tony's going on about some guy he's been fucking, how this might turn into something. I listen patiently. Finally, when Tony winds down for a second, I clear my throat. "I had this weird encounter this morning," I say. "I can't get it out of my head."

Tony looks at me expectantly. "Somebody hot?" he asks, grinning.

The absurdity of Tony's comment makes me laugh. I shake my head. "It's nothing. Skip it." Tony continues talking about his new boyfriend.

It doesn't take long before I'm sick of him, of the idea of spending the next few hours sitting next to him in a movie theater. I clear my throat. "Look, Tony," I say. "I'm sorry. I'm just not in the mood for a movie. Do you mind if I take a rain check?"

The blood rushes up to Tony's face. "Hell, yeah, I mind. We made plans. I drove to the city to do this."

"I'm sorry," I say. And I am. But all I want to do is get away.

Tony leaves, none too graciously. I put my hands in my pockets and start walking. I'm in an upscale commercial district, the streets flanked by department, jewelry and clothing stores: Macy's, Gump's, Saks, I. Magnin. And yet, in every doorway, figures are huddled under blankets and beat-up sleeping bags. I pass by a woman panhandling in front of Tiffany's, a small girl in her arms. The girl watches me with shrewd, bright eyes. *Where the fuck am I?* I think. *Calcutta?*

When I reach my car, I climb into the driver's seat. I sit there for a long time, my hands grasping and ungrasping the steering wheel. "Shit!" I mutter. I stick my key in the ignition and start up the car.

My headlights make a tunnel of light under the highway overpass. Everything on either side of me is pure darkness; the only other light source is from a street lamp over a block away. I cruise down the street slowly, peering out the window, trying to make out the details of the forms I see lying on the pavement. My nerves are raw. I half expect some crack addict to pull out a Saturday night special and blow my head off. I finally spot Jerry sitting in his wheelchair, wedged into a concrete corner. He squints into the headlights.

I get out of my car. "Hi, Jerry," I say. "Remember me?"

Jerry looks at me for a long time. "Sure," he finally says. "How ya doin', Paul?" If he's surprised to see me, he doesn't show it.

I talk fast, before I have a chance to change my mind. "Look, if you want a place to spend the night, I can take you back to my apartment. I have a fold-out couch you can sleep on."

Jerry gives me a hard, shrewd look. A full thirty seconds of silence passes. "Okay," he finally says.

I wheel him to the passenger side of the car and open it. He slides into the front seat with surprising agility. I open my trunk, and after a hard struggle, I get his rusty, beat-up, piece-of-shit wheelchair folded up. By the time I close the trunk, sweat is dripping down my forehead.

We ride back in silence. I keep my mind blank. Every time a thought tries to rise to the surface, I push it down savagely. I don't speak to Jerry until I've pulled into the garage of my apartment house. "There's no elevator," I say. "I'm going to have to carry you up the stairs."

Jerry regards me calmly, like we do this every day. "Okay," he says.

Jerry is not a small man, and I stagger up the stairs with him in my arms, praying to God that I don't drop him. Up close, the smell of stale sweat from his body is almost enough to make me gag. His torso under my arms is powerfully built. Fuck, he ought to rent out his wheelchair as a workout machine. I deposit him on the sofa and then go back down for his wheelchair. When I'm back in the apartment, Jerry is the first to speak. "Mind if I take a bath?" he asks.

"No problem," I say.

I help him into the bathroom and turn on the faucets for the tub. Steam rises into the air. Jerry peels off his clothes and drops them on the floor. His torso is packed with muscles. There's a tattoo on his left arm of a growling bulldog, with U.S.M.C. written underneath. The ink under his skin has started to run, blurring the image. A scar runs from his left pectoral down his side. Jerry sees me staring at it. "I got that in a knife fight with some coked-up street crazy," he says. He lowers himself slowly into the tub. "Sweet Jesus, that feels good!" he groans.

I pick up his clothes. "I'm going down to the laundry room and throw these in a washing machine," I say. Jerry is too busy soaping down to answer.

When I come back, Jerry is sitting naked in his chair, toweling himself dry. The water in the tub is several shades darker. I reach in and pull the plug, and then throw Jerry a terrycloth robe. "You want something to eat?" I ask.

Jerry looks at me with half-lidded eyes as he slips on the robe. *What does it take to get a rise out of this guy?* I wonder. "Okay," Jerry says.

Over dinner, Jerry starts loosening up a little. He tells me about life on the streets, about the crazies he runs into, how he got his arm broken four years ago in a fight over his cashed disability check, and how it never really healed right. It surprises me to realize that he's a handsome man: the skin around his eyes is puffy, and his face is lined, but his features are regular, his mouth well-formed, his chin strong, his gray eyes fierce and intelligent. There's a no-bullshit, direct way about him, stripped of self-pity. He laughs once over some story he's telling me about life on the streets, and in that instant he looks years younger.

Shortly after dinner, I open up the sofa bed and make it up for Jerry. "I'm going to bed," I say. "Let me know if you need anything."

Jerry shrugs off the robe and slips naked under the blankets. He folds his hands under his head, his biceps bunched up like meaty grapefruits. "Why don't you hang around for a minute?" he says. "Keep me company." He grins. "These new surroundings have got me all wired."

His grin is so boyish and good-natured that I'm immediately suspicious. He doesn't look "wired" at all. If anything, he looks completely in control. Uneasiness floods over me. *I don't know anything about this guy!* I think. *What the fuck was I thinking of, bringing him into my apartment?*

Jerry waits patiently, his eyes trained on me. I sit down next to him, my body rigid. He reaches up and squeezes my shoulder. I flinch. "What's the matter?" he says. "Do I make you nervous?"

"Yeah," I say. "As a matter of fact, you do."

We sit silently for a few beats, Jerry's hand still kneading my shoulder. He pulls me down, and we kiss, first gently, and then with growing fierceness. Jerry's tongue pushes deep into my mouth. I slide my hand across his furry chest, feeling the hard pectorals, the nipples. I pinch one and feel it swell. Jerry sighs. "Yeah," he says, "that's good. Play with my tittie."

I lean forward and flick his nipple with my tongue, then nip it gently. Jerry's body stirs. He reaches down and cups my crotch with his hand, giving it a squeeze. He pulls back and looks at me, his eyes hard and shrewd. "Why don't you get naked?" he says.

I stand up and pull my clothes off as Jerry watches. *This is fucking insane!* I think. But my dick is fully stiff and my heart is hammering hard enough to crack a rib. I can't remember when I've felt this excited.

When I'm naked, I slip into the bed, next to Jerry. He reaches over and pulls me against him, wrapping his huge arms around my torso. We kiss again as Jerry presses our bodies together. I can feel his hard dick rub up against my belly. He increases the pressure of his hug, and I find myself struggling for breath. Jerry's eyes gleam with a wolfish light, and suddenly I'm scared shitless. I'm a strong guy myself, but I can't break free. If Jerry wanted to, he could snap my spine in two right now. But he just releases his grip, laughing.

"What was that all about?" I ask.

"Nothing," Jerry says. "I'm just fuckin' with you."

"Oh, yeah?" I say. I grab his wrists and pin his arms above his head. Jerry doesn't resist, and his eyes gleam with amusement. But I don't kid myself. That if this were a real brawl, I'd probably be fighting for my life right now. "Why don't you just suck my dick for a while, tough guy?" I growl.

"Okay," Jerry says, laughing. All of a sudden he's as mild as a spring day. I release his wrists and sit up, pressing my thighs against Jerry's torso. My dick sticks straight out, inches above his face. He opens his mouth, lifts his head, and I slide my dick in. His lips nibble down the shaft, and his tongue wraps around it. I don't stop until my balls are pressing against his chin. Jerry takes it all like a trouper. I start pumping my hips, fucking his mouth in long, slow strokes. Jerry twists his head from side to side, sucking on my dick with noisy gusto. He wraps his hands around my balls and tugs on them as his head bobs up and down. I reach back and start jacking him off. His dick feels meaty and thick in the palm of my hand, and the pre-cum that oozes out helps me slick it up nicely.

I whip off the blankets so that it's just our naked bodies on the bed, with no covers to hide under. I want to see Jerry's body. I pull back from him and sit at the foot of the bed. Jerry shows no sign of self-consciousness; he lays there, his hands once again behind his head, watching me calmly as my eyes drink him in. I lean forward and run my hands over his arms, tracing the bulge of his biceps. I knead the muscles of his torso, feeling their hardness: the powerful pecs, the hard, furry abs; then run my finger along the length of his scar, noting the texture of the rubbery red skin. I place my hands on his hips and slide them down over the stumps of his thighs, massaging the flesh. Jerry's dick lies hard against his belly, twitching slightly, a drop of pre-cum oozing out of the head. Jerry has a beautiful dick: red and meaty, thick, veined, the head flaring out. His balls hang low, covered with a light fuzz. I lean forward and press my face against them, breathing in their faint musky smell, feeling the hairs tickle my face. I open my mouth and suck them in, rolling the loose scrotal flesh around with my tongue. I look up, my mouth full of ballmeat; Jerry is watching me intently, his eyes narrowed, his eyebrows pulled down.

I drag my tongue up the length of his dick and around the flared, red head. I open my lips, and slowly, inch by inch, I take Jerry's dick full in my mouth, sucking on it, wrapping my tongue around it as my lips nibble down the shaft. Jerry exhales deeply, the rasp of his breath a hairbreadth shy of a sigh. I start bobbing my head up and down, and Jerry pumps his hips in synch with my mouth, thrusting his dick hard into my mouth with each downward swoop of my head. I run my fingers through the forest of hair on his chest and twist his nipples hard. This time, Jerry does groan, and when I glance at his face, I see the composure beginning to break, the eyes widening, the mouth opening as he breathes harder. Jerry firmly grips my head with both hands and starts plowing my mouth in earnest, his thrusts hard and deep. With a sudden, quick movement, he pivots us around, so that I'm on my back now, with Jerry straddling my chest. His huge hands grip my temples with greater pressure now, and the head of his cock is banging against the back of my throat like it's knocking on Heaven's door. This suits me fine, I can't get enough of his dick in my mouth, I'm feeding on it like a shark on chum. I reach behind and grab his ass cheeks, feeling their muscularity, how they relax and harden with each thrust of his dick.

Jerry's face looms over me. His lips spread wide in a savage grin. "I would really love to fuck that pretty ass of yours, baby," he growls.

I pull his dick out of my mouth and return his grin. "Just hold that thought," I say. I slip out of bed, make a run to the bathroom, and return with a condom and a jar of lube.

Jerry leans back, propped up on his arms, as I roll the condom down his dick. I give my hand a liberal squirt of lube and grease his dick up good. Jerry pushes me back onto the bed and hoists my legs over his powerful shoulders. He works his dick into my asshole with killing patience, inch by slow inch. I push my head against the pillow and close my eyes. When he's full in, Jerry just lays motionless on top of me for a few beats. He looks down at me and grins. "I just want my dick and your asshole to get acquainted first," he says, "before they start dancing together." I laugh. Jerry begins to grind his hips slowly at first, almost imperceptibly, and then with increasing thrust. It doesn't take long before he's giving my ass a savage pounding, his balls slapping against me.

I throw my head against the pillow. "Oh, yeah!" I groan.

Jerry bends down and plants his mouth over mine, his tongue snaking back in as his dick works its way deep into my ass. I meet him stroke for stroke, squeezing my ass tight against his dick, matching his rhythm. My heels dig in between his shoulder blades, and my hands hold on to his hips for purchase. We're both working up a sweat now; drops trickle down Jerry's face and splatter on me, mingling with my own sweat. Jerry's chest is heaving, and his breath comes out in ragged gasps. He pauses long enough to squirt a dollop of lube on his hand and starts jacking me off: it doesn't take long before my groans are mingling with his. Jerry's teeth are bared, and, with each thrust of his hips, his grunts become louder and more drawn out. Finally, he shoves his dick in hard and cries out. I feel his body shudder, and he leans down and kisses me hard as the orgasm sweeps over him. Jerry's greased strokes on my dick never slow down, and it's just a matter of seconds before I'm groaning and squirting my load out as well, the thick drops splattering against my chest and belly. Jerry collapses on top of me, smearing his body with my come. I feel his chest rise and fall, and we kiss again. He pulls his softening dick out of my ass and nestles against me, his face nuzzling my neck. After a couple of minutes, he starts snoring. I drift off to sleep soon afterwards.

I wake up early the next morning and get dressed for work. Jerry is still asleep. My mind is full of ideas: contacting social agencies, finding Jerry some kind of permanent place to stay, getting him off the streets. After a while, Jerry wakes up. His eyes follow me around the room.

"I'll be leaving for work in a few minutes," I say. "You're welcome to stay here a while longer."

Jerry shakes his head. "Once you leave, I won't be able to get out. You'll have to carry me down those stairs."

I stop and look at him. "Why don't you just stay here for the day? When I get back, we can talk about figuring some way of finding you a place to stay."

Jerry smiles wryly. "Thanks, but I got things to do."

I carry him down to the sidewalk outside, sit him on the stoop, and get his wheelchair. "I'll be back from work around 5:30," I say. "You going to be here?"

Jerry shrugs. "Yeah, sure."

He's not there when I return that evening. Somehow, I'm not surprised, though I stay indoors in case he shows up. Later, I drive by the overpass, but he's not there, either.

Every evening, for a couple of weeks, I make a ritual of cruising under the overpass, searching out in the dim light for a figure in a wheelchair. I never find him. Maybe the thought of some do-gooder trying to get him off the streets is so abhorrent to Jerry that he's moved on to another place where he can't be found. Eventually, I give it up.

But I can't get the son of a bitch out of my head. It's not lust or pity; it certainly isn't love. I don't know what the fuck it is. But Jerry, wherever you are, hustling passersby with your "will you push my wheelchair for me?" routine, I hope you're doing what you want to do. And I wish you luck, man. I wish you luck.

# Monster's Gangbang

Charley McPherson throws his "gangbangs for straight guys" on the third Saturday of every month. It's just about the only action in this podunk Tennessee town, and the boys lucky enough to snag an invitation make sure they stay in Charley's good graces. Charley hosts these little orgies in his rec room, a large, open space in his basement with oak veneer paneling and crummy, beat-up furniture that he doesn't worry too much about getting stained.

I walk through the door, and Charley waves to me from the other side of the room. "Hey, Monster!" he calls out. "Glad you could make it!" Charley has tagged me with the "Monster" label since my first time here, when he first got a gander at the slab of beef I carry between my legs. Now, each time I get naked, I have to put up with all the usual "third leg" and "meat packer" jokes from the rest of the guys.

"Yo, Charley," I grin back. "Good to see ya." Charley is buck naked and leaning over his pool table, screwing one of the three hookers he hires for these occasions. I remember her from before, short and freckled, with frizzy red hair, named Shirelle, or Shirley or Cheryl, something like that. I take in the sight: Charley's tall, lean body, cut and defined, his hips pumping, his good-natured, hound dog face red from the exertion.

Charley thrusts hard and lets go with a long whimper. He catches my eye again and winks. "Grab yourself a beer, Monster," he gasps. "They're in the cooler by the wall." He laughs. "And get naked, dammit! This ain't a spectator sport."

"Sure thing, Charley," I laugh back. I'm later then usual, and there's already a good crowd gathered: about a dozen guys, all naked, some milling around, some standing in little groups, watching the other men screwing the hookers, yelling out encouragement or good-natured wise-cracks, waiting their turn. Charley makes it clear that his parties are for straight boys only (nobody has ever accused Charley of being "open-minded"), and so I keep my preferences to myself. The funny thing, though, is that in spite of this, Charley invites nothing but hot looking men. I wonder about this, not for the first time, as my eyes scan the room. There's Vinny Rossi, the car mechanic down at Rossi's Auto Works, sitting spread-legged on a couch, being sucked off by another of the hookers, his tight, muscular body gleaming with sweat, his handsome head thrown back, eyes closed, panting as she works his dick. Rufus Taylor, the town's assistant deputy of police, is plowing her from behind, his broad back narrowing down to tight haunches, his thick, black dick thrusting in and out. Eddy Pendergast, home for Spring break from TSU, is standing next to them, cheering them on; his back is to me, and I take in the smooth mounds of his pretty, pretty ass, the tight crack, the swing of his low hangers between his parted thighs. Every one of the naked men in this room is a hot motherfucker in his own way, and I can't believe that that's just an accident on Charley's part.

And, then there's me. I can work up enough of a heat to fuck a hooker or two if that's what it takes to get invited. Hell, I certainly don't have to worry about being *aroused*. All I have to do as I'm plowing pussy is look around at the crowd of naked, bull studs packed in this room, adding new stains to Charley's nasty, skanky couch, and my dick gets as hard as fuckin' rebar. Yeah, I'd much rather being plowing the ass or mouth of one of those sexy fuckers, but shit, the hot show they put on for me every month is a hell of a lot better than anything else I can hope for in this crummy town.

I strip off my boxers, kick them aside, and look around the room. Without bragging, I've easily got the biggest wanker in the house. Semi-hard, it sways heavily between my thighs, damn near half-way down to my knees, red, meaty, the head a fleshy little fist of meat. It's an awesome cock, my pride and joy, and as I thread my way through the crowd, the guys part to let me through like I'm fuckin' royalty.

Darlene, the third working girl, is being plowed on the braided throw rug by Scooter Pendergast, Eddy's older brother and the local "bad boy": hair greased back slick and black, lean torso heavily tattooed, cigarette dangling from his mouth. He looks around the room with half-lidded eyes as he pumps her, and when his gaze catches mine he nods and motions me over. "Join the party, Monster," he says. "I'm getting lonely over here."

I walk up to them. "Hey, Darlene," I say, looking down and smiling at her. "You think you can give me a little head to get me started?"

"Sure, Monster," Darlene says, flashing me her professional smile. I squat down and she takes my dick in her mouth and starts working it expertly, nibbling down the shaft, rolling her tongue around the bulbous head. I keep my eyes pinned on Scooter's muscled body pumping away, and I feel my dick swell and harden in Darlene's mouth. Darlene pulls my foreskin back and probes her tongue into my piss slit. I close my eyes for a second, and when I open them, Scooter is looking at me, grinning. "No one sucks dick like Darlene," he says. He gives another hard thrust and slaps her playfully on the ass. "Ain't that right, darlin'?"

Darlene takes my dick out of her mouth and looks back at him. "I haven't been hearing any complaints," she says. She goes back to my dick, and Scooter and I pump away in silence for a few beats. After a minute of this, he nods to the door behind me. "It looks like we got a newcomer," he grunts.

I turn and there's some guy I've never seen before, standing in the doorway and surveying the scene in front of him. He's my age, maybe a couple years older, late twenties at most. He's a big motherfucker all right; his frame fills the doorway, well over six feet, wide-shouldered and long-legged. He's too bundled up for me to get a good idea of what his body's like, but his face has the lived in, craggy look of the naturally masculine man.

"Yo, Rick!" Charley calls out, always the perfect host. "It's about fuckin' time you showed up!" Rick nods but doesn't say anything. Charley looks around the room. "Everyone, this is Rick. This is his first gangbang, so make him feel welcome." Rick waves and gives a lopsided grin, and he looks so sexy that my dick gives an extra throb in Darlene's mouth. *Where does Charley find these guys?* I wonder. I keep sneaking glances as Rick strips off his clothes. His torso is hairy and powerfully built, maybe ten or fifteen pounds away from being really cut. His arms are heavily muscled, and his biceps curve up impressively. He's wearing boxers with a diamond pattern, the kind that come in a Fruit of the Loom three-pack, and when he pulls them down, Charley barks a laugh. "Hey, Monster," he calls out to me. "You finally got some competition!" And he's right. Rick's dick sways heavily between his thighs like one of those salamis in a deli, red and veined, the bulb of the cockhead peeking shyly from his uncut foreskin. Charley has the furnace cranked on high, and the heat of the room makes Rick's balls hang low in his fleshy ballsac. A picture flashes through my mind: Rick straddling my chest, dropping those juicy balls into my mouth, slapping my face with that red, fleshy club of his . . .

Scooter starts groaning, and his body spasms. He pulls out quickly and his load squirts out of his pulsing dick and splatters against Darlene's back. "Fuuuuuck," he sighs.

"Jeez, Scooter," I say. "You gotta learn to pace yourself. The night's still young."

Scooter shakes the last couple of drops of jizz out and grins at me. "Don't worry about me, Monster," he says. "I'm good for at least a couple of more squirts tonight." He wanders off, and it's just Darlene and me. After a while, Rick comes up to us. I feel my throat tighten as I try to keep my eyes from zeroing in on that fat, red wanker of his.

"How does this work?" he asks, his voice a deep baritone. "Can I just join in?"

Darlene takes my cock out her mouth and looks at him. She rolls her eyes. "Jeez, I'm taking on the two biggest dicks in the house. I'm earning my money tonight."

"I'll ride you nice and gentle, " Rick laughs.

"Honey," Darlene says. "If I wanted 'gentle' I'd tell you. Just plow me good, okay? I can take it."

"Yes, ma'am," Rick says.

Darlene goes back to working my dick as Rick mounts her from behind. He meets my gaze with friendly brown eyes and winks at me. "Howdy," he says.

"Hi," I say. "Welcome to Charley's."

Rick does a deep thrust and grinds his pelvis, and Darlene gives an appreciative groan, muffled by my dick in her mouth. "Thanks, man," he says. "What's your name?"

I clear my throat. "Well, they call me Monster here."

Rick looks down as Darlene licks and nibbles on my crank. "I can see why. That's a beaut."

And the way he says this, just so natural and easy about admiring my dick, makes me want to hook my hand around the back of his neck and plant a big wet kiss on his mouth. "I think we're an even match," I say, glancing down. Now that he's fully hard, I can appreciate just how fuckin' huge his cock really is. *Damn!* I think.

"We'll have to measure them side by side later on," Rick says, winking. "Just to make sure."

I shoot him a sharp glance, and Rick looks back at me innocently. *He couldn't have meant that the way it sounded*, I think.

We don't say anything for a few beats, but we lock our eyes together as we fuck Darlene from both ends. Rick's gaze bores into me, and there's this *tension* between us; it's unmistakable. I forget about subtlety as I check out how his pecs mound up, how his nipples stand at attention like little toy soldiers. A drop of sweat trickles down his flat belly, and my eyes trace its path. Rick's mouth is open, and his eyes are half-lidded as he thrusts his hips back and forth. His gaze slides up and down my torso. "You got a nice body," he says. "You must work out."

Darlene's hand is wrapped around my cock, and her fist follows her mouth up and down my shaft as she bobs her head. "Yeah," I pant. "I have a set of weights in my basement. I pump iron every day."

"It shows," Rick says.

Darlene takes my dick out of her mouth. "Look," she says. "Do you two boys want me to leave? I don't want to be a fifth wheel here." Rick and I laugh, but I realize I better cool it. I don't want Darlene reporting back to Charley that he may have a ringer in the crowd. I let a couple of beats go by before I step back. "I think I'm going to take a breather," I say.

"Okay," Rick says, his face expressionless.

I look down at Darlene. "Thanks, Darlene," I say.

"Any time," she says dryly.

I wander around the room a while, and then head on down the hall to the john. I stand before the toilet, pissing out all the beer I drank earlier, my back to the open door. "Damn, but you got a pretty ass, too," that deep baritone voice says.

I look over my shoulder, and there's Rick, leaning against the door jamb, grinning, slowly stroking his big, fat dong with his right hand, his left hand clenched in a fist. I feel my own dick begin to swell and lengthen in my hand. "Well, hi, again," I say.

Rick's still wearing that sexy, lopsided grin. "Didn't we say something about measuring dicks?" he asks.

I shake out the last drops of piss and turn around. "Well, shit, man," I laugh. "I didn't bring my measuring tape with me."

"No problem," Rick says. He drops down to his knees and looks up at me slyly. "I can swallow up to eight inches. We'll just add whatever's left over." He wraps his hand around my dick, and I sigh as his lips slide down my cock. Rick gets about halfway down the shaft, shifts and angles his head and slides down a couple more inches. He stops a couple of inches shy of the base. He pulls back, and looks up at me, his eyes watering from the effort. He wipes the back of his hand against his mouth. "They gave you the right name, Monster!" he says. He opens the fist of his huge hand, and I see a couple of condoms and a small jar of lube in his palm. "I think it's time we really start partying," he says.

We find what looks like a small storeroom a little further down the hall. As soon as I close the door behind us, Rick is back on his knees, slobbering over my cock. I seize his head with both hands and begin fucking his face with some serious intention. Rick meets me stroke for stroke, bobbing his head up and down, my balls slapping against his chin. I push him down on the floor and straddle his chest, dropping my balls in his mouth. He rolls his tongue over my nut sac, sucking noisily as his hands reach up and knead the muscles of my torso.

I pivot around and take Rick's dick in my mouth. We both get down to the serious business of fucking each other's face, eating each other's cock. Rick has one of those torpedo dicks that widen at the base, and my lips stretch apart as he thrusts his hips up and shoves that fat, hard dick all the way down my throat and then out again. Rick's hand slides over the smooth mound of my ass and burrows into my crack. His finger pushes up against my bung hole, playing with it, flicking it lightly. He pushes in, working his finger up my chute knuckle by knuckle.

I start sucking on Rick's balls. I love it when a man's balls hang low, and Rick's fleshy pouch spills into my mouth as he rubs his huge dick all over my face. He's got a second greased finger worked up my ass, now, and he finger fucks me with quick, short jabs. "You gonna let me fuck that pretty ass of yours, baby?" he croons. "Really plow you good?"

I raise my head and look at him. "Fuck yeah," I gasp.

We break free for a moment, as Rick tears open a condom packet and rolls the rubber down his shaft. He gives me a gentle push so that I'm on my back, and then he seizes my ankles and spreads my legs open. His cockhead pokes against my asshole, and I let out a deep sigh, willing myself to relax.

Rick's cockhead enters me with an inaudible "pop", and then he slowly pushes in, inch by inch, his eyes never leaving mine. I keep on breathing deeply, easing my muscles, taking him in. I feel like I'm being impaled by the Father of all Cocks, and I give a low groan. Rick stops. "Just relax," he urges, his gaze still locked with mine.

I take a few more deep breaths, letting my muscles loosen. Rick bends down and kisses me, pushing his tongue deep into my mouth as he slides in a couple more inches. He wraps his arms around me, and I feel his body rise and fall against mine with each breath he takes, his cock full up my ass. After a couple of more beats, Rick begins gently pumping his hips. "That feel okay, Monster?" he whispers.

"Yeah," I gasp. "And my name's Bill, okay?"

Rick grins. "Sure, Bill." He deepens his thrusts, and I close my eyes and groan again.

"Open your eyes," Rick growls. "I like to look into a man's eyes when I slam my dick up his ass."

Rick and I lock gazes as he pumps his hips in long, deep strokes, plunging into my ass, then out just to the tip of his cockhead, and then sliding full back in again. Rick quickens the pace, pounding my ass in rapid fire strokes, his balls slapping against me with each thrust. I've got my hand wrapped around my dick, and I match my strokes with each of his thrusts, jacking my cock furiously. Rick's face drips with sweat, and drops of it splash down on me. Our bodies slip and slide against each other as Rick pounds away at my ass like he's churning butter. I keep Rick pinned in my gaze, and I feel like I'm falling into those dark brown eyes.

"I could pop any second now," I gasp.

"Yeah, me too," Rick grunts.

Rick pulls out almost completely, takes a breath, and exhales deeply as he slides his dick full up my ass. I squeeze my asshole tightly, pushing up to meet him, and that does the trick. Rick shudders and groans loudly. He bends down and kisses me fiercely, as his body spasms and his load pumps out one squirt after another into the condom up my ass. I give a low muffled groan, and my cock throbs in my hand as it pumps its load of jizz out between my fingers. We thrash around on the plank floor, squirting our loads, our bodies pressed tight together. When I'm done, I roll off Rick.

"Damn!," I say. Rick laughs. We lie there for what feels like a long time.

Rick raises his head and looks at me. "We better get back to the others," he says. "Before those straight boys start suspecting something."

I chuckle. "I wonder just how 'straight'. Shit, you can't get any queerer than that gangbang. All those hot, naked guys getting off watching each other plow pussy."

Rick raises an eyebrow. "You think so?" He gives his lazy grin again. "Maybe we should tell Charley to get rid of the hookers and just keep it stag next time."

"Not a chance," I say. "The hookers are what keep these gangbangs 'legit.' Charley and the others would sooner swallow hot coals then admit how queer all of this really is." I stand up. "It looks like you and I are the only ones here with enough balls to call it like it is."

Rick reaches over and gives my nutsac a playful tug. "And such nice, meaty balls too."

We kiss and then walk back to the rec room to join the others. Rick takes his hand off my ass just before we walk through the door.

# Inspection

Ross Plating Shop is on a desert road five miles outside of Oracle, Arizona. I can tell at a glance that it's a two-bit operation: a low, squat cinder block building next to a dirt parking lot. A company truck is parked in the lot, with some guy standing in the flatbed, tossing sacks down onto the ground. I pull up alongside him.

It's August, and as soon as I step out of my air-conditioned car, the desert heat slams into me like a mule kick. I shade my eyes and look up at the guy on the flatbed. "Excuse me," I say. "Can you tell me where I can find the owner?"

The man looks down at me, his eyes narrowed. He's a few years younger than me, early twenties maybe, and he's just wearing a T-shirt and a pair of denim cut-offs. His biceps push against the cotton sleeves of his shirt, and his calves are bunched with muscle. *Keep your focus,* I tell myself. *This is business.* "We're not looking to buy anything," he says. "We're happy with the suppliers we already have."

I walk up to the flatbed, pull my credentials out, and hold them up. "I'm not a salesman," I say. "My name's Steve Purcell. I'm a hazardous waste inspector for the Environmental Protection Agency."

The man takes my credentials and scans them. I fight the temptation to look up his shorts and see if I can catch a glimpse of something interesting. He hands the credentials back to me. "Did we do something wrong?" he asks.

I shrug. "This is just a routine inspection."

He considers this. "My dad's the owner, and he's in Tucson on business," he says. "There's nobody in charge here but me. You'll have to come back tomorrow."

He turns and picks up another sack, as if that's the end of the matter.

"I'm afraid that's not how it works," I say mildly. "I'm on a tight schedule, and this is the only time I have available."

The guy drops the sack on the ground and looks at me. His expression isn't so much annoyed as speculative. He pushes back a damp lock of sandy hair. "I've got a shit load of things I'm supposed to do today," he says.

"I'm sorry," I say. "I'll try to make this as quick as possible."

He jumps off the truck and faces me. His eyes are slate gray and wide, and there's a spray of freckles across his nose. He's fuckin' adorable. "Okay," he says. "What do you want to know?"

"Well, maybe you can start by telling me your name."

"Gary," he says. "Gary Ross."

It's late morning, and the desert sun is pounding down on us. My shirt is already plastered to my back, and sweat trickles down my face. "How about we go inside and talk, okay?" I say.

Gary regards me for a couple of beats. "We can use my dad's office," he says.

The office is a small, untidy room with manuals and stacks of papers piled on the desk and file cabinet. I sit down on a folding chair and mop my face with my handkerchief. Gary leans against the door frame, looking at me. "We got a soda machine out in the warehouse. You want a Coke or something?"

Right now a Coke sounds like the answer to every problem I've ever had. "Yeah," I say. "If you don't mind."

Gary grins slowly and stretches. His shirt hikes up to his navel, giving me a quick flash of hard abs. "No," he says. "I don't mind." He turns and walks away.

I lean back in my chair and look around. There's a picture on the wall showing Gary and an older man, his father, I guess, grinning and standing on a pier, holding up a string of fish. Another picture shows Gary standing on an outboard, legs spread apart, as he's struggling to reel in a fish he just hooked. I get up to take a closer look. The picture's taken from behind: Gary's wearing nothing but a pair of Speedos, his back is arched, and his ass cheeks are clenched tight as he struggles with his fish. Now I've been on the road doing inspections for two weeks, eating greasy diner chicken and spending the nights staring at the walls in my motel rooms. At this point I'm more bored and horny than I can ever remember being. I think about all the things I'd like to do to that pretty ass.

"That was taken at Lake Powell," I hear Gary's voice behind me. "Dad likes to take the family up there fishing whenever he can."

I turn, and Gary hands me a can of Coke. "How much do I owe you?" I ask.

"Don't sweat it," Gary says.

I pull out my wallet and take a dollar out. I hand it to him. "Thanks," I say. "But we're not supposed to take gifts while conducting inspections."

Gary laughs. "It's a fuckin' Coke."

"I'm sorry," I say, still holding the dollar out to him. "Agency rules."

Gary takes the dollar and puts it in his back pocket. His mouth is pursed like he's trying to suppress a smile. He's really getting under my skin. He goes behind his father's desk and sits down on the upholstered, swivel chair, his legs propped up on the desk. "So what do you want to know?" he asks.

I go through the standard litany of questions: what does the facility do here? What kind of waste does it generate? How much on a monthly basis? Is any of it hazardous? Gary's answers seem straightforward enough, but his eyes bore into me with all this fuckin' *intensity*, like there's something going on between us that has nothing to do with hazardous waste. The Arizona sun streams in through the office window, and the hairs on his legs glint like spun gold. I fight the temptation to run my hands up his calves, squeeze his thigh muscles. . . .

"So what's next?" Gary asks, after I've asked the last of my questions.

"We walk through the facility," I say.

"Cool," Gary grins.

It's a small operation, just like I expected, with just a few plating and rinse tanks. There's a sludge drier out back and a waste storage yard, which I check out with Gary by my side. I examine the waste drums, check out the labels, watch the workers go through the plating operations, take notes. We're back in Gary's dad's office in less than an hour. I go over my observations with Gary, ticking off the points one by one;

257

which waste drum needs a locking ring, which drum label isn't completely filled out, the standard stuff.

"You'll get my report in a couple of weeks," I say.

"So, did we pass?" Gary asks.

"Yeah," I say. "The stuff I found wrong was minor. Just get it taken care of, and that should be the end of it." There's a couple of beats of silence. Gary keeps looking at me with that expression of careful calculation. "Is there something else?" I finally ask.

"You know, I was just thinking," Gary says. "There's an old, beat-up shed way out back. I haven't been in it in years, but I seem to recall some drums stored inside. God knows what they're filled with. You might want to check it out."

I shoot him a hard look. "I don't remember seeing any shed."

"It's tucked away in an arroyo that runs behind the company lot. You wouldn't see it unless you knew it was there."

The last thing I want to do is climb down some fuckin' arroyo in this heat. But it's my job to check out *everything*. I pick up my notebook and stand up. "Let's go."

Gary leads me around the building to the back lot. We hike across the desert for a couple hundred feet. The temperature must be in the high nineties, and after a while my body is soaked with sweat, beads of it trickling down my face. All I can think of is getting back to my motel room and taking a long, cool shower, followed by a cold beer in the bar across the highway. We finally reach the arroyo Gary talked about, a narrow gulch, bone dry and flanked by banks of hard scrabble.

"Hell," I say, exasperated. "This isn't even on your property."

Gary shrugs. "I never said it was." He points down below, off to his left. "There it is," he says. Sure enough, there's a wooden shack a little ways off in the distance on the arroyo floor. *Fuck,* I think. I start scrambling down the gritty bank, kicking up clouds of dust. I am not a happy camper. Gary follows right behind. When we get to the arroyo floor, we hike out to the shed, which is nothing more than a weather-beaten pile of boards loosely nailed together. I climb up the plank steps, yank open the door and walk in.

Sunlight streams in between the warped boards, and falls across the floor in stripes of light and shadow. The place is completely empty.

I turn to Gary in exasperation. "I guess you remembered wrong," I say. I don't bother hiding my irritation.

"I guess so," Gary says. I turn to walk out the door. Gary reaches over and gives my crotch a squeeze.

That stops me short, all right. I grasp his wrist and pull his hand away. I let a couple of beats go by. "Look," I say slowly. "You got the wrong idea. I don't do this kind of thing while working." Gary is standing close enough so that I can smell his sweat. His T-shirt is plastered against his body, hugging his lean, muscled torso. The heat pours in through the shack door like thick molasses. In spite of my words, my dick slowly hardens.

Gary's mouth curls up into a lazy smile. "Hey, the inspection's over, Mr. EPA. You said so yourself. You're on your own time now." He squeezes my crotch again. This time I don't pull his hand away.

*The boy's got a point,* I think. I stand there, weighing the ethical implications, while Gary squeezes and plays with my dick. *Fuck it,* I think. I shove Gary against the wall and kiss him, my tongue pushing deep into his mouth as I grind my hips against him. I can feel his boner beneath the denim of his shorts. "Is this where you fuck all the inspectors?" I growl.

"Yeah, right," Gary laughs. "OSHA, the fire marshals, the guys from the water board, all of them." He unbuttons my shirt and slides his hands over my torso, tugging at the skin, pulling at the muscle. "Nice," he murmurs.

I pull Gary's shirt off. His torso is smooth and chiseled, the nipples two pink circles set in tawny flesh. I bend down and run my tongue over his right nipple, sucking on it, flicking it, nipping it gently. "Fuuuuck," Gary groans, and I give his left nipple the same attention. I slide my tongue down his torso, across the bands of his abs, while dropping to my knees. Gary unzips his cut-offs, and I tug them down to his ankles. His dick springs up, fully hard, pink, fat and cut, the head a spongy little fist of red flesh. His balls hang low in the heavy heat, downed with light blonde hairs. I bury my face in his ballsac and inhale deeply, smelling the ripe, pungent stink of his sweaty nuts. Gary entwines his fingers in my hair, tugs my head back and drops his balls in my open mouth. I suck on them greedily, rolling them around with my tongue, my eyes locked with Gary's as he rubs his stiff dick over my face.

"Yeah, that's right," he croons. "Work those nuts."

I slide my tongue up Gary's wanker and swirl it around the meaty knob, giving his shaft a good squeeze. A drop of pre-jizz oozes out, and

I lap it up. I milk a couple more drops out, and then slowly work my lips down Gary's shaft. Gary thrusts his hips forward and slides his dick full in, until my nose is mashed against his pubes. I hold that pose for a couple of beats. I fuckin' love it when my mouth is full of dick. I start bobbing my head, working Gary's cock, making hungry love to it as Gary pumps his hips and fucks my face.

Gary pulls his dick out of my mouth. "Get naked," he says.

I climb to my feet. "Sure," I grin. I unzip my pants and step out of them kicking them aside. I pull my boxers down, nice and slow, giving Gary an inch by inch display of my hard dick. I got a long one, thick and over eight inches, and I always love showing it off to an appreciative audience. When the cloth finally clears my knob, my dick springs up and sways gently. I squeeze my ass, and my dick jerks up again.

"Jesus fuck," Gary whispers.

"You like it?" I grin.

"Don't ask stupid questions," Gary says.

We stretch out on the gritty floor, both of us sucking dick and fucking face. Gary pivots so that I'm on my back, the wood planks scratching against my skin. I bury my face in his ass crack and rim his asshole hungrily and then work a finger in, knuckle by knuckle, twisting it as I slide it in. Gary gives a heartfelt groan, and his body shudders against mine. "You feel like fuckin' my ass?" he growls. "Sticking that big inspector dick right up me?"

"Jesus," I laugh. "Who writes your dialogue?"

Gary reaches for his shorts and pulls out his wallet. For a crazy second I think he's about to offer me money to fuck him. But he fishes a condom out of one of the compartments and tosses it to me. I roll it down my cock, slick it up with spit, grab Gary by the ankles and pull him toward me. I probe my cockhead against his bung hole, feel the little "pop" as it pushes in, and slide my dick full up his chute.

Gary and I lock gazes as I pump my hips in long, deep strokes, plunging into Gary's ass, then out just to the tip of my cockhead, and then sliding full back in again. I quicken the pace, pounding his ass in rapid fire strokes, my balls slapping against him with each thrust. Gary's got his hand wrapped around his dick, and he matches his strokes with each of my thrusts, jacking his cock furiously. The desert heat presses down on us, pours over us, gives us the feeling of fucking under warm water. The air seems to vibrate, and none of this feels real. Sweat drips down my face and splashes onto Gary's, our bodies slip and slide against each other like a couple of otters. I keep Gary pinned in my gaze, and I feel like I'm falling into those slate gray eyes.

"I'm just about ready to squirt," I gasp.

"Go for it," Gary whispers.

I pull out almost completely, take a breath, and exhale deeply as I slide my dick full up Gary's ass. Gary squeezes his asshole tightly, pushing up to meet me, and that does the trick. I groan loudly as the orgasm sweeps over me. I bend down and kiss Gary fiercely as my body spasms and my load pumps out one squirt after another into the condom up Gary's ass. Gary gives a low muffled groan, and I look down to see his spunk ooze out between his fingers. We thrash around on the plank floor, squirting our loads, our bodies pressed tight together. When I'm done, I roll off Gary.

"Damn!" I groan. Gary laughs. We lie there for what seems like a long time, just letting the thick heat roll over us.

When I'm back in the car, Gary leans into the open window. "How much longer are you going to be around here?" he asks.

I give him a rueful smile. "I'm flying back to San Francisco tomorrow morning. This was my last inspection."

"Well, maybe I'll see you next time around," Gary says.

"Sure," I say. There's no point in telling him that I'll probably never make it out here again. There's a lot a territory to inspect and only a handful of inspectors. Gary quickly looks around to see that we're alone, then bends down and plants a wet one on my mouth, throwing in a little tongue for the hell of it.

I switch on the ignition. "Like I said, you'll get my report in a couple of weeks," I say.

Gary grins. "I can hardly fuckin' wait."

I laugh and peel out toward that cool shower and cold beer that are waiting for me back at the motel.

# Moonlighting

Rick bangs open the screen door of the barracks, strides to his bunk and starts pulling off his fatigues. I follow behind him. "We gotta hurry, Eddy," he says. "I told Jerry we'd be there by 17:30." We've been working all day in the motor pool, and we're sweaty and covered with grease.

I kick off my boots and start unbuttoning my shirt. "I dunno, Rick," I say. "This might not be such a hot idea."

Rick lets his pants drop down to his ankles, steps out of them, and shucks his boxers off. He turns to me, grinning, his blue eyes wide and friendly. I feel my throat tighten. Jesus, do I ever have a hard-on for the guy. "Eddy, Eddy," he says, pulling a towel out of his locker. "You can't flake out now. Everything's all set up." He laughs. "Besides, it'll be a hoot. It'll be the easiest $200 you'll ever make."

Rick turns and heads for the showers, the towel clutched in his hand. I grab the opportunity to take in the broad shoulders, the tightly muscled back, the ass so perfect my eyes water just from the beauty of it. *I'm not doing this for the money, Rick,* I think.

As soon as we clear the base gates, Rick floors the accelerator of his piece-of-shit, '94 Datsun until it starts shimmying like a motel vibrator bed. "So, tell me about this Jerry guy again," I say.

Rick glances over at me, amused. "What's to tell? I heard about him through a friend of a friend. He's just some guy who shoots porno films using Marines and hookers. I show up at some motel room, he films me fucking the hooker he's got lined up for me, I squirt a load, he pays me

$200 and I'm out the door." He winks at me. "It's just moonlighting, Eddy. A way to make ends meet."

I look out the window at the stretch of run-down bars and strip joints whizzing by. I shake my head. "This is so fuckin' weird." But the thought that there's a video out there somewhere of Rick fucking makes my dick give an extra twitch.

Rick reaches over and squeezes the back of my neck. "It'll be fun. The guy wants two marines and a hooker this time. Kind of a tag team thing. You're my best buddy, Eddy. When he asked me if I knew anyone who'd be interested, you were the first guy I thought of." I don't say anything, just keep looking out the window. "Marine Porno!" Rick says, in a deep, booming voice. "It's not just a job, it's an adventure!" I turn my head, my eyes meet his, and we burst out laughing.

Jerry is pudgy and middle-aged, with horn-rimmed glasses, and a red and blue aloha shirt with serious pit stains. He introduces us to Shandrelle, the hooker, who's pale and blonde and a little chubby, and about halfway between "plain" and "kind of pretty." She looks at me with eyes that give away nothing. Jerry gets the three of us onto the kingsize bed. We wait patiently as he makes adjustments, shifting the lights and playing with the camera lens. It seems that Jerry believes in keeping things simple. As soon as he's satisfied with everything, he lifts his head up from the camera and looks at us.

"Okay, kids," he says. "Go for it."

I just follow the example of the other two. We roll around on that huge bed, Shandrelle kissing Rick, then me, then Rick again. We drop off our clothes, piece by piece, until Rick and I wind up naked, sitting side by side, while Shandrelle trades off giving us blow jobs. It's the first time I've seen Rick's dick hard, and it's a beaut: a thick, veined club with a knob like a red, rubber ball. I watch with more than a few pangs of envy as Shandrelle sucks and licks it. Rick pumps his hips, sliding his dick in and out of her mouth, and I try to imagine what that must feel like, having that meaty root banging against the back of my throat. When Shandrelle gets around to me again, I close my eyes and imagine it's Rick's mouth I feel sucking on my balls and sliding up and down my dick shaft. My dick throbs in her mouth. At Jerry's suggestion, Shandrelle sucks the two of us off at the same time. I feel Rick's fat cockhead pushing against mine in the warm, wet confines of Shandrelle's mouth, and I almost squirt right then and there.

Rick fucks Shandrelle doggy style, while I plow her mouth, facing him. Rick winks and gives me a wide grin. He's so fuckin' sexy. It's all I can do to keep from reaching over and tweaking his nipple, or hooking my hand around the back of his neck and frenching him until my tongue is halfway down his throat. "You havin' a good time, buddy?" Rick asks, and, because I can't trust myself to speak without my voice cracking, I just nod 'yes.'

Jerry turns off his camera. "Okay, kids," he says. "Time for a little DP action."

"What's DP?" I ask.

Shandrelle gives me a "what an amateur" look. "Double penetration," she says, like it's something any moron would know.

*Holy shit,* I think. Jerry tosses Rick and me condoms.

Jerry turns his camera on again as Rick lies on his back and Shandrelle slowly lowers herself on him. Rick starts fucking her ass with long, slow strokes. I sit there, so caught up watching them, or rather Rick, that I forget I'm part of the act until Jerry motions at me impatiently. I straddle Rick's legs and slowly penetrate Shandrelle's pussy, my balls pressing against Rick's low hangers. I start pumping my hips, the two of us fucking Shandrelle, and I can feel Rick's hard dick through the thin skin that separates the two of us. This is such a fuckin' turn-on! I speed up my thrusts, churning my hips, slapping my balls against Rick's, feeling his thighs press against mine.

Jerry wraps up the filming with Rick and me whacking off, our cocks a couple of inches above Shandrelle's upturned face. The idea is to give Shandrelle "a facial," as Jerry puts it, but Rick overshoots, and his jizz arcs across Shandrelle and splatters all over my belly. "Oops," he says.

I squirt a few seconds later, and I deliberately aim so that my load slams onto Rick's chest. "Oops, yourself," I say. I watch my load trace a sluggish path down across Rick's six pack. Rick scoops it off with his fingers and flicks it at me, laughing.

Jerry is happy with our performance. "You guys are naturals," he says, as he counts the twenties into our outstretched hands. "You interested in doing some more work together?"

Rick glances at me, and I shrug, trying to hide my excitement. "Sure," Rick says, grinning. We make a date for next Tuesday.

When we return to the motel room that next Tuesday, Jerry is alone. "Where's Shandrelle?" Rick asks.

Jerry is fooling with one of the lights. "No Shandrelle today," he says, not bothering to look at us.

"What, you got another girl lined up?" I ask.

Jerry turns his head and looks at me, his face expressionless. "No girls, today. Just you two."

"What the fuck!?" Rick exclaims.

Jerry turns his deadpan stare onto Rick. "It's no big deal," he says with exaggerated patience. "All the two of you gotta do is get in bed and jack off together." He pulls a video out of his canvas bag. "I got a porn movie you can watch. It'll be a cinch."

Rick just stares at him. "Who's going to buy a video of a couple of guys beating their puds?" Jerry gives him a long-suffering look. "Oh," Rick says. "Yeah."

"I make videos for all sorts of audiences," Jerry says, underscoring the point. Rick looks doubtful. "I'll still pay you both $200," Jerry says.

Nobody says anything for a few beats. Rick shoots me an inquisitive look. "Whatdaya say, Eddie?"

"Sure," I say, my heart racing. "Why not?" The thought of being naked in bed with Rick without the complication of Shandrelle excites the holy hell out of me. My dick is already hard, beating against my zipper and yelling to be let out.

"Attaboy," Jerry says, smiling broadly. He pops the video into the VCR, and the scene of a blonde and a brunette in a lesbian clench fills the T.V. screen. Rick still stands there, dubiously, but I can see that the video has hooked his interest. Jerry nods toward the bed. "Now get in bed, guys." His tone is almost motherly.

Rick and I climb into bed, fully clothed. In the video, the brunette is going down on the blonde. Rick unzips and pulls his cock out, which, even half-hard, is a beautiful sight to see: fat and spongy and pink. I do the same. Rick's eyes are trained on the video; he starts stroking his dick, slowly at first, but then speeds up as he slides into his jack-off mode. He stops for a moment to pull off his T-shirt. I do the same. Things are warming up.

"Why don't you guys get completely comfortable?" Jerry says, and we take the hint and pull off our jeans and boxers. We lay there naked on the bed, leaning against the headboard and whacking off. The only sounds in the room are the moans from the video and the slapping sounds of our fists sliding up and down our dicks. Rick is fully hard now, and I sneak a peek at his beautiful boner, at how his low-hangers bounce up and down with his rapid-fire strokes. I look up and catch Jerry watching me watching Rick. He looks amused, and I feel the blood rush to my face.

"Scoot in together a little closer," he says. "I can barely get you in my lens." Rick and I dutifully shift closer together. "Nice," Jerry says softly. He looks up from his camera. "Eddy, why don't you drape your leg over Rick's?"

Rick tears his eyes off the video. "Hey, wait a minute," he says.

Jerry theatrically rolls his eyes. "Jesus, Rick, don't make a big deal out of it, okay?"

Rick doesn't say anything, but I can see this is a new wrinkle he wasn't expecting. "It's okay with me, Rick," I say, trying to echo Jerry's casualness.

Rick looks at me, and then back at the video. The lesbians are going down on each other, and he lets his attention get snagged. He sinks back into his jackoff rhythm, stroking his cock with his eyes locked on the screen. I don't know what the fuck to do. Without taking his eyes from the screen, Rick shifts his leg so that his thigh lightly touches mine. Jerry looks at Rick and then at me and smiles slyly. Holding my breath, I lift my leg and drape it over Rick's. Rick continues staring at the video like he doesn't know any of this is happening. I go back to beating off, my dick harder than ever as I feel the heat of Rick's naked flesh against my thigh. I'm openly ogling Rick's dick now, not even making any pretense that I'm not. Rick acts like he's too caught up in the video to notice. I glance once at Jerry, and he just smirks back at me.

"Okay, boys," he says easily. "Why don't you start beating each other off?"

I don't even give it a second thought. *What the fuck,* I think, and I reach over and wrap my hand around Rick's fat, red boner like I've been wanting to for the past three months. I'm beyond caring about consequences. Rick looks at me, his eyes shrewd, and then damn if he doesn't do the same, sliding his fist down my hard cock and beating me off with slow, lazy strokes. I look into Rick's eyes, and he just returns my stare boldly. I spit in my hand and slide my saliva-slicked hand down his crank. Rick groans, pushing up with his hips, fucking my fist. I keep my eyes trained on his face, locking my gaze with his, feeling the throb of his cock in my hand and the warmth of his own hand around my cock. Rick's mouth is slightly open, and his breath comes out in short gasps. I lean forward and plant my mouth on Rick's, and we kiss long and hard, our tongues pushing together.

Rick breaks away. "Suck me off, Eddy," he croons. "I got such a nut to bust."

"Sure, baby," I say softly.

I'm only dimly aware of Jerry and his whirring camera. I shift down to the foot of the bed, and Rick spreads his legs open into a wide V. His fat, veined cock lies hard against the six-pack of his belly, his balls hang so low, they cover the crack of his ass. I bury my face in them, inhaling deeply, breathing in the heavy, musky scent of ballmeat. I open my mouth and suck them in, rolling my tongue around them, giving them a good bath. I look up across Rick's hard, muscled torso and stare into his blue eyes as I suck on his nuts. Rick gives me a slow, lazy grin, and rubs his cock against my face.

I slide my tongue up the thick shaft and swirl it around the fat, red knob. I give Rick's cock a squeeze, and a clear drop of pre-cum oozes out of his piss slit. I lap it up, and then, with my lips stretched around Rick's cock, I slowly nibble down the length of his shaft. Rick pushes his hips up, and his cock slides full inside my mouth. I hold that position for a few beats, savoring the sensation of having my mouth full of cock. *Rick's* cock. Jesus Christ, I never dreamed this would ever happen, and I am so fuckin' *excited!* My cock feels like it could drill through steel plating.

I make slow, hungry love to Rick's dick, sucking it, squeezing it, slobbering on it, pulling on his heavy, fleshy ballsac. I flip onto my back, and Rick straddles my torso, propping himself up with his elbows and fucking my mouth with long, deep strokes, his balls slapping against my chin. I reach up and twist his nipples, and Rick's eyes narrow and grow hard with the look of a man with a serious load to blow. With my other hand I'm beating off furiously, fucking my fist with the same crazed tempo that Rick uses to fuck my mouth.

Rick pulls his dick out of my mouth and drops his balls in. I suck on them again eagerly. Jesus, I love Rick's balls as much as I love his dick, their fleshiness and heft. I bathe them with my tongue while Rick beats off. Sweat beads his forehead, and drops splash on my face. Our eyes burn into each other like laser fire. Rick's breath is coming out in quick gasps. "I could squirt any moment, Eddy," he pants. "How about you?" I've got a mouth full of ballsac, so all I can do is grunt my agreement.

"Okay," Rick pants, "then here goes." He arcs his back and groans loudly as a volley of jizz squirts out of his cock and splatters against my face, one round after another. I thrust up and give a few quick strokes. I groan loudly, my voice muffled by ball meat, as my own spunk shoots out, slamming against Rick's back. We buck and heave on the bed, our dicks pulsing out our loads, Jerry recording every moment of this for posterity on his video camera.

Rick collapses onto the bed beside me. "Jesus H. Christ!" he groans.

"A-fuckin'-men," I answer.

We lay there, side-by-side, catching our breaths. "Damn!" Jerry mutters, awed. "That was fuckin' incredible!"

After we're dressed, Jerry doles out the cash. He tips us each an extra $50. "You guys are great together," he enthuses. "I want to work with you again for sure!" I give a non-committal shrug, and Rick doesn't say anything. My mind is racing, going over just what happened between me and Rick, and wondering what the repercussions are going to be.

Afterwards, driving back to the base, Rick reaches over and turns the radio on to an oldies rock and roll station. Bob Seger's "Hollywood Nights" blasts out the speakers. I glance at him, but he has his eyes trained on the road ahead, and I have no idea what he's thinking.

Rick shoots me a look. "So, Eddy," he says. "You feel like doin' that again?"

I shrug. "Yeah," I say, trying to sound casual. "I could go for another session."

"Cool," Rick says, grinning.

We tear down the highway toward the base, the late afternoon sun throwing long shadows across the road ahead, and I sink back into my seat and watch the buildings whizz by.

# Escorts

The phone on the nightstand next to me suddenly rings, and I damn near have a heart attack. I pick up the receiver. "Hello, Roger?" a baritone voice asks.

"Yes?" I say.

"This is Doug. I'm stuck in traffic and I'll be about 15 minutes late. Is that okay?"

I take a deep breath. "Yeah, sure. No problem."

"Room 28, right?"

"Yeah, that's right."

"Great, see you in a little while." Doug hangs up.

I glance at the clock on the nightstand. It's a quarter to ten. Zero hour is now pushed back to thirty minutes. I still can't believe I'm doing this. All during the sales seminar today, all I could think about was what it was going to be like with Doug tonight. I mean, hell, I don't even know what the protocol is in something like this. Do we make conversation first? Do I just tell Doug what I want him to do? Do I pay him up front, or afterwards? When I finally hear a knock on the door, I seriously consider not answering it. But my Midwestern politeness wins out. I put my head between my knees, take a deep breath, and then get up and open the door, my heart pounding hard enough to wake the dead.

Doug stands framed in the doorway, dressed in jeans and a light blue tank top that hugs his torso like a second skin. He doesn't look real. In fact, he looks something like a Macy's Thanksgiving Day balloon, biceps pumped up like cannonballs, pecs that threaten to rip his shirt open, shoulders like a fuckin' bull's. I have never in my life seen a man so muscular. He regards me with calm, blue eyes.

"Hi, Roger," he says, holding out his hand.

"Hi," I say back. We shake hands. Doug's grip is firm but cautious, as if he knows that he could squeeze my hand to pulp and is making an effort not to do so. He walks into the room, and looks around. He has the air of returning to familiar surroundings.

"You've been in this room before?" I ask.

Doug smiles. "A couple of times."

*Okayyyy*, I think. Doug has the corn yellow hair and broad face of the Swede farmers I see back in Green Bay. His hands are the size of dinner plates. He sits in a chair, crossing his right ankle over his left knee. I sit opposite him. We look at each other.

"So, Roger," he says. "What brings you to L.A.?"

I clear my throat. "A sales seminar. I work for a publishing firm in Wisconsin. We do 'inspirational' books. Like 'Losing the Loser Within You.' That was a big seller. Maybe you heard of it?"

Doug smiles blandly and shakes his head. "Sorry," he says.

"How about 'Be a Winner, Not a Whiner'? We killed with that book."

Doug shrugs. "I'm not much into reading," he says.

A silence lies between us like a dead flounder. "You ever been in L.A. before?" Doug asks.

I grab at the conversational line he throws me. "No. In fact, I've never been out of Wisconsin before." I clear my throat. "I've never done *this*, either. You know . . ."

"Hire an escort?" Doug gives a slow, lazy smile.

"Yeah." I let a beat go by. "I can't believe I'm doing this." Doug just sits there, looking at me calmly. "I flew in last night," I go on, speaking faster now. "And I picked up this gay paper at a bar across from the motel. And there were all these *ads* in the back. All these hot guys for sale. I never saw anything like it!" I glance at Doug. "It was just a spur of the moment thing. Here I was, loose in this city, and I just wanted to do something I'd never done before. Something crazy."

"Cool," Doug says. He looks bored.

"I'm sorry to talk so much. I'm kind of nervous."

"Don't sweat it," Doug says. He stands up and nods to the bed. "Shall we get started?"

"Yeah, sure," I say. I hesitate. "But, could you . . ."

"Yeah?" Doug asks.

I swallow. "Could you put on a strip show for me? Just let me watch you as you take everything off?"

Doug grins. "Yeah, Roger. Sure." He hooks his thumbs under his tank top and slowly peels it off. His torso is cut and sliced so that every sinew is out there on display. Amazing. His nipples stand out like little pink fireplugs. Doug kicks off his shoes and pulls his socks off. He unbuckles his belt, pulls down his zipper, and slides his jeans down thighs as solid as tree trunks. He's wearing white cotton briefs underneath. The bulge in them lives up to the promise of his huge hands.

He steps toward me. "Okay, Roger," he says, stopping in front of me. "You do the rest." He stands so close to me that I can feel the heat rising from his body. After a couple of beats, I hook my fingers under the elastic band of Doug's briefs and slowly pull them down, past his dark blonde, neatly clipped pubes, past the thick base of his cock, past inch after inch of the fat, pink shaft that follows. Fascinated, I trace the course of a vein until I get to the ridge of Doug's cockhead. The thin cotton fabric snags on that briefly and then clears it. Doug's half-hard dick springs up and sways slowly in front of my face.

"Jesus," I mutter.

Doug's dick is fat and spongy and candy pink, with blue veins snaking up the shaft. His cockhead flares out into a rubbery, red fist of flesh. Doug shakes his hips and his cock swings from side to side in a slow, pendulous motion. His ballsac hangs low, furred by a light dusting of blonde hair, the right nut lower than the left.

"You like it?" Doug asks.

I look up into his wide, blue eyes. "Hell, yeah."

Doug turns and walks back to his chair. His ass is high and firm, the color of pale cream, the crack a thin, tight line. He sits down, his legs spread apart, his balls hanging so low they cover the crack of his ass. "Come here," he says gruffly.

I slide out of my chair and crawl across the carpeted floor to Doug. He sits still, his eyes fixed on me. I reach up and run my hands up his thighs, feeling the hard muscled flesh under my fingertips.

"Yeah," Doug breathes, "that's right, go for it." I lean forward and bury my nose in the soft fleshiness of Doug's ballsac and inhale deeply. A scent of musk and fresh sweat fills my nostrils and flows down into my lungs. The scent is strong and heady, and if the evening consisted of nothing but me sniffing Doug's balls, I'd be content. I press my lips against the loose folds of the fleshy pouch and tongue it, sucking on one ball and then another as Doug rubs his cock over my face.

Doug raises his legs and exposes the pink pucker of his asshole to me. I tongue that too, something I've never done before. I slide my tongue past his balls and up the thick shaft, as I reach up and squeeze his nipples. Doug's body squirms under me. "You can squeeze harder," he murmurs, and I increase the pressure of my fingers. I push my tongue into Doug's piss slit, tasting the drop of pre-cum that dribbles out, and then slide his cock into my mouth, nibbling down the shaft until my chin presses against his balls.

Doug lays his hands on either side of my head and proceeds to fuck my mouth with long, deep strokes. His dick widens at the base, and each time it slides down my throat, my lips pull back. I look up across the expanse of muscled flesh into Doug's light blue eyes. Doug regards me calmly as he pushes his hips up and fucks my face. *This is just another day at the office for him,* I think. *How fuckin' strange!*

I pull his cock out of my mouth. "I would love you to suck my dick," I say, without any real hope that Doug will do so. But Doug pushes himself out of the chair and stands up, pulling me up with him. He undoes my belt, pulls down my fly, and tugs my pants down past my hips. Doug kisses me lightly on the mouth and then kneels in front of me, wrapping his huge hand around my dick, stroking it slowly. He bends his head down, and I feel his lips work their way down the length of my shaft. Doug bobs his head faster, jacking me with his hand as his mouth slides up and down the shaft. I run my hands through his thick, yellow hair.

"Fuuucckkkk" I groan. Doug gives great head. He presses his lips tightly around my shaft and twists his head from side to side, sucking me off with genuine enthusiasm. I arch my back, eyes shut tight, feeling him draw me closer to orgasm. I push him away just before I shoot.

"Not yet!" I gasp.

Doug looks up at me, his eyes bright. "Let me fuck you," he growls.

"Sure," I say, laughing.

It just takes a minute for Doug to grease up and sheathe himself. I pull him onto the bed, on top of me, and he slings my legs around his torso as

I guide his dick to my asshole. He slides his dick in all the way until I can feel his balls press against me. Doug starts pumping his hips, slowly at first, but then with increasing tempo. There's a mirror that runs across the length of the wall next to the bed, and I watch Doug's reflection fuck mine, his smooth, dimpled ass pumping up and down, his dick sliding in and out of my asshole. Doug's face is inches above mine, and I turn and meet his gaze, looking deep into his eyes. Doug is fucking me with a hard, driving energy, his balls slapping against my ass with an audible *thwack*, but his eyes keep that same deep, level calm as they peer into mine. I crane my neck upwards and kiss him, and Doug slides his tongue into my mouth. I stroke my dick in time with his thrusts, bringing myself to the brink of shooting, but holding back, waiting for him. Sweat trickles down his face and drips down on me, his eyes are hard and deadly serious now, his lips pulled back into a soundless snarl.

"I want to watch you squirt your load," I pant, and Doug nods. A few more thrusts and he quickly pulls out of me.

"Here it comes," he growls, pulling the condom off his dick. He straddles my chest as his dick squirts its load hard against my face, one blast after another. I open my mouth as the thick drops rain down on me, onto my cheeks and chin and eager tongue. A few strokes trigger my own orgasm, and I cry out as my spunk pulses out and sprays Doug's back.

Doug looks down at me, grinning. When the last spasm passes through me, he rolls off onto his side and kisses me lightly.

"Well," he says. "Did you have fun?"

I just laugh, without saying anything.

The next morning, at the seminar, while the other students learn about marketing strategies for midsized publishing companies, I sit in the back and pore over the escort ads of the gay newspaper, hidden away in my course manual. I'm in the grip of some crazy, wild energy; it's like I'm possessed.

I make a phone call during the class break and that night, I'm visited by Carlos, who describes himself in his ad as "a punk with attitude." Carlos is short and muscular and theatrically contemptuous, with dark eyes that burn with a bright cynicism in his brown, handsome face. He wears a gold cross around his neck; his left bicep is tattooed with a big-titted, naked woman riding a crescent moon, and his left with Santa Guadalupe. Carlos fucks me mercilessly, spewing out a steady torrent of abuse. "You like that, cocksucker?" he growls, as he thrusts deep into my ass. "That feel good, you pussy bitch?" He's like a goddamn force of nature, his hands all over me, his thrusts deep and sure, his liquid, dark eyes glaring down into mine. When I finally come, groaning loudly, Carlos startles me by placing his mouth over mine and tonguing me fiercely. The orgasm that sweeps over me lifts me up like a swelling breaker and slams me down hard against the mattress. When Carlos shoots his own load into the condom up my ass, he thrashes wildly in the bed, tearing the blankets off, crying out in Spanish. He leaves fifteen minutes later with my money stuffed in his back jeans pocket, slamming the door.

When I scan the escort ads the next day in class, my eye snags on "Spike: Trailer Trash From Hell." His photo lives up to the heading: stringy, long hair, two-day beard stubble, a surly scowl, a lanky, tattooed, muscle-packed body with just the first fringe of pubes before the photo crop. He's hot in an inbred sort of way, like the slow-witted, scary-looking but hunky third cousin you always find at a big family reunion, the one who works for a living scraping up road kill. I dial the number listed in the ad as soon as I get back to my motel room.

Spike picks up on the third ring. "Yeah?" The voice is deep and pure Tennessee backwoods.

"I'm calling about your ad," I say, putting some attitude into my voice. "You mind if I ask a few questions?"

"Shoot," Spike says. He sounds . . . not bored, just not all that concerned about selling himself to me.

"Well, I guess I'd like to know what I'd get for my money."

Pause. "Well, what d'ya want?"

"Do you make out?"

"Sure. Unless you're really gross. That doesn't happen often."

I decide to cut to the chase. "Would you suck my dick?"

"Yeah," Spike says. "Probably."

"Let me fuck you?"

"No," Spike says. "I don't do that. But I'll plow your ass if you want. Plow it good."

I have my dick out, stroking it. "Would you sit on my chest and beat off for me? Drop your balls in my mouth and let me wash them with my tongue?"

"Yeah, yeah," Spike says. There's an edge of impatience to his voice. "You can suck on my balls for as long as you like."

I'm stroking faster now. "How about fucking my mouth nice and slow? Then squirting a load on my face and licking it off?"

"Hey, are you jerking off?"

"No," I say, pulling my hand away from my dick. "I'm just trying to get some information."

"Yeah, right. If you want to set up an appointment, fine. But if you want to fuckin' whack off over phone, call the sex hotline."

I let a beat go by. "How about tonight?"

"It's possible. What time?"

"How about eleven?"

"Yeah, that'll work."

"Okay," I hear myself say.

"Cool. Where you at?"

"Room 28 at the Palms Motel at La Cienega and Hollywood. You know it?"

"Yeah. It's a dump. I'll see you then. By the way, my fee is $200."

"Yeah, sure. No problem."

I hang up and sit on the bed, looking at my reflection in the mirror. *You are one crazy, out-of-control fucker*, I think.

The man's standing over by the cigarette machine, nursing a Bud. He's wearing a black tank top, and his bicep rounds nicely as he brings the bottle to his lips. The light is dim, and it's hard to guess his age . . . late twenties maybe. He's wearing side burns, and his black hair is short and spiky. He looks good.

It's a little after ten, and I'm in a bar on Santa Monica Boulevard, in West Hollywood, killing time until my appointment with Spike. The sound system is blaring some hip hop shit, and I can barely think, the music's so loud. The guy by the cigarette machine has been eying me now for the last twenty minutes. Damn if it doesn't look like he's coming on to me, but I'm finding that hard to believe; there are younger, better-looking guys packed in the crowd around me. Yet, when he sees me returning his stare, he raises his bottle to me in toast and smiles. After a couple of minutes, he threads through the crowd to the spot next to me.

"Howdy," he says.

"Hi," I reply cautiously. Up close, he looks older. And scruffier. But still hot, his eyes dark and intense, the torso beneath the tank top lean and muscular.

"I'm Randy," he says, holding out his hand.

We shake hands. "I'm Roger," I say.

Randy flashes me a smile. He's missing an eyetooth. I don't know why, but I find that sexier than if he had a set of perfect teeth. "You don't look like you belong here," he says. "You look like you're from out of town." He lets a beat go by. "And lonely."

"Oh, yeah?" I say, not denying either.

Randy's smile widens, becomes more intimate. Yet his eyes keep their shrewdness. "I thought you might like some company."

"Well, maybe," I say. I quickly scan his body. *This is too good to be true,* I think.

I'm right. "My rates are reasonable," Randy says, still smiling. He puts his hand on my thigh and squeezes gently. "And I'll show you a good time for sure."

*Sweet Jesus,* I think. *Is there anyone in this city who just has sex for the fun of it?*

"Well, I don't know," I say. "I kind of have other plans later on tonight."

Randy's hand slides down my thigh and cups my hard dick. "Why don't you break them?" he said.

I glance at my watch. It's almost ten thirty. Spike's probably already on his way. "No," I say. "It's too late." I give Randy a level look, taking in the tight body, the seedy handsomeness. My dick is pushing against my jeans, and I do *not* feel like walking away from the wild little scene this could turn into. Randy returns my stare and gives me a gap-tooth smile. "Tell me, Randy," I ask. "Are you into threesomes?"

"Fuck yeah," Randy says.

We get back to the motel room around a quarter to eleven. When I close the door, I make sure it's unlocked. I pull Randy toward me and we kiss. Randy's breath smells of cigarettes and beer. His tongue snakes into my mouth and his hand slides under my shirt and squeezes my nipple. He breaks away. "I thought this was going to be a three-way," he says.

I run my hands up his muscular torso, tugging on the hard flesh. I look up at him. "Yeah, well, we're just warming up until my buddy gets here."

I unzip Randy's fly and slowly pull down his jeans. Randy's not wearing any underwear, and his dick springs up, half hard, dark, and uncut, the dripping knob peeking out from the puckered foreskin. His balls hang tight and plump, shaved smooth. *Fuckin' beautiful,* I think. I wrap my hand around his dick, pull the foreskin back, and give a squeeze. A clear drop of pre-jizz oozes out, and I lean forward and lap it up, rolling my tongue around the dark, fleshy head, probing into the slit. I work my lips slowly down Randy's shaft, feeling it stir and harden in my mouth.

"Yeah," Randy sighs. "That's right. Work my dick." He holds my head in his hands and thrusts his hips forward, sliding his dick down my throat. I run my hands over his ass cheeks, squeezing them as he fucks my mouth, feeling them clench and unclench with each thrust of his hips. Randy pushes me back onto the bed and drops his balls in my mouth. I suck on them as Randy rubs his dick all over my face.

I go back to sucking his dick again, pulling off my clothes as he fucks my mouth with slow, easy thrusts. When I'm naked too, I pivot around on the bed. Randy takes the hint and slides his lips down my hard dick as I continue to suck him off. All I can see is Randy's ballsac hanging above my face, all I can feel is his thick dick sliding down my throat and his hot mouth working my own dick. Randy's finger presses against my asshole and then enters it, knuckle by knuckle. I groan loudly, my voice muffled by a mouth full of cock.

There's a knock on the door. Randy looks up expectantly. I take his dick out of my mouth. "Come in," I call out.

The door opens, and Spike stands in the doorway, looking at the two of us with narrowed eyes. He's wearing an old Navy flight jacket, tattered 501s and a pair of snakeskin boots. I train my eyes on him. Spike steps in and closes the door behind him, takes off his jacket and lets it drop to the floor. He's wearing a wife-beater shirt, which hugs a lean, muscled torso. Wordlessly, he balances on one foot and pulls off a boot, and then does the same with the other foot, his long, stringy hair falling into his face as he bends over. I glance at Randy and see him taking Spike in with a cool, level gaze. By the way his dick twitches I can tell he's as excited about this new development as I am.

Spike walks toward the bed, shedding clothes with every step. By the time he reaches us, he's buck naked. He still doesn't say anything, just grabs my head and pulls it toward his crotch. I bury my face in his balls, breathing in their stink, and then take his still-soft dick in my mouth. It hardens as I work my tongue around it, and Spike holds on to my head and starts mouth fucking me with short, quick jabs.

Spike's skin is pale, and his dick is like a peeled tuber, a thick fleshy root with blue veins snaking up the shaft. The cockhead flares out like a red toadstool, the piss slit deep and pronounced. It's an evil dick, a dick that no decent, civilized man would ever have, and I could happily spend the rest of my life with it crammed hard down my throat. Spike obligingly plows my mouth with that horse dick, thrusting full in and churning his hips. My nose is pressed up against his pubes, and I'm gagging for air. He proceeds to face fuck me mercilessly, until my eyes start tearing and my jaws ache. His balls hang low in a meaty, red pouch, and they slap against my face with each thrust.

I have to break away for breath, and Randy spells me off on Spike's dick. Randy may be playing for pay, but he throws himself into deep-throating Spike with a full-throttled enthusiasm, swallowing Spike's dick whole as Spike pumps his hips. I lean back on my elbows and take in the hot, sexy show they're putting on for me.

"Stand up," I say. Spike and Randy stand in front of me, hands at their sides, their hard dicks twitching, one cut, one uncut. They take turns fucking my face; first Randy, with deep, long strokes, then Spike with his piston thrusts. My hands wander over their bodies as I work their dicks, tugging on their flesh, tweaking their nipples, squeezing their asses. I take both their dicks into my mouth at the same time, my lips stretched wide, my tongue rolling over the thick shafts, feeling the rubbery cockheads pushing against each other.

Spike pulls his dick out and gives me a mean, yellow-eyed stare. "You got rubbers?" he growls. This is the first time he's said something. His voice is sandpaper on rusty iron.

"Yeah," I gasp. "Over on the dresser. And a jar of lube, too."

Spike walks over toward the dresser. "I'm done fuckin' face," he says over his shoulder. "It's time to plow some ass."

It only takes a minute before I'm on the bed, face down in the pillow, ass up. I can feel Spike's lube slicked finger slide down the crack of my asshole. It pushes against the pucker of my asshole and then enters me.

"Fuuuuck!" I groan.

Spike twists his finger as he slides it up to the third knuckle. "You like that, motherfucker?"

"Fuck yeah," I groan again.

Spike pulls his finger out and then thrusts two in. He curls them inside me, and then corkscrews them in and out. I give out a cry that dies down to a trailing moan.

"Okay, motherfucker," he says. "I'm goin' to fuck your asshole raw now." I turn my head and watch as Spike rolls a condom down that evil dick of his and greases it up good. He pushes me onto my back, grabs my ankles and slowly impales me.

"Aw, fuck, easy, man," I gasp.

"Just take it like I give it," Spike grunts. He pushes on in until his dick is full up my chute. I feel like I have about two feet of cock crammed in me. Spike's holding my ankles, spreading my legs wide as he pauses for a moment. He slowly pulls his dick out until I can feel the ridge of the head rub against my asshole and then thrusts full in again. I groan once more. "Yeah, suffer," Spike snarls. He picks up his speed, fucking me hard and fast, his balls bouncing against my ass. Randy joins the fun, squatting down and dropping his plump balls into my mouth as he slaps my face with his hard dick. He pulls his balls out and slides his dick into my mouth. It eases in like butter on a hot skillet; I can't get enough of it, and I suck and slobber over it as I wrap my hand around my dick and start jacking.

I sink into the feeling of sweaty bodies pressed against mine, hands stroking my flesh, dicks pummeling me. Everything is sensation: my holes stuffed by these hot fuckers, the feel of sweat-slicked flesh on flesh, the tingles that ripple up from my cock each time I fuck my lube-smeared fist . . . I turn my head and look into the mirror beside my bed, watching my reflection get stuffed with cock from both ends by these two hot, sleazy guys. A thought flashes through my head before it gets drowned out by the next wave of sensations. *Holy shit!* I think. *For once in my life I'm finally getting enough* dick! And it's true! It seems like I've been craving dick every moment of my life, and this is the first time I'm feeling . . . truly . . . fuckin' . . . *satisfied.*

Randy squeezes Spike's nipple, and they lean over me and give each other a lingering kiss. Spike is making little sex noises now, whimpers and grunts that became louder with each thrust. He gives a hard, deep thrust and lets fly with a long, dragged-out moan as his cock slides up my ass. I reach behind and tug on his balls. They're pulled up tight and full to bursting.

"You about ready to squirt, buddy?" Randy asks hoarsely.

"Yeah," Spike growls. "I could pop my cork any second."

"Fuckin' A, man," Randy murmurs. "Me, too."

Spike pulls his dick almost completely out, just to the tip of the head, and then, with a long, hard thrust, slides full in me. I squeeze my ass muscles tight, pushing up to meet Spike's thrust. Spike groans mightily, and his body shudders against me. He churns his hips hard, and I can feel his dick pulse inside me, pumping its load of jizz into my ass. "Ahh, yeah, jeez," he groans. With a few quick strokes, my groans mingle with Spike's and my load squirts out between my closed fingers.

Randy pulls his dick out of my mouth and starts jacking. "Damn!" he sighs, and the first volley of spunk squirts out against my face, followed by another, and another still. "Yeah, fucker," Spike growls, twisting Randy's nipple as Randy shoots his wad. Randy arches his back, and his body spasms with each spurt. His thick load sluggishly drips down my cheeks and chin, and Randy bends down and licks my face clean. I stare up at the two naked men kissing each other as their dicks slowly soften. A spermy thread dangles from Spike's cockhead. It's all one fuckin' hot sight.

After a short while, Spike and Randy climb out of bed and pull on their clothes. Spike glances over at Randy as he thrusts his arm into his bomber jacket. "You wanna go get a beer?" he asks.

Randy grins. "Okay." They wait as I pay them, and then walk out of the room together.

The following Monday, Jerry, my boss, walks into my office. "So how was the seminar, Roger?" he asks. "Did you learn anything useful?"

"Yeah," I say. "It was very productive." I slide a brochure lying on my desk toward him. "In fact, there"s going to be another, more advanced training seminar a couple of months from now. It might be a good idea for me to go."

"We'll see," Jerry says, looking at the brochure. But Jerry's a sucker for these seminars, and I'm pretty sure he'll bite. After he leaves, I pull the gay newspaper out from my briefcase and turn back to the escort ads, already fantasizing about who I'm going to pick the next time around.

# The Canadian Censor

The alarm wakes me up at seven o'clock, and I can tell right away that it's going to be a good day. An overall feeling of well-being pulses through me. Sunlight is streaming through the window, and I can smell the coffee from the breakfast Anne is fixing for me. God bless her. Who could ask for a better wife?

I get up, shower and shave, and dress carefully. My appearance is important; as an employee of the Canadian Department of Decency, I have to set a good example.

While reading the paper, I eat my breakfast of Canadian bacon and hot cakes (with lots of maple syrup). My good mood clouds for the moment: all these muggings, murders and rapes. This country is getting more like its neighbor to the south every day. It's sad, but at least I can console myself with the knowledge that, in my own small way, I'm in the trenches, fighting the good fight for the forces of decency.

When I'm done eating breakfast, I kiss Anne good-bye; she tries to slip her tongue in, but I keep my lips firmly pressed together.

Outside, I see Timmy working on his hot rod next door. I chuckle to myself. That kid! He's always bent over that engine, covered with grease. Timmy's family has lived next to us for as long as I can remember, and I've seen Timmy grow up over the years from a freckle-faced, pug-nosed kid to the strapping teenager he is today.

Timmy sees me walking out the door, and he straightens up and waves. "Good morning, Mr. Robinson!" he calls out.

I walk over to him. "Good morning, Timmy," I say, smiling. "Still working on that bucket of bolts, I see."

"Bucket of bolts, my foot!" Timmy says indignantly. "I can outrace any car in this neighborhood, including that overpriced heap you drive!" We both have a little laugh. "By the way, aren't you going to congratulate me?"

"Congratulate you? What for?"

Timmy rolls his eyes. "Gosh, Mr. Robinson, you mean you forgot? Today's my 18th birthday!"

I stare at him. "Let me get this straight," I say. "You're 18 years old as of today?"

Timmy gives an exasperated sigh. "Didn't I just tell you?"

"You're absolutely sure about this?" I ask, my voice low and urgent. "You are 18 years old today?"

Timmy nods. "Uh-huh." He gives an impish grin. "It's still not too late for you to give me a present."

I give Timmy a long, hard look. With a shock I realize what a handsome young man he's grown into. His torn, greasy T-shirt fits his muscular torso like a second skin, and I can see the swell of his pecs pushing against the thin fabric, how his biceps bunch up and ripple with each movement of his arms. He's wearing cutoffs that he's clearly outgrown; his taut young ass strains against the confining denim, and the bulge of his crotch threatens to split the zipper of his fly wide open. I think of all the hormones and juices surging through his tight, muscled young body, and I feel my throat constrict and my dick stir to hardness.

I reach over and squeeze Timmy's crotch. "I'll give you a present, you sexy little bastard," I growl. "Just follow me into the garage and close the door behind you."

Timmy's mouth curls up into a sly smile. "Sure thing, Mr. Robinson," he says.

Timmy stands in the shaft of sunlight that comes streaming in through the garage's one window. Dust motes drift lazily around him. I look at him, taking in the firm, muscular body, beautifully proportioned but with just the slightest padding of baby fat; the smooth face; the wide, vacant eyes. *Young, dumb, and full of come,* I think as I sink to my knees in front of him and slowly pull down the zipper to his fly.

Timmy's dick meat spills out, already half hard: thick, veined, cut, a good eight inches long at least. I reach inside his fly and pull out his balls as well; they fill my hand nicely—candy-pink, plump, furred by light blonde hair. Squeezing them, I look up into Timmy's sky-blue eyes.

"You got a load in there for me, Timmy?" I croon. "Some nice, sticky jizz you can splatter my tonsils with?"

"You betcha!" Timmy says.

I open wide and slide my lips down Timmy's dick. Timmy groans, and his dick immediately swells to full hardness. Eight inches, my ass! That sucker's got to be a least nine, maybe more! Timmy lays his hands on both sides of my head and begins pumping his hips, fucking my face with slow, lazy thrusts.

My hands slide under his T-shirt, kneading the flesh of his young torso. I find his nipples and give them a good squeeze. Timmy groans loudly.

"Gee, that feels good, Mr. Robinson!" he sighs. "Really good!"

I lightly slide my hands down Timmy's back and across his tight, young ass, feeling the play of muscles under my fingers. His ass cheeks feel smooth and warm, like sunbathed stone. I burrow my fingers into his crack until I find his hole. I push lightly against it.

"Oh, yeah!" Timmy says. His dick is deep down my throat now, his balls pressed against my chin, and he grinds his hips against my face. I work my finger into his ass and push, sliding up the warm, velvety chute. I massage Timmy's prostate, and he groans loudly. His body shudders violently.

"Oh, jeez, Mr. Robinson, I'm going to shoot!" he gasps. He pulls his dick out of my mouth just as a creamy load of jizz spurts out. It splatters my face, coating my cheeks, my mouth, my chin. I close my eyes and feel the warm, sticky drops sliding down.

I look up, and my gaze meets Timmy's. "Happy birthday, Timmy," I say, smiling.

Timmy just gives me a shy, boyish grin, his face turning red. What a nice kid. A nice *18-year-old* kid, that is.

Later, while driving to work, I realize that my encounter with Timmy has just whetted my appetite for more. After all, it was Timmy who shot his load, not me. I know just the place to go: that run-down old gas station on the corner of Main and Elm. I pull into the vacant lot next to it and walk over to the men's room at the back of the building.

If the timing's right, this place can be a hotbed of activity. No one is at the urinals, but I see a man's legs under the partition of one of the stalls, his jeans and briefs down around his ankles.

As I walk into the dank, piss-smelling room, the stall door slowly swings open. The man sitting on the toilet is sporting a hard-on, stroking it slowly with a greasy hand. I recognize him immediately as Jake, the garage mechanic.

Jake has an unpleasant face, his mouth loose and moist, his eyes shrewdly piglike, his nose broken, his chin stubbled with a two-day beard. A scar beginning at his left ear zigzags down across his cheek like frozen lightning. Yep, that face of his could stop a clock, all right.

But his body is quite another story. Jake works out, as he'll be the first to tell you. Every time I stop for gas or take my car in for maintenance, I have to listen to him go on in detail about his lats, abs, delts, pecs, quads, biceps—you get the picture. He's a jerk, but the payoff is clearly there.

Underneath his matted black chest hair, his pectoral muscles are thickly developed and beautifully defined, his belly cut like Baccarat crystal. Tattoos work their way up his arms and spill over onto his shoulders: snakes, dragons, skulls, bloody knives, leering demon faces, devil girls with big tits. The man has to be seriously depraved. His nipples are set wide apart and stand out like little fireplugs, begging for a good chewing.

And that dick of his! Dark, swollen, and evil, gnarled with veins, the head flaring out like a cobra's. His balls hang down obscenely in their fleshy sac, swaying heavily to every stroke of his hand, his nuts like meaty little eggs.

"How ya doin', Mr. Robinson?" he growls. "You want your dick sucked?"

I shudder with revulsion, remembering Timmy's clean-cut wholesomeness and now having to interact with this . . . this . . . *pig*. But my dick has another take on the situation. It springs to life, pushing hard against the fabric of my slacks. Oh, well.

I yank down my zipper and pull my hard cock out. "Sure, Jake," I smile. "Be my guest."

Jake gives me a loutish grin and wraps his greasy fingers around my dick. He bends forward and slides his wet lips down the shaft, long ropes of saliva drooling from his mouth. I lean back and start pumping my hips, fucking Jake's face with determined abandon.

"Hey, Jake," I say. "How about letting me fuck your ass?"

Jake pulls my dick out of his mouth and looks up at me. "Sure, Mr. Robinson," he sneers. "I was hoping you'd ask."

He lumbers over to the condom machine on the wall and smashes it hard with his fist. A condom package falls out of the slot and into Jake's meaty paw. He hands it to me and then leans against the wall, his arms outstretched, his palms flat, his hairy ass exposed and waiting. The pose definitely shows Jake to his best advantage: I can drink in his beautifully toned body without looking at his butt-ugly face.

I slide the condom down the shaft of my dick and lube it up as best I can with my spit. I pull apart the fleshy cheeks of Jake's ass, exposing the pucker of his hole. I push my dick against it. Jake groans with anticipation. The head of my dick slides in, and then, inch by inch, I slowly skewer Jake until my balls are pressed against him.

Jake groans again. "Fuck, that feels good!" he moans.

I start pumping my hips, sliding my dick in and out of the grease monkey's asshole, my hands kneading the flesh of his torso, slick with grim and sweat. I seize Jake's nipples and twist them viciously. Jake whimpers, and his body convulses with pleasure.

I shove my dick in as far as it'll go and grind my hips against him. His whimper escalates into a full-fledged groan. I proceed to truly trash his ass, fucking him with hard, savage strokes that make him cry out with each plunge of my dick.

"*This* is for charging me $192 for changing my spark plugs!" I grunt, slamming into his ass viciously. "And this is for the $278 to reline my brakes!"

Jake whimpers pitifully.

Finally, when I'm ready to shoot, I pull out to the point where my dick head is just inside his sphincter. "And *this* is for the $84 to rotate my fuckin' tires!" I snarl.

I hold firmly to Jake's hips and plunge in hard. The orgasm sweeps through me like an electric shock, my body shaking as my dick pumps what feels like several quarts of jizz into the condom up Jake's ass. I cry out.

"Yeah," Jake growls. "Shoot that load!"

When I'm finally done, I pull out, my dick still half hard. Jake turns around and drops to his knees before me, stroking his dick furiously. "How about pissing in my face while I drop a load, Mr. Robinson?" he growls, his mouth twisted in a salacious leer.

I pull myself up to my full height and stare down at him, shocked. "Jake," I say to him sternly, "we don't do that kind of thing here in Canada."

The color drains out of Jake's face and then rushes back in, turning it bright red. "I-I'm sorry, Mr. Robinson," he stammers. "I didn't mean that the way it sounded." He gives me a sickly smile. "Honest!"

I pull up my pants and zip my fly. "Well, I certainly hope not!" I give him a hard look. "The body's excretory functions are *not* a proper venue for sexual expression!"

Jake flinches.

I walk out of the tearoom with what I trust is the proper amount of dignity and skewer him with one last look. "Save that kind of depravity for the perverts who live south of the border."

Jake looks like he's going to cry.

I make it to the office just barely on time. It's a good thing I left home a little early this morning.

The receptionist smiles at me as I walk in. "Good morning, Mr. Robinson," she says brightly.

I smile back at her. "Good morning, Lynn."

There's a pile of magazines on my desk—the usual filth. I sit down and pick up the first one, opening to one of the stories inside. Christ, another one about a humpy telephone installer; can't these writers ever come up with an original plotline?

I read carefully, red-ink pen in hand. In the middle of the story, the installer lashes down the apartment tenant with a telephone cord and merciless assfucks him. My dick springs to hardness, but I ignore it. I slash a giant red *X* across the cover of the magazine and drop it into the reject bin. I reach for the next magazine.

Tony sticks his head into my cubicle. "Good morning, Dan," he says. "You got a second?"

I swing my chair around to face him. "Sure, Tony," I say, smiling. "Come on in."

Tony sits in my one free chair. "My kid's selling tickets for his school raffle. To help pay for wrestling mats for the gym." He looks at me with raised eyebrows. "You interested in buying one for a dollar? First prize is a color T.V."

I take out my wallet and extract a $5 bill. "Hell, give me five, Tony," I say. "It sounds like a good cause."

Tony flashes me a bright smile. His teeth gleam white in his dark face. He really is a good-looking guy. "Thanks, Dan," he says. He hands me five tickets. "You want to do Mexican today for lunch?"

"Let's do sushi," I say. I pat my belly. "My pants have been getting a little tight lately. I have to start eating lighter."

Tony laughs. "Sushi it is. I'll see you at noon." He glances at his watch. "I gotta go. I got to get ready for my meeting with the boss." He ducks out of the cubicle.

I have a productive morning poring over the cheap, sleazy porn that crosses my desk, making sure that anything that strays from vanilla winds up in the reject bin. God, I love this job! It gives me such a glow of . . . well, purpose. Today I feel particularly driven, and it doesn't take long before I work my way to the bottom of the stack. I glance at my watch: it's nearly 11 o'clock. Too early for lunch.

I stand up and stretch, then walk across the hall to Mr. Willoughby's office.

Lynn stops me at the door. "Mr. Willoughby is in a conference now," she says. "He told me specifically that he didn't want to be interrupted."

"Now, Lynn," I say, smiling. "I believe he has a shipment of magazines from Los Angeles that needs to be checked. I just want to run in and grab it." I give her a conspiratorial wink. "It'll just take me a second." Before she can protest, I open the door to his office and walk in.

I'm not prepared for the scene that greets me. Tony is kneeling on the conference table, his shirt unbuttoned and his fly open. Mr. Willoughby is crouched before him on his knees. Their heads jerk up when they hear me enter.

"I'm terribly sorry," I say, blushing. "I'll come back later."

Mr. Willoughby straightens up. "No, no, Dan, it's quite all right." He smiles. "As a matter of fact, I was thinking about calling you in to join us."

Mr. Willoughby is stripped down to his boxer shorts, and I take in his solid, muscled body. I see Mr. Willoughby often at the company fitness center, so it's no surprise to me that he's in the shape he's in: the broad shoulders, the nicely swelled pecs, the powerful arms. His chest is covered with a light dusting of grayish brown hair that trails down across his flat belly and disappears tantalizingly beneath the elastic waistband of his shorts.

Tony's lithe brown body is a nice contrast to Mr. Willoughby's. He's more a cheetah to Mr. Willoughby's bull: hairless, tight, compact, each muscle defined but not overdeveloped. His dick juts straight out from his open fly, gleaming with Mr. Willoughby's saliva. For some reason the necktie that hangs against his bare chest strikes a note I find almost unbearably erotic. He looks at me with his warm, brown eyes and smiles. "Yeah, Dan," he says. "The party's just begun. Come on in!"

Well, who am I to resist an invitation like that? I close the door behind me and join the other two. Tony and Mr. Willoughby start pulling off my clothes, unbuttoning my shirt, unzipping my slacks. It's only a matter of seconds before I'm naked.

Tony pulls me toward him and kisses me, his tongue pushing deep into my mouth, and Mr. Willoughby starts sucking on my dick. His lips slide up and down the shaft, and he twists his head from side to side, creating sensations in me that make my knees tremble violently.

"Jeez, Mr. Willoughby," I gasp. "I had no idea that you could give such great head!"

Mr. Willoughby looks up at me and grins, his hand wrapped around my dick. "How the hell do you think that I got to be head of this department?" He stands up and pulls off his underwear. "Okay, boys," he says, "it's time we shift this party into higher gear." Naked, he walks over to his desk and opens the top drawer. "Let's play out a little fantasy, here. Dan, I want you and Tony to tie me down to the conference table."

Tony and I exchange startled glances. "Wait just a minute, Mr. Willoughby," I say. "You know very well that we can't engage in sexual acts involving the use of ropes or any other kinds of constraints, no matter how safe and consensual."

"Yeah," Tony chimes in. "Canadians don't use ropes in bondage sex play. That's just *wrong!*"

A smile creases Mr. Willoughby's handsome face. "But you see, boys," he says, reaching into the open drawer, "these aren't just *any* ropes. These are very *special* ropes." He withdraws his hand from the drawer and holds . . . nothing. "These," he says, "are my special *Canadian bondage* ropes." He winks. "You can't see them because they're *invisible*."

Tony and I look at each other and then both of us turn toward Mr. Willoughby. "What I hear you telling me," I say cautiously, "is that you willingly want to participate in a completely consensual sexual fantasy involving being 'tied down' with 'invisible' Canadian-bondage ropes. And that any time you want the fantasy to stop, all you have to do is say so, and we'll immediately 'untie' you. Is that right, Mr. Willoughby?"

"Of course," Mr. Willoughby says, frowning. "You surely don't think I was suggesting a sexual act that actually involved even the slightest degree of coercion, do you?"

"No, no, of course not," I say hurriedly. I make the motion of tossing a length of rope to Tony as Mr. Willoughby climbs onto the table.

Mr. Willoughby lies down on his back, his arms and legs dangling over the edges. Tony immediately starts pretending to tie down his ankles as I work on his wrists. It doesn't take long before we have Mr. Willoughby securely "lashed" to the conference table.

Mr. Willoughby looks at the two of us, his arms and legs splayed across the table, his thick dick hard and twitching, his balls hanging low between his legs. "Let's start by the two of you coming over here and fucking my face good," he growls. "Just cram both your dicks in my mouth at the same time."

A look of distress passes over Tony's face, no doubt mirroring mine. I clear my throat. "Um, Mr. Willoughby, I'm sure I must have heard you wrong," I say, keeping my tone respectful. "I know that you would never consent to an act as degrading as having two penises in your mouth at the very same time." I smile helpfully. "Perhaps what you really want is for Tony to fuck your face while I plow your ass?"

Mr. Willoughby looks embarrassed. "Yes, yes," he says hurriedly. "You're right, Dan. That's exactly what I want." He nods toward his desk. "You'll find condoms and lube in the top drawer."

It only takes me a moment to get tubed and lubed, and I climb up onto the table between Mr. Willoughby's legs. Tony is situated on the other end, squatting down, his balls swinging just above the boss's face. Tony is now wearing nothing except the tie around his neck. He starts loosening it.

"No, Tony," I say. "Why don't you leave it on?"

Tony gives me a sly grin. "Jeez, Dan, you're such a fetishist."

But he humors me and lets the tie alone. Christ, he looks sexy! He squats a little lower. "All right, boss," he growls. "Why don't we start with your giving my balls a nice bath?"

Mr. Willoughby cranes his neck up and sucks Tony's balls into his mouth. Tony pulls back his head and closes his eyes as Mr. Willoughby tongues his sac. I pry apart Mr. Willoughby's ass cheeks and generously lube up his hole, inserting a couple of fingers. Mr. Willoughby groans, his voice muffled. I rub my dick head around his sphincter, poking against it without penetrating, teasing him. Mr. Willoughby squirms his hips, squeezing and relaxing his ass in anticipation. His arms and legs strain as if they were restrained by ropes.

"Oh, my God," he whimpers. "You're not going to fuck my virgin ass with that . . . that battering ram, are you?"

*Oh, puhl-e-eze*, I think. *Somebody get this guy a ghostwriter.* I put on my fiercest frown. "Shut up!" I snarl. "Whining little pigs like you make me want to *puke!* You'll take whatever I give you!"

Grasping his hips with both hands, I proceed to impale Mr. Willoughby, pushing my dick in inch by inch. Mr. Willoughby moans piteously. I start pumping my hips.

"Yeah," Tony growls. "Plow his ass good!" Tony shifts his position so that he's got his dick crammed into Mr. Willoughby's mouth. Mr. Willoughby sucks on it noisily, and Tony plunges deep down Mr. Willoughby's throat. He reaches over and tugs on the boss's nipples, squeezing them hard between his thumbs and forefingers. Meanwhile, I have a lube-slicked hand around Mr. Willoughby's dick, and I'm stroking it hard, sliding up and down the thick shaft. Between the two of us, we're working the boss over but good.

Tony's face is just inches from mine, and I lean forward and kiss him, pushing my tongue between his lips and into his mouth. Tony returns my kiss with equal enthusiasm.

We settle into an intricate choreography of sex: me plowing Mr. Willoughby's ass while stroking his dick; Tony fucking Mr. Willoughby's face while working his nipples; the two of us heavily tonguing each other above Mr. Willoughby's body. After a while, we match our rhythms and fall into synch, moving our bodies in unison like the parts of a well-oiled sex machine. Each thrust, suck, and stroke pushes us all closer to the edge. The room is filled with our grunts, groans, and sighs.

Perspiration beads on Tony's forehead and begins to trickle down his face. I taste it as I slide my tongue over his cheeks, his nose, his chin.

I pull back to get a better view of Tony, drinking him in with my eyes. His body is truly beautiful—dark, muscled, and lithe, gleaming now with a sheen of sweat. We hold each other's gazes as we plow Mr. Willoughby's respective orifices, and it's as if I can feel each of Tony's thrusts myself, actually tasting that magnificent, thick dick of his as it's shoved down Mr. Willoughby's throat.

Tony grins at me and winks, and the joy in his face is enough to break my heart. I make a mental note to set up something with Tony some time in the future.

Tony pulls his dick out of Mr. Willoughby's mouth and squats over his face. I watch as Mr. Willoughby enthusiastically eats Tony's ass while Tony beats off, fucking his fist with quick, short strokes. Tony's eyes are glazed with pleasure, his balls are pulled up tight, and I know it won't be long before he starts shooting.

I reach over and twist Tony's nipple, and that does the trick. With a loud groan he comes, his load gushing out and splattering against Mr. Willoughby's chest. Squirt by squirt, it shoots out, and every time I think I've seen the end of it, damn if more doesn't ooze out. Tony's body is racked with spasms, and his mouth is pulled back into a grimace of pleasure.

When he's finally done, Tony grabs me by the back of the neck and pulls my mouth against his. I kiss him tenderly, my lips working against his.

Mr. Willoughby is groaning louder with each thrust of my dick up his ass. His body is drenched with sweat, and his dick throbs in my hand with the hardness of a steel bar. I think about the promotion I'm up for and decide to give him an orgasm he won't easily forget.

His body begins to tremble, and I immediately press down hard between his balls. Mr. Willoughby arches his back and cries out as the first load of spunk spews out of his dick. I shove my dick hard up his ass, grinding my hips, and Mr. Willoughby cries out again, even louder. I imagine the office outside is getting quite an earful.

Mr. Willoughby is spewing a veritable geyser of jizz, splattering it against his chest and belly, his body still writhing as if his wrists and ankles were tied to the legs of the conference table. I give another savage thrust up his ass, and that's all it takes to push me over the edge.

I quickly pull out and whip the condom off, and my own load spews out. Tony is watching all of this with bright, appreciative eyes. My cries mingle with Mr. Willoughby's, my tenor to his bass, as we shoot our loads in unison.

When we're finally done, Mr. Willoughby is a dripping, oozing swamp of spunk, the combined loads of all three of us puddled together in all their spermy glory.

There's a moment of silence. The three of us exchange glances and then burst out laughing.

"Damn!" Mr. Willoughby says, shaking his head and grinning broadly. "Sex just doesn't get any better than that!"

*Just remember that when we discuss my promotion next week,* I think as I act out untying the ropes around his ankles.

Tony and I finish "freeing" Mr. Willoughby, and the three of us get dressed. Mr. Willoughby smears our jizz into his chest, making no effort to clean it off. "I have a budgetary meeting with the division head this afternoon," he says. "I want to feel your dried, caking loads on me while I'm discussing material acquisitions."

Tony and I exchange looks. He slaps me on the back. "I think we have a date for some sushi," he says.

"You boys just get out of here then," Mr. Willoughby says, chuckling. "Let the old man get back to his work."

When I get home again, I give Anne a big kiss at the door.

"How was your day today, dear?" she asks, smiling.

"Just great!" I say. "I had three different sexual encounters. All partners were 18 or over, all sex acts were entirely consensual, no excretory bodily functions were involved, and at no time did more than one penis ever wind up in anyone's mouth!"

"That's just wonderful!" Anne says, beaming. She helps me take off my coat. "I made a special treat for dinner tonight. We're having sushi."

*Oh, well,* I think. *No day can be completely perfect.* "Swell!" I manage to say.

While washing my hands in the upstairs bathroom, I look out the window at Timmy's house. His bedroom light is on. Probably doing his homework.

Timmy confessed recently that he's having a little trouble with algebra; maybe after dinner I can offer to help him. I make a mental note to bring along plenty of condoms. I dry my hands and start whistling a cheerful tune as I head on down to dinner.

# Psyched

The light on the phone console starts blinking, and I pick up the receiver. "Psychic Hotline," I say. "This is Balthazar speaking." I was Vladimir for a while, but the Russian accent I took on made me sound too much like Boris Badenov, the spy in the Rocky and Bullwinkle show. Dead silence. "Hello?" I say.

There's a sound of a throat clearing. "You know, I've never done anything like this before", a man's voice says. It's a deep baritone with an accent that is pure Texas. Very sexy. And somehow . . . familiar.

"That's okay," I say. "I'm here to help."

Another pause. "So you can, like, read minds and stuff? Predict the future?"

"I've been blessed with psychic gifts," I say, slipping into my patter. There's another pause. These first timers are such a pain in the ass. "What's your name?" I coax.

"Well, why don't you just read my mind and tell me?"

*Oh, jeez,* I think. *A real smart-ass.* Still, the feeling that I know this guy keeps getting stronger. "Look," I say, putting an edge to my voice. "This is your nickel. If you want to piss it away playing games, then go ahead."

"Okay, take it easy. The name's Clint."

That's when I make the connection. *Damn!* I think. *I know this guy!* It's Clint the bartender over at the Badlands. There's no way I could mistake his voice. This would not be as big a coincidence as it might seem. This psychic hotline is a two-bit operation, just a local line, and the people who call in all live in the area. I feel my dick start to stiffen. Hell, I've had a hard on for Clint since the first beer he served me. The fucker's so damn hot, with his easy smile and blue, blue eyes, his lean, rangy body, his powerful arms and tight haunches. Not to mention an ass you could write poems over and a bulge in his 501s that promises all sorts of fun times.

"I sense that you are having some trouble with . . . your love life," I guess.

"Is that the best you can do?" Clint snorts. There's a pause. "Look, maybe I should just hang up."

"What's your hurry?" I say. "Your shift at the bar isn't for another four hours."

That gets his attention. "How did you know I tend bar?" Clint's voice is suddenly wary.

"Gee, I don't know, Clint. Maybe it was just a lucky guess." I've just scored a bullseye, and I can afford to cop an attitude.

"What else can you tell about me?" Clint asks. I've got him hooked now.

"I know you're from Texas."

"Sheeit, anybody can tell that just by the way I talk."

"You grew up in Canyon," I say calmly. "Some podunk town just outside of Amarillo." I once heard Clint talking to a bar patron about himself one noisy Saturday night at the Badlands. I was belly up to the bar, waiting to order a beer. I doubt if he'd even remember me. "And, let me see, you got a black dog, half lab, half all-American. And his name is Skippy . . . no, Skipper."

Silence. Then a low whistle. "Holy shit," Clint says. He laughs. "Man, you are *good!* Maybe you *can* help me out."

"I'll do what I can," I say, all modesty now. But the gears in my brain are spinning fast. This guy has been churning my gonads for almost a year, and now he's on the line hanging on to my every word. *How can I use this to my advantage?* I wonder. Hey, fuck you—if I were principled, I wouldn't be working this psychic scam to begin with.

"I got a offer to tend another bar," Clint says. "The pay is good, and it's got a upscale crowd, so the tips would be high. But it's in fuckin' El Cerrito, and I don't want to have to drag my ass over there every night. I've been wondering if maybe I should just stay where I am. But still, man, I could use the extra money."

"Hang on," I say. "Let me consult the Tarot cards." This is normally where I put the client on hold and let the phone charges mount up, like my boss has trained me to. As the minutes tick by, I think about Clint, that sexy fucker. I'm feeling very horny, right now. And also a little pissed. I'm willing to bet a month's paycheck that if I walked up to Clint this evening at the Badlands he wouldn't know me from Adam, even though I've been buying drinks from him for months now.

I pick up the receiver. "This is really strange," I say.

"What, what?" Clint asks, all ears.

"I don't see anything in the cards about your job."

Another snort. "Some psychic you are."

"All the cards talk about is sex."

Long pause. "No shit," Clint finally says.

"Yeah, no shit," I reply blandly. "I've never seen the cards so . . . obsessed with the subject. It's amazing."

"What do they say?" Clint's all eagerness now.

"I really can't answer your question," I reply, my voice reluctant, "without saying some things that are . . . well . . . personal."

"That's okay! Be personal."

"Okay," I say, my tone all matter-of-fact. "The first card drawn, the one that marks your identity, is the Knight of Swords. The Knight is shown charging on his horse, his sword held out straight in front of him. That's you, man, charging forward, stiff dick in hand. Right above, in the space that represents your immediate future, is the Ace of Swords, your dick again, this time crossed with the Ace of Wands, another stiff dick. To your left is The Hanged Man and to your right is The Moon, which means that tonight, when the moon is high, you'll encounter a well-hung man. Below you is The Devil, the card of lust and sensuality, telling you just what kind of night to expect. I've never seen a Tarot reading like this before, so *reeking* of sex. You are going to get your rocks off in a major way tonight."

"No fuckin' shit!" Clint says, awed. "Where's all this going to happen?"

"Hold on a second, I'm getting a psychic flash." I let a couple of beats go by. "I see a small park, on top of a hill, overlooking a playground."

"Yeah, there's a park like that just down the street from where I work. It's a big, after-hours cruising area."

"Well, there you are," I say. "I predict that if you go there after the bar closes tonight, you'll have a sexual adventure that'll blow your gaskets out."

"Damn!" Clint says. There's a brief silence. "How will I know who this 'Ace of Wands' guy is?"

"I see a tall, lean man with a goatee and hooked nose," I say, describing myself. "That's the guy. He's waiting by the swings." I let a couple of beats go by. "He's kind of ordinary looking, but trust me, we're talking hot, hot sex here. The cards never lie."

"Damn!" Clint whispers.

*Sucker,* I think.

I glance at my watch. A quarter past two. I've been hanging out by the swings for nearly an hour now, watching the late night cruisers move in and out of the shadows, anxious that one of them doesn't intercept Clint before I can get to him. The full moon has finally cleared the trees, and the open park is bathed in light. *Where the fuck is Clint?* I think. I wait a while longer. Right when I'm about to call it quits, I see Clint's lean figure loping up the hillside. He pauses for a moment, looks around, then changes his direction toward the swings. His pace slows as he approaches me. I wait until he's only a couple of feet away before I speak.

"Howdy," I say.

Moonlight is pouring full on me. Clint regards me for a couple of beats. His face is in shadow, and I can't read his expression. "Just like Balthazar said!" he says, his voice low. "Fuckin' amazing!" It's a warm summer night, and Clint is just wearing a pair of jeans and a T-shirt that stretches across his muscled torso. All the months-long lust I've been feeling for this guy fans through me like prairie fire.

I decide to cut to the chase. I reach down and squeeze the bulge in his jeans. "Come on," I say, my heart hammering. "There's a clearing behind those bushes where we can have some privacy."

Clint doesn't answer at first, and for a moment I think he's going to refuse. But he finally nods. "Okay," he says quietly.

When we're in the clearing, I feel a sudden shyness. But Clint pulls me toward him and plants his mouth on mine. His tongue snakes into my mouth, and I respond eagerly, wrapping my tongue around his, frenching him for all that I'm worth as we grind our hips together. I slide my hands under Clint's T-shirt, squeezing the smooth skin of his torso, feeling the muscles under my fingertips. I brush across his nipples, and then squeeze them, not gently. Clint gives a low sigh. "Damn," he mutters. He pulls off his shirt, and I replace my fingers with my tongue, running it around each of his nipples, feeling them stiffen in my mouth. Clint bends his head down and shoves his tongue in my ear. I unbuckle his belt, unzip his fly and tug his jeans and shorts down. His half-hard dick sways slowly in the cool night air. The moon pours light down on us, and I take a moment to take in Clint's naked body, something I've been fantasizing about for months. Clint's torso is smooth and pale, and in the moonlight it looks like it's been chiseled in stone, the pecs sharply defined, the abs cut like crystal. His dick is fuckin' awesome. It swells up from the dark pubic patch, thick and heavy, roped with veins, its head flaring out darkly like a cobra's hood. His balls are plump and firm, a pair of bull nuts hanging ripely from the base of his shaft.

*Sweet Jesus,* I think. I wrap my hand around Clint's dick and start stroking. It swells to full hardness, lengthening and thickening within the circle of my fingers. "Yeah," Clint sighs. "That's right. Stroke the fucker." He reaches into my unzipped fly and pulls my dick out. We jack each other off as we kiss. I slide my other hand over Clint's body, tugging on the hard flesh, feeling the ripple of muscles under my fingertips. I lightly run my fingers down his back, over the smooth hardness of his asscheeks, between the tight crack. I feel the wrinkled pucker of his asshole and press against it. "Ah, yeah," Clint whispers.

I drop to my knees, bury my face in Clint's ballsac, and inhale deeply, smelling the heady scent of musk, and fresh sweat and sex flesh. I part my lips and Clint's balls drop into my mouth and I roll them around with my tongue as I continue stroking his dick. I give his dick a squeeze, and a clear pearl of pre-jizz oozes out of his piss slit. I slick up his dick with it, and as my fist slides down his shaft I push inside his asshole with my other finger, up to the second knuckle and twist it. "God . . . damn!" Clint groans. He reaches down and pulls my shirt over my head. "Get naked," he says gruffly.

I pull off the rest of my clothes, and Clint pushes me down onto the ground as he stretches out on top of me. His naked skin is against mine, his thick, hard dick dry-humping my belly. "Swing around," he growls. "Let's both fuck some face."

He doesn't have to ask me twice. I pivot around, and we both start eating dick, Clint pumping his shaft down my throat as I do the same to him. I look up the length of Clint's lean body, watching my dick slide in and out of his mouth. It's a fuckin' hot sight, and my dick gives an extra throb as I fuck his handsome cowboy face.

Clint takes my dick out of his mouth and looks over at me. "I'd like to plow your ass, now, buddy. You up for that?"

"Shit, yeah," I say. "Go for it!"

Clint pulls a condom packet and small bottle of lube out of his jeans pocket. It just takes a moment for him to lube and tube up, and then he grabs my ankles and spreads my legs apart. I feel his dick head poke against my asshole, and then Clint slides his shaft in, slowly, inch by inch. "Fuck!" I groan. Clint holds the moment, his dick full up my ass, his eyes locked with mine. He begins pumping his hips, slowly at first, his cock shaft sliding out of my ass to the very tip and then plunging full in again. Clint picks up speed, pumps his hips faster now, and I push up to meet him, matching my pace with his.

As Clint's dick thrusts into me again, I squeeze my ass tight. Clint moans. I do it again with his next thrust, and Clint's body shudders. "Fuck!" he groans. "That feels so damn gooood."

I laugh. Wrapping my legs tightly around his torso, I push my body up and over, so that Clint is stretched out on the ground with me on top. Clint never breaks rhythm, his cock still ramming in and out of my ass, riding me with a hard, driven tempo. I bend down, and we kiss, our tongues wrapped around each other, our bodies pressed tight together, squirming. Clint spits in his hand and starts jacking me off, each stroke in synch with the thrust of his dick up my ass. I close my eyes and groan deeply.

"Keep your eyes open," Clint growls. "I like to meet a man's gaze as I fuck his ass."

I obey, locking eyes with him. His mouth is pulled down in a snarl, and his eyes gleam with a fierce, wolfish light. His thrusts take on a piston tempo, hard and fast, and his face is streaked with sweat. I reach behind and tug hard on his balls.

"Yeah," he snarls. "That's right. Give my balls a good pull."

I do just that, adding a little twist as well. Another shudder runs through Clint's body, and he gives a long, trailing groan. He cries out and arches his body up, and I feel his dick throb, pulsing out its load into the condom in my ass. He pulls my head down and kisses me fiercely as he shoots. My own orgasm sweeps through me, my come oozing out between my fingers. We thrash around in the grass until both our orgasms have played themselves out. I collapse on top of Clint. We lay there together in silence, flesh pressed on flesh. I roll off finally, and Clint pushes himself up on his elbow. "Thanks, buddy," he says, as he pulls on his shirt. "That was great fun." A couple of minutes later, he's dressed, and I watch him push his way through the bushes.

Clint calls the hotline the next day. "Howdy, Balthazar," he says.

"Hi," I say, my heart racing. "How'd it go last night?"

Clint laughs. "Just like you said. You've got the gift, man."

"So you going to see this guy again?" I ask, trying like hell to sound casual. I'm envisioning a long string of nights of having my ass plowed by Clint.

"Naw, I don't think so."

This pulls me up short real fast. I let a couple of beats go by. "Why not?" I say. "Didn't you have a good time like I predicted?"

"It was all right," Clint says. I can almost hear the shrug in his voice. "But I don't think I want a repeat performance. The guy really wasn't all that good looking."

I feel myself doing a slow burn. "Maybe he'll grow on you if you give him a chance," I say. I can hear the pissy tone creeping into my voice.

"I don't think so," Clint says coolly. A couple of beats go by. "Actually I called to see if you could pick up anything about whether I should take that job in El Cerrito."

"I just got a psychic flash," I say. "It says you should go fuck yourself." I slam the phone down and glare at it for a couple of beats. *You schmuck!* I think.

The next call is from a woman who thinks her boyfriend is seeing someone behind her back. I tell her yes, that's true, and that she should dump the cheating bastard.

# Queer Survivor

DAY 1, 10:00 a.m.: This is the diary of Jason Wheeler. They told me I could bring one item with me, so, of course, I chose my notebook. I plan to chronicle every day faithfully, capturing the dramas as they unfold, be a witness to every little event. I figure that with my skills as a writer, plus my keen insight into human nature, I'll be a natural at this.

I am here on this remote island about three hundred miles southeast of Bora Bora with my fellow "queer survivors." There are seven of us, four gay boys and three dykes, left here for 18 days. "Queer Survivor" is a scaled down version of "Survivor": like the name implies, all the players are queer, and every three days we boot one of us off the island, until there are only two of us. At that point, the last two people to have been booted off are flown back, and they decide who gets a half million bucks.

Right now, I'm writing these words sitting on the beach where we're setting up camp. The others are foraging for materials for the shelters (we are given almost zero supplies: a few sacks of rice so we don't starve, a couple of knives, rope, fishing hooks, a carton of condoms and a case of lube—"just in case"). The ladies are giving me dirty looks, so I better start helping. No sense in getting off on the wrong foot. After all, I plan to stay till the end and win that money!

DAY 1, 1:00 p.m.: Okay, I'm beginning to get a little feel for the dynamics here. Two of the guys here are fuckin' drop-dead gorgeous. Jorge is this Brazilian stud: tall, dark mocha skin, soulful brown eyes, and a body so sliced and chiseled he could draw blood just by walking through a crowd. Sky, on the other hand, is blonde and lean, with the piercing blue eyes, Nordic features, and tight body of a Norwegian ski instructor. The three of us hit it off immediately, talking about our workout routines and what supplements we take. These guys are definitely my kind of people: hot, sexy, cultured. I can see me playing out all sorts of tropical island fantasies with these stud muffins. However, the fourth guy, Bill, is a total zero, a skinny little dweeb with zilch social skills. I think he's from Ohio or something. A complete loser. No matter; we'll vote his scrawny ass off the island the first chance we get.

DAY 1, 2:00 p.m.: The dykes are giving us all sorts of attitude. I can tell they're real ballbusters. Jorge, Sky and I want to build the shelter right on the beach. I think it'd be so romantic, listening to the waves at night, feeling the sand under us. One of the girls, Jennifer, is pissing and moaning that the beach is too exposed, that we should build the shelter under the protection of the trees. The others agree with her, I'm sure more out of "sisterhood" than anything else. Hello? This place is a tropical paradise. What kind of "protection" do we need, for Christ's sake? That traitor, Bill, agrees with the dykes. Apparently he does a lot of camping back home in Butt Fuck, Ohio, or wherever he's from, and says the beach is a bad idea for a shelter. Your days are numbered, Bill!

DAY 1, 4:00 p.m.: Okay, we've worked out a compromise. Jorge, Sky and I have built a shelter on the beach just like we wanted to. The style's very minimalist: a few branches tied together covered with palm fronds. I feel so Robinson Crusoe! The dykes and The Dweeb (as we've taken to calling Bill) have joined forces and built some tacky little hut in the jungle, out of sight from the three of us. Good riddance!

Jorge has stripped down to his thong briefs and has begun sunning himself just a few feet away from me. By the bulge in his pouch, I can tell he's got a real mouthful there. He keeps giving me these significant looks, and I make sure to give them right back. There's some serious eye fucking going on here.

A few minutes later, Sky comes out of the jungle with a bunch of coconuts. "Hey, look, guys," he calls out. "Ripe coconuts!" He's wearing his short shorts and nothing else, and he's pure eye candy. I drink in the tight, firm body, the creamy skin (he better make a habit of putting on plenty of sun block while we're here!), the pink nipples just begging to be chewed on. I can tell by the way the shorts hug his hips he's got to have just about the prettiest ass this side of the International Dateline. There'll be no shortage of quality dick as long as Sky and Jorge are on this island.

Sky cuts open one of the coconuts and passes it around. I pull off a piece of the meat inside and start chewing on it. "Where'd you find these?" I ask.

Sky shrugs. "The Dweeb gave them to me." He laughs. "I guess even The Dweeb has his uses." Jorge and I crack grins. We really do get along great. Jorge drinks from a coconut, spilling milk down between the firm mounds of his pecs. It looks like someone has just squirted a load on his chest; I fantasize about leaning over and lapping it off that smooth, brown skin. Jorge sees me eying him, and he grins widely, his teeth flashing white.

DAY 2, 10:00 a.m.: Hot damn, what a night I had! It started at sunset, the three of us sitting on the beach, watching that fat, red sun slowly sink below the horizon, the sky turning all these shades of pink and coral, studly Jorge on my right, sexy Sky on my left. Jorge put his arm around my shoulders and then Sky laid his hand on my knee, and before I could blink an eye we were buck naked and rolling around in the sand, kissing and stroking. I was right about Jorge; his dick is a fuckin' miracle of nature, thick and long as a baby's arm, uncut, the head flaring out like a juicy, brown plum. Sky's cock is all pink and blue veined, the balls hanging low and heavy, downed by blonde fuzz. Damn, did I ever feed on dick that night! The two studs stood in front of me, and I just spent the night sucking cock, switching from Jorge's mocha shlong to Sky's fat, pink fuckstick. I got drunk on dick, feeling those fleshy tubes slide down my throat, the heavy pouches of ballmeat slamming against my chin. Nobody can suck dick like I can, and I drove those studs wild, bringing them to the brink with my hands and mouth, then easing up just before they squirted. I made them beg! I finally let them shoot their loads, jizz showering down on me from both sides, dripping down my cheeks and chin, caking my face. Afterwards, Jorge and Sky slowly licked my face clean. The full moon was just sinking below the horizon when we finally crawled back into the shelter and curled up together in a tangle of arms and legs, listening to the dull roar of the ocean before drifting off into sleep. Fuckin' magical!

DAY 2, 11:30 a.m.: The Dweeb has stopped by with an armful of mangoes he found. They're underripe and have almost zero flavor; if that twerp thinks he can buy his way into our little group with them, he's even stupider than he looks. Jorge gives him a curt nod, and Sky doesn't even bother to look at him when he takes a mango. I almost laugh. I guess The Dweeb eventually gets the message, because he mumbles something about "going fishing" and wanders back to Camp Dyke. Still, the mangos do give us a little variety from this fuckin' rice.

DAY 2, 2:00 p.m.: Jorge has rolled some boulders over to the campsite, and the three of us have improvised a workout routine, pressing different size boulders while taking turns spotting. It isn't exactly Gold's Gym, but it's the best we can come up with. I've resigned myself to losing some muscle mass before all of this over (of course, I'll gain it all back as soon as I get back to the States!), but I'm hell bent on keeping it down to a minimum. Afterwards, we strip and have a circle jerk, just for the hell of it. It's so hot watching Jorge stroke that fat, brown dick of his, seeing Sky's balls bounce up and down as he pounds his pud. I'm the first to shoot a load, but the others are right behind me. We then run into the ocean, laughing and horse playing.

DAY 2, 5:00 p.m.: Jorge and I have gone looking for firewood. As soon as we're out of sight of the beach, Jorge pulls out a condom packet and tube of lube and fucks me right there on the jungle floor. I can't get enough of his dick slamming my ass! We thrash around under the coconut palms, Jorge sliding that battering ram of his in and out of my ass, our mouths fused together. The light filters down through the palm fronds, all green and shimmering, like we're fucking under water. Jorge gives a long, trailing groan, and his body shudders against mine as he pumps his load into the condom up my ass. I squirt, too, jacking off while Jorge twists my nipples. Afterwards, as Jorge kisses me, he murmurs that he's crazy about me, that he has been since he first laid eyes on me. Jesus, I think I could fall in love with this guy!

DAY 3, 11:00 a.m.: The first vote tonight! Jorge, Sky and I have gotten together to figure out our strategy. We'll pick off the lezzes first, then go for The Dweeb. Of course, if the dykes and The Dweeb join forces, we're screwed. We decide that all three of us will vote against Jennifer, so that she can go back to driving her diesel truck or cracking boulders into gravel, or whatever the fuck she does back in the States when she's not busting balls. If we pull this off, we'll rule the island!

DAY 3, Midnight: Hot damn, we've won! It was almost too fuckin' easy! The dykes and The Dweeb are totally disorganized. Jorge got one vote, Sky got one, I got two (!), but ol' Jennifer got our three votes. She's history now!

On the way back to our camp, Jorge and I straggle behind Sky. Jorge pins me against a coconut palm, and we start making out like crazy: kissing, tonguing, stroking each other's cocks. Jorge tells me he's totally ga-ga over me, that after we've voted off all the bitches (he said "beetches"; that's so cute!) and The Dweeb, we'll knock off Sky. We shoot our wads there, in the moonlight, under the palms, Jorge's dick pumping its load into my hand. He is so fuckin' hot! Nothing personal, Sky, but after The Dweeb, you're next!

DAY 4, 10:00 a.m.: The wind got a little heavy last night, and some of the thatching has blown off our shelter. I ask Jorge and Sky if they'll help me rethatch the roof, but they just grunt and say "maybe later" and then hang around the beach, bench pressing rocks together. Finally I go off into the island, get some palm fronds, and rethatch the fuckin' roof myself. I keep shooting dirty looks over toward both of them, hoping to guilt trip them into helping me, but it's like looking at fuckin' stone.

DAY 4, 1:00 p.m.: The Dweeb has just come by with a basket of fish. Apparently he's been going out to the reef with the snorkel and spear in the early mornings, learning where the fish hang out and how to spear them. I can't tell you how good that fish looks! We've been eating pretty much nothing but rice and coconuts for the past couple of days, and it's getting old fast. The Dweeb may be a total goon, but at least he's been showing a little initiative! Unlike two other guys who shall remain nameless.

The Dweeb and I scale the fish, start the fire, and cook them (again, without any help from Jorge and Sky). Jorge and Sky may not have lifted a finger getting the fish ready, but they sure haul ass to help us to eat it! Fuck, it tastes great! I thank The Dweeb, and Sky just rolls his eyes and shakes his head at me. After The Dweeb has left, Sky turns to me and says "Jeez, Jason, use your head! If you start making friendly with The Dweeb, he'll want to hang out with us!" I'm beginning to think that Sky isn't as cool as I thought he was.

DAY 6, Midnight: Well, we've just voted off another dyke. I think her name was Amy. Nothing can stop us now!

DAY 7, 10:00 a.m.: The Dweeb has just come by with some tapioca root he found, along with the fish he's been bringing us every morning. He also has some mangos, and this time they're ripe! He stays and helps me fix them all up into a meal, along with the inevitable rice and coconut. You know, The Dweeb really isn't that bad of a guy. I mean, don't get me wrong, he's a complete nerd, but in his own way he's a decent enough fellow. And God knows, Sky and Jorge haven't exactly been busting their asses to find food. I'm going to feel kind of bad when the three of us vote The Dweeb off the island. But, that's the way it's got to be.

Sky is eating the food The Dweeb has brought but doesn't even thank him, much less talk to him. I'm beginning to suspect that Sky is something of an asshole, no matter how pretty his damn ass is. You know, when it finally gets time for Jorge and me to vote Sky off the island, I don't think I'm going to mind all that much.

DAY 7, 2:00 p.m.: Jorge has gone off into the jungle with me again to help me "find firewood", our codeword for fucking our brains out. Jorge is so damn good at fucking ass. He slides that big cock nice and smooth up my ass, like butter on a hot griddle, keeps it up there, churning his hips, really getting me used to the feeling of being full of dick, and then gives me the pounding of my life. Jorge tells me that there's nothing he loves better than fucking ass, and I believe him! When he's slamming into me, his balls slapping against my ass, his eyes glazed over and all-dreamy, I know I'm being worked over by a pro! This time, when he comes, he pulls out of my ass, rips the condom off, and squirts his load onto my face. I've never had sex that hot! Jorge tells me that he wants to keep on seeing me after we get back to the States, that he doesn't even really care that much about the money anymore.

DAY 9, Midnight: Well, tonight we booted off, Carol, the last of the dykes. She knew it was coming, and she just sat there, glowering at us, as the votes were counted. Sky got one vote and I got one too. I wonder if it was The Dweeb who voted against me? Surprisingly, that kind of hurts my feelings to think that. Well, no matter. The Dweeb is the next to go.

DAY 10, 7:00 a.m.: SHIT! Last night has got to be about the fuckin' worst night of my life! A storm blew in, dumping buckets of rain on top of us, and it took only a couple of minutes of this pounding before our shelter was scattered in all directions! FUCK!!! The three of us grabbed whatever we could and hightailed it into the jungle. We spent the night huddled together under some palm trees, which offered abso-fucking-lutely no protection! The rain only stopped about an hour ago. We've walked back to the camp to see what we could salvage. Everything we didn't take with us—clothes, pots, knives, provisions—got swept out to sea. Sky is making snotty comments about how I should have grabbed a couple of bags of rice instead of my fucking diary. If that bastard doesn't ease up on me real soon, I'm going to cram a coconut up his ass!

DAY 10, 9:00 a.m.: The Dweeb just came by a few minutes ago. Amazingly, his shelter survived the storm. I can see now that he and the dykes were right, building their shelter in the protection of the trees. They also did a helluva better job thatching it into something sturdy, unlike the piss-ass job we've done. The Dweeb says that since the ladies (his words) are gone, there's room for the three of us if we want to move in. He also says that with the fruit and fish and remaining rice he's been able to stockpile, we should be okay in the provisions department.

Sky mutters in a real snotty tone that if he moves into The Dweeb's hut, The Dweeb better not "get any ideas" and keep his hands to himself. I think maybe I *will* shove that coconut up Sky's ass after all! The Dweeb just smiles and shrugs his shoulders.

DAY 11, 11:00 a.m.: I've gone out early this morning with Bill (I'm not calling him The Dweeb anymore) to catch fish. Bill shows me all the fishing techniques he's learned, and the best places to look for fish among the reefs. He's real encouraging, and when I finally bag a fish, Bill's as pleased as if he had caught it himself. We catch two more that morning. Sky and Jorge are still sleeping in the hut when we come back, so Bill and I scale and clean the fish and cook them by ourselves, along with some rice and coconuts. The others smell the food cooking and come out afterwards to eat. No thanks or anything!

DAY 11, 2:00 p.m.: Jorge and I have gone out into the woods "to gather firewood", and my ass gets another good pounding! This is the first time we've fucked since the storm, and it's great to feel Jorge's dick in my ass again. This time, when I shoot my load, I splatter Jorge's face but good, and we both laugh as I lick my jizz off. Jorge tells me he thinks he loves me, that the money means nothing to him anymore, only that we've found each other and can now create a life together. I tell him I feel the same way! Jorge talks a little about tomorrow, about how we're going to vote The Dweeb (his term now) off the island. I don't say anything, but I feel rotten thinking about it. Still, it has to be done. I mean, that's our strategy, right?

DAY 12, 11:00 a.m.: Bill and I have gone out fishing again this morning. I really have a good time with him when we do this; it actually feels like a vacation. We snag four fish today! Bill says I'm a natural fisherman, that all I needed was a little practice. He really is a sweet guy. I feel bad about the shitty way we've all been treating him this past couple of weeks. And, I tell you, diary, I feel like a real stinker about voting him off tonight. But what else can I do?

DAY 12, 5:00 p.m.: THAT MOTHERFUCKER!!! THAT SON OF A BITCH!!! THAT TWO-TIMING PRICK!!! I've gone out into the jungle to the place where Bill said the mangos grow and have stumbled onto Jorge and Sky fucking! They don't see me at first, and I listen while Jorge tells Sky how much he loves him, and how once The Dweeb's gone they'll vote me off the island and split the money!!! THAT ASSHOLE! Well, I step out into the clearing and in spite of how pissed I am, I almost laugh at the expression on Jorge's face. He looks like he just shit in his pants! I guess I kind of lose it, because I wind up shouting every name I can think of at Jorge. I then tell Sky that Jorge has been giving me exactly the same line of bullshit. Jorge is too fuckin' stupid to lie well, and one look at his face is all Sky needs to see that I'm telling the truth. When I stalk off, I can still hear Sky screaming at Jorge, his voice hitting that nelly little pitch it gets whenever he's excited.

DAY 12, Midnight: It's unanimous. Jorge was voted off the island tonight. The prick!

DAY 13, 11:00 a.m.: Bill and I have gone fishing again. I really look forward to these times now; they're the most fun I have on this island. Sky just sulks around the camp, this petulant little look on his face. When Bill is out of earshot, Sky refers to him as "The Dweeb." I tell Sky that the next time he calls Bill that, he'll be spitting his teeth out. Sky glares at me but has the good sense to keep his goddamn mouth shut.

DAY 15, Midnight: Well, to nobody's surprise, Sky has gotten booted. What a relief to get rid of him! Now it's just me and Bill.

DAY 16, 5:00: Bill and I are spending the day exploring the island. Bill shows me all his favorite places: the pool with the waterfall, the mango grove, the lookout point. I'm actually having a lot of fun with him! He's a sweet, no bullshit guy. Smart, too. He's not pumped up like Jorge and Sky, but his body is lean and tight. If he got rid of those dorky horn-rim glasses and got a decent haircut, he wouldn't be that bad looking.

In two days, Jorge and Sky will be flown back to vote for who gets the half million dollars. In spite of my falling out with them, I know there's no way they'll vote for Bill; they think he's such a loser. It may be unfair, but at least I reap the benefit of it.

DAY 17, 9:00 a.m.: The sky is overcast today, and the wind is whipping up whitecaps. I don't like the look of this at all.

DAY 17, 1:00 p.m.: We're in the middle of another goddamn storm! As I write this, Bill and I are holed up in the shelter, listening to it outside. It just seems to get worse and worse.

DAY 17, 8:00 p.m.: This storm is much bigger than the last one! I'm still in the shelter with Bill, listening to the wind howling and the rain drumming on the thatched roof. So far, the shelter is holding, but who knows how much longer it can take this beating? I'm fuckin' freaking out!!! Jesus, all I want is to be in my bed back home, with four strong walls around me, and none of this Robinson Crusoe shit anymore. I'm sick of it! Oh, jeez, a blast of wind just hit the shelter, and I thought we were goners for sure. I hate this! I FUCKIN' HATE THIS!

DAY 18, 9:00 a.m.: It's still raining outside, but the winds have died down and the rain is little more than a drizzle now. Thank God, the worst is over! If it hadn't been for Bill. . . . He could tell I was freakin' out with that storm raging outside. I thought we were going to fucking die!!! Without saying anything, he came over to my side of the hut, lay down next to me and wrapped his arms around me. Damn if he didn't just calmly reach over for a condom, "suit up," and fuck me slow and easy, while he held me tight. It wasn't "hot" sex, like with Jorge, but sweet and tender, Bill whispering reassuring things in my ear as his dick slid in and out of my ass, his hands stroking my torso, beating me off. We came together, Bill shooting up my ass while I squirted a load in his hand. It was exactly the right thing to do. I calmed down, and even eventually fell asleep, Bill's arms still wrapped around me. He's about the sweetest guy I ever met. I'm going to feel kind of bad when Jorge and Sky vote tonight that I get the money.

DAY 18, Midnight: THOSE VICIOUS, MOTHERFUCKING QUEENS! THOSE SONS-OF-BITCHES! I CAN'T BELIEVE THEY DID THIS TO ME! JORGE AND SKY VOTED AGAINST ME!!! THEY JUST SAT THERE, SMIRKING AT ME WHILE

## THE VOTES WERE COUNTED! FUCK THEM!!! AND FUCK THIS FUCKING DIARY!!!

Hi, this is Bill. Jason just threw his diary into the jungle, and I don't think he'll mind that I retrieved it so that I could get a chance to write something myself. I'm sorry Jason was so upset that the others voted for me, but I did think that was a real nice gesture to me on their part. And I have to admit, I sure can put that money to good use! Now Greg and I can start up that hardware business that we've been dreaming about. And I can finally buy my folks a decent house to live in instead of that old, broken-down place they live in now.

I hope Greg won't get too upset when I tell him about having sex with Jason that last night during the storm. It was just that Jason really was going off the deep end, and it was the only thing I could think of to calm him down. I swear, my eyes were closed, and I was pretending it was Greg all the time. Greg knows he's my honey bear. Anyway, this was all a very interesting experience, and I really did enjoy meeting the guys and the ladies, and I hope nobody has any hard feelings. And if they ever make it to my neck of the woods, Jennifer and Amy and Carol and Sky and Jorge and Jason are always welcome to look me up so that we can reminisce about our fun adventures on this beautiful tropical island. Oops! Gotta go. The chopper just landed.